Autumn of Dixie

Harryett Burden Hyde

For my wonderful husband, Glenn,
who never doubted that his wife
could actually write a novel.
Thank you for your love and support.

And to Linda and Caleb Pirtle,
without whom my novel
would still be in a
drawer.

Chapter One

Manassas, Virginia, July 21, 1861

Confused by what was to him, virgin terrain, Jedediah Thomas half walked, half stumbled through the twilight of a quickly approaching night. Losing his footing, he grasped for something to brace against the fall, but the object he sought to steady himself served only to repulse the officer in gray. As he fell backward, his errant hand found the body of a fallen comrade. Horrified at the sight of a faceless man, Jed silently cursed his own cowardice. Shameful of his reaction to the corpse, he swiftly looked to see if his response held notice to any of his men.

Had the truths been known, all twenty of his troops were in various degrees of mental detachments brought about by the scene of carnage that was Henry House Hill on that July evening.

Stewart Kane, his lieutenant and lifelong friend, drew near enough so that their conversation was audible to no others. Both towering close to six feet in height, the two were opposites in appearance. Naturally tanned, young Kane's dark hair was a mass of ebony strands, while the fair-haired Jed easily betrayed his emotions by the flush of his facial features.

"God Almighty, Jed. I've never seen anything like it. Men, horses, all torn apart, and we actually tried our damnedest to be here!" he added incredulously.

"Considering the condition of our troops, we can be thankful that these poor excuses for roads held us back. None of us would have survived the initial charge."

Both glanced over their shoulders at the men, boys by most standards. It was only a few weeks earlier that they had been boasting of their prowess in a Charleston tavern, making wild bravadoes concerning the vast number of Yankees they would kill. They were university volunteers who had been anxious to assign themselves to the commands of these officers who were but a few years their senior. Jed's father's position as the owner of the largest passenger/shipping company in the United States had assured Stewart and Jed officers' commissions, and a seasoned general had determined that these twenty-seven-year-old "officers" could do the least damage leading a handful of young gentlemen scholars to this, the threshold of hell.

Ezra Thomas had always seen to it that Jed and Stewart reaped the benefits of his fortune. From the time Stewart had come to live with the Thomas family during an influenza epidemic some fifteen years earlier, Ezra had bought them the best horses, clothes, schools, and entrances into the good graces of only the most influential of society's hostesses. Thomas' money had not only armed them with the best rifles available, but it had supplied the expensive tunic coats of Confederate gray, which now proved entirely too warm and cumbersome for the July heat that reflected off the double rows of gold buttons. Blue trims upon the cuffs designated their status as infantry soldiers. Citing the dignity of prestige of the cavalry within the military caste, the elder Thomas urged the boys, as he called them, to become a mounted unit. Caught up in the fervency of war fever, they could not be dissuaded from the infantry where they would undoubtedly see more action and opportunities to kill their enemy. Those loathe to admit it aloud, to a man, each soldier of this Charleston band had begun to question the wisdom of his impulsive youth.

"What's that coming, Jed?"

Straining their eyes, the image of a single rider focused.

"He's a Reb!" came the jubilant cry of Private Parker. "We're Southerners, too!" he yelled to the approaching soldier.

"Name your regiment and commander," ordered the man on horseback.

"I'm Captain Jedediah Thomas of Charleston. My men and I had hopes of attaching ourselves to General Beauregard's command, but I fear we have arrived too late to be of service to the Cause."

The rider dismounted and shook Jed's proffered hand.

"Sergeant Miles Davis of Virginia at your service. My orders were to come back to check once more for survivors before the burial details begin at dawn." With great enthusiasm he added, "Ya'll missed a hell of a rout! Yes Sir, those Yankees turned and ran like scared rabbits to hide behind Old Abe's coattails."

"Did we capture Washington?" one of the men excitedly questioned.

"Damn near! We'll take it by noon tomorrow if we can find any of the cowards to fight. Ya'll shoulda seen 'em. A supply wagon overturned on Henry House Bridge and blocked their retreat. They were so scared they crawled all over each other getting away." Enjoying himself immensely, Davis continued to captivate his audience. "Yes Sir, when Early's boys arrived by train and reinforced our ranks, well those Yanks made the big skedaddle, all right." Seeing the disappointed look upon the face of a Charleston private, Davis attempted to rouse his spirits. "Ya'll ain't missed the war." He slapped his newly discovered comrade good naturedly. "We're still pushing towards Washington. Night will slow us a mite, but there's plenty of action for tomorrow." His lightheartedness changed to a more solemn tone. "Though God knows why any of us would be anxious to have a hand in it."

As his eyes traveled the battlefield, the raw recruits shuddered, some unable to look at the blood-soaked soil and the faces and forms distorted by the agony of violent death.

Stewart interrupted the Sergeant who had continued to retell the battle with vivid descriptions of the disorderly Yankee withdrawal.

"And that was, of course, after they saw Jackson and his men as a stonewall…"

"Sergeant, would you direct us to General Beauregard? We have message of importance from President Davis and the Secretary of War."

"It'll be my pleasure, Sir. I'll walk my horse and give him a rest," said the young soldier.

The Rebels moved more swiftly and steadily under the Sergeant's guidance and the newly rising moon that shone to illuminate the serene farmland turned battlefield. At the edge of the Stone Bridge, a movement underneath it caught the sharp eyes of Davis.

"Take cover! There's Yankees under there!"

Amid the scratches of drawing sabers, a shrill, female voice cried, "Please we're women! We aren't soldiers; we swear!"

From under the bridge two young women emerged. One neared hysterics as they struggled to maintain some degree of dignity trying to scale the incline amid hoops and yards of skirts.

"Where are my manners, Ma'am? Let me be of assistance." Lehman Mason, son of a Georgian planter lunged forward to grasp the arm of the woman who shrank from his touch with such force that she tumbled down the slope in a wild motion of arms, legs, and pink muslin. Laughter erupted as much in amusement as in relief to find the "Yankees" they had feared.

"Catherine, are you hurt? What has that spiteful Rebel done to you?" Helping Catherine to her feet, the second wheeled around to direct a steel-cold gaze which met the eyes of Captain Thomas.

Within the span of mere seconds, Thomas had appraised one of the most striking women he had ever seen. Streaked by dirt and tears, the face was nonetheless classic in its beauty. Cascades of dark hair encircled the flawless face which was enhanced by her animated, hazel eyes. At the moment, those same eyes were defiantly locked with his, expressing a dominant force, demanding recognition and respect.

"How dare you stand there laughing at us, you backwoods hooligans?"

"Allow me to assist you and your friend. I am Captain Jed Thomas of Charleston and your servant, Madam." Jed extended his hand, clothed in a gauntlet-styled buck glove. Raising her up to his level, their eyes met again, this time in a moment of mutual attraction that she allowed to last for only an instant.

Obvious to the young Captain, this was no farm girl. Everything from her clothing to her poise alluded to the fact that she was a lady of refinement.

"What are you doing out here?" questioned Kane, who had been even quicker to appreciate the beauty of their "prisoners," focusing his attention on the humiliated Catherine whose arm he had taken as a means of assistance.

"Please escort us home!" wailed the girl on his arm. "We came for the picnic and to watch the battle." Her voice pleaded with her captors for understanding. "Then, everything went awry. Everyone was running and screaming, and we were separated from the others. Please, please take us home."

"Catherine Jackson, have you no shame, groveling to the enemy? Must you degrade yourself so?" scolded the dark-haired beauty. "If you will excuse us, we will be making or way back to Washington," she said, addressing the Confederates. "Our families must be frantic with worry over our absence."

Though inwardly fearful of the dire predicament that fate had thrust upon them, Clarissa Morgan exuded a haughty, supercilious air of superiority which had carried her through a most difficult childhood. The only child of a frail mother and a loveless father disappointed by her sex and his own inabilities to secure a personal fortune, she assumed the role of protector for her vulnerable mother against her father and any outside forces that threatened.

Now as a woman of nineteen, her mask of strength was donned unconsciously, a reflex which shielded her from the sex she mistrusted as a user of women but whose recognition she tirelessly sought in order to exercise her power and to entice the men she left smitten and rejected. Instinctively she knew that the Southern captain was hopelessly under her spell, and she would prove to herself that all men, Reb or Yank, were hers to control.

"I'm afraid you'd better reevaluate your travel plans, Miss..., Miss..."

"Morgan, Sergeant. Miss Clarissa Morgan. And how dare you presume to dictate our plans to us? I'll have you know I am the niece of Secretary of War Cameron."

"Begging your pardon, Miss Morgan, but there's danger lurking behind every tree. Why, there's pillagers, skulkers, and God only knows what kind of deserting rapscallion that could cross your path." He shook head firmly. "No, your circumstance is not an enviable one by any means. Don't ya'll say, boys?"

"True enough, Miss," added Parker. "I was ready to shoot you myself if you hadn't called out. Next time you might not be so fortunate."

"Indeed, Ma'am," agreed another Charleston soldier. "We are gentlemen and guarantee your safety. If I may be so bold as to say," he removed his cap and bowed in one sweeping motion, "it will be our pleasure to guard two such lovely ladies to the safety of the headquarters of General Beauregard himself."

Gathering her muddy skirts, Clarissa Morgan tossed her head to the right, looking up at Thomas with a coy smile that won his heart. Had he known that same smile had charmed and manipulated both young and old for much of her life, he'd have been less beguiled.

Reassuringly she addressed her companion. "It's quite all right, Cathy. No doubt the General will offer us escorts to the Capital." To the soldiers she said, "Gentlemen, we are in you debt. How truly fortunate we are to be in the company of such able and valiant soldiers."

Jed was unsure whether he detected a faint note of sarcasm in her last remark.

Catherine followed suit, only momentarily confused, for she had witnessed Clarissa's captivating charms at work on numerous occasions and had every confidence in their abilities

to maneuver these unsuspecting Rebs into carrying them to
Jeff Davis, himself, had Clarissa Morgan the notion to do so.

*****

Battle weary, but nonetheless buoyant, Beauregard's
troops were engaged in all manner of preparations for the
morrow's fight. None of the horrors which they had witnessed
upon the field of combat led them to expect such a humorous
sight as that of a small group of Confederates escorting their
"prisoners" into camp.

"So the Yankees are sendin' their womenfolk agin us now!"

"We heard tell of 'em changing to civilian clothes durin' the
retreat, but we didn't expect they'd dress as no women!"

"Careful men. There's liable to be Yanks behind those skirts."

The Charleston recruits were just young enough to enjoy
the attention of these combat veterans who but a few hours
prior had inflicted without a thought unspeakable carnage upon
their fellowmen. Somehow the ludicrous capture of two
Northern socialites momentarily blotted these atrocities from
their minds.

The unmistakable sound of a voice of authority brought the
camp to silence.

"What the hell is going on here?" barked Colonel Adam
Dupree, an aide and advisor to Beauregard. "You men weren't
this agitated in the heat of..., heavens to Betsy, where did
these women come from?"

Seizing the opportunity to take control of the situation,
Clarissa stepped forward, placing her arm through that of the
colonel.

"Oh, Colonel, how grateful I am to see you. I am Secretary
of War Cameron's niece, Clarissa Morgan. My companion,

Miss Jackson, and I were victims of a most unfortunate circumstance."

Always in awe of her friend, Catherine watched as she battered her long lashes and flashed her charming smile.

"We were separated from her family during the retreat, and in order to survive the battle, Catherine and I hid ourselves in a washed out embankment under a bridge. Too frightened to move, we remained there until dusk, when these men came to our rescue." Releasing the Colonel's arm, she returned to Catherine's side. "Now, if you would do us the service of providing horses, we can find our way back to the city."

Jed's gaze was riveted to those eyes which seemed to speak more expressively than her voice. He'd never encountered anyone like her before. Thinking about his fiancée, Amanda Mallory, he was certain that Mandy would never have taken charge in a crisis with the confidence of Clarissa Morgan. She'd have stood in the middle of the battlefield experiencing the vapors and whining for Maizy, her childhood nurse, to bring her salts. Not that he thought less of Mandy, gentility was part of the attraction of a Southern belle. Still, Clarissa Morgan's self-assurance and aggressiveness was refreshingly new and not to a small degree intriguing.

A more gallant sort would have offered a ride through the enemy lines just for the honor of escorting a woman like Miss Morgan to her doorstep; however, Adam Dupree was not such a man. A veteran of the Mexican War, Dupree had risen through the ranks of the United States Army quite literally by his bootstraps. Distinction in combat earned him his present command. The outbreak of hostilities suited his purpose well. Himself a Virginian, he might have joined either side, but the Confederate Army offered the better opportunity to further his career. In actuality, the cause for which he risked his life meant little. He possessed no desire to protect the rich planters' slaves or uphold the sacred rights to the states. Rather, Adam Dupree was in this war with loyalties to no one other than himself.

Since his appointment to aid Beauregard, his disgust with the Confederate system had become more pronounced. What sort of army could distinguish itself with scattered bastions of soldiers who were merely rich men at play? That a rank could be purchased irked him, and he lost few opportunities to belittle and shame the toy soldiers whose money brought them the titles they so proudly held. These, he surmised of Jed and Stewart, were no different than the hundreds he had already witnessed. The Southern routing of the Yankees evidenced only that the United States Army was less competent because of the loss of true officers like himself.

Clarissa felt the pressure of the Colonel's arm uncomfortably encircling her own. It became more unpleasant and possessive as he spoke.

"My dear young woman, do you take us for fools? Surely you do not believe us to be so gullible as to allow two Yankee spies to ride out on our own mounts to inform the enemy of our strengths and weaknesses. The callousness of the Union leaders never ceases to appall me, but the use of their women to infiltrate our camp is beneath contempt."

His last remarks had been addressed to the audience of men. "No, Miss Morgan, I will not allow you to find your way to Washington."

Still directing his eyes to the spirited woman he issued his command. "Sergeant Lummus, I want special guards for these ladies, and be certain that none are representative of that weak type of man whose duty can be obscured by the devious seductions of a Yankee spy in hoops."

Furious, Clarissa jerked her arm free, slapping the shocked Dupree across the cheek all in a single motion, its sound reverberating within the circle of onlookers.

"My uncle will hear of this, and when our Army defeats you spineless Rebels, I'll see to it personally that you will pay dearly for this."

It commanded all his fortitude to control himself. Remembering his men and the fact that she was, after all, a woman, Dupree walked over to the defiant woman and stared coldly into her blazing eyes.

"Lummus, it is the practice of the Confederate States of America to execute spies, is it not?"

"Uh… yes, Sir…Colonel… but … I…"

"And did we take other prisoners today?"

"There's close to a couple of hundred men in a makeshift internment area just in our camp alone, Colonel Dupree."

Unable to break Clarissa, Dupree turned his attention to the obviously weaker Catherine who was leaning on the arm of Stewart Kane...

"Then they won't mind the company of these women, do you think?"

Her mouth incapable of more than the motions of speech, Catherine drew back in horror, the vindictive grin of the Colonel enhancing her fears.

Undaunted, the stronger woman moved confidently toward the weaker, taking her arm. "Come along, Catherine, I much prefer the company of our soldiers than the continued companionship of these so-called gentlemen for another instant. By the way Colonel, I recommend that you read Samuel Richardson. I understand his Sir Charles Grandison would be a worthy pattern. Sergeant Lummus, if you will direct us?"

"Colonel Dupree, I am Captain Jedediah Thomas of Charleston, if you will permit me this observation? These are young ladies of quality, not unlike our own sisters and wives. Surely we would not want it said that the Confederate Army treated them in any manner that would rob them of the respect due ladies of their station?"

"I see your point, Captain. Perhaps a private tent with round the clock guard will suffice. Sergeant Lummus, see to a tent near the center of the camp."

"Yes Sir. Ladies, this way please."

Jed looked to Clarissa, hoping to detect a note of gratitude in her expression. Instead, she picked up her tattered organdy skirt as she tossed her flowing hair in a defiant manner. *A woman with determination thought* Jed, an appreciative grin crossing his face.

As Lummus led the women toward the center of camp, Clarissa silently thanked heaven for the handsome Captain's intervention. "Don't worry, Cathey," she said reassuringly. "Our troops will overrun this camp before long, and we'll be home with an exciting adventure to tell."

Catherine hardly appeared convinced by Clarissa's abilities as a seer, and she scolded herself for having allowed Clarissa to influence her to leave her family for a closer view of the battle. Ever since Clarissa's arrival in Washington to live with her aunt and uncle while her parents lived in England, she had cajoled her into one awkward situation after another. That two young women so inherently different could bond a friendship rivaled by few sisters, puzzled even Catherine herself. Yet, it was Clarissa's poise and independence that drew shy, withdrawn Catherine, "Like an insect into a web," as her father put it during his rebuking of the girls following their attendance at a meeting of Washington ladies who were striving to give women the right to vote. What would he say when they returned? Still, the encounter with the handsome Lieutenant outweighed any of her father's rantings.

When the prisoners disappeared into the darkness, Jed spoke. "Colonel, I have a special message directly from President Davis. My instructions were that Lieutenant Kane and I should deliver it to General Beauregard personally,"

Dupree appraised the young men, "I am the General's aid. Feel free to deliver the message to me."

"Begging your pardon, Sir. Our instructions were quite specific."

"Very well. Davis, quarter these other men while I see to these officers." Highly doubtful of the claim, Dupree decided to let them hang themselves in Beauregard's presence.

"Thank you, Sir," said Jed.

"My pleasure. You boys hungry?"

The banter of the men drifted as Stewart, Jed, and Dupree walked in the opposite direction. Rows of tents bearing "CSA" formed an informal street. Through the coarse material, lanterns illuminated the path. Occasional laughter and the toasting of metal cups were overheard as the three strode in an icy silence. Stewart's feelings were reminiscent of a similar walk the two friends had taken with Ezra Thomas when they were in their early teens. The elder Thomas had come to bring them back home following a brawl at a local gaming establishment. *The only difference,* mused Kane, *is that I ache from traveling instead of the blows I'd taken.*

Outside the tents, exhausted men lay upon oil cloths and covered themselves with blankets, sleeping through the irregular artillery fire that testified to the South's cautious pursuit of its enemy. Louder than the cannonading, the profane oaths which followed the rolls of dice in crap games pierced the night. Body slaves passed, carrying food they had prepared or the freshly blackened boots of a master they attended. The scene reminded Jed of the pages of King Arthur's knights, though he considered the need of a valet at an army encampment as bordering upon the ridiculous.

It was not that Thomas was opposed to slavery. At the Thomas household, a small number of slaves performed the duties necessary to its upkeep and the family's needs. Though Ezra and his wife Isabella availed themselves of personal servants, the boys were denied the constant companionship of a body slave, unlike the majority of the young men of their station. Having grown up poor, it was Ezra's belief that a young man's character was shaped by hard work, which taught reliance upon self, a trait lacking in those softened by slaves available to answer every whim. To that end, he had employed the boys as laborers in most every aspect of his shipping enterprise.

Though such had not been his intent, Ezra had created the paradox that was Jed. Intrinsically Southern by virtue of each aspect of his privilege, the boy's exposure via Thomas Shipping's involvement with the Northern and European customers planted the seeds of blasphemous change within Jed's soul.

Laboring alongside those for whom life was a daily struggle to secure the barest of necessities or witnessing the plights of the slaves throughout the South, Jed's sympathies grew. Expressed only to Stewart, Thomas' personal battle raged. To speak of a southern society devoid of slavery was unthinkable. All those to whom he owed respect could not be openly challenged. He was one youth opposing the venerabilities of wisdom, and for what end? Disgrace, ridicule, and most assuredly the collapse of a fortune amassed by his father.

Thus, Jed Thomas stood in a Confederate camp, prepared to fulfill all duties, to give his life and take others for a society he could not honestly defend, even to him.

At a particularly large tent, two armed sentries snapped to attention as the three approached. Upon recognizing Dupree, the soldiers allowed passage into the tent.

The Charleston officers were taken aback by the contents of the quarters. Far from the spartan conditions expected, they saw the general dining on china plates at a wooden table covered by linen cloths. There was a folding bed, complete with steads, whose covers were invitingly turned down in hope of luring Beauregard into some much deserved rest. Dressing in serving attire, the Black man close to the General's age seemed to dote over the Confederate commander, anticipating his need through the conditioning of long years of service.

Seated around the General's table was a representation of his most trusted officers, Barnard Bee, Francis Bartow, and Shanks Evans. The newly christened "Stonewall" Jackson and Joe Johnston were still in pursuit, though their orders were to fight only if provoked until the morning could bring sufficient light and fresh troop replacements.

Jed had never been formally introduced to General Pierre Gustave Toutant Beauregard, but his foreknowledge of the General provided by his father, prepared him to deal with a vain and boastful man. Only five feet seven inches, Beauregard was nonetheless imposing as he presided over his war council, his tone pompous and uninviting to opposition.

"I must say that our railhead at Manassas Junction proved itself worthy of the energies expelled to establish it."

There was hearty agreement.

"The Lord is truly the provider of those in need," inserted Bartow. "From the rifles, cartridge boxes, and other supplies confiscated by my details after the battle, the reinforcements arriving as we speak will have sufficient arms to bear."

"I must praise the efforts of a rather clever young lieutenant of mine," added Bee, his pleasure at being able to outdo Bartow much in evidence. "Young Rutherford, freshly out of Virginia Military Institute, spotted the supply wagons as the Yankees were fleeing; I can hardly term such a disorganized example of personal cowardice a retreat."

Agreement in the form of laughter permeated the tent.

"As I was saying, Rutherford ordered his men to direct their fire at the horses and drivers of some of the wagons, resulting in the capture of arms, food, ammunition, and the wagons themselves."

"An excellent job. You are to see to it that Lieutenant Rutherford and his men are duly recognized," noted the General.

"With pleasure, Sir."

"General," questioned Evans, "has the rumor of a captured Union supply train been substantiated?"

"Indeed it has; however, it should be several more days before the provisions reach us. There is a small distance to surmount, and, of course, we keep adding to it," triumph marking his last statement. "And of the morrow, gentlemen?"

"Jackson and Johnston's scouts report the Capital most vulnerable toward the south and west," announced Bee.

"And of your informers in Washington?"

"Mrs. Greenhow proved highly accurate in her reporting prior to the battle. Other sources attest to the facts that the city is in a state of turmoil and the army in disorder. If any troops can be mustered, their ability to fight as a cohesive body is seriously in question."

"Very well, then we are prepared to follow our plan of action until we reach the city." Directing his attention from his council,

Beauregard acknowledged that others were present for the first time. "What was so important that it necessitated an interruption, Colonel Dupree?"

"These officers tell me that they have a message from President Davis," Dupree sarcastically explained.

"Gentlemen?"

"Sir, we are Lieutenant Kane and Captain Thomas of Charleston. We command a small number of volunteers from the university. Delayed by poor roads, we arrived too late for this morning's defeat of the enemy. My father, Ezra Thomas who is a personal friend and counsel to the President, gave me this message from Montgomery just before our departure. He emphasized the importance of delivering it personally to you, Sir." He glared at Dupree, accentuating the last few words.

Kane moved forward, removing an envelope bearing the CSA crest of the Presidential office. His return to Jed's side allowed Beauregard sufficient privacy to examine its contents.

General Beauregard,

I pray that the Lord will grant you safety and a victory for our glorious cause. These young officers, Kane and Thomas, are the ward and son of Ezra Thomas. I believe the two of you to be acquainted.

When our Army prepares to take Washington, I want these men to lead a special unit of your most trusted men through a series of ramped passages within the White House. Knowledge of the passages rests with these men for their days as laborers for Thomas Shipping. Through these passageways, the unit's ultimate assignment will be the Presidential Office from which they will abduct Abraham Lincoln. Should the mission prove successful, Lincoln should be spirited to a location well within our lines where, God willing, negotiations

*will bring a conclusion to the hostilities and a victory for the
Confederacy.*
    God be with you and our Cause,
                                    Jefferson Davis

Without betraying the contents of the message, the General
leaned back in his wooden chair. "Captain Thomas and
Lieutenant Kane, are you aware of the contents of the
President's letter?"

"No Sir," Kane quickly answered.

Taking a few bites of his late supper, Beauregard continued.
"Are you familiar with some fort of back tunnels at the White
House?"

Kane grinned broadly, "Indeed General. My muscles are
still strained from distributing cargo to various rooms and
offices. The system is really quite ingenious, having been built
for the renovation of the White House after the British set fire
to it during the War of 1812. A virtual labyrinth of ramps, its
convenience led to its enclosure and subsequent use for
delivering and undetected travel by governmental officials."

"Then I can assume that these passages are fresh enough
upon your memories to lead a unit through them to any point
within the mansion, perhaps even to the office of the President?"

Looks of astonishment immediately crossed the faces of
all present within hearing distance.

"Without a doubt, the service ramps are lighted, wide, and
clearly marked, and the President's office is the last room
accessible," Kane voiced exuberantly.

Stewart was already several steps ahead of his commander,
allowing his enthusiasm to obscure the obvious dangers of
such an undertaking, especially with city under siege. In his
youthful heart, so ready to serve, a trek behind enemy lines

and into the very bowels of its headquarters was no less a lark than stealing melons from a neighbor's garden.

Still skeptical, General Beauregard regarded the silent, young Captain. "And how would you, as senior officer, propose to complete such a mission, as say to abduct someone from an office through these tunnels?"

Jed's mind raced in search of the identity of one important enough to warrant such risks.

In a voice he barely recognized as his own, Jed replied. "Our only experience was in delivering freight. It secured us access once, and should serve us well a second time. We would dress ourselves as dock workers and employ Odysseus' Trojan horse ruse. The necessary arms could be concealed within the packing crates, and the individual could be hidden within the same crating."

Dupree could keep silent no longer. "And you expect even a Yankee to believe that a delivery is being made to the White House during a battle? The entire plan is ludicrous." Addressing the General he tried to dismiss Jed's proposal. "I suggest a swift charge of fire power to gain entry…"

"And alert the entire White House, which will undoubtedly be under heavier guard during a siege," snapped the brash lieutenant.

"But if we were removing rather than delivering," mused his friend.

"Helping Mrs. Lincoln outdo Dolly Madison by saving more of the nation's treasures?" Dupree challenged. "That should prove a perfect plan to confuse the enemy. Go back to your daddy's business and leave the execution of a Rebel victory to veterans," growled the cynical Colonel.

Kane leaped to the defensive. "It's only natural that there would be things the Yanks wouldn't want to see fall into

Confederate hands. Why, there must be sensitive documents within the White House…"

"And such information would require the evacuation to prevent capture by an invading army," finished Jed, gaining confidence in his own strategy.

A look of pleasant approval betrayed Beauregard's amazement with a plan the Charleston friends had accepted with the zeal of a boyhood prank.

"An excellent ploy, Gentlemen, I will have an aide assign you quarters. You will need a good night's sleep, for tomorrow you will lead an historic mission which will involve the abduction of Abraham Lincoln and his safe arrival within Confederate lines."

"Abduct the Mr. Lincoln?" Jed had considered a cabinet member or perhaps a high ranking officer, but the President of the United States?

Beauregard addressed his meal. "Exactly," placing the silver across his dinner plate he calmly explained. "By removing the leadership of the North, the cohesiveness of its government is lost; precipitating confusion from its highest echelons down through the very ranks of the army we seek to defeat. He is," the General seemed somewhat irritated to remind his officer, "the commander-in-chief. With Lincoln in our pocket, he is at the very least an invaluable pawn with which to bargain a swift conclusion to this war, and we, gentlemen, can return to our lives, having silenced forever the interference of our northern brothers in our affairs."

Dupree saw little chance of dissuading Beauregard. *So be it*, he thought. *Let the rich boys have their fun; their use of the battlefield would have proven minimal at best. When their capture is reported, let their father buy their release*. He turned angrily, leaving them to the General.

*****

Catherine and Clarissa spent a fitful night for differing reasons. Catherine's dreams were frightening scenarios which placed her in front of a firing squad and at the mercy of Mrs. Stowe's overseer. For Clarissa, the night had been passed in various plots of revenge against Dupree. After disposing of the arrogant Colonel in a variety of humiliating methods, all of which concluded with him on his knees begging for mercy, Clarissa's mind took an occasional turn to the handsome Captain Thomas who had now saved her twice. He was, in her estimation, unquestionably an aristocrat. Even his arduous journey failed to disguise his rugged yet patrician features. That the South had also produced Dupree was explainable only by the existence of that type of Confederate who was the abusive slave owner. She could easily picture Dupree's sadistic smile approving torture of the defenseless.

Having lived the life of the defenseless, unable to prevent her father's domineering cruelty, she vowed that as a grown woman she would never fail to control her own fate. Hers was a fierce determination to direct her own life, regardless of the cost. To that end she set about to engineer an escape not only for herself but also for her sleeping companion. She had coaxed her into venturing further into the field, reassuring her of their safety, all the while aware of Catherine's fears.

The early morning stir of a camp preparing itself for battle awoke Catherine and Clarissa. The girls rose, wrapping the coarse woolen blankets that served as their only bedding around their shoulders against the chill of the dawn. Though the sun was barely crowning, the activities of the encampment were proceeding as if it were high overhead. From the boisterous sounds, the women inferred that the troops would be marching within the hour. Peaking through the tent folds, Clarissa could make out the forms of the armed sentries.

"Ma'am, I'll be asking you to remain inside your tent."

A farm boy, thought Clarissa. She was living the plot of a stage comedy. *Wouldn't the ladies of my literary circle be appalled that Cathy and I passed the night in such close proximity to two backwoods Rebels?* Picturing their reactions caused Clarissa to smile.

"Let me see," demanded Catherine, attributing her momentary happiness to a corps of blue coated cavalry to achieve their rescue.

"There's nothing to see, unless you count two farm boys standing guard against the dangerous wiles of women spies.

"Shish, they'll hear you. Haven't we enough trouble without..."

"Let them hear." She spoke even more loudly. "If all they can do is to protect the Rebel army from us, I hardly fear their wrathful retaliation.

"Excuse me, ladies. It's Lieutenant Kane. Might I have a few moments with you?"

For reasons of his own, Kane also passed a restless night. War lent itself to death and cruelties, thus was its nature; however, he was unprepared to mistreat women in so vile a manner. Deeming Dupree's conduct reprehensible, his visit to the prisoners would be his last opportunity to alleviate their discomforts in whatever small way he could before the mission that might well take his life.

Immediately Catherine's hands flew to her auburn hair, performing useless motions to tidy her impossibly disarrayed tresses.

"Of course, Lieutenant," came Clarissa's pointed response. "I suppose we could spare the time for a brief audience. Don't you agree, Miss Jackson?"

Too distracted to worry over her disheveled appearance, Catherine ignored her companion, concentrating her attentions to her mud-splattered, slept-in frock. Finally recognizing the hopelessness of her efforts, she drew her blankets tighter, obscuring as much of the dress as possible.

Kane entered, hat in hand, making a graceful bow. "I've come to inquire about your welfare. Is there anything which I might do to see to your comfort before we march?"

"Oh, Lieutenant, we are perfectly delirious over our quarters." Gesturing wildly, Clarissa proceeded to feign the motions of someone delightedly pointing out her most prized possessions. Indicating the ground upon which they'd slept, "Why, this bedding is beyond the realm of reality. It's like sleeping on nothing at all. And these toiletry articles just defy description."

"Clarissa, please. Lieutenant Kane is trying to be kind to us." To Kane, Catherine said, "It is so thoughtful of you to remember our needs as you prepare for battle."

Normally, Catherine Jackson would never have been so bold as to openly flirt with any man, but in Stewart Kane she sensed a gentle, understanding soul. By some miracle, he was immune to Clarissa's wiles and instead seemed genuinely attracted to her. Feeling her cheeks flush, she remembered the thrill of walking on his arm back to the Rebel camp. *Oh Lord*, she silently prayed... *see him safely through this war.* Quickly, she looked back at Clarissa, as if her friend had heard treasonous prayer just uttered.

Her arms crossed and face distorted in rage, she angrily tapped her soiled slippers. "You are expecting another encounter with Union forces, are you not?" Clarissa questioned.

"I do realize the primitiveness of these circumstances, and I do wish that I could correct them. Perhaps I can be of some assistance. The generals say that we will be within Washington before long. If you would give me the locations of your homes, I might try to see that short messages from you could be delivered to alleviate the anxieties of your families."

"How exceedingly gracious of..."

Clarissa interrupted, forcibly turning Catherine from her ardent admiration of the Lieutenant.

"Have you been rendered senseless? It is perfectly obvious what he's doing."

Directing her remarks toward the startled officer, she continued. "He's hoping to gain our confidence with this kindness. Then, he will prod us for information concerning, say Washington barracks location. No, Lieutenant, we have no messages."

Referring to his attire of a worker rather than a soldier, "Perhaps your time would be used more wisely changing into suitable battle attire, or is this uniform of backwoods Rebels?"

Caught off guard and fearing that he could compromise their plan, he hurriedly excused himself, leaving the women arguing over the exchange.

"How could you be so rude?" demanded Catherine.

"Well, someone had to save you. Really Catherine, I don't believe I have ever seen you behave so shamefully about a man, and to do so to the enemy!"

From the indignation in Clarissa's voice, she knew better than to argue. "I thought," her voice barely a whisper, "that I might improve our lot by getting along."

Of all the experiences introduced by Clarissa, the Morgan girl's attitude toward men puzzled Catherine most. Even so clearly an expression of kindness took on an aura of ...of challenge to Clarissa, as if the mere suggestion of what she might do became transformed into an invitation of rebellion.

Still, men flew to her side with the ardor of bees to flowers, that when repulsed could not resist returning.

"You aren't fooling me, Cathey. You're smitten with him."

"No more than you are with Captain Thomas." Catherine's words touched an all too tender wound. Whether she wished to admit it to her friend or even herself, Catherine's observation rang true.

Hers would not be the only traitorous prayer offered for a Rebel's safe return.

*****

The side boarded wagons burdened with several large crates lumbered down a seldom traveled road toward Washington. Inside the crates, a cache of revolvers, rifles, and their necessary ammunition was buried under blankets and tenting materials.

A force of ten men, including Kane, Thomas, and Davis were attired as civilians. Purposefully, Davis guided the wagons away from the advancing Confederate forces. The plan called for the kidnappers to enter the Capital removed from their comrades, thus lessening the chances of detection as enemy soldiers.

Jed was pleased with his men. All were eager and brave enough to withstand the pressures of the mission. Strict orders had been issued to the men by the General regarding the purpose and importance of their task.

"We'll be successful as long as no one lapses into his Southern speech," muttered Jed to no one in particular.

"Don't ya'll worry none, Sir," drawled a private. Then changing his accent he continued. "We'll be the best damned Yankees you ever heard."

Those within earshot laughed heartily.

Once underway, Jed's indecision concerning the mission dissolved. Duty, so ingrained into a gentleman and now a soldier, pervaded any misgivings about their Cause. A man's personal convictions could not interfere, lest the price for such vacillation prove too great.

After traveling a few miles, the unmistakable cacophony of cannon fire echoed in the distance, but as they neared the city, the sounds were foreign.

Wagons, carriages, carts, and any other means of conveyances were streaming from the city. Many were loaded with treasured belongings which had been hastily strapped and were suffering such damage in transit as to render them unusable at whatever destination they reached. The aura of panic in the evacuation was unsettling to the disguised Rebels for it was impeding their progress, the carefully detailed timetable now useless.

As the small convoy reached the outskirts of the Capital, a sentry stopped them. As planned, Thomas and Kane took charge of the volatile situation. With looks of impatient disdain, Jed spoke to the guards whose makeshift roadblock of whitewashed siding stood between them and their goal. Had the Rebels but known, these men, as well as the majority of the uniformed soldiers they would encounter, were an impromptu militia pressed into service to allow what seasoned fighters that could be mustered to be sent to the front. The young man's instructions as to the loading of his musket had been hasty. In fact, the gun upon which his life depended would not have fired had he found the cause to use it.

"Look here soldier, we've got to get through. We're under orders to take these moving crates to the White House."

"Let's see those orders. This is a highly secured area."

"Secure my ass," chimed Stewart. "There's Rebels closing in on us from all sides, people are stampeding to the countryside, and you are telling us this area is anywhere close to being held? Why, McDowell and his boys will be passing the women and children by evening."

The second sentry, angered at Kane's all too accurate accounting of the Union army's prowess, had aimed his rifle toward him.

"Just what the hell gives you the right to call us cowards? I don't see no uniform on your back," came the fervent response.

"We're wasting time here," shouted Jed in an effort to diffuse the situation. "How close do you figure the Secessesh to be?" he inquired of the first picket.

"The last report was over an hour ago. Don't know if it bears repeating, but a medical wagon driver who was evacuating the wounded said we'd be lucky to hold them off until nightfall."

"Then we've no time to spare. The important documents we were told to remove must not fall into Rebel hands."

"Your orders?"

Feigning aggravation, Jed extracted folded papers from his pocket. The men inside the wagons made inconspicuous movements toward the weapons hidden within the cargo. The more skeptical soldier, whose rifle had yet to be lowered, inched toward his partner. Stealing glances to the papers and back to the wagon, he appraised the forged orders.

"Don't look like no orders I ever seen."

Kane quickly interrupted, "Great heavens, do you think anybody has time to get things prettied up! Beauregard will be sleeping in Lincoln's bed because of men like you who are more interested in official-looking papers than getting the job done."

At that exact moment a shell landed a few streets over, sending the horses into frenzy. It was all Jed and his counterpart in the second wagon could do to keep them from bolting.

"Damnation, let us pass!" screamed Jed through clinched teeth.

Thrusting the orders at Thomas, he threw his rifle down and began moving the boards that had hours before graced a Washington home. Seizing the opportunity, the Southerners urged the horses forward, the lurch sending an off-balanced passenger to his knees.

Safely out of hearing to the sentries, Jed shouted, "That shell was a gift from God Almighty. Those two were easily convinced as to what we'll face at the White House. You men say your prayers."

Jed's words proved less than prophetic as the men drove without further resistance to the rear of the President's mansion. The bewildered band of kidnappers stole silent glances of disbelief. Unbeknownst to them, events transpiring at the formal entrance, acknowledged God's second intervention on their behalf.

Privy to the most accurate information and a personal plea from General Scott, the President had made the agonizing decision to send his family to a safer location. As each shell fell, he became more convinced of the wisdom of his choice. Amid the furor of Mary Lincoln's ranting, he struggled to kiss his sons, assuring them of his own safety and urging Mary to board the carriage. Every possible man had been recruited from the White House Corps to safeguard the first family. Putting himself at great risk, Lincoln issued the order leaving the mansion all but unguarded, since the greater portion of the security force had joined those men at the front hours earlier.

His great shoulders sagged as he watched the carriage disappear from sight. Prayers for their well-being and the success of the army dominated his thoughts. Only at the urging of his aide and friend, Colonel Ward Hill Lamon, did he slowly move toward the entrance.

"How does the tide change so rapidly?" Withdrawing the crumpled telegraph message which had been the first news received of the previous day's conflict. It read, "Great victory."

Before Lamon could offer a response, Lincoln posed yet another question.

"Ward, what will happen if McDowell is unsuccessful at his attempt to defeat the Confederates?"

"There's really no cause for such speculation. Our reinforcements will attack from the rear, squeezing them into easily breached lines."

The conversation trailed as the men entered the mansion closely followed by an escort of two raw recruits. Approaching the desk of his secretary, Mrs. Kennedy rose to accompany him into his office. In her hands were several sheets of paper all inscribed with perfect penmanship.

"Mr. President, the cabinet arrives within the hour."

Lincoln stepped behind a small pigeon-holed desk in the center of his office and directed his words to the primly dressed matron. "Mrs. Kennedy, I feel it necessary to alleviate you of your duties for the next few days." Seeing her dismay, he explained. "Only until we are more certain of the outcome of the hostilities.

"It is most unnecessary…" began Mrs. Kennedy.

Uncharacteristically, his tone rose authoritatively. "I insist that you return to your family and do whatever you feel is called for in light of the Rebel advance. Colonel Lamon will personally escort you. There will be no further discussion."

"But I cannot leave you unguarded. Any number of the remaining sentries will be only too proud to accompany Mrs. Kennedy to her home," objected Lamon.

"I appreciate your concern; however, the soldiers on duty will suffice. Please, be on your way."

Mrs. Kennedy and the aide exited the office, leaving the commander-in-chief of the United States Army protected by a skeletal force of frightened recruits who winced at each explosion of the enemy's artillery.

Unobserved, the ten had unloaded the large crates onto wheeled carts for entrance into the series of ramps. The Lincoln boys were known to play hide and seek with them, and the President often utilized the tunnels to protect himself from the throng of office and petition seekers who lay in wait in the public halls. Only the First Lady avoided the "catacombs," as she dubbed them, preferring the attention paid her as she passed through the crowds.

The memories of Jed and Stewart served them well, guiding the men to a ground floor entrance partially obscured by flowering shrubbery. A young picket in an ill-fitting set of Union blues aimed his rifle at the approaching men.

"Halt! State your business."

Jed emerged from behind the cart, removing the orders from his breast pocket, he offered explanation. "We have been sent by Secretary of War Cameron to remove sensitive documents to prevent Rebel capture in the event, God forbid, a defeat of our troops."

With little heed to the orders, the soldier allowed passage into the bowels of the executive mansion. The boy, barely sixteen, would not have recognized a genuine order, having entered the service of his country the day prior against his mother's vehement objections.

Proceeding with caution, they wheeled the ammunition laden cargo through the dimly lighted maze of ramps. Arriving at the last accessible doorway, a silent signal alerted the men to remove their weapons and stand against the tunnel walls, obscured by the shadows.

Captain Thomas knocked cautiously at the door to what he recalled to be the Presidential office.

"Yes?"

Kane and Thomas eased the door open. A quick survey of the French gray papered office left them momentarily dazzled by their good fortune of finding Lincoln alone.

"Mr. President, Sir, I hope Secretary of War Cameron notified you of our coming."

Jed extended his hand to Mr. Lincoln as he continued. "We are to remove any sensitive documents lest they fall into Rebel hands. The Secretary instructed us to conceal them inside the crates we have in the passageway. Once we have left the White House, the crates will be loaded amid other cargo aboard a ship bound for New York."

It seemed as though his words failed to gain the President's full attention. His eyes fixed on the window, only a small twitch had registered in his expression when an artillery shell burst. The man was too deeply in thought, concerned for the welfare of so many on both sides of the conflict, to allow another of Cameron's usurpations of authority to distract him.

Stewart Kane appraised the most powerful man in the United States, assessing him as taller than expected. He was also struck by the physical plainness of Old Abe. Kane almost laughed as the thought occurred that he had seen mules with far more handsome countenances. Had women the vote, mused the Lieutenant, Lincoln would still be defending farmers in Illinois.

Slowly Lincoln looked into the eyes of the young man. "My personal papers are few at this time; however, I will turn them over to your able hands."

"I'll fetch the crating."

Kane hastily approached the door, admitting his comrades. Half the force remained, guarding the ramp way. The President rose and stood gazing at the half finished Capitol dome. This melancholy, which had invaded his soul from the moment he had read of the first shots at Fort Sumter, resulted from the personal responsibility he assumed for the death or injury of every soldier, regardless of uniform. The President's mind was constantly consumed with which alternatives might save the nation and prevent more wholesale slaughter.

Ever observant, Stewart recognized the heavy obligation of a president whose army was in the throes of defeat. There was no envy in the younger man's heart.

As Lincoln pondered, a staff physician, selected especially for his knowledge in anesthesia, drew a bottle and a white cloth from his coat. He timing was critical, for osmosis would permeate the distinctive odor throughout the room.

At his captain's signal, Dr. David Cantrell's seasoned hand poured the premeasured liquid. Immediately he pressed the cloth over the President's face. As if alerted to the danger, Lincoln turned to face the doctor as he was about to reach around the President's body. His back to them, Thomas and Kane grabbed his long arms, allowing the doctor easy access.

The listless President was unceremoniously placed within the confines of a crate.

As an afterthought, Stewart placed Lincoln's distinctive stovepipe hat beside his limp form.

"Are you sure he will remain asleep until we are outside the city?" Jed addressed the physician.

"He'll doze for several hours, at which time I can always administer more. It's really quite harmless if you disregard the nausea. I do suggest that we open the windows to eliminate the tell-tale odor."

Joining the troops on guard, the crates were moved down the ramps without incident. The decoy crate easily exited the passage into the afternoon sky, but the second crate, weighted by the sleeping President, balked at the doorstep.

Seeing the struggle, the unwitting Union picket set his gun aside to offer his shoulder. He provided the necessary momentum thereby helping to deliver Abraham Lincoln to the enemy. This bit of irony would haunt him the rest of his days.

Chapter Two

Washington, D.C., one hour after the President's abduction

Secretary of war Simon Cameron paced the floor of the Presidential office. He abhorred tardiness in others and made his personal punctuality a point of pride. "This is absolutely disgraceful. The enemy is knocking at our door; decisions must be made."

Naval Secretary Gideon Welles sat calmly in an overstuffed chair and relit his cigar. "All of us appreciate your impatience, Simon. The loss of your niece and her friend has been a great shock to your family and to us all. The deaths of Union sons were expected, but the deaths of its daughters..." his voice trailed into silence.

All around the room, Lincoln's cabinet members made vain attempts to busy themselves by reading newspapers or messages from the front. For the most part, they had been silent the better part of the hour; however, the quiet was punctuated by the staccato gunfire, artillery, and Cameron's outbursts, all of which seemed directed to no one in particular.

Shifting in his seat, the thickly set Welles could not accustom himself to his surroundings. A reformed Democrat, the fifty-eight-year-old silently fumed over Cameron's remarks, noting that the circumstances called for unity rather than more division. Turning to Edward Bates, the Attorney General and one he suspected as a true ally of Lincoln's, he shook his head signaling disgust with the Secretary of War's remarks and impatience.

The voice of Edwin McMasters Stanton, the Secretary of State was heard to agree, as was most always the case, with Cameron. "The original gorilla has kept us waiting long enough." He pounded a nearby table as if his insulting pronouncement deserved added emphasis.

What a difference William Seward's refusal of the position of Secretary of State had made upon this cabinet, contemplated Welles. *If only Seward had not been so determined to influence Lincoln's appointments to this group.*

A shell burst only a few blocks away. Secretary of the Treasury Salmon P. Chase, and Postmaster General Montgomery Blair rushed to the window.

"I swear," remarked Blair, "that was close enough to unseat Jackson." His attempt at levity in reference to the equestrian statue of the former President, which sat across Pennsylvania Avenue in Lafayette Square, garnered few smiles.

To a man the cabinet stared as the door to the office burst open, admitting a winded Colonel Lamon. Following a quick survey of the office, a puzzled expression crossed his face.

"Please excuse me. I was not expecting that your briefing would be so lengthy. Will the President be returning soon? I have the latest information from General McDowell."

"The President," Cameron curtly remarked, "has not shown us the courtesy of keeping his appointment. It would seem that he and Mrs. Kennedy are noticeably absent. In an effort to bait Lamon, the Secretary's next statement was delivered with an accusatory tone. "Let me recall. I did hear that Mrs. Lincoln and the children were no longer in residence."

Chase's features broadened into a wide grin. The notion of Abe Lincoln as a ladies' man was vastly amusing, but the image of one of Mary Lincoln's tirades unleashed upon her husband and the demure Mrs. Kennedy led to his private amusement.

"I have just returned from escorting Mrs. Kennedy to her family," snapped Lamon, failing to appreciate Cameron's remark. "It was my impression that he was awaiting your arrivals in the office." Crossing to the President's highly polished desk as he spoke, he retrieved several papers from a neatly placed stack. "Here are the notes he prepared for your meeting. I'm sure he's only left for a few moments and been delayed by some sort of crisis elsewhere."

Cameron and Stanton, allied in their belief that each was more deserving of the Presidency than Lincoln, approached the Colonel. "Then, I suggest you locate him immediately. This war and the needs of the government do not pause for his meanderings," demanded Stanton.

"My heavens, our brave men are being slaughtered at an alarming rate, and the Army awaits the directives from this office." With each word Cameron had closed the distance between Lamon and himself. By the end of his speech, the two were face to face.

Lamon had never cared for either man, sensing the Secretaries' disloyalties to the administration. It was his personal opinion, one he had deliberately kept private, that Cameron or Stanton was capable of any act that would embarrass or discredit the President he had sworn to protect.

Such hypocrisy had placed the Colonel on his guard from practically their initial introductions.

"I'll initiate a search of the grounds." Lamon turned and exited the confines, feeling the eyes of the cabinet boring into his back.

Colonel Ward H. Lamon's emotions ranged from confusion to frustration and ultimately to concern. The dispatching of every available man and servant at the Presidential mansion had uncovered little knowledge of the President's whereabouts. Returning to the office, he informed the cabinet of his findings.

"It would seem that Mr. Lincoln has 'disappeared.'" The last word was delivered by the Colonel in a soft tone which betrayed his lack of confidence in his own investigation. As he explained the exhaustive measures he employed, the men of power murmured among themselves, offering possibilities of which none seemed of substantial basis to convince even its author of its feasibility.

"Regardless of the circumstances of President Lincoln's absence, we have no other recourse but to summon Vice-President Hamlin. The War must be uppermost in our minds." Pragmatically, the Attorney General took control of the chaos.

Even Cameron could voice no dissention, and Hamlin was summoned and summarily briefed on the gravity of the situation. As the Vice-President and the Secretaries took the reins of the government, Lamon, his presence of no import, left the office via the ramp way.

*****

Often looking at the flooring to reassure his steps, he proceeded cautiously. From the moment he had entered the passageway, a pervading odor had pierced his senses. Had he been in any other surroundings, the Colonel would have identified the source immediately; however, the absurdity of its location and the prevailing sense of bewilderment over Lincoln's disappearance caused him to dismiss the fact. Making his way round the corner, his eyes caught a wadded white cloth the doctor would never realize was lost. Bending over the fabric, the Colonel allowed the realization to take hold. Drawing his pistol, he raced through the labyrinth, stumbling occasionally in the semi-darkness.

Throwing open the door to the White House grounds; he frightened the young sentry who momentarily believed the Rebels were attacking his position from behind.

"Oh, Colonel, you scared the life out of me!"

"Private, has anyone exited here since you have been on guard?"

"Well, no, I don't remember anyone except our boys who were taking those papers to hide from the Rebs. I had to help them get the last one out. It was some heavy load."

Lamon's shoulders and countenance fell. "By heavens, son. You've help abduct the President!" The Private's face acknowledged his confusion.

Chapter Three

Alexandria, Virginia, July 24, 1861

Night fell on an abandoned barn where the fate of an entire nation rested on the events that would transpire within. The wearied band alternated sentinel positions at the door and in the surrounding woods.

Since his abduction, the President of the United States had passed his days resolved as to the folly of escape, but exceedingly anxious to learn of news from the front and affirmation of his family's safety. Allowed to walk freely within the confines of his "prison," Lincoln appreciated the humane treatment exhibited by his captors, developing a rapport for the young Captain during long conversations which served to pass the dreary hours of isolation.

Always cautious, lest he betray their location and any events of the War, Thomas was extremely candid about his background and his personal opinions regarding secession and slavery. Were all as resolute as Jed Thomas, Lincoln speculated, the Army of the Potomac would never emerge the victor. Jed, too, had grown to appreciate Lincoln, enjoying his homespun humor and the endless parables he recited to make a fitting point to any circumstance. The President, having just finished such a tale concerning a wise farmer and a citified banker, was in the midst of his distinctive laughter.

Suddenly the barn door swung open to admit six riders. Jed left the President in the loft and hurried down to the floor. A closer inspection revealed that two of the riders wore blindfolds, their hands bound to the saddle horns.

During the dismounting, the cap of one of the prisoners was knocked from atop the head. A mane of dark hair cascaded to the shoulders of a face that Jed laughingly recognized. As a Rebel soldier united her hands, Clarissa Morgan launched a stream of complaints concerning the women's treatment, attire, and forced ride. Colonel Dupree, long since weary of the troublesome Miss Morgan, refused comment. His refusal incensed her all the more. It appeared that a blind ride through the night and three days of captivity had done little to break her spirit.

Jed rushed to retrieve her fallen cap. "Why, Miss Morgan, I believe you have dropped your stylish new bonnet." As he rose to give her the fallen article, he took her hand and kissed it. "How kind of you to brighten our dismal surroundings."

Clarissa Morgan rudely removed her hand from his. "The fact that I am a lady precludes me from expressing my sentiments, Captain Thomas."

The arms offered Catherine Jackson by Lieutenant Kane were gratefully received, as he helped her dismount. "Lieutenant, how wonderful to see a friendly face. I was greatly concerned for you during the battle."

Seeing Dupree's eyes scanning the barn, Davis nodded in the direction of the loft. "He's up in the loft with Doctor Cantrell.

Other than being a mite sick to his stomach, he's fine. Should I bring them down?"

"By all means." Dupree, speaking to the men who had accompanied him, "Escort the ladies outside. We'll let you know when to reenter."

"Ladies," beckoned a soldier. "You heard the Colonel."

"It seems all I have heard for an eternity is the Colonel. What a grand diversion to be able to hear from someone else, complained the high-spirited prisoner as she and her friend were ushered out the door of the barn.

"Miss Morgan, I shall do my upmost to grant your wish this very evening. Your delicate ears will sample the wisdom of someone you least expect to hear," responded Colonel Dupree.

Clarissa wheeled about. "Then tell Jeff Davis to go to hell and save him a trip out in the damp!"

Jed could contain himself no longer. Clarissa's bluntness and the irony of the entire situation were beyond endurance. Steward joined in, and soon the aged rafters echoed the laughter of everyone, save the Colonel

The creaking of the wooden door broke the mood of the merriment and signaled Davis and Cantrell to escort the President to the center of activity.

"Mr. Lincoln, I am Colonel Adam Dupree. It is my extreme privilege to represent President Jefferson Davis in welcoming you to the Confederate States of America. I trust you have not been greatly inconvenienced by our 'invitation' to meet here this evening."

As they shook, the hands of the President engulfed those of his captor. The Colonel continued, "I am pleased to inform you that our Army has pushed within the boundaries of Washington. The loss of life numbers in the thousands on both sides." Pleased with the effect his words wrought upon Lincoln, he added. "By this hour tomorrow, the C.S.A. will be in control of the strategic buildings in the Capital."

Cheers erupted from the men who had not yet learned of the Southern success.

Dupree sat himself upon some bales of hay that men had arranged as makeshift furniture. "Were I in your place, Sir, I would be extremely skeptical of my words; therefore, I have brought some means to persuade you of my truthfulness." One of his men withdrew a newspaper from a saddlebag, handing it to Lincoln. As the President examined a dated copy of the *Washington Constitution*, a slight tremor of his hands was discernible to those nearest him. Three bold headlines were emblazoned across the newsprint: "Rebs hold city outskirts," "Army in full retreat," and "Casualty lists." The list of wounded and dead brought tears to his eyes.

Looking up at Dupree, he spoke. "What assurance do I have that this publication is genuine?"

"Other than my word as both an officer and a gentleman, you are well aware that the *Constitution* office is located in the section of Washington opposite the Manassas area."

Dupree allowed his words to achieve the desired effect before proceeding. "President Davis has empowered me to offer you the South's terms for a Northern surrender. These were drafted some weeks ago in anticipation of a victory for our glorious Cause. If you will permit me to extend to you the terms?"

Lincoln merely nodded his assent.

"In order to prevent further loss of military and civilian lives, the Confederate States of America respectfully offers these terms of surrender:

1. Union soldiers will lay down their arms without further conflict.

2. The United States will recognize the Confederate States of America as a separate and sovereign nation and will afford it equal status with all nations friendly to the United States.

3. The United States agrees to return all fugitive slaves.

4. The United States will allow for popular election by voters to determine whether territory on the North American continent will become Union or Confederate.

5. In full faith, the Confederate States of America agrees to return all conquered areas and prisoners, provided that no further interference with the Southern way of life is forthcoming from this date forward.

6. Withdrawal of Southern forces will begin upon approval of these terms by both branches of the Legislature."

The President appraised the surrender agreement; however, he felt the term "surrender" was hardly applicable. As the South often proclaimed, it sought not to be an aggressor nation, asking only for its independence and expressing its desire to be free of federal controls. Taking a second look at the newspaper, he scanned the casualty roster and noted the dismay the havoc precipitated in the city of artillery blasts, fighting in the street, and the many fires resulting from the conflict. *Thank God that Mother and the boys are not in residence,* he thought.

A long pause preceded his next words.

"To what extent has the government been made aware of my status? If they believe that I am dead, Vice-President Hamlin will have assumed the Presidency, rendering my signature invalid."

Dupree smiled, enjoying the control he held over Lincoln. "That fact has been taken into consideration."

"Davis, bring them in."

The President's eyes focused on the door. As it opened, Clarissa and Catherine gratefully sought the shelter of the barn. As their eyes met those of Lincoln, even Clarissa was dumbfounded by what she saw.

At length the Colonel began, "Miss Jackson, Miss Morgan, may I introduce you to your President?"

"The introductions are unnecessary, I assure you. Clarissa? Catherine?" Lincoln extended his hands, clasping first one single hand then another. "It is unbelievable that we should meet again under these circumstances." He turned to his captors. "Have you men no consciences?" To steal these women from their homes and use them in such a degrading manner is beyond the realms of decency, even in times of war."

Stewart was quick to avenge the honor of the Confederacy. "Let me assure you that such was not the case."

Before he could explain, a torrent of words gushed from the dark-haired woman. So frenzied were her expressions and gestures that the entire scenario resembled a schoolgirl relating a hateful prank to her headmaster. To her credit, she did accept responsibility for their presence at Manassas, but she squandered few opportunities to make their interment seem all the more vile. "They dressed us as men, and then..." As if some fleeting thought had suddenly penetrated her clouded mind, she stopped in mid thought. "But Mr. Lincoln, how did you ever get here?" Momentarily off guard, she combed one face to another searching for some semblance of reason for the absurdities of the moment.

"This is really quite enough of your ravings. You have an uncanny ability to try a man's patience." Dupree stood before her, slapping a riding crop at his gloved hand. "Suffice it to say that Mr. Lincoln was 'removed' from the White House and has become a prisoner of the Confederacy."

Addressing the President he said, "When the document is signed, I will personally see to it that these young ladies are taken to the Union lines and released. Miss Morgan will present the surrender to her uncle and attest to its authenticity. When the Confederate battle flag is raised above the Capitol, we will release you and withdraw all hostile forces."

Lincoln sat back on the hay bales, contemplating the fate of the United States. When asked years later about that night's events, Jed Thomas would estimate the time as infinite. He was able to recall with great clarity the bowed head, lined face, and despondent carriage as the great leader pondered the fates of thousands of soldiers. In silence, Lincoln dipped his pen in the India ink and initiated the first letters of his sprawling signature.

Upon realization of their victory, rousing Rebel yells shook the rafters of the old farm structure. Only Dupree resisted the temptation to join in the celebratory cheers. In an uncommon gesture of compassion, he shook Lincoln's hand and patted him gently on his slumping shoulders. Audible only to the President because of the delirium, Dupree spoke to the dejected leader. "I know how difficult this was for you. Rest assured that many mothers, wives, and fathers owe you the lives of their men folk. You have made the correct decision, and history will bear you out.

The great man's expression exhibited no emotion or gratitude for Dupree's kindness, though he would later tell his wife of the Colonel's graciousness to a surrendered foe.

"Quiet men! The war must still be won." As the noise abated, he told the women, "My men will escort you as close to the Federal lines as possible. Since it will be daylight by the time of your arrival, your safety will be assured; however, you will be provided a flag of truce under which you will be able to deliver these documents to the government and verify the authenticity of the President's signature. We await the signal flag over the Capitol."

Her eyes clouded with tears, Clarissa fought the urged to drag her claw like nails across his smug face, yet somehow she knew from the first day at Bull Run that the War had been lost on the battlefield. Without protest she submitted to the blindfold.

When she was astride her horse, Jed walked over and said, "You are a brave woman, Miss Morgan. I feel quite strongly that our paths will cross again under more pleasant conditions."

Though she never acknowledged his words, Jed saw her lips quiver as the tears fell from the folds of cloth that covered her eyes. The horse followed the tug at its reigns, and he watched her disappear into the darkness, leaving him an emptiness that he could neither quench nor explain.

Chapter Four

The Union line, hours later

A picket stared, rubbed his strained and sleepless eyes, and again bored into an early morning fog.

"Get the Major, quickly!"

As if by fate, Major Gray was making his first rounds after another restless night. How long his volunteers could hold off the sharpshooting Secessionists, he estimated to be a day or so at most. The inexperienced Union Army was no match for the Confederate forces led by nine major officers seasoned on the battlefields of the Mexican and Indian Wars. To his knowledge, Major Gray could name only one of the three Union division commanders and three of the nine brigadiers who had even faced an enemy in battle.

The thought of another day of casualties and suffering preyed upon his very being. When a young private alerted him to his picket's request, he hurried his steps. Sergeant Edison was an experienced man with whom he had been in service in Texas.

"What is it, Edison?"

"I'm sorry, Sir. I supposed it's the strain and lack of sleep, but I swear that I saw two women on horseback waving a white flag."

The men entrenched nearby began to laugh. Gray was about to suggest a respite far away from the front, when strident voices pierced the fog. "We're women. Don't shoot. It's Clarissa Morgan and Catherine Jackson!"

The soldiers in the trenches rose and squinted. Everyone was awestruck as the Sergeant's apparition took on a tangible form.

At least, thought Edison, this War hasn't left me completely daft.

Harold Gray was astounded by the tale woven by Clarissa Morgan. The occasional additions by Catherine Jackson underscored the horrors these women had experienced. The more beautiful of the two had allowed him to take charge of their activities, a move which he mistook as weakness and a need for a masculine tower of strength upon which to depend. In actuality, Clarissa was exhausted by the ordeals which had begun at Bull Run.

Gray thought it more expedient to take the women to the Cameron household. Himself a product of the Washington social set, he knew Cameron well as a power that moved within the government. With the President gone, Cameron was the one individual Gray felt competent enough to take charge, and he was, after all, the woman's uncle.

As the horses maneuvered the vacated street, Catherine and her friend were horrified by the damage rendered by the Southern artillery shells. Crater-like holes gapped the broad thoroughfares that would ordinarily have been bustling with carriages ferrying businessmen and politicians to their destinations within the city. Clarissa reined her mount to stare at a home on Pennsylvania Avenue near her own whose front room had been blasted away, its heavy draperies flapping in the wind. On many houses, a mourning wreath had been placed to designate it as the home of one of the dead, while others bore holes where stray bullets had found their marks.

So dazed was Clarissa that their arrival at her uncle's home escaped notice. Catherine had already dismounted before Clarissa felt a hand upon her arm. She jumped in a reflexive response when the door flew open and the Cameron's maid, Kathleen, emerged screaming loudly in her heavy Irish brogue, alerting neighbors on the block.

"Mrs. Cameron, come out here! Miss Clarissa is home! Hurry, Mrs. Cameron!"

Partly from fatigue and from her aunt's impropriety, Clarissa fell to her knees laughing. It was a rare occasion when her aunt ventured past her bedroom door in her dressing gown, and here she was on the street of Washington, her gown tail flying.

Hugging both girls, she took no pauses between words. "Claire, oh my child, what have they done to you? Catherine, your parents have been devastated with the Rebels attacking and you missing. Thank God you're both safe. Where have you been?"

Before either girl could answer, the slim frame of Simon Cameron appeared. Seldom an emotional, man, his eyes blurred with tears at the sight of the girls. Kissing them both, he carried Clarissa into the house, while the Major assisted Catherine.

Their story related, Mrs. Cameron insisted that both girls retire for a bath and much needed sleep. The Secretary sent his carriage for the Jacksons; however, the damage to most of the streets made direct routes impossible and travel time lengthy. To conserve time, the Major and the Secretary rode on horseback to the White House where the remainder of the cabinet had been summoned.

With the Southerners plunging deeper into the city and the President in Rebel hands, the cabinet members saw no alternative, in light of Lincoln's surrender, an act Stanton and Cameron labeled as symbolic of the man's character. Within two hours the few legislators who had not fled the advancing Confederate forces voted. Beauregard's stars and bars flew proudly over the Capitol of its conquered territory.

Chapter Five

Washington, D. C., July 28, 1861

As he closed the lens of his square, gold-rimmed eyeglasses, Edwin Stanton's mind was occupied with the same thoughts that had invaded his waking hours since Lincoln's cowardly surrender to the Confederacy. Clearing his desk of the morning's paperwork, he prepared for a meeting requested by Cameron.

Also at the Secretary of War's request, the other cabinet members were to be kept unaware, a practice to which Stanton was no stranger. As with most politicians, he considered it a common practice, if not a governmental necessity, to hold a backroom session to cement one's ideas with his allies before facing the opposition.

A sharp knock announced Cameron's arrival. Upon answering the door, the Secretary of State was surprised to see Salmon Chase accompanying Cameron. Chase, by no means Lincoln's ardent supporter, seldom expressed solidarity with Cameron or him, either.

As the men seated themselves before his desk, Stanton allowed himself the opportunity to delve into the past of the Treasury Secretary in search of a motive for his presence. Chase was an ambitious politician, hardly a character flaw to Stanton, who admired such a trait, provided that his own best interest was furthered by such aspirations. Also no secret were Chase's major disappointment precipitated by Lincoln. He ardently sought the cabinet post awarded Stanton, electing only to settle to the treasury position when he discovered that Lincoln had announced his acceptance without consultation.

Lacking the arrogance of a Seward, he assumed the post, fuming over Lincoln's betrayal. Of course, as with the men who completed the trio, Chase obsessively desired the Presidency. Losing the office to better men was palpable to some extent; however, to forfeit the position to the tale-citing rail splitter was a humiliation too great to bear.

Despite the location, Cameron seized control of the agenda. To have expected otherwise would have marked a fool. Political manipulation was an art form well perfected by Simon Cameron.

Since his destitute family allowed a physician to adopt the ten-year-old Simon, the Secretary began to collect friendships and favors for use at appropriate times. His reputation was built in Pennsylvania politics. The Secretary never forgot a friend or an enemy, which proved, at times, difficult for observers to differentiate.

"Gentlemen, I trust that Lincoln's degrading surrender of our forces weighs as heavily upon you as it does on my own heart?" Without waiting for a reply, he continued. "In the past few days, I have dwelt upon no other concern than the restoration of the honor of this nation through retaliatory measures that will bring the South to its knees."

"As Secretary of War," interjected Stanton, "surely you must recognize the folly of renewed warfare?"

Cameron's retort tore bitterly at his colleague. "I am all too aware of the military's shortcomings, for which I can hardly be held accountable."

"I don't think he meant to imply…" began Chase who was ignored by the others.

"There are other means of warfare, Edwin."

"Such as?" queried Stanton.

"Economics, my friend."

His interest thus aroused, he allowed Cameron to continue unimpeded.

"I have arranged for several backers who would use the means at their disposals to sabotage the economy of the Confederacy. Think for a moment, Gentlemen. The South is, for the most part, devoid of industry and totally dependent on two elements: cotton and the slave labor necessary to produce the crop abundantly."

He sat back in his chair to provide the suspenseful pause needed to underscore his next pronouncement. "By reducing their labor force, the production of cotton, tobacco, and food stuffs will plummet, sending the South into an economic chaos from which it will be unable to recover without our help. The United States will be only too pleased to assist our Southern brothers," his tone heavily laced in sarcasm. "Of course, this aid will be on our terms."

His pleasure with the genius of his strategy brightened his usually somber face with a twisted smile.

Contemplating the feasibility of Cameron's proposal, Stanton prepared questions which he began to jot down on the paper he always provided himself when discussing business matters.

"But such a course of action will violate the terms of the surrender," Chase added more as a question than a statement. He began to rise. "I want no part of such a plan."

"Sit down!" demanded Cameron. "We owe no allegiance to a paper signed by a coward seeking to save his own life." He raised his hand, index finger pointing in Chase's face. "You will procure funds from such treasury sources as you can transfer without detection."

"And if I refuse?" Chase headed for the door.

"Then the two of us will swear to your part in the inception of this venture."

Chase's eyes darted to Stanton in hopes of securing an ally against the obviously demented Cameron. Stanton peered over his spectacles, nodding his assent.

As Chase slowly reclaimed his seat, Cameron continued to outline his plan for the next two hours. Each portion of the strategy was intricately detailed, leaving Stanton scant room for suggested improvements.

At the conclusion of the discussion, Chase and Stanton were well versed on every aspect of Cameron's scheme, save his most important objectives.

The Secretary of War envisioned a Confederacy humbled by economic hardships so severe that an influx of Northern Republicans could easily gain complete control of its lands and politics, especially if a stipulation for the Confederacy's readmission prohibited the vote to any Rebel soldier or office holder.

This Republican stronghold coupled with the admiration of a grateful nation, would bow to his influence, and, depending upon the time frame, he would see to the impeachment of Lincoln or his own election. Then and only then would the death of his brother at Bull Run be avenged.

Chapter Six

Outskirts of Washington, D.C., August 1861

Click! The sound echoed from the beams of the ruggedly constructed roadhouse. The owner, and old friend for the right price, had been easily persuaded to forego normal business practices this warm afternoon. Cameron placed his watch into his pocket, knowing before he even looked, that the agreed upon hour had not yet arrived. Still, he was hopeful that the necessary minutes had elapsed.

In mulling over his agenda for this encounter, Cameron's thoughts traveled to the first cabinet meeting following the President's release and subsequent return to Washington. Cameron spoke on behalf of the members, offering an obligatory statement which expressed their great relief at his safe return. So convincing was his performance that the Secretary wondered if he had perchance embarked upon the wrong career. But were they so different, politicians and actors? Both demanded facades to impress an audience and to make them believe the words they uttered were true measures of their hearts.

The President acknowledged the Cabinet's good wishes, wearing his usual rumpled, black suit, which appeared to be the same clothing he had worn throughout his ordeal.

"It is the consensus of this body that the United States adopts strict policies regarding trade with the Confederacy, charging high tariffs against their goods which enter our borders and demanding that businesses charged higher prices for manufactured goods shipped to the South. Thus the costs of the War will be exacted from the Rebels," stated Stanton.

Lincoln sat silently, the sounds of the hurried heels of boots against the flagstone wooden walkways on Pennsylvania Avenue clearly evident through the open windows. As if for a source of strength, the President gazed at the gild-framed portrait of Andrew Jackson which hung near his seat. "No," he spoke in a deliberateness not often heard. "I envision a reuniting of our nation in the future. Ill feelings run high enough without adding fuel to the flames. We will be as cooperative and solicitous as possible with our Southern brothers, and let us not forget the terms of the treaty." Lincoln looked squarely at first one official and then the other as he stated his position. "As victors, the Confederate States were well within their rights to laud over a conquered foe, yet they chose not to do so. To be less gracious than they would be as disastrous as it was to the indebted servant in our Lord's parable."

As Cameron's thoughts returned to the business to be discussed at the tavern, he removed a small, leather ledger from the pocket of his coat. As he leafed through its crisp pages, the names of several men bolstered the Secretary's faith in his plan. He had personally led the search for these catalysts necessary to avenge the Union's defeat. A scant few recommended by Stanton or the ever difficult Chase, these recruits represented a diverse grouping. Had an unwitting observer scanned the list of names, he would have been hard pressed to detect the common strand that bound them.

The opening of the heavy door roused Cameron from his ledger. An impeccably dressed gentleman in his late forties emerged from the brilliant sun. Cameron's attention was diverted by the refraction of the sun's rays by the facets of a large diamond stickpin adorning the man's cravat. In his left hand he grasped an ebony walking stick adorned by a golden head. To the last detail, Solomon Edwards was the consummate financier. As President of New York's Manhattan Bank and Trust, he, to a large extent, controlled the financial pulse of the nation. To have such a man further convinced the Secretary of War of both the feasibility and the justification of his quest.

Cameron pulled out a wooden chair which reflected the rustic décor of the tavern. Extending his arm, he silently offered Edwards seating.

"Mr. Secretary," Edwards lightly patted a leather carrier, "I am confident that I have the required figures and documentations to set things in motion."

Cameron smiled broadly complimenting himself for enlisting Solomon Edwards' expertise.

Edwards continued as he spread balance sheets and documents across the roadhouse's tabletop. From time to time he designated certain portions and made further notations as he explained his movements to the Secretary of War.

"I have transferred one million dollars into an account under the name 'Union Fidelity Holding Company.'" Both men appreciated the wit the title implied. "From this account only you and I will be authorized to make withdrawals. You will sign this power of withdrawal sheet with the name 'Daniel Adamson.' It empowers me to act as your representative at the bank. I will expect all further correspondence from you to bear this pseudonym. If my calculations are accurate, the successful implementation of the plan will require at least another half to another million additional dollars." Looking up from his paperwork, "I trust you have made the financial arrangements of which we previously spoke with Secretary Chase?"

"Indeed, Chase has made the deposits in several banks under these names." Cameron withdrew a folded sheet of stationery from his coat and offered it to Solomon. As Cameron continued, Edwards scrutinized the entries. "You will note that the monies have been diverted from the designated budgets under such expenditures as blankets, horses, food stuffs, and a host of other governmental expenditures." He sighed. "Chase has proven less successful than we anticipated. He feels that he cannot safely redirect subsequent amounts; therefore, I have taken the liberty to set in motion other means of securing funds."

Edwards assessed the stern features of the Pennsylvania-bred politician. In doing so, he appreciated his status as the man's friend. To have so formidable a foe, meant sure and swift destruction. The financier did not doubt the Secretary's abilities in the area of creative finance. Well known were his transactions as a member of the commission appointed to settle the claims of the Winnebago Indians. At the time Cameron was the founder and cashier of a bank in Middletown, Pennsylvania, upon which he saw that the notes for Indian claims would be drawn.

That admirable bit of stratagem won Edwards' respect, lo those many years ago. Perhaps that explained Cameron's ability to lure him into the intriguing cabal. True there were a few opportunities for personal profit and some for the bank; however, the risk, if the undertaking were exposed, was indeed great. But Solomon Edwards had secured great wealth was a risk taker. That he would bring ruin to the fortunes and lives of a nation weighed lightly on his conscience. Bankers, he had often expressed, exorcised their consciences when they assumed their occupations. To have Simon Cameron in his debt would be of great benefit; after all, the man would become President in the very near future.

Edwards was about to press the Secretary for further details when a door behind the bar opened to admit a small, balding gentleman. Walking the length of the expansive bar, he was dwarfed in comparison. His profile captured in the mirror, revealed a face lined by age and exposure to the elements.

"Mr. Edwards, may I present Bill Harrison. Bill is a printer of extraordinary merits."

As Edwards shook the hand of the printer, he had cause for the first time in their lengthy friendship to doubt his word. The hands of the smaller man were heavily calloused as if he had performed more demanding labors than printing. Harrison bowed his head in shame as though he read the banker's mind.

Cameron sensed the tension. "Mr. Harrison has been a 'guest' of the Federal government for the past five years."

Harrison blushed to the top of his sparsely covered head, as he dragged another of the heavy chairs across the planked flooring.

Solomon's eyes widened in recognition. "The Bill Harrison who successfully counterfeited thousands of dollars? Of course, how remiss of me not to remember. My own tellers unwittingly circulated a great many of your bills. We lost quite a tidy sum."

Cameron questioned the New York executive, "Then I need not extol his talents. You will agree that there is no one better qualified to duplicate the Confederate currencies and flood the South with worthless paper money?"

"None more eminent, but how do you guarantee the loyalty of a ..." Edwards fumbled for a euphemism.

"Of a criminal?" Mr. Edwards. You have no cause for fear of my betrayal of your project. I'm sixty years old and would not have lived out another year at hard labor in a Federal prison. No Sir, just the thought of freedom, returning to my family, and my wife's cooking will keep me in tow."

"Operatives have purchased space for Mr. Harrison's printing business here in the Capital. To insure upmost security, his operation will be a small one; however, I have no doubt that it will be effective." Addressing the newly released convict, Cameron asked, "How long will the designs require?"

The smaller man studied the ceiling. "Depending upon the intricacies of the bills, I should have the first copies ready for distribution in say, a month."

"You spoke of other methods of obtaining operating funds?" inquired the financier.

"The second is far more risky and will require a special individual. As yet, I have not secured the cooperation of anyone I deem equal to the enormity of the task; nevertheless, I do have in mind the perfect man. It will be some time before I contact him. Like a fine pearl, just the right amount of irritation and incubation will have to occur. For a man to be moved to treason, his frustrations must be allowed to seethe within his egotistical personality."

Edwards leaned back in his chair to absorb Cameron' cryptic statements, as Harrison busied himself counting the currency that would put him back in business.

Chapter Seven

Charleston, South Carolina, October 1861

From his office window the Battery and its surrounding waters dominated the picturesque view. His uniform traded for a newly styled suit and cravat, Jed Thomas stared at the graceful incoming ships. He was always spellbound by the beauty of the docking vessels, several of which he owned. Yet his mind was far from business and trade. He could still feel the talon hand as the President was released to Union soldiers. The Captain and Lincoln ceased to be captive and prisoner.

"Jed, I want you to meet Mother and my boys," he remarked as they shook hands that last time. "I expect you to call at the White House when you return to your business ventures; however, this time I trust you will use the more formal means of entry."

His remark was the closest the somber Lincoln had come to levity since signing the surrender terms.

"Jedediah, Jed Thomas, join the world!"

Jed whirled about to meet the cheerful expression of Amanda Mallory. Amanda was truly a vision. Strands of strawberry blonde hair escaped the netting that held her chignon in place. Her milky, smooth skin contained the faintest flush from the autumn winds which swept in from the water. As always her appearance exhibited the loving care with which Maizy had ironed her frock, styled her hair, and selected the appropriate hat, gloves, and parasol for Amanda's outing.

Jed crossed the room and took her delicate hands in his. He raised them to his lips. As he whisked his lips across the lace gloves newly arrived from Paris aboard a Thomas ship, he affirmed that which Mandy was already aware. "Mandy, you are breathtaking today."

"Only today?" she teased.

"Always, my darling, always."

No one would have disagreed with his assessment of Amanda Mallory, nor would they have argued that he was without a doubt one of the luckiest men in the South. Not only was his fiancé a beauty who possessed both wit and charm, but she was also the daughter of a prominent plantation owner. As his only daughter, she had served as Bellmead's hostess since she was fifteen. Such experience would complement any gentleman of means, his mother reminded him on numerous occasions. The premature death of her own mother thrust Mandy into the position of plantation mistress at that early age, a grueling responsibility for any woman, but an obligation she assumed without shedding the mystique of a Southern belle.

The aura of Southern womanhood was such that they feigned weakness and total dependence, thus perpetuating the myth that gentility rested upon the premise that women were incapable of grasping the politics and business of a man's world. Succumbing to the vapors became an art form and the fan a tool from behind which to flirt, tease, and flatter men. In actuality, Southern women were pillars of strength and masters of organizational skills. So cleverly had Amanda Mallory masked her resourcefulness, that her future husband considered her a fragile flower to be shielded from the "indelicacies" of life by ushering her into the ladies' parlor for polite after dinner conversation while the men retired to a more masculine counterpart where smoking and serious discussion were fit for their masculine ears alone.

As Jed would discover when Mandy became his wife, her days as a pampered belle ended with Celia Mallory's death. Her mornings began early with Maizy attentively seeing to "her baby's" toilet. Over breakfast she conferred with Mose, the household slave who served as majordomo and saw to it that her orders outlined the night before at her mother's cherry desk were executed by the slaves in his charge. The remainder of her day was occupied by the incessant needs of the slaves. A back room of the big house contained a clothing station in which she and the most skilled seamstresses of the plantation toiled to produce the clothing required to provide seasonal attire for Bellmead's seventy-five slaves. Later she saw to the distribution of food and household needs for the slaves and purchasing of the necessities of the big house. Often her day extended into the night when she acted as nurse and midwife.

Since Jed's return from the War, Mandy had not been able to resist the temptation of these unannounced visits, for they somehow reassured her that Jed had come home alive and whole, unlike so many of the former beaux, maimed by the Yankee Army or the scalpels of Southern field surgeons.

"And what scheme did you employ to get into town today?"

She flashed a coy smile that never failed to melt his heart.

"Oh, there's any number of excuses a girl can use when her wedding is two days away," she drawled. "I have only one last fitting with Mrs. Chancellor." She paused, and her voice became high pitched with excitement. "And I should be able to take it home today." Such was the delightfulness of Mandy; she was part woman, part child.

"I've just a few minutes to chat before I'm to meet Mother Thomas and Mrs. Rutledge at the Spotswood for luncheon. Those two have outdone themselves in making our wedding a social event to be remembered for some time to come. Mrs. Rutledge terms it the only real wedding of consequence since the War. How she berates those, as she calls them, 'tawdry, rushed affairs' that preceded Manassas." Tapping the wide brimmed hat whose ribboned streamers reached the small of her back and matched the pattern of her afternoon dress, she sprightly announced, "I must be off, my darling." She held her hat as she threw her head backwards to receive a parting kiss.

As Jed watched her leave, he decided that he was content with his life. The fragrance of jasmine lingered after her and reminded him of her for some time to come.

A shark, double rap at the door needed no response. Stewart's signal was a pretext of a mannerly gesture. Sniffing exaggeratedly he proclaimed, "I sense that our Miss Mallory has made her daily check of your whereabouts."

Both men laughed at the notion that Mandy distrusted her fiancé to the point of personal inspections.

"She's all aglow with wedding dress fittings." Pretending to give the matter great thought, "Perhaps we should be more excited about our attire?" Had the longtime friends their choice, the minister would have performed the ceremony after supper without all these formalities.

"I wanted you to see the letter I received this morning from my favorite prisoner," Stewart said.

Jed took the blue stationery from his friend.

At the top of the page he noted the scroll worked monograms "CJ."

Dear Lieutenant Kane,

In these past weeks following the conclusion of the War, I have had many opportunities to reflect upon those days Clarissa and I passed in your company. Though at the time I was positive that we were being cruelly dealt with, I have since realized that the most fortunate circumstance was our discovery by true gentlemen.

How ungrateful we must appear to you! So often you inquired about us, came to our aid, and saw to our safety. The purpose of my letter is this. I owe you so much, as does Clarissa, though she is loathe to admit it. I pray you will allow me to repay this debt. My parents and I hope that we may in some small way return these kindnesses by extending to you an invitation to be our houseguest.

Sincerely,

Catherine Jackson

Looking over the pages, Jed teased, "I told you she had an eye out to marry you. Will you allow her to entangle you in her web?" Jed's eyes danced as he questioned.

"There are less pleasurable ways to die. Besides, those contracts for the foundry materials from Austin Steel need finalizing. I could negotiate in person, while I allow the Jacksons to express their gratitude."

"Better approve it with Father. Since I'll be on my honeymoon, he'll have no one here to be at his beck and call."

"Get Miles up here. It's time he learned the true difficulties that face a rising young businessman."

The rest of the afternoon was passed creating scenarios in which Miles Davis would be the victim of the elder Thomas' pointless errands and endless stories.

Chapter Eight

Bellmead Plantation, two days later

B ellmead was aflutter with activity and had been for weeks. The marriage of the master's only daughter would be the largest celebration the plantation had seen since Old Hickory himself had spoken during his bid for the Presidency. President Jackson and every guest who happened to pass idle hours on Sidney Mallory's plantation just outside of Charleston found the setting pastoral and its host gracious.

From the winding rural road, the two-storied mansion was visible for miles. Standing upon a hill, its sloping lawns and meticulous gardens offered the approaching visitor a glimpse of the beauty and serenity to be found within the confines of the big house. An elevated, graveled drive was lined with stately oaks and fragrant magnolias for the entirety of the mile that led to the Mallory home. Jutting into all directions was similarly paved paths leading to the slave quarters and work buildings of the plantation.

The big house, built in three obvious projects of construction, had expanded as had Sidney Mallory's fortune and family. Centermost was the two-storied structure to which Mallory brought his young bride from her Charleston home. Separate white columns supported the wide veranda for the lower floor and the balcony of the second. One of the few bricked homes of the South Carolina gentry, its second and third additions equally complemented either side of the original construction, raising the number of rooms to fourteen.

Mose was dressed in a new suit of which he was immensely proud. He counted himself fortunate to have been singled out by Miss Celia when he was twelve. Somehow she alone had seen the potential in the ragged slave boy, teaching him to read each afternoon in her parlor. He would learn to read, write, and speak properly, she told him, and someday he would be in charge of the household slaves at Bellmead. She would not have him greeting her guests speaking like a field hand or running to her for instructions that she could more easily write out for him each morning. *Miss Celia*, he thought, *Lordy but she would have been happy to see this day*.

As Bellmead's majordomo, Mose's position on the plantation placed him somewhat above his fellow bondsmen. The jealousies of the field hands and lesser house servants segregated him and prevented the development of close ties with the other slaves. Still, he was respected by them for his intelligence and his efforts to make things easier for his kinsmen. Many were the evening Mose brought food from the manor to an ailing slave or a cast-off toy to a child. As he neared his thirty-sixth birthday, Mose knew that his life had been richly blessed when compared to others of his race, yet he yearned for more. Sidney Mallory had chastised his wife for tutoring the boy.

"He'll never be content with his life when he becomes educated. Leave the boy in blissful ignorance."

To a certain extent, Mister Sidney's prediction was true. Mose dreamed of the world outside Bellmead. From the leather-bound volumes in Bellmead's library, he learned of faraway places like Egypt with its pyramids and sand. He longed to travel the ocean on a ship like Mr. Jed's and see the wonders of ancient Rome, but all his dreams were for naught because they required the one thing he lacked: freedom.

Mose looked up to see Maizy standing at the end of the curving staircase that dominated the foyer and grand hall of Bellmead. Flanked by the ribbons and candles which festooned the banisters, he found her a lovely sight. Though he'd never spoken to her of it, he was in love with her, but he had witnessed the tragedy of slaves who loved, married, and had children only to see their lives torn apart at the whim of a master.

"My Miss Maizy, if you don't look a vision? Did you make that frock yourself?"

"No Suh," came the quick retort, "my Mandy had did dis here dress special made at the dressmaker's in Charleston. She say it wuz my weddun present from her. Ain't my baby the sweetest chile?"

For Maizy's sake and his own, he was grateful that Mr. Jed agreed to live at Bellmead, not that he didn't have a grand home in the city, but he knew that Mr. Sidney depended upon her too much to have her living anywhere else. Besides, Isabella Thomas was an overbearing woman, unaccustomed to sharing her home and its rule with anyone, especially a sweet, sensitive young lady like Miss Mandy. Mr. Jed's mother was the only drawback Mose could see to Miss Mandy's choice of husbands.

"Everything ready?" Maizy questioned, determined that all would be perfection.

"I was about to call in everyone to inspect them and go over their duties one more time."

"Maizy, I need you!" rang from the second floor railing. Both looked overhead to catch a glimpse of white satin as the bride returned to her bedroom. Maizy scurried up the stairs, her white turban bobbing.

The doubled oak front doors opened to admit a handsome man in a Confederate uniform that came across the polished hardwood floors of the foyer. The enormity of the entry and grand hall was such that the second floor railings were exposed for the length of the house on either side. First time guests were dwarfed by the initial view of Bellmead for the entry reached to the second floor ceiling. The officer's eyes searched the panoramic view in a familiar manner.

Andrew Mallory, the third of the Mallory sons had elected to remain in the military. A soldier's life suited him, for he had always been the most aggressive Mallory, a trait Sidney Mallory tried in vain to comprehend. As an officer, Andrew had begun to realize a place of importance in life which he had heretofore been unable to acquire. It was understood that the eldest male, Dorian, would one day assume their father's position as master of Bellmead, a post Sidney had groomed Dorian to attain practically from the cradle. Dorian was his father, their bearings, gesture, and facial features almost identical. When their voices sounded in the halls of the manor, even family members were at a loss to distinguish between the two.

Andrew always believed these common characteristics resulted from constant contact rather than family lineage. As the third son, he often felt a rejection, unintended by his father, who was merely guiding Dorian in the ways of plantation management.

Unlike the second Mallory son, Skylar, Andrew had never been a successful or an avid scholar. As a child, Skylar tagged behind old Dr. Panell whenever he could and had turned a breached slave baby, saving its life and that of its mother when he was sixteen. The old doctor declared when he arrived that he could not have done a better job himself. Thus it had been sealed; Skylar Mallory would become a physician.

There were those in Charleston who would not frequent his practice because of Skylar's unfailing dedication to treat the slave populations near and in Charleston. This had proven of no small contention among his wife, Juliana's, aristocratic family.

For the youngest son there had been no such niche, until the War. Away from his home, he carved an identity removed from the shadows of his father and brothers.

"Where's the bride? Am I too late?" called Andrew.

"Mr. Andrew we were all afraid your duties would keep you away."

"Now Mose, even the Confederate Army couldn't keep me away from my baby sister's wedding." He gave the house an appreciative notice. "Absolutely beautiful." He put his arm around the family's most trusted servant. "You are a wonder."

"Thank you, Sir. Only the best for our Miss Mandy. I wanted her wedding day to be something special, though I could have done better without the help of a certain woman."

Andrew needed no further explanation, giving Mose a sympathetic nod. Isabella Thomas was someone you wouldn't wish on anyone.

At that moment Sidney Mallory emerged from his office. "Andrew, I thought I heard your voice." He embraced the son he had not seen since the tearful day he had left for the War. Only his letters and those of the commanders who had written praising his valor had kept the family apprised of his whereabouts and safety.

"Well Father, I did have to offer Bellmead as a rendezvous point of sorts to get a furlough."

The older man stared at his son with a perplexed expression.

"I'll have to explain more fully later, but there will be some prestigious guests for Mandy's wedding. General Lee and his aide will arrive in the guise of wedding guests; however, they intend to speak with Jed concerning matters of great importance to the Confederacy."

"But on his wedding day, surely…" The men had no more opportunity for discussion. The first of the invited guests were arriving.

When the grandfather clock struck the hour, Jed and Stewart walked up to an arbor covered with ivy, joining Reverend Ames in the parlor. As he scanned the crowd that was gathered around the room and the hall, he saw a mixture of the most influential citizens from across the South. It was almost equally divided among Thomas Shipping associates, Mallory friends, and mutual acquaintances. Behind them, dressed in their best clothing, Bellmead's slaves craned their necks for a glimpse of the ceremony. As the bride and her father appeared at the top of the stairs, two uniformed men slipped into the throng. The identity of the older officer was unknown to Jed and Stewart, but the second was unmistakable. The audience assumed the two were discussing the bride as she made her way to the arbor. In reality, each was questioning the presence of Colonel Adam Dupree.

*****

The endless procession of festive guests formed a colorful, serpentine progression. Entertained by a noted performer seated at the rosewood piano, each awaited his or her turn to shake the hands of the gentlemen of the wedding party and to kiss the cheeks of the ladies. Peals of laughter and the tinkling of fine crystal blended with pockets of conversations to fill the air. The fathers, Isabella Thomas, and finally the bride and groom exchanged pleasantries with each individual.

The new Mrs. Thomas was radiant in her gown of embroidered satin. In the scoop of her neckline hung a diamond necklace whose facets glittered under the French chandelier. The necklace had been her mother's and was her father's wedding gift to her. Feeling it around her neck, Amanda sensed closeness with Celia Mallory. From her position in the foyer, Mandy could see the Gilbert Stuart portrait of her mother which hung in the middle of the parlor. It was her hope that she resembled her as much as others insisted.

Amanda attempted to adjust the pouf sleeves of her gown. As she looked toward her father, she realized that the ordeal of receiving her guests was at an end. Abruptly, Dupree and the other officer, a general, began a deep exchange with Jed, their tones too muffed to be clearly overheard.

"Mandy darling, go and have some punch while I talk with these officers for just a moment. I won't be long; I promise."

The bride started to object, but the combination of fatigue and the heat of the overcrowded house made the suggestion of refreshment all too tempting.

The three men slipped unobtrusively into the library. Jed spoke as he slid closed the heavy double doors. "General Lee is in indeed an honor to have finally met. I trust you are pleased with your new command, though I am sure that you would not have wished it under such a painful circumstance."

"The loss of General Beauregard saddened us all. He was a brave and noble man who will be sorely missed." As the men were seating themselves in the overstuffed furniture, the General continued. "Had Colonel Dupree not been placed at my disposal, I would have regretted his passing all the more."

Dupree feigned a slight smile, inwardly cursing his luck to be sharing a room with these two men, one of whom had usurped his command and the other his glory. Was it not enough that Jedediah Thomas had been credited with every aspect of his plan and the execution of the events which altered the course of the War, when a mission of that import should have been his to command? He, Adam Dupree, should have been the hero of the Manassas campaign, not a pampered schoolboy, and now he was forced to endure the endless platitudes of Lee, the man given command of the entire Confederate Army instead of him. Dupree felt the constant sting of the oversight. As Beauregard's aide, he had assumed the promotion he deserved, coupled with his invaluable expertise and experience, would entitle him to the post after Beauregard succumbed to wounds sustained in the last hours of the War.

"President Davis feared that his presence at your wedding would attract unnecessary attention, thus the Colonel and I were dispatched. You see, the President is greatly troubled by events abroad."

Jed addressed his remarks to Lee. "I fail to see what could have led the President to interrupt my wedding."

"Several of the South's largest cotton importers are refusing shipments. As you are very well aware, the economic survival of our nation is contingent upon the price of cotton. As both a businessman and a proven strategist, the President enlists your aid in this matter."

"I don't see what I can do," began Jed.

Frustrated by Jed's repeated opportunity to make himself the Savior of the South, Dupree blurted out his next words. "You are to go to England and France to negotiate the sale of our cotton reserves and latest harvest."

Stunned, the new bridegroom stammered, "But… it's my wedding day. My honeymoon is set for a tour of Mandy's relatives in Georgia and New Orleans; this is really quite impossible." Even as he spoke, he knew that he would be aboard ship rather than spending lazy afternoons with the Georgian cousins.

Chapter Nine

Philadelphia, Pennsylvania, October 1861

The Congregational Meeting Hall of the Friend's Church had been ablaze with the fury of the abolitionist rally conducted by the Reverend Jonas Armitage. A fiery orator, the gray-bearded preacher had God's gift to persuade an audience to repent lest an eternity in hell's fire await; however, tonight's listeners had been no flock of lost sheep. On the contrary, the frequent "Amens" and "Praise Gods" were from the voices of a dedicated crowd of anti-slavery advocates.

"Each of you has his mission. With the word of God, we will triumph over the Devil's handiwork." He spread his arms out over the congregation, conjuring up images of Moses as he parted the Red Sea. "God be with you."

Jonas watched the last of his devotees exit the sanctuary. In his twenty years in the pulpit, he had never felt so confident about the dedication of an audience to carry out the will of the Lord without regard for personal cost. Theirs was a dangerous but vital undertaking. Within the next months they would relocate to one hundred fifty strategic points throughout the South, primarily at and near the largest plantations. Once there they would insinuate themselves with those oppressed, and at his signal would lead the slaves in a massive revolt to freedom.

Ever since he had seen the scarred back of a slave who had made his way North, Armitage had vowed to put such human suffering to an end. His supporters had been few in number at first until the publication of Harriet Stowe's novel which so vividly brought the atrocities of slavery to the forefront. Placing the notes from which he had made his speech in the pocket of his worn frock coat, he relaxed for the first time in weeks.

Never had he dreamed that his contribution to the debacle of slavery would be on so grand a scale unil that Sunday evening when a message had been discreetly placed in his hand following his lesson.

He'd been skeptical yet curious of the cryptic summons, and he had allowed the messenger to escort him to the back door of a garish hotel located in one of Philadelphia's less desirable neighborhoods. In a dimly lit pantry a table and two chairs had been placed amid the stench of garbage and the scurrying feet of cockroaches. It was here that he met the Secretary of War.

"Reverend Armitage, I apologize for the conditions of our meeting, but I assure you of the need for secrecy." Cameron pulled out one of the rickety wooden chairs. "I have long been in sympathy with your cause."

Armitage was truly moved by the man's words.

"Placing all my faith in the success of our Army, I avoided lending my public support to the abolition movement before now; however, the War's outcome has affected my decision to use my substantial influence to further the cause of freedom for the Negro."

At that point Cameron outlined his proposal of a simultaneous slave rebellion. "My position of prominence prevents me from standing in the forefront of this noble cause," he warned. "For a governmental office to be privy to such a revolt would violate the terms of our treaty with the Southern states."

Thus Cameron easily convinced Armitage to act as his representative. Amazed by the degree of thought and planning that Cameron had already done, Jonas agreed to set the plan in motion, voicing but one reservation. "Mr. Secretary, our anti-slavery forces have raised some funds for the Underground Railroad, but we will need time to amass the funds to relocate our people."

An envelope was removed from Cameron's pocket and placed in Jonas' hands. "One hundred thousand dollars has been placed in your name at the Manhattan Bank and Trust. Should it not prove sufficient, you need only to mention my name, in private, to Mr. Solomon Edward, the bank's president and an abhorrent of slavery."

Armitage never questioned the source of the funds or his own choice as facilitator. One does not question God when He is answering prayers.

Chapter Ten

Washington, D.C., two weeks later

Stepping off one of Mr. Pullman's most modern cars, Stewart Kane surveyed the bustling mass which hastened in every possible direction, each confidently intent on some foreordained destination. Normally a man of daring, it was with no small amount of trepidation that he arrived in the city to which his comrades had so recently laid siege.

The journey from Charleston provided ample opportunity to contemplate the seriousness of his decision to travel north. Hostilities born of neither defeat nor any form of retaliation was of no consequence and, in fact, had never entered his thoughts. His insecurities were the result of his contradictory emotions regarding Miss Catherine Jackson and the implications that might be drawn by his visit. Initially Stewart convinced himself of the innocence of this trip to Washington, deluding himself that business was indeed his priority and that his intentions toward the lady in question could not possibly be misconstrued.

Outside the station, a liveried driver approached, "I beg your pardon, Sir. Might you be Mr. Stewart Kane?"

Stewart's nod set him at liberty to proceed. "Miss Jackson awaits in the carriage." His gesture indicated an impressive conveyance, the cost of which inferred considerable wealth to the Southerner.

What began as an awkward journey to the Jackson home found the riders comfortably at ease with one another at its conclusion. Emerging into the sunlight once again, Kane observed the Jackson house as he took Catherine by the hand. Set on a fashionable avenue, the three-storied brick structure closely resembled those of its neighbors. Lacking the wide verandas he so enjoyed on plantation homes and their smaller versions in the cities, it offered little by way of an entry. A short, white fence served no more purpose than to discourage a wandering dog from venturing too closely. Also visible were several servants' quarters which were constructed behind the man structure.

Once inside, he was not surprised to discover it filled with the ornate and torturous furnishings to which Yankees, and the British they strove to emulate, subjected themselves.

At the foot of a steep, green-runner staircase, Mrs. Margaret Jackson stepped forward, offering her hand to her houseguest. Upon his return from the textile mill established by his own father, Walter Jackson counted it a pleasurable duty to rescue Stewart from the ladies. Throughout the Southerner's stay in his home, Jackson altered his hectic schedule to include Stewart Kane in more masculine pursuits, a practice the enamored suitor soon regarded as a plague rather than the blessing intended.

As the days passed, Stewart no longer questioned his motivation for remaining in the Capital. His business soon concluded, Kane postponed his return to Charleston for a singular reason, his deepening affection for Miss Catherine Jackson. Hard put to articulate all the charms which so attracted him to this woman of such dissimilar background, he recognized her comely feature, wit, and grace.

Privy to the most sought after invitations in the city, the couple was never at a loss for diversions. The second evening of Stewart's sojourn, the pair accompanied the elder Jacksons to a lyceum where Ralph Waldo Emerson lectured to the audience on his views of the conduct of life.

At an informal reception hosted by a Massachusetts senator, the lecturer desired an introduction upon discovery of Stewart's role in the Lincoln abduction, a feat he regarded as nothing short of incredible. The conversation soon evolved into a discussion of the Confederacy and its hope for survival.

"The citizens of the Confederacy are united in purpose," explained the former lieutenant. "We are a determined and resilient people. As we never doubted a victory at Manassas, our ability to solidify into a stable nation goes without question."

"Then I can only applaud your will and dedication, Mr. Kane. It has long been my belief that doubts are conquered by faith. Have your people such a faith in your Mr. Davis?" questioned Emerson.

Stewart smiled, "A wise man once said that great men teach us to correct the delirium of animal spirits, make us considerate, and engage us to new aims and powers. Let me assure you that Jefferson Davis is such a man."

The philosopher chuckled. "One of the disadvantages of age is that our words are often recalled, perhaps to our own embarrassment. I fear that if the statement of all men were so recorded, it would remind them of their follies in logic and judgment, resulting in a quieter and more thoughtful world."

Calling to a friend, Emerson engaged him, leaving Stewart and Catherine to themselves.

*****

Stewart sat, abandoned, in the small but comfortable library reading Hawthorne's fiction. When no footsteps were evident in response to the door, he placed the novel face down on the widow seat and passed into the entry. A boy attired in the uniform that bespoke of his employ, offered Kane a package from one of New York's more distinctive stores.

"That'll be a total of eleven dollars, Sir."

Scanning the bills removed from his pocket, Stewart offered the amount requested.

"What are you trying to do to me? This ain't no money I've ever seen," cried the boy in disgust.

"Those bills are perfectly acceptable, Son. Your employer need only take them to a bank, where they will be exchanged for Yankee greenbacks. I've done so myself on several occasions since my arrival from Charleston."

A look of realization crossed the delivery boy's young face. Grabbing the parcel from the man's grasp, he threw the bills on the porch. "I won't take no Confederate money."

Unobserved, Catherine entered the foyer and became a party to the encounter. Placing her hand on Stewart's shoulder, she directed her comments to the boy. "You'll accept Mr. Kane's money or rest assured that your behavior will not go unreported."

Trapped, he grudgingly reclaimed the discarded bills and returned the package with no further comment.

As they watched the boy turn the corner, Stewart looked down at Catherine. "What has secession done to ease the tensions between North and South if we have taught another generation to hate a man for his place of birth?"

In an effort to cheer, Catherine took his arm, leading them into the parlor. "I just know this is the mink muff advertised in the *New York Times*. I can't believe my luck. Though it's too early, it will be carried to the Charity Ball this evening."

"No Cathey, the muff remains here," was Stewart's adamant pronouncement.

Hurt, Catherine was set to question him when he added, "I'll not have you drawing any more attention to yourself, lest the Prince steal you away from me. And I will have every dance." He kissed her lightly on the cheek.

"Oh Stewart, the Prince of Wales has far more beautiful and interesting women vying for his attention." She settled back excited by the gossip she was about to impart. "Why, I hear Harriet Lane is to be on his arm this evening. Besides," she added, "you are my prince."

Their embrace was interrupted by the entrance of Walter Jackson already dressed for the gala. "Catherine, you had better hurry and dress..."

"Of course," she stammered as she veritably flew from the room.

"I had no idea of the hour," Kane excused himself, avoiding the displeasure of the protective father.

Only the men felt the strain as the two couples rode to the ball. Aglow with light, activity, and music, the ballroom's spectacular décor was overshadowed by the finery of Washington's women. Charity affairs, which were still quite novel, were becoming a popular diversion among the affluent set. Conversation seldom waned, for the women chattered about gowns, accessories, and the prospect of a glimpse of the Prince of Wales. No expense had been spared to don the most fetching gown. Walter Jackson remarked to himself that these balls were a God send for his mill as well as the jewelers and dressmakers of the city.

The throng around the Lincolns, the Prince, and Miss Lane prevented even the briefest view of the royalty who recently had begun his twentieth year. Disappointed, Catherine abandoned any hope of presentation, agreeing to dance to the strains of a waltz. During the orchestra's intermission, a uniformed British office interrupted the couple's conversation.

"Mr. Stewart Kane?"

"I am he."

"His Royal Highness, the Prince of Wales, requests the opportunity to meet one of the men most directly responsible for your nation's victory."

Catherine emitted a stifled gasp with the prospect of presentation, evoking the ire and jealousy of those ladies close enough to have overheard the officer's request. News traveled more swiftly than the pair and the escort as heads turned and lips were hidden behind fans to disguise their remarks.

Guided to a parlor off the ballroom, they entered. Seated upon a settee placed in a comfortable proximity of a hearth carved with airborne angels, the Prince and the vivacious Miss Lane were engaged in an exchange of gossip about the Lincolns. Having served as mistress of the White House, during her uncle's administration, Buchanan's niece boasted sources on the White House staff and was relating a particularly embarrassing tale at Mary Lincoln's expense.

Though several years his senior, the Prince found Miss Lane all the more captivating. He spirited her away from the crowded room as soon as the opportunity presented itself. When she had casually mentioned the Rebel guest in their midst, he immediately dispatched his aide.

The formalities of presentation concluded, the Prince beckoned for the couple to sit opposite him and Harriet Lane. An affable conversation ensued until Edward rose, his remarks dumbfounding his companions.

"I dare say that American balls are equally as boring as those I have had the misfortune to endure at any European court."

"And where would you rather be, Your Grace?" queried the violet-eyed socialite.

Contemplating his reply, not as one unsure of his answer, but as one accustomed to the granting of his every wish seeking to exercise caution lest it result in some error in judgment, he replied, "Playing at tenpins." Amused with his own candor, he began to laugh with his confidants.

"It happens that I am quite a champion at the game," added Harriet, "and no doubt a formidable opponent."

Unfamiliar with the challenge, especially from a female, the Prince of Wales scoffed at her declaration, spawning an exchange during which both boasted both proficiency and certain victory.

"Then we will compete this very evening," insisted Victoria's eldest son. "Where shall we play?"

"Perhaps I can impose upon the head mistress of Mrs. Smith's Institute for Young Ladies? Their gymnasium will prove adequate, Harriet cried, basking in the excitement of the adventure at hand. Pausing a moment she dismissed her own suggestion. "Of course, this is all for naught; we do have our obligations.

"All be damned," exploded the future king. "Never will it be said that Edward, Prince of Wales, withdrew from a contest."

Thus, the four wilily eluded the confines of the ball at which the visiting British heir would fail to fulfill his promise to preside over the auction of various gifts whose purchase prices would benefit the city's poor.

Lambasted in the morning press for his unforgivable affront, the Prince sat amused in a massive four-poster bed savoring tea and recalling the defeat he suffered at the skills of Miss Harriet Lane. "Ah, if she were only a European princess," he sighed aloud.

*****

The Jackson dining room featured an ornately carved buffet and an elongated oak table which was set for three rather that its usual five. Mrs. Margaret Jackson presided at the lower end of the table. Sitting on her right, her elder daughter was Catherine, and on her left, her houseguest, Mr. Stewart Kane of Charleston.

As was her daughter, Margaret Jackson was entranced by the story Stewart was telling of his and Jed's boyhood antics. It was a relaxed meal, minus the chatter of her younger children, Dollie and Silas, who were in school. Today Stewart elected to remain with Catherine and Margaret rather than to accompany Mr. Jackson to his textile mill, a decision Margaret regarded as a good omen. In her opinion, Cathey could do far worse than the handsome young man at her left whose inheritance was immense and business future secure.

Since Stewart's arrival, she had pushed and prodded the romance along, arranging for the couple to be left unescorted for walks along the neighborhood, carriage rides, and intimate suppers. Such manipulating left her nearly exhausted, but she persevered. Her husband deemed her shameless, but the risk of scandal was inconsequential. In truth, Margaret had, until Stewart's arrival, held little hope of a grand match for her daughter. Oh, Catherine was pleasing enough to the eye, but she lacked the vivaciousness of women like her daughter's friend, Clarissa, who could ensnare the most desirable of catches. *There*, thought Margaret, *was a girl who future was insured. With the right introduction that girl could be the wife of a President one day.* She prayed Catherine's friendship with the Morgan girl would prevent her from spiriting Stewart away.

One night she even dreamed that Stewart and Catherine were married. In her fantasy, Cathey held court in an exquisitely decorated parlor of imported furnishings. Wearing a French gown and draped in pearls, Catherine reclined on a chaise, surrounded by slaves eager to do her bidding. Margaret awoke with renewed determination that Stewart Kane would become her son-in-law.

"Excuse me, Mum,"

Mrs. Jackson turned in the direction of her English housekeeper, Elizabeth, to acknowledge her intrusion. Before she had to the opportunity to speak, the quiet luncheon was overpowered by the imposing energy of Clarissa Morgan.

Barging into the dining room she spoke, "I am sorry for coming unannounced, but this is urgent!"

"Clarissa, wouldn't you like to join us?" Margaret asked, sure that the girl was out to create havoc of all her plans for Catherine's future.

Gesturing with her gloved hand, Clarissa waved away her invitation.

"I haven't the time, really. Actually, I am here to see Stewart."

Margaret sure that her worst fears were becoming reality, looked to her daughter to urge her into action, but Catherine needed no coaxing for her eyes were taking on a decisively green tint. She angrily watched her friend, who had yet to remove her cape and gloves, sit down next to Stewart and monopolize his attention.

"Stewart, you are the only one who can help me." The young man's expression registered his surprise and confusion.

"My father, as you know, is in service to our government in England." She pulled a letter from her drawstring bag. "I received a letter this morning in which he informs me of my mother's failing health."

"Oh my dear, I had so hoped that living abroad might improve her condition. You must go to her immediately," Margaret said, seizing the opportunity to whisk Clarissa as far away from Kane as possible.

"Unfortunately, the reverse has been the case. The damp climate further restricted her breathing."

Catherine interrupted, "Stewart is hardly a physician. I don't see how he can possibly be of help."

"Cathey, I am well aware of that fact," Clarissa shot back, miffed by her ridiculous statement. "He is, however, a high-ranking employee of Thomas Shipping." Turning back to address Stewart once again, "I did hear you say that Mr. Thomas has a private cabin onboard all his vessels?"

"Yes, it enables him to travel on any of our ships from whatever port he wishes at a moment's notice.

Clarissa released a sigh of relief. "I sent Kathleen out early this morning to book my passage to England, but there are no immediate bookings to be had. Your ship the *Victoria* sails in the morning. If I could have Mr. Thomas' cabin, then I could sail without delay."

Stewart was on his feet without hesitation. "Go home and pack, Clarissa. You sail in the morning."

Clarissa relaxed in her chair, having achieved her objective once again.

Chapter Eleven

Bellmead Plantation

T he carriage of Miss Alicia Beaumont maneuvered Bellmead's drive in virtual silence. No less perfection was demanded by the oldest daughter from Vermillion, an adjacent plantation. Horses reined, the doors of the big house opened, and Mose offered his assistance.

Purposefully avoiding even polite gratitude for his gesture, Alicia mounted the front steps, crossing the veranda, and entered the foyer.

As she removed her gloves, Mose questioned, "In which room will you be most comfortable?"

"You needn't bother with formalities. I'll announce myself," was her curt reply. Gathering her skirts, she hurried up the staircase toward Clarissa's room, where the two had spent many hours since childhood. There are ever so many things I'll change when I am Bellmead's mistress, she assured herself. Starting with that obstinate Mose and, she knocked upon

Mandy's door, ending with the insistence that Mr. and Mrs. Thomas remove themselves to the Charleston residence.

"Come on in, Alicia. I saw your driver pulling the carriage around back."

The women embraced.

"My dear Alicia, isn't your frock a bit… daring for a morning call?"

Unscathed, Alicia retorted in the same cold tone with which she addressed Mose or anyone white or black for whom she held even momentary disdain.

"We've all the charm of a disagreeable old matron already."

Alicia began removing her hat, which she tossed carelessly upon the floor.

Adjusting her bodice to reveal a bit more cleavage, she added in order to soothe the feelings of a woman she desperately needed to achieve her desires. "And how else do you propose I catch a husband?"

"You ninny," she laughed. "You know full well that you can have your pick of any of your beaux. Why, Bowden Cantrell told Jed that he had shamed himself most dreadfully by begging for your hand on any number of occasions."

"But you know that Bowden is not who I want." A sly expression crossed her face. "Just where is Dorian this morning?"

Mandy pinched her cheeks, surveying her appearance, and then grudgingly wondering why she bothered. Jed's abandonment stung like an overseer's lash. Crying, pleading, she'd called upon her every wile to dissuade him from the trip or to convince him that she be allowed to accompany him.

"You'd distract me from my duties," he'd said. "I'd never be able to tear myself away from quarters aboard ship if you were with me." But he'd been able to leave their bedroom in

Charleston easily enough. Thus the new bride foundered in an emotional sea of self-pity, confusion, and frustration.

"I haven't the faintest. I made him swear to meet us for croquet."

The women walked beside each other down the broad staircase. Awaiting their descent, Mose spoke to Mandy, ignoring the haughty Miss Beaumont. "Mister Dorian is waiting at the court."

"Wonderful." Mandy winked at her friend. "Please see to it that Edna prepares us some juleps."

"Of course, Miss Mandy."

Dorian Mallory sat at a garden table, bemoaning his fate. It was no secret that Alicia Beaumont was shamelessly interested in him.

She was certainly pretty enough, but a colder, more calculating female had never drawn breath. Rising as they approached, he placed an obligatory kiss upon her cheek. As he offered the women their mallets, they selected their colored wooden balls.

Two slave boys held parasols over the women, lest they mar their skin in the South Carolinian sun.

Successfully past the first wickets, two balls hit, the sound of wood against wood unmistakable. Viciously, Alicia attacked Mandy's red ball to the outer edge of the grass court.

With Dorian to herself she began, "You really should have exercised your obligation as a brother and forbidden Jed Thomas from degrading poor Mandy so. Polite society is abuzz with the scandal."

"Need I remind you that a man's country is his first duty, Miss Beaumont? His ball gently tapped hers before it rolled to a stop. Positioning it next to hers, he placed his foot atop it, driving the yellow sphere within a few feet of Mandy's.

"You spiteful ole thing; I'll get you yet," she vowed, flashing a coy smile before following the path of the errant ball.

Skillfully, Dorian progressed through the permanent wickets installed when croquet had been introduced to the Charleston area and become the rage. Since then, many relaxing afternoon had passed under the magnolia boughs as young and old delighted in the sport. Today, however, was different for Dorian. A sport more desirable beckoned.

As the ball glanced off the final pole, he abandoned his mallet. "You ladies finish the game. I really must attend to a pressing matter." Disregarding their protests, he disappeared from view.

Furious, Alicia threw her mallet across the court where it accidentally struck a tree, splintering the croquet stick.

"You really must learn some patience with men and their ways, Alicia," advised Mandy.

"Like you?" she snapped in retort.

Mandy felt her face redden with rage and humiliation.

"Yes, exactly like me," she expressed in uncharacteristic forcefulness. "You don't for an instant think that a wife will ever be of paramount importance to any man? Men just have more, more … distractions." She reached for a mint julep and took a seat at the table.

"When I do become Dorian's wife, I will maintain his interest, and for longer than a few days. Tell me, Mandy; are you naïve enough to believe that our national hero is spending lonely hours pining for his lady love when there are salons of flirtatious women?"

"I do indeed."

Alicia sat back in the chair, fanning herself between sips of her drink, her tone more subdued. "For your sake, I sincerely hope you are right, but I harbor the gravest reservations, Mandy dear," her voice reminiscent of a mother, "you've grown up without the proper tutorage in feminine wiles. Let a man think he has the upper hand, but never allow him out of your sight for too long," She paused. "That invites trouble, Mrs. Thomas."

"But I pleaded to accompany him. What was left to do?"

"Why, book passage yourself and surprise him." She rose, "Follow him and drive away whatever distractions are separating you, exactly as I am doing now."

Calling to her back, Mandy questioned, "Is that always wise? Suppose your interruption is unwelcome? Won't you suffer his anger for your trouble?"

Alicia Beaumont pivoted, her hoops catching in the motion. Shaking her head slowly, she addressed her pupil. "Mandy, Mandy, you've ever so much to learn. I'll return to continue your lesson." Then reconsidering she added, "Or perhaps I'll be too distracted."

Failing to locate Dorian in his office, she asked of his whereabouts several times. During the fruitless quest, Alicia found herself near the oldest and least used part of the cotton warehouses. Of a Black boy pulling weeds she queried, "Tell me, boy, have you seen Mr. Dorian?"

In awe of the strange woman and her hostile manner, he said nothing but pointed toward the warehouse.

Gathering her skirts, she eased open the squeaking door. "Dorian, Dorian… where have you disappeared to?" Adjusting to the dimmer light, she called out again.

Convinced that she was again mislead and chastising herself for listening to a brainless boy, she decided to leave. Just then, a sound toward the back of the building drew her attention. Looking toward the floor, lest she trip over some object in the scant light, she ran into Dorian Mallory, who caught her arms with his hands. Even in the dim warehouse light, she detected his disheveled appearance.

Somehow, without a word exchanged, she knew. Pushing past him, she peered into a small room to discover a makeshift bed of cotton. Beside it lay the hastily abandoned bandanna of a slave woman.

As she passed him on her way out, she tossed the article at him and ran toward the big house. From the sound of his mistress' voice as she called for him, Desmond threw down the cards he was playing and hurried toward the freshly fed and watered horses.

Dallying would only feed her wrath.

Feigning ignorance at Mandy's inquisition concerning Alicia's sudden departure, Dorian listened to his puzzled sister's accounting of her friend's intention of finding him.

Shrugging her shoulders, Mandy continued with her daily routine. Countless were the times Alicia Beaumont had gotten herself in a snit, leaving without a word.

Amanda Thomas learned her second lesson from her visiting mother-in-law a few days later as she enjoyed a light luncheon with all the Mallory family.

"My dear," she breathlessly said, "the city is just aghast at the scandal of it all. It is all too tawdry and beyond even wartime escapades."

"Whatever are you talking about, Mother Thomas?"

A gut-wrenching foreboding stopped Dorian as he raised a silver fork to his mouth.

"Why, the elopement of Alicia Beaumont and Bowden Cantrell. They ran off to Richmond like white trash. Of course, her mother is indisposed, refusing even my call."

Dorian sighed, relieved that his secret was safe, confident that Alicia's pursuit would trouble him no further.

*****

The deckhand had lost count of the trunks he and his co-worker had labored to bring aboard, but he counted it worthwhile when he saw their fashionably dressed owner step aboard the paddle wheel and steam driven vessel. His interest was aroused to an even greater degree when he was ordered to deliver them to Mr. Thomas' private cabin. Mr. Thomas, he recalled, had no daughters.

When he returned to the deck to resume his duties, he watched the attractive woman draw her cape around her to ward off the chilling winds, stealing admiring glances whenever possible.

Clarissa remained on deck until they were moving out into the water. Watching the crewmen perform their duties, she marveled at their precision and the endless number of preparations necessary to put a ship like the *Victoria* out to sea. She hoped that her excitement was not in evidence, for she would hate for the other passengers to guess that this was her first crossing. The decision to remain in Washington while her parents lived in England had been her father's effort to economize, but Clarissa viewed it as yet another in his long line of rejections.

Finally giving in to the stinging winds, she asked for assistance from a crewman she instinctively knew was unable to keep his concentration directed at this work. Maneuvering her skirts down the narrow passageway, Clarissa paused before the door of her accommodations.

With the help of the attentive sailor, she stepped into a magnificent suite lined with rosewood paneling. Her feet literally sank into the Brussels carpeting which reached into every crevice of the sitting room. Setting her purse upon a table, she caressed its top of Bocatelli marble. I simply must try to be kinder to Stewart, she thought, especially since Cathey is so smitten by him. The portholes covered in stained glass next caught her eye, and she secretly hoped that the voyage would last longer than the predicted three weeks.

Dismissing the crewman, she sought the second of two doors behind which she assumed was located her bedroom. throwing open the door, she stopped short, the image of Jed Thomas in the midst of his bath rendering the unique effect of leaving Clarissa Morgan at a loss for words.

Chapter Twelve

San Antonio, Texas, October 1861

Even in October the heat and dust had not entirely abated causing the dirt to cling to his face. He could now agree with the general in charge of the United States forces during the War with Mexico who had stated his preference of hell as a place of residence rather than Texas. Wyatt Humphries' rotund form freely perspired, and his hand fumbled for his handkerchief. This humid, stale air had not been anticipated by the Northern envoy.

He tried to question the driver of his ancient landau, finding it a wasted effort since the aged Mexican man spoke little English. Cursing the driver and himself, he thought of the Washington gaming house where he could have been, had he not been so intent in gaining Cameron's favor. It struck him that he was, in fact, involved in just such a high stakes game of chance.

When the Secretary of War approached Humphries, a minor member of the Secretary's staff, he entered into the greatest gamble of his life. There were some who might regard his mission as treasonous. Still he had accepted the challenge and cast his lot with Cameron. It was one thing to ante with one's career, but when the stake was life itself, even a seasoned gamester like Humphries had cause for concern. Would the profit be worth the risk? To Wyatt Humphries it was, for he had seen what Cameron could do for or against his fellowman.

Arriving at the Menger Hotel, he paid his driver and entered the lobby. Nearing the desk, Wyatt was greatly relieved to observe the finest amenities offered by any Northern hotel. His train ride from New Orleans convinced him that Texas was a primitive outpost. Never had he experienced a railway with only one class of seating. Sharing the crowded car with screaming infants, a case of chickens whose feathers clouded the air, and cowboys fresh from the trail, the journey became a hellish nightmare. Coupled with the oppressive heat and humidity and lack of drinking water, Humphries repeatedly questioned the wisdom of his decision.

"May I help you, Sir?"

At least, thought Wyatt, the desk clerk speaks English. "I have a reservation in the name of Daniel Adamson."

"Of course, Mr. Adamson, your business associate has been anticipating your arrival. I have been instructed to tell you that he dines in the hotel dining room promptly at six each evening." The hotel employee called Humphries' attention to a large wall clock. Since it is so near that hour, I will see to it that your bags are placed in your room."

"Thank you, the Menger is a welcomed oasis after my arduous journey."

As the clerk watched the man head toward the dining room, he could not help but laugh to himself. Humphries had been appraised as yet another Yankee come to Texas in hopes of making a quick fortune. This one will never last, the clerk told himself.

Humphries followed the direction given him into an elegant salon, brightly lighted with imported crystal chandeliers. The tables were set with fine china and silver. A gentleman in evening attire approached Wyatt.

In a heavy French accent the man offered his services.

"I am Daniel Adamson. A business associate who has been dining with you each evening at the hour is expecting me." Upon the realization of the absurdity that businessmen would not know the names of their associates, Humphries silently cursed his own stupidity at allowing himself to become involved in Cameron's escapade.

If the maître d' found his situation questionable, he registered no expression, facial or spoken. Unknown to Wyatt, the anonymous contact paid him in American dollars to escort a heavy set man to his table.

As they made their way past the other patrons, Humphries imagined all eyes were upon him. In actuality, no one paid more than a fleeting interest to yet another dusty traveler.

Toward the back of the room sat a lone Hispanic man. His dark, handsome features accented by a thin moustache. As he offered his hand to Wyatt, the poorly paid governmental employee was drawn to the man's expensive clothing.

"Thank you, Claude. Daniel my friend, I am pleased that you have finally arrived."

As Claude withdrew from them, the man continued. "I am Lorenzo de Zavala, Mr. Adamson. We can freely discuss our business here. Claude will see to it that no one is seated too near our table."

"It's my pleasure."

"I trust you will find my tastes satisfactory. Claude has been instructed to send us a waiter who speaks no English to serve us and to bring you a duplicate entré."

Humphries, who had forgotten his hunger in the excitement of locating his contact, greedily eyed the steak and fresh vegetables which de Zavala had only begun to eat.

De Zavala continued, "Your proposal?"

"Very well," Humphries proceeded despite the uneasiness he felt at being rushed immediately to the purpose of their meeting. "I represent a certain interest within the United States that is unhappy with the terms of the surrender treaty with the Confederates."

Wyatt searched for an indication of surprise from the man who sat across from him, but de Zavala kept his head bent over his plate, seemingly more interested in the steak than his business with the American. "It is the belief of this party that the rebellious states will be unable to survive as a nation for more than a few years, a decade at the outside. The longer it is allowed to exist apart for the United States, the rift that led to the separation will only widen. Therefore, it is our plan to see to it that the Confederacy falls, hopefully within the span of a year or two."

"As President Juarez has stated before, he has no desire to interfere with the internal problems of your country, Señor."

Humphries shook his head, "Such a pity! The benefits for your country would have been substantial. You see, we would ask only that he make certain 'demands' upon the Confederates."

The Mexican's interest was such that he put down his silverware and regarded Humphries' remarks before speaking. "With such demands there must be penalties for failure to comply, and these could breed liabilities. We are a poor nation and unwilling to risk such liabilities," he said with a sly grin, "unless guaranteed of potential gains."

Wyatt was overcome with an immediate distrust for the Mexican representative and wished that he was authorized to deliver Cameron's proposal to anyone else. "The interest that I represent is well aware of Mexico's rather precarious financial position. I think that you will agree that there are also elements within your own country that resent Juarez's liberal stance. For both these reasons, we believe that your President will find our request of great benefit."

"I am intrigued, Señor Adamson."

The waiter's arrival with Humphries' meal temporarily halted the conversation. After pouring the wine, de Zavala ordered him in Spanish to leave the bottle. His service would no longer be required.

Wyatt grudgingly postponed cutting into the tantalizing meal in order to finish his negotiations. "What would be Juarez's reaction if you were to inform him that Mexico could restake its claim to Texas?"

De Zavala's eyebrows arched, his eyes narrowing. "But Mexico is bound to the terms of the Treaty of Guadalupe-Hidalgo."

"You are forgetting," he paused, baiting his prey, "that your treaty was with the United States government... to which Texas no longer swears allegiance."

Placing his ornately carved silverware across the china plate, Lorenzo de Zavala folded his linen napkin. He paused an unnecessarily lengthy amount of time, as if to let the intent of the bureaucrat's words become clear. In fact, the man was no one's fool. At the mention of Texas, he had calculated the American's next move. *I must measure my words carefully,* he thought. *A successful negotiation on my part will insure my worth to Benito Juarez and perhaps fatten my own pockets as well.* "But Señor Adamson, if my government declares Texas as its territory once again, the Confederates will wage war to protect it."

Well versed by Cameron, Humphries delivered the most tempting aspect of the Secretary's plan. "You must agree that Juarez is not the darling of all his subjects and under constant threat of revolutions led by his fellow countrymen and foreign governments."

Confident that de Zavala would carry Cameron's recommendations back to Mexico City, Humphries began to enjoy his meal, speaking at his leisure. "I can think of nothing that solidifies a country more than a popular war. Your people have been slow to forget the defeats suffered at the hands of the Texicans and the United States. Regaining this territory can be a rallying cause to unite your divided people, especially when the prize is enough land to reward all the President's most loyal supporters."

"But war is such a 'costly' endeavor for a nation such as ours that is already deeply in debt to its allies." Leaning across the table, he posed his next question. "Where would we find an ally willing to back us as we attempt to reclaim what is rightfully ours?"

"It is our belief," began Humphries, "that the rebellious states will not be anxious to wage a war with Mexico. The South is hardly in any position for mobilization to its outermost regions in order to fight such an experienced, highly trained foe as your soldiers would prove to be." Humphries leaned back and surveyed his companion. "No, Señor de Zavala, we can almost assure your President that the Confederacy will be inclined to 'purchase' your rights to Texas in exchange for your assurance that you will never again lay claim to the land beyond the Rio Grande." Content that he had presented his case well, Wyatt returned to this first palatable meal in days. Taking a drink of the excellent wine, he proceeded. "Nor is a fledgling nation financially solvent to the extent that it can withstand an outlay of millions of dollars for land that it sees as its own. Our recommendation is that President Juarez demand somewhat less than the value of the state. Perhaps five million is within reason?"

"Five million is less than half its worth," snapped de Zavala. "Why would President Juarez agree to such a pittance?

"A profit of five million dollars for selling something he does not own or control, or the promise of a war that will gain him the admiration of his people while its expenses are partially paid by others," stated Humphries matter-of-factly.

Pouring the contents of the wine into Humphries' and then his own, he raised his goblet in salute.

Chapter Thirteen

Bellmead, November 1861

M aizy shook her head in disgust as she trudged down the stairs to iron yet another evening frock for her mistress. The others lay discarded across her canopied bed. "One night wid dat man, she grumbled to herself, an she da debil to deal width. I swears my Mandy ain't nebber been so disagreeable. Iffin Mastuh Jed doan git home soon, dis whole house gwanna be crazy."

"Maizy, you hurry up now!"

As she passed Edna, the cook, she declared, "Grieben after him ain't doin none of us no good." Edna agreed.

Maizy knew the ache in Mandy's heart. Once she too had been married, at fifteen to Lamar a field hand who had lost his life trying to rescue one of the Mallory's thoroughbreds from a burning barn. She missed him still, and the gnawing shame that he left her childless compounded her sorrow. When the mistress delivered a healthy daughter later that year, she poured her emotions into caring for the pink-faced infant. With three young sons and her plantation duties, there were days when Miss Celia saw her baby only at feeding times. So she delighted the baby's constant care to the loving and capable Maizy. A knock at the door stopped her in mid step. Failing to hear Mose coming to answer, she plodded to the door, frock in hand

Maizy bid greetings to a tall, white man who held a well-worn hat in his hand. Her expert appraisal assessed the tanned man as working class, probably a farmer, but surely not a peckerwood or sharecropper. As a mammy to the master's daughter, Maizy held nothing but disdain for a white man without the wherewithal to own the land on which his family lived.

"Morning' Suh."

"Is Mr. Mallory home? I'm Jasper Erwin, the new overseer."

"Step in da pahlor; an I'll see iffin Mastuh Dohaian free fuh callehs."

After leading him into the least formal of the parlors, which she deemed appropriate after the incident a few months prior of a thieving sharecropper helping himself to a silver candlestick while he awaited the eviction Mr. Dorian was about to deliver, she left the man gaping at the richness of his surroundings.

Examining the patrician poses of the Mallory ancestors whose faces adorned the parlor walls, the artists' signatures of Stuart and Samuel Osgood failed to impress Erwin as much as the comfortable sofa upon which he chose to sit. Also escaping his notice were the alabaster vase and marble busts which added dignity to the room's décor.

On the way down the main hallway, Maizy met Mose and told him of the arrival of Jasper Erwin. Mose made his way to the parlor to explain the cause of Mr. Dorian's tardiness. "Excuse me. Mister Dorian is out for a while. If he was aware of an appointment, he did not inform me of it."

"You're Mose, aren't you?"

Taken aback by the stranger, Mose was slow to reply. Sensing his confusion, Jasper explained. "I made a point of finding out all I could abut Bellmead, and you are an important part of it."

Not entirely sure of how to reply, Mose merely nodded a nervous affirmation.

"Folks say you're pretty smart. The way I hear it, you run this whole house."

Dorian Mallory's arrival interrupted a rather one-sided conversation. Dismissing Mose, he inspected the newly employed overseer. The man seated in his parlor was decidedly more muscular than his employer. Just the sort of man who can keep them in line out of fear of his size, assessed the master's son. "I welcome you to Bellmead, Mr. Erwin. Your letters of introduction and recommendation were highly impressive. May I commend you on your loyalties, and services to your former employers?" He offered his hand. "I trust your employment at Bellmead will be equally as productive."

Jasper acknowledged the comments of Dorian Mallory, silently praising the skills of the Reverend Jonas Armitage. Where and how he secured such missives were mysteries to him.

In reality, Jasper Erwin had been raised the son of a Tennessee farmer. His staunch Quaker upbringing had reinforced the ills of the slavery system which he had often encountered. When he came of age, he joined a Quaker minister working for the abolitionists' cause. Ultimately, his path crossed with that of Armitage. Their religious differences notwithstanding, the two men maintained a relationship deeply grounded upon the premise that men were not destined by God into bondage. As a result of this mentorship, which closely resembled hero worship, Jasper sat in the tastefully decorated parlor of the Bellmead plantation, impersonating an overseer.

"At his point, we should meet the other overseer, Henry Monroe. You will answer directly to him. The majority of your duties will be in the areas of stock and distribution of goods to the slaves. Shall we tour Bellmead?" Underscoring the rhetorical intent of his question, Dorian had already come to his feet before posing it.

The two left the white-columned mansion, proceeding through immaculately landscaped gardens. Erwin's mind began to fill with the colors and fragrances of such a garden in full bloom. It was the type of setting he dreamed of as a boy. On occasion he had visited plantations near his home when he accompanied his father to deliver crops to the landowners. It was on one of these trips that he witnessed the beating of a slave near his own age. There were still times when his screams invaded his nightmares.

Just to the left and behind the big house and the cook and smoke houses, Erwin caught sight of the rows of slave cabins laid out in symmetrical "streets." Literally dozens of ragged children roamed and played. Jasper wondered how they could project such a semblance of normalcy when their lives belonged to their white master. As they neared the end of the row, several Negro workers were piling log upon log and filling the crevices with daubs of clay of what would be another clapboard roofed quarter. Behind each modest house a well-tended garden plot produced vegetables for the family living inside. The small pens of pigs and chickens that the Mallory family allowed its slaves to tend were situated near these gardens. A tottering, old slave, his white hair protruding from a tattered hat, emerged from a cabin, a coon dog at his heels.

"How was hunting today, Eli?"

"Ole Bluebell done his job right an bagt us a possim."

Dorian continued, pointing out one Bellmead landmark after another such as the huge wooden structures that served as barns, cotton warehouse, and tool storage buildings. Everywhere, or so it seemed to Erwin, were slaves both male and female working various jobs. He was surprised by the master's recognition by name of each one. "You know them all?" queried Erwin.

"I made it a point," was Dorian's emphatic reply. "Most all of them have been on Bellmead since birth, and we consider it poor business to separate families. Grieving slaves are less likely to work productively and are tempted to run for freedom."

"One of your jobs will be to distribute food stuffs weekly to each family. Normally, each adult receives four pounds of meat, one peck of meal, and one quart of molasses; however, we supplement the diet with seasonal produce. They have their own chickens for eggs, and the dairy will see to milk and so forth." They stopped inside one of the warehouses where Dorian inspected a barrel of rice before finishing their tour. "My sister has seen to these duties for some time now. Since she was recently married, we expect that before long she will… ah… be confined."

"Of course," Jasper replied deeply embarrassed by Dorian Mallory's open discussion of his sister.

"You'll be meeting by brother, Skylar, on Monday. He's a doctor in Charleston, and he spends each Monday at Bellmead seeing to the slave population." His expression must have registered surprise for Dorian Mallory remarked, "Most folks are taken aback by our practices, but our productivity far exceeds every plantation in the state." They walked a little farther in silence. "There is also a third brother, Andrew, who is serving in the military." The oldest son added with pride, "He distinguished himself at the Manassas campaign and was decorated by his commander."

As he was speaking, Henry Monroe, the longtime overseer of the Mallory's plantation approached astride a bay. He reined his horse as he came along side his employer and the stranger.

"Henry, I'm glad you're here. You can finish the tour with your new man. Make the acquaintance of Jasper Erwin."

As Jasper greeted the rider, he could not help but notice the menacing whip encased within the rifle holder on his Western saddle. Henry Monroe was a rugged, fiftyish man, well tanned from his many hours in the sun. A long, jagged scar dominated his left hand. Realizing that the new man lingered too long upon his hand, he quickly withdrew it from view.

"I am returning to my work. Again, Mr. Erwin, I trust our association will prove memorable." Dorian turned and began the walk back to his accounts. The trip made all the more lengthy by his desire to stray toward the fields. Bellmead was his life's blood, his heritage, his love. Not that Dorian Mallory had squired his share of South Carolina's most desirable belles; somehow none had convinced him of her mutual love for his land. So he remained, as Mandy informed him, the South's most pursued bachelor.

"The man says you're from Tennessee," Monroe said as the two watched Dorian Mallory head toward the big house.

"That's right. My father had a farm there."

"Guess you've worked Darkies before, but I'll tell you how I see it. Darkies are best kept down and fearful." Henry spit tobacco from the opposite side of his mount, wiping the excess with his shirt sleeve. "I'll be seeing to it that you carry one of these." He stroked the whip at his side. "Make sure you're never without it, and don't never trust one of 'um. Mr. Keitt's brother, a doctor down in Florida, murdered in his sleep by his own Darkies." He spat again. "And poor old Miz Witherspoon, smothered in her own bed. They'll turn on you in a minute." Monroe made a reflexive rub across his scarred hand. He stopped and looked coldly into Erwin's eyes. "I hear from Montclair's overseer that there's some Yankee do-gooders about trying to stir up the slaves. Damn Yankees, I'll kill the first one of 'um sets his feet on Bellmead." Before Jasper could comment, Monroe took the conversation down a different path. "You married?"

"No, Henry."

"Me and my woman been married nigh to twenty-five years now. Live over there." He pointed to a two-story framed house. "Got six youngins. All but one's up and gone. My wife would be pleased to have you to supper." He patted the new man on the back. "You can meet my daughter, Alice." He smiled at the best prospect he'd had in a long while to take Alice off his hands.

Chapter Fourteen

Richmond, Virginia

A smarting pain in his foot distracted Jefferson Davis from the game in progress and the approach of two men. Since Buena Vista, the wound which he sustained and endured throughout the battle had plagued him, informing him, as it did now, of impending changes in the weather.

Though his health prevented his active participation, the President had developed a love for Mr. Doubleday's novelty. Allowing himself to be swept into the activities of players, he managed to escape the responsibilities of his office and his personal affairs.

Increasingly, he was discovering the difficulties of managing a plantation in the new South, especially when the master was in absentia. At least he was spared the negotiation and sale of his crops by the new law he believed to be imperative if the Confederacy were to survive. In fact, he insisted upon the provision before accepting the office, his greatest fear being an unstable economy manipulated by the greed of his own kinsmen of the landed gentry. Envisioned by Davis was a South in which the predominantly agrarian economy could equally benefit the privileged as well as the common man.

Such an idea had not gone without opposition, since the vast majority of the politicos were plantation owners. Still, the loyalty he commanded precluded a vocal opposition. For the time, the Yankees loomed as a larger enemy than an unproven theory and a united front a psychological preference. Now, however, the unforeseen interference by the enigma of one Daniel Adamson had ignited those claiming to have condemned the law from its inception.

The force of a blow jarred Davis back from his thoughts. "Mr. President, what a fortuitous happenstance to find you at this afternoon's contest."

Howell Cobb was planting his trademark slap across Davis' back as he continued to expound upon the falsehood of a "chance" encounter. An exhaustive search and a well-placed bribe of a household slave had located the President at the baseball game between two army units.

"I was mentioning to Henry how much pleasure I derive from watching the boys play ball." Though uninvited, Cobb and Foote positioned themselves on either side of the President, their torsos engulfing the plank supported by neighboring tree stumps. The unevenness of the supports produced a slanting, which forced the President and Foote in perpetual efforts to avoid nudging Cobb off the crude settee.

As the game resumed, the three turned their attentions to a particularly strong young private who was hurling the ball with speeds that left the batters swatting at the wind. Whether in disgust or as a vain attempt at strategy, the next hitter allowed four perfectly hurled balls to pass him while he made no attempt to swing.

Cobb was on his feet, screaming for the man to take his chance and swing. Sitting back on the plank, he angrily expressed to the others, "It's long been my contention that there should be someone to assess the penalty of a strike when a batter refuses to swing at a pitch thrown with such precision."

Davis smiled, "Howell, the boy just didn't feel those pitches were right for him. A man cannot be forced by the judgment of another to act against his heart."

The opportunity thus afforded, Cobb betrayed the true intent of their presence. "You are so correct, Mr. President. How clearly your words ring true. They bring to mind the outcry of the citizens of this nation, whose letters reach me daily, pleading for the Congress to repeal the unnatural law which prevents them from selling the fruits of their own fields."

"Sir," added the heretofore silent Foote, "did we not secede in opposition to the tyranny of a Federal government that sought to ignore the sovereignty of each state?"

Davis' eyes remained focused on the players. Watching the young pitcher, he remarked, "It is a credit to these men that they rely upon the thrower as one does a leader to perform to the best of his ability." As he pointed to the fielders he added, "You see, gentlemen, how they await his moves and cheer on his efforts? No doubt each would perform differently were he in his shoes, but he remains loyal, eager to do his part when the need arises."

His point thus made, Davis began to wave his soft felt hat as a man at the home base produced a Herculean effort, sending the ball far into the outer field. Backtracking, the fielder managed to snatch the ball from the air, saving the game for his team. Turning to the men still seated, Davis pronounced, "And the nine bask in the glory as a whole."

Cobb stood beside the President, his voice firm. "But when the men become discontented with their leader, what then? The ego of one cannot be fed to the detriment of the whole."

Undaunted, Davis retorted, "Then let them leave the game."

Foote rose and began to walk away from the field. "The strength lies in the numbers, Sir. When the majority abandons the one, he is left alone as the others seek to replace him."

Watching then leave, Jefferson Davis suddenly turned, frantically searching in each direction. The game concluded, the players and spectators dispersed, leaving the President of the Confederate States of America gazing at an empty playing field.

Chapter Fifteen

Aboard the Victoria

Under the carved ceiling of the Thomas suite, Clarissa finished setting the table for two, stepped back, and admired her handiwork. She'd actually begun to anticipate these evening meals prepared by the *Victoria's* onboard chef. Unfortunately, there were no stewards available at the busy dinner hours, but seeing to her needs and these light household duties served to pass the hours at sea.

It was not that she found her first crossing tedious or boring, quite the contrary was true. Basking in the comfort of the steam-heated apartment, she read Shakespeare, Thackeray, and Hawthorne from the endless volumes shelved in the seaboard library.

A knock sent Clarissa Morgan on a ritualistic pass before the gold-leafed mirror. She checked her hair, her dress, and pronounced herself fetching, at which point she opened the door to her cabin, knowing full well who stood behind it.

Jedediah Thomas entered the cabin that by all rights should have been his. Following the startling incident that reacquainted them, Jed insisted that she accept the cabin, while he shared Captain Whitney's quarters. Since then Clarissa had taken their evening meals in the suite, dining in the salon being an impossibility.

The close confines of a ship easily lent itself to the exchange of gossip, and the discovery of the newly married Mr. Thomas spending his honeymoon with a young lady who was not his wife would surely have set the tongues wagging. The crew, suspicious from the onset of the voyage, considered their employer's sharing of the captain's cabin as an unnecessary ruse, a mistress making a crossing with her wealthy companion not uncommon. The ensuing weeks of the voyage had done much to quell the hostilities that had flared during their War encounters. An unfamiliar observer would have believed them to be old friends or future lovers, so close had become the ties, and therein lay the problem.

"You look exceptionally beautiful tonight, Clarissa. Why so formal this evening?"

"Why, you told me that tonight would be our last before docking." She turned and needlessly busied herself with the table setting, "And I wanted it to be memorable. My mother had this ball gown made for me in Paris. Lord only knows why I decided to bring it on a nursing mission. At least I'll put it to some use tonight."

She looked up, her eyes sparkling. The ball gown had been an effort to cheer herself over the fact that she would be giving up Jed in the morning. Though she would have denied it adamantly, she was falling in love.

Jed drank in the picturesque vision reflected by the candlelight. Her emerald gown of mull muslin was cut quite low and accented with point lace. Since that night at Manassas, he had admired her beauty and courage. Now he had a lengthy list of attributes that made Clarissa Morgan all the more appealing. Jed found her well-read and versed upon politics and economics, knowledge she attributed to dinner conversations of her uncle's many and varied guests. Unlike the majority of Southern women he knew, she lent her opinions freely, arguing them with confidence as though she held a genuine interest in each one.

He smiled remembering an incident when the voyage was in its second day. On an afternoon stroll, Clarissa passed the men's smoking salon. Though quite unspoken, it was frequented by males. Perhaps the segregation stemmed from its masculine décor of dark walnut paneling, paintings of hunting scenes, and the presence of a hand-carved bar, from which brandies and other spirits flowed.

Jed, Jerold Sikes of Natchez, and David Wesley Hale of Montgomery were engaged in conversation extolling the South's efforts to see slavery extended into the territories, thereby recruiting more states into the Confederacy. Overhearing Hale's remark about the sanctioning of slavery by God, Clarissa was unable to contain her contempt. She burst into the room, shocking the half dozen or so men in attendance.

"And what makes you believe that God upholds such an abusive institution as slavery?" she demanded.

Hale, detecting from her speech that the young lady was no daughter of the South, replied, "Young woman, in the South a female is reared with grace and a sense of decorum which guides her conduct. Most assuredly she would not intrude where she is unwelcome, nor would she attempt to interject herself into a conversation about which she knows nothing."

Watching the fire raging within, Jed sat back, crossed his legs, and awaited the inevitable retaliation.

"Thank you, I will be pleased to join you," she spouted contemptuously as she seated herself opposite Hale. "Now if you have the manners so often professed by Southern men, you will answer my question."

Seeking to put this virago in her proper place, Hale obliged. "I reference you, Miss…"

"Morgan."

"Miss Morgan, to the Holy Scriptures. You are familiar with them in the North?"

"Indeed," she said with an icy overtone.

"You will agree that slavery in the days of our Lord was widespread?"

She nodded her assent.

"Then cite for me one example where slavery was condemned and explain to me why the slave, Onesimus, was told to return to his master?"

"There are no verses that condemn slavery; however, Christ did command us to love and serve our fellow men. Now which of you is willing to follow the Lord's example of love and servitude to His apostles by placing himself at the mercy of a Southern master?" As she spoke, she twisted herself in her chair until she had addressed each man present. "Surely you would suffer no ill effects at the hand of your Christian neighbor and brother." She awaited a reply, which was avoided by bowed heads or averted eyes. "As I thought." She rose. "Now if you will excuse me, I shall retire to join your other slaves across the hallway."

Jed wanted to burst into applause. Hale and his companions, left speechless by her remarks, remained as staunchly pro slavery as before. Only Jed possessed an inkling of doubt that he attributed not to the words but to the speaker.

Entering the velvet portiered women's parlor, Clarissa surveyed the women who sat like queens upon their brocade thrones. Some embroidered, and others chatted as games of backgammon and wisk were in progress. Sensing no kinship with these women who allowed themselves to exist in a state of blissful ignorance of the world outside their own, she walked back to her cabin.

Had she been a male, Jed was certain that Clarissa Morgan would have made a formidable politician, attorney, or businessman.

"Jed, there's something I have avoided telling you, mostly due to my own inability to admit when I am wrong." Jed seated himself at the table and awaited her revelation. "This has been weighing heavily upon my conscience these last few days. Before we had this opportunity to become friends, I resented you and the others at Bull Run just because you represented a way of life that I abhorred. I'd heard such God awful tales of slaveholders and Rebel politicians that I let them prevent me from judging you as a person." She looked sadly at the man opposite her. "You were all such gentlemen to Cathey and me, but all I did to return your kindnesses was to be caddy and difficult when I should have been grateful." She thrust her hands into her lap, obviously frustrated by the great difficulty she was having in expressing herself. "What I'm trying to do is apologize, but I've not had much practice at doing so."

Reaching across the table, he took her delicate hand in his. Her heart beat madly. "You were frightened, Clarissa. Captured by the enemy, lost behind the lines, how were you supposed to react? I admire the way you survived despite the dangers."

"But I…"

"Let me finish. You showed more bravery and spirit than I thought possible of a woman. Why, Mandy would have had the vapors when…"

At the mention of his wife's name, Jed quickly removed his hand, a look of guilt crossing his face. The awkwardness of the moment was interrupted by the cook's announcement that their meal was ready for Clarissa to claim.

In her absence, Jed thought back to the conversations they had held over previous suppers. One such discussion began over the recently published dime novel, *Seth Jones*, of which Jed was especially fond and had encouraged Clarissa to read. He praised the skills of Edward S. Ellis which transported the reader to such exciting episodes as the hero's capture by the Indians. While Jed's enthusiasm for the orange-backed novel was hardly shared by Clarissa, she nonetheless feigned an interest, the effect being that Jed fancied himself and his comments to have rivaled the most famous lecturers of the day. Only once had their discussions touched upon the point which most clearly divided them. The subject of New York had given rise to the topic of plays. By chance she mentioned *The Octoroon*. A vehement argument ensued in which Clarissa underscored the fact that their differing philosophies on slavery were directly related to geography.

"I really do not comprehend," Clarissa raged, "how living south of an invisible line can so jade the thinking capacities of people that they are able to believe in the superiority of one people over another. How dare you presume to own someone like you would an animal or a piece of land?"

"The plight of the slaves is preferable to that of the Irish, Polish, or other immigrants that starve in your cities and wander the street in search of places to lay their heads."

"At least," she emphasized, "they made their decisions to come here of their own free will. Besides, your system is doomed to the failure of all feudalistic societies. Even one of your own kind, Hinton Helper, admitted as much."

Jed was familiar with the writings of the North Carolinian turncoat's *The Impending Crisis of the South: How to Meet It.* Though loathe to admit it to his dinner companion, Jed had found Helper's points thought provoking. As the author outlined the great economic liabilities of slave ownership, he admitted that in its youth the system had been a boon; however, the support of aging slaves, the overuse of the land, and the effects of moral decay wrought upon the people of the South had become more costly as the system grew in years. Regardless, it was the South's dependency upon the North's industries that frightened Jed the most. If a time came when the Confederacy could not trade its cotton for manufactured goods, it would devastate his country.

That dispute had continued until Jed departed in a fit of anger, but he returned the next evening, the issue of slavery left unmentioned and unresolved. For the last few evenings they had taken turns read aloud *Minister's Wooing* by Mrs. Stowe. The romantic novel soothed the feathers ruffled from their previous disagreement.

Clarissa returned with the meal, and they sat down to enjoy their last night at sea. The conversation turned to their individual plans upon reaching port. After Clarissa cleared the dishes, she returned to her companion.

"Jed, I want to dance."

Rising quickly to his feet, he headed toward the door.

"Where are you going, Jedediah Thomas?" She demanded.

"There's an old sailor with a fiddle; I'm going to provide an orchestra."

"Don't be silly," she laughed as she ran across the cabin to bar his exit. "We have a virtual symphony right here." Opening an armoire, she removed an ornate music box. Lifting the finely carved lid, the strains of a waltz flowed.

Jed made an exaggerated bow which Clarissa answered with a curtsy. She felt his strong arm raising her to her feet and became lost in the moment, the envelopment of his arms, the manliness of his scent, and the motion of the ship. As they danced, not a word was exchanged. A mutual fear prevented so much as a glance. Then, as if cued by an unseen force their eyes met. Jed bent to kiss her forehead, then her lips. The woman's response told him the captain would have his quarters to himself for the first time since setting sail.

Chapter Sixteen

Liverpool, England, the next day

Clarissa, accompanied by the men laboring under the burden of her trunks, disembarked. Upon reaching the dock, she turned, searching the railing for a last look at her lover.

There were no regrets on her part. Waking in his arms erased the stern warnings concerning mortal sin issued by her mother and her aunt. As to his wife, Clarissa purged the woman's existence from her consciousness.

A slight wave of the hand solicited a prudent nod from Jed Thomas, whose reflections were the antithesis of the woman boarding the hired carriage. Unaccustomed to the pangs of misgivings which gnawed at his stomach, Jed's trust in himself had heretofore been implicit, yet he had been inexplicably compelled to posses Clarissa Morgan. After she drifted off into a contented sleep, he struggled to grasp what manner of guile, what basal instincts had coerced him to betray the wife he so dearly loved. He discovered none, save an allure which permeated all his senses, rendering him powerless against it. Yet, as he watched the barouche disappear into the British mist, he was certain that he would appear at her door, as agreed. Left with no further enticement, he vacated his position at the railing to claim his belongings.

What should have proven an adventuresome delight eluded Clarissa. The unique quaintness of the English city escaped her fancy as she dwelled on the new direction her life had taken. Thus preoccupied, she gave little heed to her surroundings. The driver's tapping on the carriage drew her thoughts and urged her into the motions of exiting the coach and paying the man his fare.

Finding herself outside a row of dwellings which alluded to the station of its inhabitants, Clarissa was struck by her parent's home. Far from humble, the structure, at best, was common and bore the markings of the middle class existence of conservative spending and tightly reigned budgets of which her father held such disdain. Her arrival drew the attention of a young maid who opened the door with a flourish.

"Oh Mum, I am ever so thrilled that you've come. It'll make the Missus so much better." Detecting a note of disbelief she added without hesitation or breath, "I seen your picture; I did."

Clarissa took an immediate liking to Sarah, who appeared to be in perpetual motion and animated of speech which was unhampered by an obligation of "her place" in the Morgan household. Her brashness and devotion to her mother endeared to Clarissa this woman that she appraised to be quite near her own age. In the short time the two were together, a kinship developed, culminating in Sarah's passage to America for which Clarissa Morgan served as benefactress.

Following Sarah up the narrow staircase, familiar objects caught Clarissa's notice. A portrait, a table, a figurine once ensconced in each of the many houses of her youth, signaled home and triggered episodes from the childhood she had banished to the deepest recesses of her memory.

Sarah was announcing her presence before the door opened. "She's here, Missus. Your girl is here to see to ya."

Unaccustomed to a robust mother, Clarissa nonetheless hesitated at the first glimpse of the more fragile version of herself that lay heavily blanketed in a tiny bed. The room boasted an ample hearth, but it failed to repel the dampness which penetrated its every crevice. My heavens, she thought. Its ten thousand wonders that she's alive.

Throwing their arms around each other, the two wept. Unperceived, Sarah dabbed her eyes with the corner of her starched bibbed apron.

Sipping the steaming tea provided so willingly by the servant girl, mother and daughter chatted, catching up on the latest news of relatives and friends. So involved was the conversation that Clarissa forgot about the lateness of the hour. Sarah's call from the hallway alerted her to her father's arrival.

"Are you well enough to come down to supper?" Clarissa inquired of her mother.

"I'm afraid not, dear. I'll nap for a while, and when you've dined, you can come back up?"

"Then Father and I will bring a tray up..."

A sarcastic laugh escaped the invalid. "I hardly think so. Your father hasn't entered this room in weeks."

"Not even to bid you a good night or to see to your welfare?" was the daughter's shocked reply.

The expression that crossed Phoebe Morgan's countenance was one of shame.

"Well," Clarissa continued, "after this evening I'll take my meals with you."

"I'm so glad you've come, Clarissa," she called as her daughter left the bedroom.

I shan't be here for long, thought Clarissa. *Nor will you, if I have any say.*

Granville Morgan sat in a wing backed chair enjoying a brandy when his only child entered the dimly lit parlor. Neither rising nor offering any sort of affectionate acknowledgement, he peered at her over his glass. Referring to her traveling attire, he remarked, "Quite an expensive ensemble you're wearing. Is that how you squander your stipend, on frivolous clothing?"

Before she could respond, he persisted. "I shall write my esteemed brother-in-law concerning his disregard for your reputation. Allowing you to paint your face with lip rouge is reprehensible."

"If my face is flushed, it is due to the drafty room Mother is forced to endure. It is no wonder that her health continues to decline. And as for my stipend, I'm sure Sarah receives a tidier sum. Uncle Simon assumes the costs of my needs, though I doubt you have concerned yourself to any great extent regarding my welfare."

Granville Morgan leaped to his own defense. "Your welfare is of foremost concern to me, Clarissa. After all, I allowed you to remain in Washington so that you might form a suitable match, one upon whom I could rely in my golden years. Instead," his voice became even more hardened, "you disgrace us by flaunting yourself on a battlefield and cavorting with damnable Rebels."

Clarissa was on her feet, eyes glaring, "How dare you…

"You've always had a smart tongue, Missy, a trait from your mother's side so aptly exemplified by the Honorable Simon Cameron, Secretary of War." He spat the words laced with the vehemence of resentment and jealousy.

"I welcome the comparison to Uncle Simon, for he is more of a father to me than you will ever be."

The argument might well have intensified had Sarah not appeared to announce their meal.

"I am dining with Mother, if you'll be so kind as to prepare a tray."

As she climbed the stairs, Clarissa called over the railing. "I am returning to Washington with Mother as soon as possible, before this climate causes her death."

Running to the landing, Morgan raged, "You will take her nowhere; she's my wife and will retain her place at my side."

The slamming of the door silenced his voice but not his thoughts. *Damn the Camerons. They have the constitutions of plow horses. If there'd been any justice, she'd have died giving birth to the girl, and I would be free to make a more advantageous alliance.* Downing his brandy, he unleashed the full fury of his temper on the hapless Sarah.

Clarissa awoke abruptly jarred to consciousness by the tugging at her arm.

"Wake up, Mum. We haven't time to waste in bed."

Groggily, Clarissa pulled herself up to a sitting position. Suddenly, she exclaimed, "Mother!"

"Not to worry. She's sleeping like a babe."

"I don't understand."

"You wasn't a poppin' off last night about taking the Missus was ye?"

"And if I were?"

"Quit being so uppity. You'll be a needin' my help, you will."

Excitedly, Clarissa leaned forward. "Would you help us, Sarah?"

"I've grown fond of the Missus, but I can't say nothing for that..." her voice trailed. "For your father. He's a cold man, that one. I'd hate to see her waste away, Mum. That's why I been to the docks this mornin' early. I brung you this." She thrust several schedules into Clarissa's hands. "We'll have to trick her for she won't be desertin' her husband, not that he's been no husband to her. Him seekin' out the wifely comforts elsewhere and all." Realizing Clarissa's shock, the maid stammered. "Beggin' your pardon, Mum."

Clarissa clasped Sarah's hand. "You've said nothing that I have not suspected long before now."

Their two heads together, the two young women began a thorough study of the sailing times of the various passenger vessels destined for the United States.

Clarissa first eliminated the *Victoria*, whose rapid turnaround was entirely too soon. According to Sarah, Granville Morgan was expected to attend a governmental dinner in two weeks, necessitating his absence from home up until the early morning hours. Thus, the packing of Phoebe's and Clarissa's trunks and their dispatch to the ship would transpire undetected.

"But Sarah, my father is sure to realize that you aided us in our escape. There is no way of knowing how he might seek his revenge."

"I wish I could be goin' with you." Sarah hung her head.

"Uncle Simon only provided the funds for two, but I swear that I will send you passage as soon as we land. Then you can join us in Washington."

"Beggin' your pardon, Mum. I don't want to seem ungrateful. I've a sister in New York City who works as a maid for a fine lady whose house covers near a city block." Sarah's eyes grew wide as she described the mansion and her sister's promise of employment if Sarah could manage passage, a journey for which Sarah had been saving for nearly two years.

Very well, New York it is, and in a first class cabin," vowed Clarissa. "Are you certain that you will be safe from my father until the money for your passage arrives?"

"The good sisters at the church will see to me. There's none to worry." She patted the hand of her benefactress.

"Then, hurry down and secure us a cabin." She called after the eager maid. "Perhaps it would be safer if we were known by the name of Thomas? We cannot make the mistake of underestimating my father."

"To be sure."

Clarissa sat back in bed as the maid hurried to the docks. As was characteristic of any quiet moment, her thoughts drifted to Jed, his whereabouts, his actions, and the joy of memory. True, they had agreed not to contact one another for several days, providing Jed the opportunity to conduct his business with the British cotton brokers and for Clarissa to assess the situation with her parents. Still, she had hope for a brief note or perhaps an invitation to a late supper.

*****

Sir Basil Smythe adjusted his wire-framed spectacles. For the better part of his sixty years, he had cursed the failings of his eyes. The page cleared after a few seconds, revealing rows of neatly written figures representing bales of Confederate cotton that he had carefully stockpiled when the permanent rift between North and South seemed inevitable.

Leaning backward, the chair omitted a discordant squeak. The cotton merchant's mind wandered into the past, settling upon a meeting a month prior.

The intermission of the opera had served to conceal the clandestine association between Sir Basil and a minor

American bureaucrat. A distaste for such commoners allowed to participate in sensitive issues had always disgusted him. Such were the winds of change that blew over the modern world, scattering the old, traditional methods of caste. He viewed such alterations as a great pity.

Seeing the discomfort of the little man who faced him in the crowded lobby, Sir Basil appraised him as one who found himself in alien surroundings. His evening clothes, obviously borrowed, were ill fitting, and his actions revealed to an aristocratic observer that he was at a loss as to the required decorum of an operatic patron.

The men maneuvered unobserved to a less occupied area of the richly decorated lobby of the opera house. Smythe appreciated the painstakingly wrought friezes which depicted scenes from famous operas. The red carpeting gave one the emanation of stepping upon air; such was its luxurious texture. Golden fixtures complemented the room, one in which the nobility was aesthetically reminded of the privileges of its station.

"John Wesley Porter?"

"My pleasure, Sir Basil."

"Of course...we have little time, as you may not be aware."

"The agreed upon prices have been transferred into your account."

"I feel an obligation to warn you of the necessity of distributing the contents of my cotton warehouse slowly, lest the margin of profit be diminished by excessive supply." After this statement, Sir Basil Smythe was momentarily taken aback by his own words. Why indeed, had he found it necessary to warn this weasel-like commoner? The money, a handsome amount decidedly above the market worth, was safely in his bank. He owed the man nothing, yet his sympathies for those less endowed and skilled had been embedded within him through his heritage, which traced to the lords and fiefdoms of Medieval England.

"The fool," Sir Basil remarked aloud, rising from his desk and walking over to a leather upholstered sofa because it afforded better lighting. Taking up the morning newspaper, he reread the item that had gained his attention earlier in the day and had sealed his estimation of Mr. John Wesley Porter as the village idiot.

The gist of the article reported a sharp drop in the price of cotton. Though not seen in print, Sir Basil personally knew of several other British and French cotton merchants who had also sold their entire inventories to the same man, and all had received more than fair exchanges. He let the newspaper drop into his lap.

How could any businessman afford to buy at such exorbitant rates and sell for such pittances? The puzzling situation preyed on his mind until his personal secretary announced the arrival of the special envoy of the Confederate States of America. Each time he heard mention of the world's newest nation, it evoked memories of one of his few underestimations.

"Mr. Jedediah Thomas of Charleston," the secretary announced.

Sir Basil rose and shook the proffered hand. "Ah, the man who kidnapped Lincoln! A singularly courageous undertaking. My congratulations."

"Please Sir Basil, I hardly completed the abduction unassisted."

"Nevertheless, it was your leadership that gave your nation the upper hand. I also understand that you are the son of a friend and business acquaintance. I do hope your presence does not signal his inability to make the crossing."

"My father is as difficult to deal with as ever," Jed laughed. "In fact, he sent you his regards and this box of Cuban cigars."

Smythe smiled broadly, accepting the gift.

"My business has no direct connection to Thomas Shipping. I represent my government."

"In that case, I trust I am in no danger of suffering a fate similar to Mr. Lincoln's?" The inquiry evoked lightheartedness between the nobleman and the younger envoy.

"If what my father has told me about you is to be believed by half, you are far too shrewd to fall victim." Jed settled back in his chair. "My country has authorized me to offer you the opportunity to act as the sole marketer of this year's cotton crop. Our Legislature has enacted a law that requires planters, regardless of size of their yield, to funnel all cotton and tobacco that is to be sold to the state. The states in turn will allow the Federal government to distribute the crops, assuring each grower a fair and equitable price for his labors."

"And the plantation owners are willing to submit to such controls in lieu of the great stock placed in states' rights?"

"The citizens of the Confederacy realize that sacrifices of some personal liberties must be made to insure the success of our Cause. If they can send their sons to die, they can send their harvests to be sold at, I remind you, a fair price." He proceeded. "The purpose of the plan is twofold. Obviously, the strategy protects the price of the South's money crop, but it also serves to encourage small farmers to contribute to the overall economy by allowing them to compete equally with their more prosperous neighbors for the first time."

Again, thought the noble, *the lower class chips away at the aristocracy's hold on its God given position.*

Jed produced legal documents, which he offered from his seat across from Sir Basil's desk. "Please examine this contract, paying special note to your sizeable commission the price we intend for you to require per bale."

Smythe examined the documents.

Certainly, his commission was tempting, and had he been a man of less honor he might have negotiated an agreement with the son of his colleague. The stated price for the cotton was several cents a bale higher than the top price from the previous year. Through exhaustive research the Englishman was aware that this year's crop was even larger than the last harvest. *Surely*, he thought, *the South realizes that much of its bumper crop of 1860 has been stockpiled? What hope could they entertain that such an asking price will be feasible in a glutted market?*

Jed surveyed the nobleman as he examined their terms. Since Sir Basil held the papers so closely, it proved impossible to see his expression and thereby gauge his interest in the proposal. After several minutes, the documents were lowered, signaling his intention of continuing their dialogue.

"Mr. Thomas, may I direct you to this notice in our morning paper."

Somewhat confused, Jed read the periodical. Magnetically, his eyes were riveted to the article which had earlier captured the gentleman's notice. Disbelieving, Jed read its contents.

"This can't be possible. The price quoted must be in error!" Jed exclaimed, slapping the folded newspaper upon the desk.

"I assure you, the figures are indeed accurate." Aware that Jed was about to refute his declaration, Smythe continued, "If you will allow me to offer an explanation? You will agree that the South's harvest of last season was approximately 3,600,000 bales? A bountiful crop, though it was some one million bales less than 1859."

A nod of affirmation was all Jed ventured in response.

"As a result, European merchants like myself hoarded cotton from this glutted market in order that we might be protected from a long, ruinous war blockade." He paused, allowing the impact of his statement to be fully appreciated. "It was, therefore, surprising to us that an independent source would offer excessive prices for our reserves. Naturally, we sold, for reports reached us of an equally impressive, if not surpassing harvest for this year."

Slowly, Jed began to piece together the import of the facts Sir Basil presented. "Undoubtedly there are some merchants who will be willing…"

The emphatic motion of Sir Basil's white head caused Jed to falter, realizing the futility of completing his query.

"A businessman would have been a fool, totally ignorant of the events, or both to agree to your terms. To a man, these merchants have made their profits and have no need of your cotton at such an excessive rate." Opening a drawer of his desk and pulling out his bank book, Sir Basil added, "Now, I might entertain the purchase of your goods at say, half of last year's price?"

Never in his business experience had Jed found himself in such a stranglehold. He wanted to tear at the unseen force that gripped his nation, placing it in such an optionless circumstance. "May I inquire as the name and nationality of the individual that has seized control of my country's economy?"

In a moment of compassion for the son of a valued friend, Sir Basil Smythe disobeyed one of his first laws of business. "It goes without saying that I will disavow having served as your source."

"Of course."

"The man, as far as I can ascertain, is new to the world market. His representative is one John Wesley Porter. The engineer of this enterprise was revealed to be a Mr. Daniel Adamson of the Union Fidelity Holding Company, and all drafts originated in Solomon Edwards' bank. I suggest you institute your search of Mr. Adamson at the Manhattan Bank and Trust." Rising from his chair, the older man indicated the close of the meeting. Jed shook the man's hand, thanking him for his assistance.

Well into the hallway, he paused and reflected upon the enlightening events. *What would the Confederacy do? I had to sell its cotton to provide revenue, yet selling at a loss would severely cripple if not lead to the collapse of cotton producers.*

He walked slowly onto the cobbled streets. *Who is the man called Daniel Adamson?* he thought.

Suddenly convinced of his course of action, he rushed to his hotel, cursing himself and Daniel Adamson, and the failure of the telegraph industry's efforts to line North America to the Continent. So intent was he to report to the President, that he never kept the agreed upon rendezvous with Clarissa. Without explanation, Jed sailed back to Charleston that very afternoon.

As days passed without a word from Jed, Clarissa was somewhat troubled, but created plausible excuses, rationalizing his silence. The days became a week, and she could contain herself no longer.

Her father at work, she feigned a shopping excursion and ordered the driver to Jed's hotel. Approaching the desk, Clarissa informed the clerk. "I am Mrs. Jedediah Thomas, and I have just arrived from London. Please be so kind as to show me to my husband's suite."

Eyeing her skeptically, he leaned closer, his voice in a hushed tone. "Mrs. Thomas, you should be aware that your 'husband' departed for the Confederacy several days ago."

Several seconds elapsed before Clarissa claimed some semblance of composure. "That is impossible. Obviously you are mistaken; we agreed to meet here."

Unmoved by the lovely, young woman claiming to be the Confederate's wife, the deskman returned to his duties, momentarily entertaining the idea of offering the 'lady' his attentions for the remainder of the afternoon.

Clarissa rashly surveyed the ornate lobby in a futile effort to locate Jed. Returning to the clerk, whose eyes greedily traveled over her body, she demanded, "There must be a message for me of our British cousin, a Miss Morgan."

Exasperatedly, he abandoned his post, roughly taking her by the arm. While unceremoniously escorting her to the street, he advised, "Not of a single instant do I believe that you are Mrs. Thomas or any other representative of the gentleman's family. The man ordered his luggage returned to the *Victoria* before he sailed. Now be gone with you; I'll not have your kind plying your trade at my hotel."

Had the revelation of Jed's departure not moved her, robbed her of speech, Clarissa would have surely forced the Englishman to withdraw his innuendo. As it was, she wandered aimlessly along the street, oblivious to passers-by or surroundings, smarting from the finality of his scurrilous gesture.

"A ride to your destination, Miss?" the hansom's driver inquired. Her response was the address of her parents' home.

On the morning the women were to sail for America, the Morgan household bustled with the secret activities. Once Granville departed, the packing began in earnest, beginning with trunks of dresses and culminating with pictures and household objects of which Clarissa knew her mother to be especially fond.

When all had been loaded into the carts hired by Sarah, Clarissa entered her mother's bedroom, a letter from Simon Cameron to his sister in hand. Anxiously, the daughter awaited her mother's reply to its contents.

Offering her the letter, Phoebe, her voice faultering, summarized the missive. "He feels you are suffering without my guidance and are in need of a mother's influence and love. I had no idea."

Clarissa crossed to her mother's bedside. "I respect your loyalty to Father."

"Which is hardly as important as that to my daughter. Simon wants us in Washington, for your sake, of course."

"And you are willing to go?"

"Without hesitation."

"Then, we sail in a few hours."

Phoebe's initial shock lay overshadowed by preparations for the journey. Writing a note of explanation to her husband, she cited her brother's promise to summon him to the Capital with all haste."

Exhausted from the ordeal of the departure, Phoebe nodded off several times during the trip to the docks. Once admitted to their accommodations, she was soundly asleep when the vessel left the harbor. It was not until England vanished from the horizon that Clarissa relaxed her guard, believing them safe from her father's wrath.

Chapter Seventeen

Bellmead Plantation, some days later

Guided by the acapella strains of a familiar hymn, Jasper Erwin drove a farm wagon down what loosely served as a road. The complaints of the boards and wheels offered a cacophic challenge to the praise, causing him to wonder if the Lord could detect the difference. At his side, bundled in a heavy shawl against the evening chill, sat Amanda Thomas. It was at her request that Jasper undertook this trek into the darkness. Given the melancholy into which she had fall on late, the overseer agreed to escort her to the tent revival.

Reigning the team beside an assortment of similar conveyances and a splattering of more elegant carriages, Jasper became aware of the lapping of the backwaters near which the tent was pitched.

Drooping flaps of the shelter served as a doorway through which an array of lanterns illuminated the modern tabernacle, producing a blinding contrast to the ebony night. Escorting Amanda down the aisle, he glimpsed an unusually diverse audience composed of members of the landed gentry, town's people, poor farmers, and sharecroppers uncharacteristically cordial to one another in the caste conscious South. United as God's children under a makeshift church, a tolerance of their inferiors emerged with exception, he noted, of the slave drivers and maids who stood in the rear singing loudly to a God so oblivious to their outcries.

The hymn concluded, the audience took its seats on benches worn by the usage of saints and sinners throughout the South. Emerging from the some sixty souls in attendance, the itinerant preacher stood before them, arms outstretched in a loving embrace. In a resounding voice given to politicians, lawyers, and such men of the cloth, the dark-haired man began his oration, clutching the Good Book as his only source of referral. During the span of a few minutes, the evangelist quoted no less than ten Scriptures wisely selected from the Old Testament so as to appeal to the variety of faiths of his attentive flock.

Since his arrival, Jasper's religious consciousness noted that the Confederacy's custom of segregation by wealth pervaded even its religion. Those closest to his station, the wage earners and small land owners, migrated toward the smaller Baptist and Methodist congregations, while their more prosperous brethren favored their Episcopalian and Presbyterian counterparts.

It was indeed difficult to ascertain the affiliation of the good brother in the pulpit. Through the nearly ninety minutes of Biblical discourse, he called the Holy Spirit from the Lord's right hand, commanding it to dwell in each soul beneath the crowded tent. Several, both White and Black, swooned and babbled as the Spirit entered their bodies, purging the devil from his strongholds. With the strength of God's Spirit, the preacher began a series of condemnations of liquor, card playing, and all seven of the deadly sins in varying degree.

One uncomfortable sinner, known to frequent the bawdy houses of Charleston muttered to his wife that the speaker had, "Quit preachin' and gone to meddlin'."

Referring to their proximity to the backwaters, the minister called for a song of invitation during which those languishing in sin could receive forgiveness and salvation or suffer the torments of hell fire for eternity.

As some ten to twelve penitent souls made way to the mourner's bench, Jasper succumbed to the urge, taking his place along side a particularly heavy matron whose immense size left him little room. Shaking the hands of each confessor, the preacher reached for those of Erwin. His head bowed in repentant humility, Erwin's eyes never met those of the man who placed the small paper in his hand. Without notice, Jasper placed it in his trouser pocket, reading it only when he reached the confines of his Bellmead room. The date of Armitage's rebellion committed to memory, he tossed the paper into the fire.

Chapter Eighteen

Bellmead, December 1861

T he Christmas season was being ushered in by a stiff, northerly wind. Jasper Erwin found himself rushing toward the granary to supervise the daily feeding of the stock. In his weeks at Bellmead, he had encountered unexpected difficulties.

Preying most heavily upon his mind was his failure to initiate any facet of his mission. At first unable to determine the reason for his lack of success, he arrived at a realization the afternoon Mr. Dorian had presented him with a magnificent black stallion. By far the most superb creature he had ever ridden, Ebony was to be his personal mount for the period of his employment. Since then, Jasper had spent every idle hour combing and caring for his horse. He had never known such a pleasant lifestyle, and that was the downfall of his assignment. Jasper Erwin was truly happy at Bellmead.

The entire Mallory family was generous and genuinely caring. Nor was this gentleness limited to its own. Not a traveler or a destitute neighbor who sought aid at the plantation left without a full belly or an opportunity to work for a wage. Bellmead would have been a paradise were it not for the slaves.

Were the Mallory slaves mistreated? Worked from sunup to sundown, they were given fair portions of food and household goods, but they reaped few fruits of their own labors. Slave cabins were small, drafty, and sparsely furnished. They knew the sting of Monroe's whip, and above all, they were in bondage.

As Jasper compared their existence to those immigrants he had seen in Northern cities or the poverty-stricken sharecroppers of the South, he viewed the slaves at Bellmead to be in somewhat more enviable circumstances. As to whether a man in slavery who was fed, clothed, and housed was better off than one who was destitute and free, he could formulate no clear opinion. It was the reality that the majority of slave holders were not as humane as the Mallory family that constantly reminded him of his true purpose at Bellmead.

Entering the granary, the overseer watched as two young slaves named Boaz and Samuel were loading the grain into a wagon. The two were wearing their new clothing, which along with two pairs of shoes, a hat, and a little liquor, had been the Christmas gifts provided by the Mallory family.

In the short time the new overseer had been in residence, the slave population had reached a consensus that he was a blessing directly sent from God. To them, he was more representative of the Mallory's attitude toward them than the oppressive Henry Monroe. Stern enough to maintain respect, not a slave had witnessed an incident when Jasper Erwin had ever raised his whip.

Watching the men work, Erwin made his decision to launch his plan, knowing that his life and those of many others hung in a precarious balance.

"Boaz!"

"Yes Suh?"

"Did I hear right? Some boys were talking about Mose. They were saying that he can read and write as well as any White man."

"Yes Suh, you dun hud right. Dat Mose waz luhnt by Miz Mandy' maw afoh she passed."

"You mean if I sent him a message on paper, then he'd have no trouble with it?"

"Nah Suh."

"I'm going to see if that's the case. I want you to run up to the big house and deliver my note to him personally. Can you do that without letting anyone see you hand it to him? I don't want somebody reading it to him?"

Immensely proud that one of their own had achieved such recognition, Boaz was willing to do whatever Jasper asked in order to demonstrate Mose's literary prowess. Quickly scratching out a note with a pencil stub, the overseer folded it and placed the paper in the pocket of Boaz's jacket.

As if on a great adventure, Boaz hurried across the grounds, oblivious of the bitter wind which swept over the open area between the warehouse and the barn.

After sending Samuel out to feed with several more of the slaves, Jasper began pacing the length of the granary alternately wishing he had never met the Reverend Jonas Armitage and replaying scenarios that would have been more clever or less dangerous ways to set his conspiracy in motion.

Arriving at the back entrance to the big house, Boaz confidently knocked upon the door. Shifting from one foot to the other in the wintery weather, it seemed as though no one would ever answer. When the door was finally flung open, he would have preferred that it had remained closed.

"Whut doz you wants?" the belligerent voice of Edna, the Mallory's ill-tempered cook drowned out the howling gusts.

"My but you looks fine Miz Edna…"

"Ah sez, whut doz you wants Nah fe'el han gots nah biznus up to da big house."

"Ah gots buznus wid Mose." Poor Boaz could detect no measure of change, nor did he entertain any hope that he would be allowed access to the servant, when Mose himself approached from the cookhouse.

"Mose, ah gots to shows ya."

Caught off guard, the older man allowed himself to be carried away from Edna's prying eyes.

"Boaz, you're hurting my arm," he complained as he vainly tried to remove the clamped hands from his forearm.

Taking several conspicuous glances over each shoulder, Boaz removed the note from his pocket and thrust it at Mose. Had Erwin the opportunity to view Boaz's attempt at secrecy, he would have mounted Ebony and headed North without a moment's delay.

Mose unfolded the crumpled paper given him by the increasingly jubilant Boaz. Holding the note in his large, black hands, he read its contents and looked up to the eager young boy. With some trepidation he spoke, "Tell Mister Jasper that I passed his test."

"Ah knewed dat!" Boaz turned, moving swiftly with the blustery winds and the desire to tell Mr. Jasper the news.

*****

All through the supervision of the Mallory's evening meal, Mose had been preoccupied by futile attempts to surmise some sort of reasoning for Erwin's perplexing message. As he stole through the shadows of the December night, he was still no closer to a solution than he had been when he first learned its contents.

Taking one last glimpse, he assured himself that he had arrived undetected. Quickly he slipped into the darkened structure. With the door securely closed, Mose stood listening to the rapid beating of his heart. The prevailing aromas of the smokehouse invaded his senses.

"Mose?"

Mose could not see anyone, but he recognized the voice of the new overseer.

"Yes Sir. I'm here. What do you desire of me?"

He heard and smelled the strike of a match. He watched as Jasper lit a lantern that illuminated the room filled with various types of smoking meats.

"I am here to propose something to you, Mose. Something that can benefit every slave in the South."

Confused, Mose listened to the words of the overseer. "I will confess to you, that your literacy skills make you a necessary ally for my plan to work. In short, I need your help in organizing a slave rebellion."

"Sir?"

"I represent an abolition movement from the North. It is our belief that given an incentive, that all slaves will be ready to revolt in hopes of freedom." Seeing the disbelief that he had expected in the slave's face, he continued. "The plan is to launch a massive slave revolt throughout the South on a designated date and time." Becoming more enthusiastic, he continued, "Don't you see, there are hundreds like me who have been sent to the major planters' slaves?"

His response marked with skepticism, "We rebel; what happens then? We have no way of escape. We'd be hunted

down like animals. You Yankees have no clue as the realities
we face here." Accustomed to the dimness, the two men could
see each other more clearly. Mose held his fists tightly
clinched, his arms perpetually in motion. "You come to the
South and want to free us from our masters, but do you offer
us anything after we're free? Tell me, Mr. Jasper how does a
freed slave make a life for himself and his family in the North?
You have any cotton fields for the men and women to work?"
Anticipating his rebuttal, "Oh, you have factories. Well what
chance does the Black man have when the only machinery he
has ever seen is a cotton gin that he probably wasn't allowed
to touch, and if he can run a machine, what are his chances
of competing for a job against a White man?"

Defensively, Erwin responded, indifferent to the
negativeness in Mose's retorts. "The hunting is done by
neighbors and town's folk, but they'll be occupied with their
own insurrections. By the time word can spread, we'll have the
people safely within the Underground Railroad or with other
sympathizers."

"Seventy-five men, women, and children cannot escape on
foot and undetected. No," he insisted, "I won't be a party to
filling their heads with false hopes and dreams."

"Fine," he snapped in exasperation, "don't help; waste your
life here as the master's boy!" Gaining control of his temper,
his tone eased somewhat. "You're no better than a slave owner,
Mose. Don't you think that just once, these slaves deserve to
make their own decisions about their lives?"

Shamefaced, Mose acquiesced, his words coming slowly.
"How do you propose that we begin?"

Chapter Nineteen

Washington, D.C., December 1861

The thirty-one room Executive Mansion was aglow with the holiday season. It boasted three towering spruces whose decoration had been scrupulously supervised by the Lincoln sons. Despite the ardent pleas from his sons, the President vetoed their notion of adorning the Jackson statue centered in Lafayette Park with holly and mistletoe. In an effort to quiet them, he did allow a banner expressing a Yuletide greeting to be strung from the Jefferson piece in front of the White House, which seemed to satisfy the children's desire to bring cheer to the rest of the nation.

With the passing of each partygoer, the tiny flames of the candles fluttered, producing a twinkling effect. For weeks Mary Lincoln had been in a manic state over each aspect of tonight's festivities, so much so that a baker and two stewards were now without employment during the Holy Season. Those who managed to abide within her good graces or who had been successful at avoiding her wrath, thanked a higher authority.

Despite her numerous last minute alterations in decorative arrangements and food, the White House was once again alive and festive, something which had been lacking since the surrender. Even the samplings cut from the draperies by souvenir hunters and the shabbiness of the East Room's pale green carpeting went unnoticed, such was the ambience and the buoyancy of spirit. Perhaps it was the city's effort to free itself from the depression of the summer's defeat. Possibly each had vowed to make merry in an effort to overcome the loss of a single loved one or half a nation of kinsmen.

Rows of liveried broughams lined Pennsylvania Avenue, inching closer to the half circled drive of their destination. Within them were the elite of Washington's society. Members of Congress, Senators, Justices, Governors, businessmen and their ladies would dance away the hours to the strains of the orchestras whose talents had been engaged.

Taking to heart the prevailing attitude of "Peace on earth, good will toward men," the President sought to institute the process he hoped would heal the wounds of the divided nation. Hostilities, Lincoln had told his cabinet, would only serve to drive the wedge of dissension deeper. It was his intent that amiable relations, like the invitations he had extended for tonight's gala, would one day lure the rebellious states back into the Union.

In the family living quarters, Lincoln was unable to abide his wife's nervous outbursts another moment. He left her finishing preparations and stopped off to visit his sons. He preferred a Rebel charge to facing Mary Lincoln as she prepared for an evening before the wagging tongues of Washington's society matrons. Such encounters only served to enhance her insecurities concerning her wardrobe and her inability to claim the position as Washington's premier hostess, which she felt should belong to the First Lady. In vain attempts to supersede the wives of the Capital's most prominent men, she had amassed debts with dressmakers, jewelers, and shopkeepers, disregarding the pleas of her husband to curtail her spending. Bracing himself, the President kissed the boys and returned to his wife.

Already the East Room was filling with elegantly clad guests, reflecting in the massive mirrors that hung at regular intervals. So lengthy was the guest list that both public floors of the mansion required musicians and dining tables to accommodate the throng.

Secretary and Mrs. Cameron were among the first to arrive. The evening's celebration served dual purposes for Cameron. Mrs. Kennedy gladly secured invitations for several visiting dignitaries at his request, thus affording the conspirators the occasion to meet without fearing discovery of their association.

Perusing the dance floor, the Secretary caught sight of the Comte de Joliet. An influential figure in his native France, the Comte had made the crossing under the auspices of Napoleon III. Through his network of sources, Cameron had become privy to the information essential to acquiring the Comte's special form of diplomatic service.

The Secretary of War was momentarily distracted by the comely vision at the Comte's side. Without question, she was the most desirable woman in the room. Her scalloped gown was marked by a series of rosettes of a deeper shade of blue than its skirt. Cut daringly low, the neckline was pinned with a costly brooch which drew attention to her ample bosom, and caused both men and women to comment for differing reasons. Decidedly younger than her escort, her flattering attention to the aging diplomat convinced Cameron of the nature of their relationship.

The Comte's partner had not gone unnoticed by the other men in attendance. When a Congressman from Pennsylvania, much to his wife's dismay, requested the next reel, Cameron seized the opportunity to approach the Frenchman.

"Merry Christmas, Comte."

"And to you, Secretary Cameron." As the two men exchanged pleasantries, even the most observant bystander failed to perceive the exchange of a single scrap of paper.

"Your Capital is fast becoming a city to rival those of Europe. Construction of the dome captures the traveler's attention for miles as he approaches. I also noted the presence of scaffolding here at your President's home. Will I see an additional wing when I next visit?"

Secretly the Comte hoped that the neglect of the White House would be corrected at long last. Regarding Americans as vulgar and tasteless, the deplorable state of its President's home somehow seemed in tune with such a nation of commoners.

Thank God the weather demanded that the windows remained closed, he thought. Recalling the unpleasant stench of a drainage canal at the mansion's side, he vowed never to return during the warmer months.

"A deletion is more accurate a term. An old ramp system is being enclosed permanently."

"Ah… the infamous tunnel that brought an army to its knees. A wise move on the government's part to be sure."

"The engineers assure us that the presence of the ramp ways will be so cleverly concealed that it will appear as though they never existed, even to the trained eye." Making a slight bow, "You must excuse me; I see my wife. My regards to the young lady." A knowing smile crossed his face.

"My sister's youngest child is a vision, no?"

"Indeed she is, Comte." With his back to the Frenchman, the Secretary laughed aloud at his ludicrous excuse. Only when he had crossed the length of the teeming East Room did he permit himself a brief view of the Comte's communication. It bore only the figure, $100,000.

As he slipped the note inside his white glove, he reflected upon the Comte's demand. *A small price for the cooperation of the French government,* he thought. *How fortunate that those closest to Napoleon III can be purchased for so reasonable a price. Let the Rebels see how long they can survive without a major ally or market for their precious cotton and tobacco.*

Simon Cameron's euphoric mood was broken by the announcement of the most recent arrivals.

When Lincoln first broached the subject of this gesture of reconciliation, both he and Stanton regarded it as absurd. What other term could describe the extensions of social invitations to those responsible for one's own abduction? The thought of the damnable Confederates being feted distracted him from his objectives for a short time. At least Davis had exercised the good sense to decline.

Stewart Kane combed the crowded ballroom, guiding Catherine Jackson toward the dance floor. Underneath her lace gloves she nervously adjusted the diamond engagement ring that Stewart had insisted she open prior to Christmas Day. Behind them Colonel Adam Dupree and Miles Davis broke into opposite directions.

Dupree, whose drinking had begun earlier at the National Hotel's well-stocked bar, looked about for a waiter so that he might continue his quest for oblivion. The irony of President Davis' request that he represent him at the White House was inescapable. Dupree considered Davis' estimation of his skills:

*He denied me the chance to lead men here to insure a victory,
but he orders me to conquer the dance floor on his behalf.*

The Colonel's inebriated condition failed to pass unnoticed.
Sensing weakness in the Southern officer, Cameron directed
his steps so as to station himself in a close proximity. Despite
the cacophonic mixture of voices, laughter, and music, the
Colonel's slurred speech was clearly discernible. From the
heated exchange between Dupree and the Rebel who had
rejoined him, the Secretary was able to turn his attention to
the other guests, firmly assured that his search for the
heretofore elusive link in his plan for the South's demise had
been discovered in the form of Colonel Adam Dupree, newly
appointed commander of the guard at the Confederate
Treasury and Mint. The appointment of such a man to protect
the nation's currency could only be attributed to the ineptness
of the Confederacy.

The strains of *Hail to the Chief* announced the arrival of
the hosting couple. Dupree maneuvered through he crowd
for his first look at Abraham Lincoln since his release. Dressed
in formal attire, his long arms hanging from his stooped
shoulders, Lincoln began extending his white glove hand to
his guests. Forced to wear them by his wife, he often ruined
a pair at each social occasion from repeated greetings and
poor fittings.

The wife is exceedingly plain, noted Dupree. Though
plumpness seemed the vogue of the North, the Colonel
preferred voluptuousness in his women, remembering
lecherously the French woman he encountered as he entered
the East Room.

At the very least, the man could have combed his hair,
reflected the Colonel as he downed the contents of his brandy
and scouted the room for a waiter.

Mary Lincoln tapped her fan nervously against her arm. Was the fur trimmed gown striking enough? Perhaps the flowers pinned at her bosom were a tasteless adornment? These and hundreds of other details prevented her from enjoying any aspect of the evening, for she was certain that each man and woman in attendance was speaking ill of her by berating her clothing, the food, or the décor.

She wished her husband would dance with her, but he avoided most dances, waltzes in particular.

With his head characteristically bowed, the President made his way to a bandstand festooned with garlands of holly. Quieting the crowd, he spoke.

"Mrs. Lincoln and I want to extend our most heartfelt wishes for the Yuletide season and the coming New Year."

He paused briefly and then continued, "1861 has been a year not without trials and disappointments for all of us. My heart aches for those families whose tables have empty chairs. The sacrifices of their loved one were not in vain, for our soldiers died for noble causes.

"My prayer during this celebration of our Lord's birth is that we heed His call to love our neighbors. The time has come to bind up the nation's wounds. Revenge and hatred are the destructive tools of the devil, and they will putrify our souls. We must extend our hands to our Southern brothers with malice toward none and charity for all. I would be remiss if I did not do all that I have asked of you. It had been my hope that President and Mrs. Davis could honor us with their presence."

Gasps of disbelief rose from the audience.

"That his duties and his wife's health prevented his acceptance, I sincerely regret, yet I am pleased to offer the hand of friendship to three who were my captors, Lieutenant

Stewart Kane, Sergeant Miles Davis, and Colonel Adam Dupree."

The President left the platform, walking to the trio of Southerners, shaking the hands of each. From somewhere in the crowd, applause originated, echoing throughout the East Room.

Simon Cameron left in disgust. At a discreet distance Solomon Edwards trailed the Secretary and passed a sumptuous buffet of *pâté de foie gras*, grouse, and salmon. Other glittering trays were ladened with hams, turkeys, and other tempting fares. Solomon reluctantly passed a queue of diners patiently waiting to reach a round table of French pastries, silently vowing to return to these delicacies after his meeting with Cameron. A cautions succession of movements afforded the men privacy in a seldom used receiving room.

"The Comte's demands are paltry, indeed," Edwards remarked upon examination of the figured paper.

"Were that all our endeavors were of such trivial proportions."

The banker looked up, noticing for the first time in their association a note of despair. "Armitage advocates an impossible proposal the slaves make their escapes by rail," a derisive laugh accompanied Cameron's statement.

"We knew that the underground routes would be far too crowded to be used effectively. I had assumed that alternative arrangements had been outlined some time ago," came Edwards' shocked response.

"How or if those slaves ever arrive any further north than Richmond has never been of monumental concern to me, Solomon. Their revolts need only leave the plantation owners without labor to work their fields." Seeking to persuade the skeptical financier he posed, "And what would the Union do with thousands more unemployed illiterates? Our cities are overflowing with just such a class of immigrants, who are at least White. No, for our purposes, those slaves are more advantageous to us dying in their escapes than showing up on our doorsteps."

Solomon Edwards was caught off guard by the callousness of Secretary Cameron's comments. Leading these people to certain death amounted no less than murder. "And you fully believe that the Reverend will continue his cooperative attitude when it becomes apparent to him that the slaves are to be sacrificed?" he queried. "I think you are underestimating the dedication of these abolitionists. They see their struggle as a crusade to free the Black man. If so driven, I can foresee Armitage exposing our roles in retaliation."

An agitated Cameron glared at Edwards, unaccustomed to less than total conformity to his views and highly displeased with the bleeding heart concern for a race of slaves. "I see, and how would you suggest that we proceed?" His question was directed with an aggrandized gesture which indicated a relinquishing of responsibility to the financier.

"I fail to see it as an insurmountable obstacle," Edwards replied matter-of-factly. "My bank holds a rather large mortgage on the Southside Railroad, which has foolishly placed much of its capital in Confederate currency. Judging from the accomplishments of Mr. Harrison, the railroad will be unable to convert its increasingly worthless paper into Yankee greenbacks, which the bank will demand as payment. The installation of a new president, of my choosing, will be accomplished far enough in advance to station waiting trains at various locales in a number large enough to aid the escapes, but small enough to be above suspicion." It was difficult to determine if he had fought for the lives of the slaves or power over Cameron.

The Secretary rose and crossed to the door.

"And of Mexico?" the banker inquired of his back.

Cameron removed his fingers from the brass knob of the door. "Juarez's cooperation was never in doubt. He is a small man with fewer loyal supporters than he has specie in his treasury. The only variable rests with Davis and whether he elects to acquiesce to blackmail or engage his army in war."

Without further comment, Cameron exited. Seconds later Edwards returned to those delights he previously desired.

Chapter Twenty

Richmond, Virginia, the last of January 1862

Nervously, Jedediah Thomas shifted through the papers to which he would refer. Speaking to the combined Houses was somewhat irregular; however, these were irregular times. Since his return from England, Jed's attempts to privately convince Southern leaders of the country's grave financial position had fallen on deaf ears, leaving him with on oppressive sense of guilt.

Guilt met Jed at every turn, shrouding his existence as if the Furies were in residence within him. There were times when he could not meet Mandy's eyes. He didn't deserve her, not after his indiscretion aboard the *Victoria*. If she suspected, there were no outward indications. Quite the contrary, his absence seemed to have made Mandy all the more ardent for his affections, yet the memories of Clarissa Morgan invaded even their darkened chamber at Bellmead. Desperately he had tried to exorcise himself of Clarissa, but her image was indelibly etched within his mind. She was alive in his waking thoughts, his dreams, and underneath him when he made love to his wife.

Poor Clarissa, what must she have thought when I sailed without a word? Before he left his hotel and many times since, he had attempted to put to paper his regrets. All seemed shallow, cold, and ultimately a tangible threat to his marriage. What sort of man could betray his wife so soon after making his vows to her and abandon his lover as well?

He turned his attention to his speech. The South was floundering in an ocean of fiscal woes. Without considering the rapid decline in the price of cotton, there were the expenditures of the new government. President Davis had great visions of a Confederate capital whose houses of government would far surpass its rival in the North in architectural majesty. Of course, there was the army to maintain. Outfitting a permanent force and the inception of a navy had exceeded even the most imaginative estimations.

Yet, it was each state's belligerent defiance of further governmental controls that most worried Jed. Such obstinacy had led to proposals ranging from individual currencies to permanent abolition of any form of Federal control, now that the United States posed no threat to the Confederacy's existence.

Thomas removed a Confederate bill from his pocket. Turning it between his fingers, he saw the Stars and Bars emblazoned across the left hand corner with the digits denoting the denomination. The signature of a heretofore unheard of Richmond woman attested to Secretary of the Treasury Christopher G. Memminger's practice of employing women to sign the bills after printing in what Jed believed to be a ridiculous deterrent to counterfeiting. "Will pay to the bearer upon demand," he wondered how easily the bearer could redeem the note's value since the bullion that constituted the Federal Treasury amounted to little more than $718,294 in confiscated gold from the Union's mint in New Orleans. True to form, each state had its own smaller reserves, which they were reluctant to relinquish. There were rumors of loans from European sources, but lenders were hesitant to speculate on an unproven country.

Silently, he thanked heaven for his father's sensibility in maintaining a large portion of Thomas holdings in a Washington bank, supposedly for use by his Northern office. Not that Ezra Thomas was unpatriotic, for he had invested a tidy sum in cotton bonds before the outbreak of the hostilities. With the ever deteriorating market value of the crop, Jedediah approximated the degree of his father's patriotism at close to a ten thousand dollar loss.

Such was the frame of mind as the driver passed Richmond's equestrian statue of George Washington and reigned the carriage to a halt in front of the Grecian-styled State Capitol which would serve as the nation's seat of government until the completion of Davis' plans for a new Confederate Capitol were brought to fruition. Thomas Jefferson had designed the edifice, which lent its influence to many another structure, both North and South. Jed always regarded Richmond as a rather spectacular city. Built on seven hills, the James River provided its southern boundary. It appeared to have little distinction between its business and residential populations near the Capitol Square. Rows of warehouses lined the banks of the James. Dotting the view were easily spotted Tredegar Iron Works and Crenshaw Woolen Mills. With the influx of office seekers and Legislators, boarding houses and hotels were filled to overflowing. Considered in poor taste before the nation's birth, even the most fashionable houses posted notices of rooms to rent.

As he ascended the steps, a familiar voice drew Jed's notice. Senator Howell Cobb of Georgia approached, his face marked with excitement. "Jedediah my boy, how's your father and your lovely bride?"

"Quite well. Mandy is here with me. We'll be going North to Stewart's wedding in a few days."

"Weren't there any belles worthy of young Kane that could have prevented him from marrying a Yankee girl?"

Protectively he insisted, "Catherine is a perfectly charming young woman. I shall look forward to introducing you when Mandy and I host a reception for them at Bellmead. After a few moments, you'll be drawn to her fine qualities and forget her ties to the Union."

Cobb was about to voice his misgivings concerning Jed's remarks when an aide neared them. "Mr. Thomas, your presence is required immediately, Sir. The session is being called to order."

The two men hurried into the already crowded assembly hall, packed with the Confederacy's twenty-eight Senators and one hundred twenty-two Representatives. From the corner of his eye, Jed noted the presence of several ladies and briefly wished that he had encouraged Mandy's attendance. The Speaker had just concluded his opening remarks, when Jed was ushered to a seat beside President Davis. His arrival went momentarily unnoticed for the noise was distracting, and Jed had been seated to the side from which Jefferson Davis had no vision. It was not until he began his journey to the podium that Davis acknowledged the younger man's presence.

As the President spoke, Thomas busied himself scanning the assemblage. Of those he could discern without rudeness, he recognized Congressmen H. W. Bruce of Kentucky, Jabez L. M. Curry of Alabama, and Henry S. Foote of Tennessee. He regarded the immaculately groomed Davis. What a contrast he was to his Union counterpart, always taking pride in his appearance. A charming man and an eloquent speaker, Davis commanded and received respect. A face neuralgia hampered his lifestyle somewhat, producing severe headaches which often required complete rest and calm.

"… My aspirations for this nation are many, but of foremost importance is the existence of a peaceful coalition of sovereign states, subject to a Federal authority which both enhances and encourages the rights of each individual state."

Cheers and applause filled the hall.

"In the infancy of the Confederacy, we have sacrificed for our glorious Cause. Many gave their sons and husbands at Manassas, the planters have given their crops in a collective effort to sustain our government, and countless more have purchased bonds and loaned money to give this nation life. Would that I could promise an end to such self-denials, but alas, to do so would be ill-advised. As with any new being the efforts which give life are not without pain, but ladies and gentlemen of the Confederacy, the rewards we reap will be our sustenance through this travail…"

Davis took his seat amid the ovation of his audience. The Speaker banged the gavel for quiet, a task requiring several minutes to complete.

"At the request of President Davis, the chair will recognize his special envoy who has recently returned from England. This son of the South proved his worth to us during the War against Northern aggression, leading his men into the White House and walking out with Old Abe in a box. The chair welcomes Captain Jedediah Thomas."

Had he not dreaded the news he was about to impart, Jed might have basked in the glory of the admiration that these distinguished men and their ladies were outpouring. With trepidation, he began to speak, causing the crowd to sit and quiet itself.

"My fellow Southerners, I do not deserve the laud and praise you have so generously bestowed, for my duty was and is to you, the citizens of the Confederate States of America. My men and I did no more than was asked of anyone and did much less than those who gave their very lives to grant us freedom. Your heartfelt greeting makes my task all the more difficult, for I must inform you of unpleasant tidings."

Jed waited as the crowd exchanged dubious words and looks. "Upon reaching my destination, I discovered that the European cotton market had been depleted and the value of our cotton reduced by more than half its worth."

There were exclamations of disbelief and profane outbursts.

"The bounty of our previous harvest afforded the European merchants opportunities to hoard surplus bales which they have now sold to a Union based concern at an inflated price. In a deliberate effort to sabotage our livelihoods, the Yankees offer this same cotton at a loss, robbing us of any hope of a profitable enterprise for this year's harvest."

Stunned by his pronouncements, the audience allowed Jed to proceed uninterrupted.

"I foresee few options gentlemen. Opening new trade agreements with South America, the Orient, or Eastern Europe will be equally costly in lieu of the increased risks and expense of transport."

Unable to contain himself further, William Lowndes Yancey, the outspoken Alabama Senator, sprang to his feet. "Such is the folly of placing ourselves under the control of a Federal government. The planters of Alabama will market their own cotton crops."

His Alabama colleagues cheered.

"We cannot divide our forces!" came the cry of Georgia's Howell Cobb.

Repeatedly the gavel rose and fell in vain attempts at order. The elected officials sought out those of common voice, like the Old Testament men of Babel.

Split upon whom to place the blame for the disastrous collapse of King Cotton, one warring faction heralded the ineptness of Davis, while another damned the Yankee for breach of the Treaty of Manassas, as yet another extolled the virtues of patience and loyalty to the new government in the face of adversity.

From each cluster emerged a leader. Davis' rival from an earlier state election, Henry S. Foote, rallied those calling for the President's resignation. In direct opposition, the Hill coalition directed its venomous outcries against the traitorous Lincoln and his Yankee horde. So heated did the arguments become than an inkstand thrown by Senator Benjamin Hill found its mark, cutting the cheek of the raving Yancey.

The Confederate Congress might well have been permanently dissolved had a winded messenger not made his way to the Texas delegation, thrusting the yellow tissue of a telegraphed message into the hands of Louis T. Wigfall. Pushing his way to the Speaker's platform, Wigfall somehow managed to make himself heard above the din.

"Gentlemen, gentlemen, we are at the brink of war!"

Debating ceased in mid sentence.

The women sank to their seats, calling slaves to fetch their salts. The now universal voices cried for an explanation for Wigfall's remarks.

"A messenger has arrived bearing grievous news. President Benito Juarez of Mexico had declared the Treaty of Guadalupe-Hidalgo invalid and reclaimed Texas as a territory of Mexico. He further states that it is his hope that another costly war can be avoided; therefore, he will allow the Confederate States of America a two month period of grace during which we may elect to negotiate a purchase of Texas at a price of five million dollars in gold." The usual clamor erupted, plummeting the assembly into chaos.

"This ludicrous claim is no more than blackmail," the words of Thomas Brock of Virginia resounded. "The Confederacy will not concede to the demands of a petty dictator who disguises his domination of the Mexican people under the title of 'President.'"

"Gentlemen, let us be practical for a moment." The audience directed it eyes to Tennessee's Foote. Sending our sons and husbands to die for the preservation of a way of life is paramount, but placing these same men in jeopardy to protect an area whose citizenry is uncultured and backwoods at best..."

"Sir, the people of Texas take great offense at your remarks!" Wigfall had rushed the platform, pistol drawn. Only the containment of Wigfall by several of the more level-headed Representatives averted bloodshed on the Congressional floor.

The Speaker, in an effort to quell the dissident sects, proclaimed the session adjourned. Exits were hastily achieved, and the disputes transferred to saloons, homes, and hotels where whiskey bolstered the arrogance and resolve of each faction.

President Jefferson Davis pulled at his sparse beard as he analyzed the events of the previous day. As he sat amid his cabinet in his second floor office of the Treasury Building, formerly the United States Customs House, he believed that Juarez was not a man to resort to blackmail, rather he struck Davis as a decisive one who took whatever he wanted. If any bartering was to be done, it came after conquest to be used to his advantage. But who influenced the Mexican leader? France, always a dabbler in Mexican affairs, proved a feasible choice; however, as of yet there was no motivation, no advantage for France in a Mexican controlled Texas.

Indecision racked Davis until the pronouncement of the political representative of Benito Juarez.

Lorenzo de Zavala, reveling in his newfound importance since the afternoon he had broached the matter to Juarez, had failed to mention to El Presidente any portion of his encounter with Daniel Adamson. De Zavala's "idea" had secured him a position close to the leader. He was, at this point, indispensable, for he had cleverly vowed to secure a sizeable sum to finance the war, should the Confederates prove foolish enough to initiate a conflict. Completely in control of the funds dispersed by the Americans, who would be the wiser if some of the money were diverted from the war chest?

There was no possibility for Lorenzo de Zavala to lose with the hand dealt him. If the South succumbed to blackmail, he would remain Juarez's darling, and if war began, he stood to become a very rich man. Arrogantly he strode into the office of President Jefferson Davis, determined that the latter would occur.

Somewhat shaken by the presence of several men he had yet to meet, the envoy acknowledged Secretary of the Navy, Stephen Mallory; Secretary of State, Robert Toombs; Secretary of War, Leroy Pope Walker; and for some unfathomable reason, the civilian businessman, Jed Thomas. It had been the envoy's plan to confer with the President alone, thus exposing those negotiations of which he was the sole beneficiary to fewer witnesses. Solemnly he began a survey of the gentlemen in which his financial security rested. The tobacco chewing Walker, he assessed to be of that aristocratic race of landed gentry in which the South placed such high regard. Whether he was shrewd and manipulative or of the heritage country gentleman variety of Southerner would soon become apparent. His uniform literally bursting at the seams, the Naval Secretary's short, fat body created the illusion that a Punch cartoon had come to life. In Jed Thomas, he foresaw the greatest potential for challenge. Surrounded by his adversaries, he sat in a comfortable chair offered by the President whose capacity for discomfort was twofold.

The President began, "The Confederacy is, of course, disturbed by your President's demands concerning Mexico's rights to the state of Texas, which has, I remind you, been free from Mexican control since Houston's defeat of Santa Anna's forces along Buffalo Bayou. It is, therefore, quite inconceivable that Juarez can entertain any hope of being paid retribution for something which is in no way his."

Sensing the urgency of an offensive stand, the Mexican diplomat left the confines of his chair, delivering his words while encircling has audience. The comparison of a schoolmaster towering over his errant students was inescapable.

"Since the independency of our country from the French and Spanish oppressors, the Mexican government has held sovereignty over Coahuilia -Texas. The citizens of Mexico were never given the opportunity to voice their displeasure with negotiations by the dictator Santa Anna in what can hardly be considered a binding treaty. The Treaty of Velasco was arranged with a prisoner, desperate to save himself. As for Guadalupe-Hidalgo, it was made with the United States of

America, not with a splintered fragment of that nation." With his hands on the back of his chair and bending forward in emphasis, he uttered his most convincing point. "If you no longer recognize the agreements which bound you to the United States, why then must Mexico?" The narrow set almond eyes of the bronze skinned de Zavala burned with triumph.

"Now see here!" Davis thundered. "You know perfectly well that Mexico has no legal claims to Texas. Juarez is an opportunistic thief who is resorting to petty blackmail in order to bolster his coffers. We will not concede a single dollar!" Davis exploded at the Mexican envoy. "Unless you abandon this thievery, the Army of the Confederate States of America will rout your men as it did those same Union forces at whose hands the Mexican military has previously suffered defeat. Our Navy, under the able leadership of Secretary Mallory, will blockade your ports as our Army closes trade on the ground."

Lorenzo de Zavala had positioned himself directly facing the man who stood poised over his desk. Looking Davis squarely in the eyes, he weighed each word with sufficient volume and intensity to produce an ominous effect. "And what Navy do you propose to employ, Mr. President? The Confederacy has at its disposal only those vessels abandoned by the Union, scarcely sufficient to blockade the Gulf."

Davis was unsettled by the Mexican's accurate assessment of the virtually nonexistent Confederate Navy.

"Your appalling lack of geography surprises me, for you are ignoring our Atlantic coastline, which can continue unimpeded by your impotent 'Navy' to supply us through our North American friend, the United States. As for your Army of obstinate gentlemen and backwoods farm boys, it will have to fight a seasoned foe without the benefit of a captured President to force a surrender. Your women would provide a more substantive challenge!"

The Secretary of War grabbed de Zavala by his shoulder, wheeling him violently in his own direction. "You insolent bastard, we will crush Juarez, and he will curse the day this extortion was conceived."

Feigning an attempt to compose himself, de Zavala collected his hat and walking stick. "I will inform El Presidente of your unfortunate refusal to negotiate a monetary settlement."

Slamming the door to Davis' office Lorenzo de Zavala was already hard at work, determining which European climate would best complement the lifestyle to which he would soon become accustomed.

Chapter Twenty-One

Washington, D.C., February 1862

Clarissa Morgan's return voyage held none of the fascinations of her initial crossing. Nursing and entertaining her invalid mother occupied her time. What free time she had drove her to madness with the memories of the night she spent in Jed Thomas' bed.

Every detail of their final night together was etched into her mind. She could feel the passion of his kisses and the tenderness of his caresses as they satisfied the desires which had been building since their first meeting amid the carnage of Bull Run. Each daydream, each reliving of their love ended with the same brutal finality. The man to whom she had given the most precious of her possessions had placed her in a carriage and walked callously out of her life.

At first she rationalized plausible circumstances that explained Jed's behavior, but as days became weeks, her hurt had hardened into a deep-seated bitterness which pervaded her every action and thought.

Though she never questioned her daughter, Phoebe Morgan attributed Clarissa's melancholy to the burdening of a vibrant young woman with the care of a helpless mother. She had assured herself that Clarissa would revert to her former vivaciousness upon their arrival at the Cameron home. With a staff and her sister-in-law to see to her physical needs, her daughter would be free to enjoy her youth and the constant round of parties available to the niece of the Secretary of War, but Clarissa had politely declined each invitation and discouraged to the point of rudeness each young man who sought her company.

The advent of Catherine Jackson's wedding seemed to revive Clarissa's spirits. As maid of honor, there were no circumstances to warrant her absences at the social courtesies that preceded the marriage of a fashionable Washington lady.

For the eve of the ceremony, a large fete was being hosted by the groom's family, Ezra and Isabella Thomas. Isabella had determined upon Stewart's announcement of his intentions to take a Yankee wife, that Washington society would long remember a ball with which a Southern family honored its son and daughter-in-law to be. The Willard, the most costly of the Capital's grand hotels had been selected as the site for the festivities. A full month prior to the event, Mrs. Thomas ensconced herself in the imperial suite from which she supervised the preparations. The guest list, which of course, rivaled an inaugural gala, included the President and the First Lady.

Isabella's singular regret was the absence of the most elite of Southern gentility. The majority excused itself, citing the winter weather, the difficulty of travel, and the length of the journey. Similar excuses would have been viewed as personal affronts had the wedding been held in Charleston or Richmond, but Isabella knew all too well the resentment embedded within the hearts of her friends, for she, too, shared their hatred of the Yankees. Had the Thomas Family hosted such an affair for any other reason, it would have been looked upon as traitorous. Instead, it was an ironic obligation which garnered Mrs. Thomas martyrdom and invited suggestions and encouragements from the grand dames of the South, so that one might have viewed the preparations as groundwork for a vengeful battle.

As Clarissa arranged the auburn curls which highlighted Catherine's face, the bride again chastised her maid of honor. "I don't understand you, Clarissa. Why won't you let Byron escort you this evening? Arriving on the arm of my baby brother is a social embarrassment reserved for the homely likes of the Danvers sisters, not one of the city's most sought after women. Ever since you returned from England, you've been so different. It is as though all your spirit has been drained." The friends addressed each other's image in the ornate, oval mirror above Catherine's dressing table. "Your mother's heal…"

"It's not her health, Cathey." She sat the brush down on the table in disgust. "Oh, I thought I could go through with this, I really did. Please don't think too harshly of me." Tears began to swell in her eyes. "I just can't stand for you at the wedding or at this ball!" Clarissa turned, sitting herself on the four-postered bed.

Catherine rushed to her friend's side, draping a quilted robe over her chemise. Taking her hands, she peered seriously into Clarissa's tear-filled eyes. "If you are going to desert me during the time I most need your support, then you owe me the truth. Whatever it is, I promise it will go no further than this room."

"He'll be there."

"Who, honey?"

"Jed Thomas," she sobbed.

"Honestly Clarissa," Catherine dismissed her friend's emotional outburst as trivial and returned to her toiletries.

"You can't possibly hold any more ridiculous grudges over our capture at Bull Run against Jed any more than you do against Stewart."

"We were lovers, Cathey," she blurted.

Catherine pivoted so quickly that the china kitten ornament on her dressing table was upset, causing her to make a desperate grab as it fell.

"I'm the first to admit that I am tragically naïve about such matters, but I know that you two weren't ever alone long…"

"On the *Victoria*!" she interrupted.

"Jed Thomas was on the *Victoria*?" asked Catherine.

Her expression reflected her confusion. "I don't understand; Stewart never mentioned Jed being aboard."

"Oh, Stewart was perfectly innocent when he offered me the Thomas' private quarters. The Confederacy sent Jed on an extremely important mission to negotiate cotton sales. So, he had no idea that Jed was on the ship or even considering a crossing."

Catherine was truly shocked by Clarissa's conduct. "And you shared his cabin for the entirety of the voyage?" She loosened her heavy robe, finding it suddenly to warm in her bedroom.

"No, only the last night! We took our evening meals together and often spent the afternoons in each other's company, but he slept in the captain's quarters!" she said adamantly.

"Clairie," she hesitantly questioned, "do you love him?"

All Clarissa could manage was a nod accompanied by a fresh torrent of tears. Gaining some semblance of control, she sobbed her words in a halting fashion.

"Don't you see? That's why I can't face him. He doesn't give a tinker's damn about me, or he couldn't have abandoned me as he did. I haven't heard a word from him since we docked at Liverpool."

The bride-to-be's mind was a clutter of thoughts. She felt terribly sorry for her friend, but her mother's warning about men, their desires, and the careless uses of foolish young girls kept reappearing.

Anger against the despicable Jed Thomas and the idea that she would have to go through a ball and her wedding without Clarissa, drove her to distraction, and she found herself barely listening to the rest of Clarissa's words.

"How he and Stewart must laugh about his tryst with the Yankee slut!" sputtered Clarissa.

Catherine held Clarissa as she cried onto her shoulder.

"It certainly explains a great deal." Momentarily, Catherine pushed the distraught woman back, holding her shoulders squarely as she spoke to her. "Clairie, do you remember what you told me while we were hiding under that bridge, the shells landing all around? You said, 'Don't be afraid. No Rebel bastard will ever hurt us while there's one ounce of strength left in my body.'"

Releasing her, she posed, "If you don't go, you'll be letting the Rebel bastard win! You must face him with your head held high in defiance."

The Morgan girl walked toward the dressing table, examining her swollen eyes and tear-stained face. As she stared at her own reflection, a renewed spirit and determination crossed the image.

Turning to the woman on the bed, she spoke with the confidence that had sustained them both throughout the ordeals of the War.

"I'm going to be incredibly beautiful tonight, and I know just what I'll say to him. I swear; I will make him suffer!"

Chapter Twenty-Two

Richmond, Virginia, February 1862

The sprawling three-storied home of the Slidell family covered the small city block. Its whitewashed cupolas pierced the sky, towering above the elm and crepe myrtles which were picked by the seasonal winds. Located on Main Street, near its intersection with Foushee, the inviting home turned hostelry was situated approximately a half mile from the center of the uptown activities. Its wide halls, typical of Richmond's architecture, courted the breezes of spring and summer, but suffered from the cold and draft during the winter.

At the onset of secession and its ensuing conflict, the city's quantity of hired rooms had increased as much through demand and through economic opportunity, for even the most modest dwellings charged inflated rates to the desperate soldiers' families and governmental officials. In the lesser neighborhoods and the city's outskirts, tents dotted the landscape as did a parasitical class of pickpockets, gamblers, and profiteers.

As John Wesley Porter searched for lodging in the overpopulated city, he was sickened by the absurd fees demanded by the so-called patriots of the South. He chanced to encounter a young captain's wife, vainly endeavoring to secure any semblance of accommodations for her brood of five children. Seeing her reduced to paying on exorbitant fifteen dollars a month for a drafty room which was sparsely furnished with discarded pieces, it caused him great concern for her welfare and those of more meager resources.

His own expenses were of minimal regard, allowing him to pay two month's rent in advance for a cheerful room at the Slidell's. Seated at the dining table, he silently acknowledged his good fortune. Passing a heaping platter of biscuits to the gentleman at his left, Porter measured his dining companions, an array of Legislators and Confederate officers. A white aproned slave, ladened with a tray of fried chicken and a variety of vegetables, emerged from the kitchen. Henry Foote baited the fifty-eight-year-old Treasury Secretary who had yet to secure suitable housing for his family. "Memminger, we will be at war with Mexico by spring." Removing a bill from his pocket and dramatically placing it on the table, he pronounced its purpose. "And this twenty dollar note will bolster my claim."

The Secretary of the Confederate Treasury took the bill from atop the starched linen tablecloth, examining it carefully.

In jest Henry Foote chided the Treasurer, his voice heavily accented by his drawl. "Sir, I consider it a personal outrage that you would question the authenticity of my currency."

A lighthearted banter, kindled by Foote's humor, added to the enjoyment of the meal for all save Memminger.

"Henry, where may I ask, did you secure this note?"

"Why, I received it in exchange from the barber yesterday. Is there some problem?" He looked around the table, garnering encouragement for what he believed to be a continued merriment.

The disturbed Christopher Memminger excused himself and proceeded to the foyer where his cape and hat hung from the hall tree. Foote followed him intent upon learning the cause of the Secretary's unusual behavior.

"Explain yourself, Memminger."

"The bill is plainly counterfeit," he whispered. "With your permission, I intend to take it to my office at the Treasury for a closer inspection."

"I'll accompany you. If someone is undermining our currency, it is of grave concern to us all."

Ordinarily Porter might have pursued the two in hopes of gaining information that would further ingratiate him to Cameron; however, his appointment this evening was crucial and would far outweigh any knowledge acquired from Memminger and Foote's mysterious exit.

If the Secretary and the Legislator's disappearance perplexed the remaining boarders, none commented upon it. Hearing the clock above the fireplace strike ten, Porter excused himself to the four remaining men in the parlor who were involved in a serious card game. Announcing his retirement for the night, he entered the hallway that led to the staircase, glancing over his shoulder to reassure himself that the card players would be unable to see him bypass the stairs and slip unperceived into the kitchen and out the back door.

Fortunately the Confederate Capital proved to be an easy city for a stranger to find his way, the numbered streets intersecting the avenues. He especially enjoyed the stately red bricked home which the city called Linden Row. As he passed Mrs. Pegram's School for Girls, he shoved his hands deeply into the pockets of his trousers to brace himself against the February chill. *If only I'd been able to risk the removal of my cape,* he thought, after a particularly stiff breeze cut through his clothing like a knife's blade.

Now, keeping himself to the back alleys, he reached the walls of the Rosemont Cemetery. From the map he removed from his pocket, John Wesley Porter navigated the lanes of tombstones, arriving at a granite mausoleum bearing the name *Beauchamp*.

Sounding the signal knock, the bronze door slowly opened emitting the shrill, grinding noise that proclaimed its exposure to seasons of harsh weather. A few seconds were necessary for his eyes to adjust to the darkness during which Porter reeled in the direction of a match strike and the opening of a lantern.

"The directions did not prove too challenging," spoke Porter as the man inside the shadowed crypt continued to busy himself with the lantern.

"You are an excellent cartographer. My compliments, Sir. Just what is the information so vital to the Confederacy that it compels us to these repugnant surroundings?"

"Actually, I think you will find our meeting extremely beneficial to your own welfare," said Porter, keeping himself purposefully concealed in the darkness. "You see, I have long admired your distinguished service in both the Mexican War and the Manassas Campaign, but if I may be so bold, I sense a measure of displeasure with your current post. Your indignation is perfectly justified. Were I in your position, I would question my allegiance to a nation that had carelessly cast me into a command which ignores my proven skills."

"Sir, a man who uses a slave child to deliver his messages and insists upon hiding himself within the darkness of a tomb has no concern for interests other than his own." Had Porter been able to see, the man with whom he spoke was wearing a holstered sidearm. "I have no need of any man who refuses to show his face."

Undeterred, Porter shrewdly proceeded to bait his trap with a most enticing morsel. "I've met few men with no need for fifty thousand dollars in American greenbacks." Receiving no response, Porter pushed further. "How many years must you serve amidst degrading rejection to earn an equal recompense?"

The lack of a reply convinced Porter of the man's interest. "Your present duties make you privy to certain information that would be of great benefit to my employer. He would consider your assistance in removing a large portion of the contents held within the confines under your control worthy of the previously mentioned sum."

"My loyalty is not for sale!" came the outraged reply.

"Very well, the decision is yours. Frankly, I apprised him of your fierce loyalties and impregnable sense of duty, thus the precautions for the concealment of my identity." Unconvinced that Simon Cameron could so misjudge the man's character, Porter allowed him time to think about his offer.

"Should you change your mind, place a notice in the *Richmond Enquirer* of a death in the Beauchamp family. Then I will contact you with further instructions."

Porter grabbed the lantern and was out the door of the mausoleum before the man could react. He left the door slightly ajar and hurried in the opposite direction of the Slidell home, confident of his success in recruiting another member of Cameron's conspiracy.

Had he remained, Porter would have seen Colonel Adam Dupree stumble from the Beauchamp tomb and frantically search the cemetery for his whereabouts.

*****

Memminger thrust a magnification lens into Foote's right hand. "Notice the discrepancies in the intricate patterns around the Roman numerals," the Treasurer instructed.

"I see," noted Foote in a somber tone.

"And the waves crashing against the ship are of a conflicting number. Finally, the fact which first drew my attention to your bill this evening, the serial number is one which we have yet to issue." He placed the note and the larger magnifying glass on his desk.

"Are you one hundred percent certain, Christopher? These other discrepancies might have logical explanations."

Shaking his head, Memminger emphatically stated, "I am quite sure. I personally select the lot numbers of the bills. This one has never been issued with my approval." Indicating a small safe in the corner, he stated, "You may consult my logs."

Waving his hand in dismissal, the Legislator assured him, "That is totally unnecessary. You have my complete trust." Leaning back in his chair, he posed the most obvious questions. "What does this mean to our Treasury, and how do you propose we stop it?"

Memminger relit his pipe, considering both his colleague's inquiries. He slowly began, "The impact of a widely distributed amount of counterfeit currency will grossly weaken the Treasury. At Davis' urging, and against my better judgment, I have already issued monies closely totaling the entire cache of the Confederate gold reserves. Naturally, these unsubstantiated bills weaken the value of the authentic ones."

"Do you mean that idiot has placed us on the verge of national bankruptcy?"

In defense of the man who could easily remove him from his post, Memminger tried to reassure the increasingly hostile Representative. "We have no way of knowing the extent of saturation of the bills, so I hardly foresee so great a disaster. How could the President have anticipated a dilemma such as this?"

Realizing that his words were of little comfort to Foote, he began a different approach. "As soon as the cotton sales are completed and revenues from taxes are collected, we will be able to cover whatever losses we might incur."

"Dammit, man!" bellowed Foote. "Didn't you hear a word that Thomas boy said? There will be no cotton sales unless we absorb tremendous losses, and the planters are in dire straights; don't look for revenue to be pouring into the Treasury from citizens who will undoubtedly feel no obligation to support a Federal government so irresponsible that it allowed one damn Yankee to control its largest money crop or an ineffective leader who authorized the issue of paper money to the very limits of our resources!"

Assuming control over the weaker Memminger, Foote slammed his fist against the desk, sending the magnification instrument crashing to the wooden floor. "Now, you listen to me, Memminger. This information is privy to no one, not even Davis, without my approval. If the news of this reaches the people, they'll be running to the banks and your office door demanding redemption in gold, and this whole currency system will collapse like a house of cards."

"But not to alert the President..."

"And just how many folks do you see believing that it was he who insisted on issuing so much currency instead of the Treasury Secretary? I'd say you're only lucky, man, that I'm here to salvage your ass."

Memminger shrank further back from the Tennessean as if he were a wild animal. Watching Foote head to the door, he realized that the night had passed, and he became aware of the noises of a new business day.

"Get in here, Son!"

Percy Newton, Memminger's secretary promptly entered. He was impeccably tailored, as always, and overly eager to please with his meticulous performance of duties.

"Secretary Memminger and I wish to meet with this young officer." Foote busied himself writing the name and location for Newton. "Have this messaged delivered, and see to it that he arrives as soon as possible."

"Of course, Sir."

His secretary's exit lent Memminger the opportunity to question Foote and his motives. "Just what are you planning to do?"

"This counterfeiter must be stopped and the sooner the better. There are very few people that we can entrust with the search; nevertheless, I am certain that the perfect choice is stationed right here in Richmond."

"And he is?"

"Major Andrew Mallory."

Chapter Twenty-Three

Washington, D.C., that evening

In the grand ballroom of the Willard Hotel, its gas-lighted chandeliers reflected from the mirrored walls to produce an illumination which rivaled the noonday sun. The Willard was indeed Washington's finest, boasting indoor toilet facilities and abundant gas lighting. Isabella Thomas' desire to impress had led her to hire extra doormen and servants now attired in the Willard's traditional maroon and black.

Ezra Thomas seated himself in a straight backed chair covered in maroon brocade. Evenings such as this bored him, though he had suffered through countless social occasions to humor Isabella's endless need to lavishly entertain. His wife, resplendent in Valenciennes lace, was currently engaged in a fervent discussion with the Willard's manager concerning the chaperones' seats. At Isabella's insistence, the seating was being arranged, despite the manager's assurance that the quaint practice, though popular in the South, was considered antiquated in the North. Apparently Stewart had not forewarned her about this difference in social mores as he had about the custom of Yankee women waltzing with men other than their relatives.

Stewart's marriage plagued Ezra, for it represented a breach of his word given the boy's father when their sons were infants. Both had sworn to care for the other's family should the need arise. Ezra sighed, *haven't I done everything possible for Stewart? Haven't I treated him equally with Jed, acquired the most renowned tutors, educated him the best schools, given him a position in the business? It was that damnable War.*

Ezra Thomas had tried to reason with Stewart about his marriage. "Rescuing the woman does not oblige you to marry her," he'd said. Elizabeth Hunter had been Ezra's choice for Stewart. Now there was a match equal to Stewart's heritage, a student of Charleston's Madam Tabrandi's French School for Young Ladies, and even a second cousin. But Stewart had spurned her for the daughter of a Yankee cloth maker. "Forgive me, my dear, dear friend," he remarked aloud.

"Who's to forgive, Father?" The entrance of Jed and Mandy had escaped his notice, so deep had been his concentration.

"For letting your mother launch her own personal battle to put the Yankees in their place with this ostentatious display, of course."

"God help the Union," joked Jed.

Mandy slapped her husband playfully with her fan. "Don't you two run on so. Mother Thomas has arranged for a virtual feast. You all will be dining tonight on all manner of Virginia ham, partridge, boned turkey, mutton, oysters, and I can't even recall the rest. I do remember that she ordered Madeira champagne as well as claret cups." She paused a moment, "And if memory serves, a fine burgundy as well." Realizing the point she had just made for her father-in-law she added, "I supposed I do see what you mean."

"Take this chair, my dear." The elder Thomas took her hand and regally sat her in the chair which became engulfed by the yards of hand-beaded fabric of Mandy's skirts. He beamed at the sight of Mandy, his demur and very Southern daughter-in-law.

"Oh, I see the happy couple has arrived. Son, get over here." Ezra held out his arms to embrace his second 'son.' 'It was just too late to contact you last evening when our train arrived." His eyes fell on Catherine. She was pretty enough, but those coarse Northern ways of hers were quite tiresome to a gentleman accustomed to the charms of Southern belles.

"Catherine, you are striking." He kissed her gloved hand, keeping it and escorting her to Mandy's chair. "This is our Mandy."

Both women nodded and donned the awkward, forced smile of someone who found meeting strangers a chore, as they appraised the style of clothing, accessories, and overall appearance of the other.

To Mandy, the guest of honor's attire left much to be desired; the blue velvet skirt appeared too full in the back for her taste. Perhaps it is the gored effect that displeases me so, she silently reflected, as well as her newly styled headdress that encircles her like a mammy's bandana only to culminate with that large bow. "I am so pleased to finally meet the woman who stole Stewart's heart," she drawled.

Catherine half expected to see sugar fall from her lips, as she graciously acknowledged her greeting, all the while considering Clarissa and praying that she could summon the strength to endure the encounter with her lover's all too perfect wife.

After meeting Jed's wife, she could not fathom the mind of a man equally drawn to two women of such diversity. Mandy Thomas resembled a porcelain figurine taken from atop a mantelpiece and somehow given life in a Pygmalion myth. Why did Southern men dote on such fragility and helplessness? A frightening thought chipped away at her own self-image. *What had driven Stewart to her?* In comparison to the delicate flower before her, so representative of her kind, Catherine felt roughhewn and vulgar.

As if sensing her self-consciousness, Stewart excused them, leaving Mandy alone with her husband. Looking up at Jed, a vulnerable expression crossed her lily white face.

"Darlin', I do feel ever so faint. Please be a love and fetch me some punch or whatever is available." She batted her dark, lengthy lashes. "Now don't you let on to your parents. Mother Thomas has much too much to do to concern herself with me."

"Let me call someone over to wait with you while I'm gone," Jed urged, with genuine care in his speech.

"Nonsense, you run along, now."

"It may take a little while," he said giving the room a quick survey. "None of the refreshments are ready, but I'll find you something." He kissed her forehead and left to fulfill Mandy's request.

As she carefully arranged the folds of her skirt, Mandy Thomas chanced to see an alluring creature embraced first by Catherine and then by Stewart.

Something about her captivated Mandy. The woman's scooped necked gown of deep purple fell gracefully to the floor. Clinging capriciously to her shoulders, the sleeves hinted of the faintest bell, tightening at her wrists. The chandeliers danced in the facets of an amethyst necklace whose stones accentuated a faint glimpse of cleavage. Jed's hand upon her shoulder, awoke her from the trance brought about by Clarissa Morgan's presence. "Jed darlin', do you happen to know the dark haired woman in the purple gown? She is by far the most attractive woman I've had the opportunity to encounter since we came North."

In a fateful moment both Jed's and Clarissa's eyes met. His heart stopped, and he felt his legs weaken. She immediately turned her back in what he mistook as a defiant gesture. In fact, she sought to disguise the pain piercing her soul.

"Jed, do you know her?" his wife repeated.

"Yes…yes Mandy honey, she's Clarissa Morgan. Both Stewart and I have spoken of her from time to time."

"Of course, the other Yankee prisoner. You two certainly never related the half of her beauty. I simply must be presented." She began to prepare her hoops and skirts to stand, but Jed gently pushed her to her seat.

"Remain seated; I'll bring her over. Here's your punch, though I am afraid it isn't properly chilled."

The expanse of the polished ballroom floor was the longest journey he had ever taken. *How does one introduce his wife to the woman with whom he broke his wedding vows?* he pondered.

The knowledge that such an occurrence must have taken place innumerable times did little to alleviate his apprehension. Momentarily standing unperceived behind her, he drank in the aroma of her perfume.

"Jed," Stewart began.

At the sound of his name, Clarissa faced the man she loved.

"It's wonderful to see you again, Clarissa." Her face was expressionless, and she remained silent, confusing Jed as he labored to read her thoughts.

Clarissa Morgan was entangled within a snare. Angrily, she reminded herself of his betrayal and the lonely weeks of heartbreak, but her body ached for his touch. Catherine's words relieved the tension.

"Isabella has engaged Mr. Matthew Brady, the photographer, to take a photograph of the four of us. Isn't that the most thoughtful gesture?"

"My mother, ever the insightful hostess," Jed responded, he eyes never leaving Clarissa's flawless face.

"Jed, escort Clarissa to the third door on the left." She pointed in the direction of a hallway. "Stewart and I will inform Mr. Brady that we are ready for his services."

Jed turned toward his wife, "I must let Mandy know." Stepping aside, he cleared a path of vision which allowed the lover a first glimpse of the wife. Clarissa stifled a tremendous urge to laugh aloud, as if this whole scene was lifted from a bawdy French comedy.

"Oh, we'll inform her," Catherine hurriedly said, already pulling her fiancé toward her. "You two go right ahead. We'll first see Mandy and then Mr. Brady."

Clarissa began walking toward the hallway before any objections could be voiced. *Thank God for Cathey*, she thought.

The passage seemed to thunder with the tapping of her evening slippers upon the hardwood flooring. Opening the door herself, despite the closeness with which Jed pursued her, they pivoted upon hearing the door's closure. With one rapid motion, she slapped him fiercely across the face, leaving for several minutes the imprint of her hand on his fair complexion.

"How dare you abandon me with no word of explanation?"

Nursing his smarting cheek, Jed responded. "Clarissa, I never meant to hurt you. God, how I have wished that I'd left the cabin of the *Victoria* before I ruined our lives so completely!"

As he reached for her hands, she jerked them behind her, staring him down, jaws clinched, fire blazing within her expressive eyes. "I had no choice," he began. "My intentions were to call on you the next day, but the news I heard from the British cotton merchants necessitated my hastily planned departure." His voice trailed, realizing the shallowness of his excuse. "President Davis had to be informed of the Daniel Adamson buy out of..."

"And I was so unimportant you owed me nothing, not even a note delivered by a hired Judas?" her words dripping the venom of resentment and loathing.

"I felt you'd understand; the fate of the nation rested on the information I had acquired."

Clarissa tried vainly to avoid looking at him, knowing that to do so would weaken her resolve. Summoning all the stamina within her, she lashed out at the man she so desperately wanted. "Of course,...I would understand that a single man could inflict such a critical blow to your precious country that you had no regard for anything or anyone else, save the Confederate States of America." The last of her words were pronounced with bitter disgust for that which had torn Jed from her arms and represented everything she deemed abhorrent. She crossed the room, no longer afraid of betraying her true feelings, the emotions so long suppressed erupting to the surface. As she collected her thoughts, she stared into the blazing hearth.

"You all have your mistresses, be they business, ambition, or even a country." Facing him, her eyes squarely addressing his, she delivered her most forceful pronouncements. "I will not become as my mother and every other woman who sits compliantly as her man rejects her for his only true love. I have watched helplessly as Mother's health deteriorated from the climates she sacrificially endured for the furtherance of a career my father valued more than her. Time and again, I've seen my aunt and her friends whisked away to separate parlors by husbands who are totally oblivious to their needs."

Fervently underscoring her declaration with every movement, she stood in a close proximity. "Make no mistake, Jedediah, Clarissa Morgan will not be pushed aside by any man. I am not your placid, Southern belle," she gestured toward the ballroom, "who doefully allows her bridegroom to abandon her on their honeymoon in favor of the fickle whims of an entity that is unable to feel and seeks only to use him. To hell with the Confederacy and you!"

Before Jed could muster a response, Stewart and Catherine entered accompanied by the acclaimed photographer. The small, bearded man set about his task of posing his subjects. As was often the case, Brady perceived a resistance to sit before his camera. He vowed to accomplish the assignment at hand with as little delay as possible and proceed with the list of photographs requested by the amiable Mrs. Thomas.

Despite the reluctancies of this oddly matched foursome, Brady achieved a splendid likeness of the happy couple ensconced by their honor attendants. Years later those captured by the artist would marvel that the emotional undercurrents which pervaded the room had remained hidden from the camera's eye.

The instant Matthew Brady freed his subjects, the purple gowned woman hurried from the room's confines, slamming the door with a violence that left the sensitive photographer wounded by her intolerance and disdain for his chosen art form.

Returning to the ballroom entrance, Clarissa discovered her path blocked by Mandy Thomas, a force with which she had not intended to reckon. The stressful episode with Jed had heightened her emotions to an unparalleled peak, and the realization that she must now exchange pleasantries with the woman whose husband she had bedded was the ultimate climactic disaster.

"Miss Morgan, I believe I have your advantage. I am Amanda Thomas, Jed's wife."

The irony of the statement escaped the angelic Amanda, but coupled with her now evident pregnancy, it served to drive Clarissa from the hotel and into a self-imposed exile which she endured for some time to come.

Chapter Twenty-Four

Richmond, Virginia, three days later

T he inconvenience caused him by the relocation of his appointment irked Adam Dupree. From the bespectacled bureaucrat who informed him of the last minute change, he received only the explanation that President Davis was suffering from a digestive malady and at his wife's insistence would conduct business from the White House of the Confederacy. Approaching the two-storied columned portico, he stopped at the wooden sentry housing. Dupree took little note of the stately mansion, whose brick had been plastered over. At the top of a Richmond hill, the Confederacy's White House bordered a picturesque, terraced garden, which also failed to impress the disgruntled Colonel.

Admitted quickly by the sentry, he entered the high ceilinged structure and was escorted through white paneled doors into the main drawing room. Braced by several glasses of whiskey, Colonel Dupree sat stoically, awaiting his interview with the President. Thoroughly dissatisfied by the protocol of the Confederate Army, he elected to bypass such formalities and present his case to Davis himself.

Amid the usual crowd of office seekers, tradesmen, and would-be pensioners, Dupree considered himself degradingly out of place, which served to prick both his anger and finally his nerves to the point that he yearned for the contents of the half emptied bottle on his nightstand.

In an involuntary movement, he recoiled with repulsion from the haggard woman and her wailing baby seated to his right. She looked in the direction of the Confederate Colonel, the gap-toothed grin in perfect accord with her tattered, homespun dress. When she shoved the sugar-teat in the infant's mouth in a desperate attempt to quiet it, Dupree slammed down a copy of the *Southern Literary Magazine,* as he sprang to his feet determined to impress upon the clerk his impatience.

Before he could do so, a timid, mouselike man emerged from an adjoining drawing room to summon him to the private reception room.

Dupree pushed him rudely aside and entered.

The President, looking healthy enough in Dupree's estimation, put aside an opened copy of the *Richmond Enquirer* to greet him by beckoning the Colonel to seat himself in a chair of black leather. "My sincere apologies for the delay I must have caused you." Waving his arm across his desk, he continued. "There are so many petitioners for my limited time that I must work amid my pains and discomforts."

"Making me all the more grateful that you agreed to see me," lied the Colonel.

Moving to the front of his desk, Davis positioned himself at an angle, supported by its marge. Crossing his arms across his chest, he addressed Dupree. "How may I be of help?"

Adam Dupree spoke without the least hesitation. "I wish to transfer from my present duty station."

Having anticipated a plea for additional troops or funds, the request for transfer was indeed surprising to the President. "On what grounds?"

"I am a military man, unaccustomed to the confines of an office," he proudly stated. "Since my days at the Point, I have served in the field, leading men, not guarding gold."

"To what post do you feel yourself more suited?"

His confidence bolstered by the President's interest, he proceeded with assurance. "I am volunteering my services as commander of our troops against the Mexican forces. My firsthand knowledge of the terrain, my fluency in the Spanish language, and my extensive combat experience…"

"Speak well of you, to be sure; however, General Robert E. Lee has been charged with that responsibility."

Dupree's tightened fist violently met the leather arm. "Lee hasn't my qualifications. Surely, you can alter such an obvious error in judgment?"

Davis returned to his desk, the intimation that his decision was in question along with the rumblings within his stomach producing an intolerance for the arrogant soldier. "The Secretary of War and I are secure in our selection of Lee. You have occupied your present command for such a short time. No doubt the wisdom of our command selections will become clearer to you over a more extended period." Without giving Dupree an opportunity for a rebuttal, Davis dismissed the Colonel. "Now, if you will excuse me, our meeting is concluded." Davis busied himself examining the contents of a document.

Seething from the abrupt closure of the meeting and the President's total disregard for his proposal, Colonel Dupree set his course for the office of the *Richmond Enquirer.*

The sheer stupidity of the man, he proclaimed in a silent monologue as he made his way to the newspaper office. *Lee cannot even converse with the enemy to negotiate surrender terms. Why he hasn't my expertise in any phase of command.* Lost in his thoughts, he ignored the greetings of passing men and rudely omitted courtesies due the gentile ladies as he threaded the maze of people less intent upon their destinations.

In front of the Spotswood Hotel, a young amputee struggling with his crutches hailed him by name. "Colonel, it's me, Asa Cook. This here's my wife, Lavinia!"

If Dupree recognized the veteran of his command, he gave no indication. Smarting from the slight, the man explained Dupree's actions to his wife, "He always was a son of a bitch; excuse me, Lavinia."

Adam Dupree entered the *Richmond Enquirer* without a qualm, believing that Davis had forced his hand. Thus, he no longer felt that he owed allegiance to a country which had repeatedly failed to recognize his talents. He approached the counter which served as a buffer to restrict the public from the visible presses and reporters' desks.

"May I help you, Sir?" questioned a matron, her pencil poised.

"Yes, it is my sad obligation to place the notice of the death of a distant cousin from Macon."

"Please accept my condolences," she expressed with practiced sympathy. "I'll need the name."

"Beauchamp."

"Ah, the gentleman said you might also come to notify us. He left a message to clarify, just in case you were unaware that the obituary had already appeared." She opened one of the counter drawers from which she removed an envelope marked "Beauchamp."

"I trust you haven't been greatly inconvenienced," she said, handing him the envelope and smiling demurely.

Expressing his thanks, the Colonel left the newspaper office. Only in the privacy of his rented room did he tear open the missive and read its message.

You know the place and time.

The date is two days hence.

Dupree tossed the paper into the fireplace, watching it curl into ash as he drained his glass in an effort to obliterate memories rather than in remorse for the deed thus committed. The chance meeting with Asa Cook had surged to the forefront the scene long buried.

Buford Hancock, one of the few men with whom Adam Dupree had allowed himself to bond, lay upon the soil near Buena Vista, Mexico, victimized by a brazen charge. Hancock's piercing cry rang through Dupree's clouded head, none the less vivid and horrifying than it had been in reality.

In the bottom of the glass, the Southern Colonel saw a younger version of himself bent over his comrade in arms. Theirs had been a natural migration, as two of the few cadets whose family wealth and power had not superseded their qualifications as future officers. Upon them fell the brunt of the abusive hazing by upperclassmen. Oh, all had felt the sting of bitter words and treatment, but the sons of privilege held dominion over the future, with the realization that in business or society, they would undoubtedly cross paths with the roles of power reversed. But to the boys of a common farmer and an Ohio blacksmith, no such certainty loomed. Yet the two had endured, even triumphed, with the giant "smith's" strength and the "farmer's" will.

How he'd been able to carry his wounded friend to the medical wagon, Adam was unable to explain. Duty, training, all focus evaporated with the smoke of a Mexican artillery shell. And Dupree was at Hancock's bedside when he broke the news of a missing leg. Even in the grogginess the expression of a man whose entire life had been robbed prevailed.

An outcast from the military and unable to ply his trade to support himself on crutches, Hancock became less than a man, living a parasitical existence dependent upon his seamstress wife. Dupree and Hancock had met only once more when a transfer allowed the officer to call. Discovering the formerly robust Hancock a shell of his former self, Dupree feigned a train deadline to escape the depression of the meager home and his once proud friend.

Adam picked up the *Examiner*, fighting to adjust his blurred vision to the printed page. Though the article itself was too small for his focus, the headline loomed clearly enough, casting the name of the man responsible for the fateful charge… Davis, Jefferson Davis, President Jefferson Davis.

Staring at the rumpled newsprint, the drunken Colonel began to "recite" from pages alive his memory. "The hero of Buena Vista… brilliant strategist…implementing the v-shaped charge." As he began to methodically shred the newsprint, Adam Dupree snarled in a thickly slurred speech, "You've lead a charmed life, Mr. President. The gods destined you. Tell me. Tell me. Would you have been placed over us at Buena Vista had you not been Taylor's son-in-law?" Raising his glass to a nonexistent companion, he toasted Davis. "My complements, Sir. Marrying the old man's daughter, then taking her to your Godforsaken Mississippi to die… a fever? Who could have foreseen it? Such a pity… This time, Davis, the charmed life be damned." As Dupree collapsed into a drunken sleep, his half-empty glass overturned, seeping into the headline, consuming Davis' name.

*****

After the passage of two days

The entrance of Major Andrew Mallory brought the Secretary and Henry Foote to their full heights. As he removed his hat, the strawberry blonde hair, which often appeared red, caught Memminger's eye.

Secretary Memminger approved of Foote's selection, a strapping man nearly six feet in height. Andrew Mallory's build would see him through any difficult situation he might encounter, appraised the Treasury Secretary.

"Please pardon my tardiness. I had a few minor details to check before reporting my findings."

Since receiving his assignment to uncover those responsible for the counterfeit bills, Mallory had labored nonstop.

Security demanded that he do the leg work unassisted, but the time had come to enlist the aid of others, if further progress were to occur.

"After leaving our initial meeting, I contacted the barber from which Representative Foote received the forged note. While he was cutting my hair, I steered the conversation toward the staggering increase in robberies since Richmond became a national capital. I urged that he not leave the till in his shop overnight."

The governmental officials hung on his every word, too absorbed to question the soldier turned detective.

"In offering his reassurance, he traced his daily practice which began and ended each day with a visit to the Merchantile Bank."

Mallory addressed the Legislator, "I believe that you were waiting outside his shop that morning when you received the bill?"

"Meaning that the note originated at the bank," Foote declared, his enthusiasm rising.

The Major did not share his exuberance. "Well, there are various other ways that the bill could have made its way to the bank, which leaves us without further leads, I fear."

"Perhaps not," Memminger opened a cabinet and removed several ledgers.

"The bill was uncirculated. You see, the Richmond banks obtain uncirculated currencies directly from the Treasury. Frantically flipping the pages of the ledger, he stopped to examine a particular page. "Just as I suspected. A shipment left the Treasury the afternoon before for the Merchantile Bank,"

"Mr. Secretary, can you guarantee the honesty of your employees?" demanded Foote.

"Before today, I would have," he admitted sadly.

Major Mallory added, "We must also investigate the bank employees and those directly tied to the delivery."

"Treasury employees make the deliveries in enclosed wagons. At the bank, the contents are relinquished to one Leslie Irons."

"I know him well," interrupted the Major. "He grew up in the Charleston area, as did I, and it would surprise me greatly if he were guilty of anything harmful to the Confederacy."

"It seems likely that the bills are entering the open market either at the mint or at the bank; consequently, we must scrutinize those in positions to substitute the fakeries. Since I am acquainted with Leslie Irons, I plan to ask him for a job to cover my presence at the Merchantile Bank. There, I will be able to conduct firsthand investigations of the personnel."

Addressing the cabinet member Andrew requested, "Mr. Secretary, can you perform similar studies of your people?"

"The Treasury and the mint employ over one hundred people. Of those, perhaps twenty-five to thirty-five have contact with the finished product. Some, of course, are the women signing the bills. Surely we can eliminate them?"

Foote voiced his opinion in his usually authoritative style, "I disagree. Any woman who must seek employment cannot have the rigid upbringing that would place her above suspicion."

The Major added his agreement. "Mr. Foote is quite right. These women may well be used by someone else because he feels that they are less likely to be suspected of wrongdoings."

"Very well then," Memminger acquiesced. "No one will be excluded. Tell me, gentleman, how do I closely monitor them all?" His question alluded to the skepticism he held of the young Major's methods.

"It may not be required," the Major announced. "If I can check the bills upon arrival, then the criminal's whereabouts will be determined immediately, thus allowing us to concentrate our efforts fully at a single site."

"Then we will expect to hear from you when there are more details to report."

Andrew Mallory left the granite Treasury Building heading downhill on Bank Street. He complimented himself upon his present situation. Not only did he find the intrigue exciting and challenging, but he was even more confident than ever that his decision to remain in the military had been a sound one. For once the third son was at peace with his capabilities and his place in life.

Chapter Twenty-Five

Richmond, Virginia, two days later

John Wesley Porter stationed himself behind the largest marker within eyeshot of the Beauchamp Mausoleum. He was not yet certain that Dupree could be trusted, and from this vantage point, he would easily detect if the Colonel was alone. Porter wondered how these faceless men and women who surrounded him would have reacted had they known that one of their own was selling his soul and his country. Was it greed? He dismissed the notion. Then what else could move a man to betray what he once held holy?

To Porter the relationship between a man and his country rivaled no other. It motivated men to die in their youth, abandon their wives and children, or he mused, *to stand amid the dead in a blackened cemetery.* As for Colonel Adam Dupree, he represented that sort of man whose pride was the dictator of his decisions.

The crackling of boot heels upon the stone path which outlined the family plot of generations of Richmond's citizenry, alerted Porter of Dupree's presence. He allowed the Colonel to pass before cocking his pistol. "Don't turn around. For our mutual protection, it would serve us not to recognize each other should we chance to pass on the street."

"Then you have no need for your weapon," called the Colonel. "You have my word that I will cooperate fully."

He released the hammer and stuffed the barrel into the waist of his trousers. "I assume your presence assures your further assistance in furnishing the information that I require?"

"And that is?"

"The best possible circumstances for robbery of the Confederate Treasury."

"Impossible," scoffed Dupree. "The Treasury is heavily guarded both day and night, and even if you penetrated the forces, it would take hours to remove the gold."

"It was never our intent to empty the Treasury, only deal the South another crippling blow."

Another blow? Dupree relaxed, thereafter exuding more self-confidence, as he realized for the first time that his anonymous accomplice sought more than personal gain. In the Colonel's estimation, he was involved in a much larger organization, a thought which served to boost his faith in his own choice as well as peak his curiosity concerning the man and those with whom he conspired. Since his first encounter with the man, Dupree had speculated as to what would be required of him, the obvious being his connection with the Treasury. Therefore, he had formulated a maneuver that would not require his physical participation and avert suspicion in the direction of others.

"Then may I suggest an alternative that would be equally devastating but with higher odds for success?" He waited for a reply, deciding to proceed before an objection could be voiced. "As you are no doubt aware, the content of the Federal Mint in New Orleans was captured after the South's secession. Its bullion has been requisitioned and is scheduled for transport to Richmond. If the shipment becomes somehow 'misdirected' it would pose a great hardship should there be an actual war with our Mexican neighbor. Rumor has it that these funds are to be used, in part, to purchase artillery and other military supplies from France. Unfortunately, the French refuse to honor Confederate currency, making this Union gold all the more valuable."

Intrigued, Porter progressed without hesitation. How Secretary Cameron wounded the South should be of little concern. Certainly Dupree's alternative was more feasible. "When will the transfer be conducted?"

"You haven't a great deal of time. It leaves New Orleans three weeks from today by rail."

"And the security measure?"

"Are a further demonstration of Davis' incompetence. It is his belief that a strong show of force will invite investigation; therefore, he has ordered that the bullion be concealed in mail sacks and flour barrels and placed in the baggage cars amid other less valuable cargo."

Suddenly the entire venture seemed riddled with coincidences too neatly tied and bowed to suit Porter.

"You're no fool, Colonel. How do you propose to protect yourself? Surely the breach of security will be traced directly to you?"

"Why should it?" retorted Dupree. "Those securing the Mint have been surrounded for months by gold they cannot touch. Prices rise daily, and I have heard of merchants who encourage the use of the more secure Union currency or gold by offering discounted rates for payment in such kind. The family men, who are of far more modest circumstances than I, must be likening their situations to that of Tantalus, encircled by what they desire but unable to grasp it. Of course," he remarked cunningly, "I shall be quite sure to point these facts out to any accusers."   Suddenly anxious to escape the cemetery's confines, Dupree encouraged the close of their rendezvous. "I have honored my pact with the devil; my reward, Sir?"

"In the flower urn by the stone of Jabez Chapman will be an envelope with half the sum agreed upon.   With the successful completion of the robbery, the second half will be forthcoming in a similar manner."

Dupree started for the urn.

"Colonel, haven't your forgotten something?"   Dupree paused in contemplation.

"The route?" asked Porter.

"The Louisiana-Arkansas Railroad," Dupree said. "Where to strike is your option. Personally, I would elect to hijack the train as its tracks parallel the River, thus affording another avenue of escape."

No further exchanges occurred. Collecting his money, Adam Dupree disappeared from sight leaving Porter wrestling with indecision. Realizing his only option, he hurried to the railway depot.

When the Union conspirator entered the telegraph office, he recognized the effects of his exposure to the February cold. His hands shook as he penciled his message. Wadding the yellow tissue paper, he tossed it into the potbellied stove which was the sole source of warmth for the drafty station. After he warmed his reddened hands before the welcomed flames, he began anew. Using the agreed upon code name, he addressed his message to Lawrence Mims.

Plans changed. Moving to New Orleans. Will buy supplies there. Travis.

At the same window, he paid for his wire and his train ticket to New Orleans. Since the train schedule left him little time, Porter had notice of his departure and a request for his belongings remain secured sent to the Slidell home.

The grinding locomotive wheels squeaked their dissatisfaction with the engineer's dictates, as John Wesley Porter sank back in the upholstered seat. Of the few passengers on that midnight train, none was aware that the man with whom they shared the journey was planning more than a leisurely visit to the Louisiana seaport.

*****

Later in the week

The enclosed wagon rattled to a stop behind Richmond's oldest banking firm. The armed guard left the driver's perch and made his way to the single rear window. Two sharp raps drew the face of one of the three men inside to the pane. Thus given the signal, he clearly heard the sliding of the heavy bolts which secured the door. Several bags of bills were presented to Leslie Irons inside the bank that was an hour from opening its door to the public. Irons looked older than his thirty-eight years. His long, thick sideburns called attention to his balding head and gave the unflattering allusion of framing his face into an elongated shape.

As he had done on so many previous occasions since the Confederacy had begun printing its own currency, he signed the pages of the now fraying ledger. Once inside the security of the bank, he sat down with a hand glass to scrutinize each bill. For the past few days, he had the pleasure of Andrew Mallory's company and assistance in the time-consuming task. He never tired of Andrew's companionship and the jovial atmosphere of nostalgic conversations about their common roots.

Today, however, was different. Frustrated by the inability to detect any fraudulent bills, other tactics had been employed. At three intervals throughout the business day, trusted government representatives posed as bank patrons. Their business transacted, they reported to Memminger who examined the bills. On three occasions, counterfeit bills had surfaced, always in a twenty dollar denomination.

Irons put down the magnification glass, silently dismissing the effort as futile. As much as he hated to accept the obvious, the bills all originated from an old, treasured employee. David Ames was a grandfatherly gentleman in the bank's employ for over a quarter of a century. That he could be jeopardizing the reputation of the bank as well as that of his own was beyond possibility, yet the evidence clearly pointed to the venerable teller.

With no breaches of security in minting or transport having been detected, Mallory and Irons began exhaustive searches into the backgrounds, movements, and daily transaction's of the Merchantile's six tellers.

The old gentleman was the last to be investigated, so impeccable were the white-haired Ames' credentials. Nonetheless, Major Andrew Mallory ordered that a close watch be kept of David Ames as well. Examining one such daily reporting, Mallory's instincts guided him to the entry denoting the call Mr. Ames had made at the railway office. Far from wealthy, the teller lived comfortably and owned a house servant who would automatically be sent to attend to such matters. That Ames imposed this duty upon himself, aroused Andrew's curiosity.

At the railway office, the Major had made discrete inquiries of the clerk who revealed that David Ames collected packages with regularity. The man drew back in surprise when asked where the packages had originated.

"Mind you," began Ames' contemporary, "normally I don't make it a practice to look into the business of others, but Mr. Ames, being an old friend and all, I engaged him in polite conversations whenever he came to claim a parcel. He told me they were from a nephew up North."

"Where up North?" asked the Major.

A bit irritated that the Major would consider him a snoop, the clerk replied, "Well, I did happen to notice the markings when I gave him his parcel. They came from Washington."

With those words, the clerk unwittingly sealed the fate of an old friend. From the station, Andrew delivered his news directly to Memminger.

Irons surveyed the stacks of Confederate currency. Hesitating for a few moments, he hurried to claim his hat and cape. He owed the old man the sight of at least one friendly face.

Agents of the Confederate States of America stationed themselves around the cramped railway office. To the most inquisitive eyes, there were no tell-tale signs that would identify them as waiting for anything save tickets or mail.   One pretended to read the day's edition of the *Richmond Enquirer*, one checked the time tables, and others chatted as if waiting their trains' departures or the arrivals of those near and dear.

A woman, child in tow, was posting a small parcel. A few travelers milled around the lobby awaiting trains. The clerk watched the familiar Major as he attempted to transact his normal duties. An uneasiness he could not quite identify darkened his mood. When David Ames opened the station door, the clerk's heart stopped with the sudden realization that Mallory, who was seated on one of the wooden benches reading the *Enquirer* was present for no other reason than to observe the bank teller.

"Good morning Evan," came David Ames' cordial greeting. "Quite chilly again."

Evan Dodd found it exceedingly difficult not to warn his friend. But what would be gained? Ames was no more capable of outrunning the young Major than he.

"Looking forward to the spring myself. Let me get your parcel." Returning, he placed the small box wrapped in brown paper and secured with twine upon the counter. "You have a fine nephew there," he remarked pointing to the package.

"Let me help you with that, Mr. Ames," offered Major Mallory.

Caught unaware, Ames stepped back momentarily, then attempted to claim his property. "Now see here," protested the indignant teller.

Three soldiers in civilian dress sought the butts of concealed pistols, lest the old man attempt an escape or draw a weapon.

Perhaps he might have made such an attempt had Leslie Irons not arrived. Identifying his colleague as assistance against the brazen young Major, Ames pursued further. "Remove your hand from my belonging, Sir. You have no right..."

"I am claiming this package on behalf of the Treasury Department of the Confederate States of America."

The old man attempted to force Mallory's hand. Fearing injury to his friend and to avoid the prying eyes of the railway patrons, Irons spoke, "Mr. Dodd, is there a back room where we might discuss this situation in private?" He gestured toward several men and women talking among themselves in disbelief at the bewildering proceedings.

"Yes, yes, of course," he stammered, leaving his stool and unlocking the door that barred patrons from the inner workings of the depot.

Mallory addressed one of the plain clothed soldiers, "Go get the Secretary and Foote." A second guard stationed himself outside the unlocked door; the third entered behind Irons, the Major and Ames.

Dodd, trembling slightly for fear that his old friend would hold him partially responsible for this obvious miscarriage of justice, escorted them to a cramped office, cluttered with unclaimed parcels, paperwork, and newspapers. The furnishings were cheaply fashioned and chipped from years of usage. A single window lit the cubicle; a small stove shed enough heat to maintain a comfortable climate.

"Let me clean off some seats," Evan nervously offered, dropping several items from his unresponsive fingers. The only two seats had been cleared by the time Memminger and Foote arrived.

Pulling one chair to the center of the room, Andrew Mallory regarded the gentleman whose fate he now controlled. "Mr. Ames, if you please."

Oddly composed, the elderly teller took the seat, removing his hat and loosening his cape for what he sensed would be a lengthy interview in the overcrowded and stifling confines.

"Undoubtedly there are duties that require your attention, Mr. Dodd." Thus the Majory unceremoniously dismissed Evan Dodd from his own quarters.

When the door was closed and blocked by the third guard, Secretary Memminger opened the parcel, voicing to the others the Washington D.C. markings. Once opened, Memminger carefully placed the contents on the seat of the second chair. Unable to contain himself, Foote retrieved one of what would prove to be five hundred twenty dollar notes. Memminger also availed himself of a bill, walking to the dingy window. Spreading the faded red-checked curtains, the Secretary took little time to pronounce his findings. "Major Mallory, may I be the first to congratulate you on your investigative skills?"

Addressing the undaunted David Ames, Mallory announced, "Sir, you are under arrest by the Confederate States of America for the circulation of counterfeit currency."

The old man's posture remained erect, his head held high, his dignity remaining intact throughout the entire ordeal.

Memminger initiated the questioning. "The identity of you 'nephew' in Washington?"

Smiling at his accusers, the old man replied, "I think you are all too aware that my Washington nephew is nonexistent."

"Then your source?" barked the Legislator.

"These parcels come to me anonymously."

Taking the elderly man by his shoulders, Foote glared menacingly into his face. "You had better consider the gravity of the situation, Ames." Sensing that his strong-armed tactic failed to impress the man, he altered his approach. "How will your dear wife face her remaining years, shamed by your actions and shunned by the good people of the South? Tell me, Ames, what future is there for the childless wife of a criminal?"

Angrily, Leslie Irons pushed Foote aside and compassionately pleaded with the old man. "By all that is holy, David, I can't imagine what led you to do this, but surely you have considered Mary Leigh. How could you have done this to her or yourself?" For the first time Ames' countenance fell. The thought of his wife ostracized, suffering from the barbed tongues of their self-righteous neighbors, caused him to question the wisdom of his actions for the first time.

"My wife will suffer whether I cooperate with you gentlemen or not," he sadly said.

Secretary Memminger, seizing the opportunity to glean the information he most desired, assured that this frail man could not have directed the scheme himself. "Were we to offer you your freedom and attribute the entire matter to a grievous error, you could spend your remaining years shamed only by your own conscience."

Ames looked up, his voice pitched with hope. "You'd be that generous?"

"If we were given the knowledge that we seek."

"Then you have my word as a gentleman that I shall tell you all that I know." He waited a few moments as if trying to determine where he should begin. "In early October, I took my morning constitutional down Third Street toward Gambel's Hill; I enjoy the view of the River so. A gentleman I had seen perhaps upon two occasions at the bank overtook me and asked to accompany me. He introduced himself as Marcus Harcourt, a salesman down from Albany."

"His description," demanded Foote.

"Portly, well-dressed, I'd say between forty-five and fifty, but with a full head of black hair that was lightly salted with gray, as was his full beard. He struck me as a knowledgeable sort, for a Northerner. The date being what it was, the conversation turned political. We discussed the War and the South's hope for survival, independent of the Union."

At that point, Ames ended his narrative about his encounter and directed his response to his own political views. "It has been no secret that I opposed secession. Granted, I was neither militant nor demonstrative in my opposition, but when asked my opinion, I voiced my beliefs in the power of a union of states. You see, I am not against the Confederacy itself, but I do believe that each citizen is best served by a powerful federal government. Divided, we are easy prey to any nation. Look at the threat Mexico has made. Would Juarez have been foolhardy enough to blackmail the United States?"

Realizing his digression, he returned to his accounting of his involvement with the counterfeiting scheme.

"As always I unashamedly voiced my beliefs to Mr. Harcourt, who admired my determination and convictions," stated the teller proudly. "We walked together for several mornings. On the last, he asked me if my faith in a union was such that I would be willing to assist those whose sworn purpose was to reunite the factions into a world power once more. You, of course, are aware of my reply. He explained my part, which was simple enough. The notes would be mailed to me at weekly intervals, and my job was to enter the currency into circulation."

It was Leslie Irons who questioned his procedures. "How did you incorporate such massive amounts without detection?"

David Ames blushed, unwilling to praise himself, considering his precarious circumstances. "I carried the bills on my person, and whenever possible, I substituted the fraudulent ones in my till or in the vault itself."

Foote shook his head in disgust. "And the true bills are resting comfortably in your personal account, no doubt."

For the first time the old man became emotional, leaving his seat and approaching the Legislator. The guard moved between them lest Ames' wildly shaking fists reach their intended destination.

"You have insulted my honor, Sir," raved Ames. "I am not, nor have I ever been a thief!"

Later Major Mallory would retell, careful to omit the man's true identity, the last remark never failed to induce laughter because of the jaded view of the accused.

In the firm grasp of the guard, Ames straightened his clothing and reseated himself. "The money," his voice heavily accentuated with indignation, "was given to various charities. The Virginia Home for Orphans, The Confederate Veterans, and my church have all benefited greatly."

Memminger threw up his hands; Major Mallory's eyes were teared by his attempts to contain his laughter. Irons was unsure whether to scold or praise his old friend.

The Secretary spoke, "Have you a way to contact this Marcus Harcourt?"

Ames shook his head. "I have no idea."

There was a lengthy pause. "Except there was an odd occurrence a few weeks ago. Amid the normal newspaper scraps used to cushion the bills, there were several scraps of a yellowish page. I fear my curiosity overtook my reason, and I pieced them together. It was a voided receipt for a Mr. Bentley from the Union Printing Services in Washington."

Memminger addressed the banker, "Mr. Irons, if you would escort Mr. Ames to his home? After such a harrowing experience, a day away from his duties might be in order." As the two passed, Memminger spoke to their backs. "It goes without saying that you will, of course, collect no further parcels from Mr. Harcourt. I am instructing Mr. Dodd to have them directed to the Treasury."

When the door closed behind the guard, he turned to Foote and Mallory. "Major, exchange your uniform for civilian dress. You leave for Washington without delay."

Chapter Twenty-Six

Washington, D.C., late February 1862

Phoebe Cameron Morgan's pale form lay heavily blanketed across a daybed. Its proximity to the oak mantled hearth made it her favored spot. Many nights she'd slept there, waking only when Clarissa crept in to check the fire.

Holding a silver hand mirror, she gazed at her reflection. Placing it face down on her covers, she let her mind wander to the days when she had been heartened by her image in the same mirror. Had it been so long ago? With Clarissa now twenty, perhaps it had been ages since she herself had been that age, courted, and wooed. And she had been a beauty, too yet not on the same scale as her only child.

Clarissa had a zest for life and an energy she'd never possessed, and that was precisely why something had to be done. Phoebe Morgan refused to allow her daughter's life to be ruined by an invalid's infirmities. A short rap on the door transported her to the present.

"May I come in, my dear?"

"Of course, Simon."

Simon Cameron never denied his younger sister, even when she requested his time on an already tightly scheduled morning. Seeing her struggle to sit up, he silently cursed Granville Morgan for reducing her to this state. The doctor warned that she could not risk childbirth, yet his lecherous desires led to two miscarriages and the birth of Clarissa, for which she had never fully recovered. A true husband would have kept a mistress or visited a bordello, but not Granville Morgan. Then it was the tropics for a while, the muggy coast, and finally England. *Thank God she's been brought home by Clarissa* he thought. When the country learned of his successful annihilation of the Confederacy and he'd won the post in 1864 that was rightfully his, he'd see to it that Granville Morgan never entered the United States again. Better yet, he'd see him dead.

Cameron bent over, kissing her cheek and taking her frigid hands. He pulled a small stool which mated the chaise near her and balanced his large frame upon it.

"I am so sorry to bother you, Simon, especially when I owe you so much."

"Now Phoebe…"

"No, let me finish. I wouldn't ask if I weren't so distressed over Clarissa."

"Clarissa?"

"I am sure you've been too busy with your many obligations and duties to notice, but she hasn't gone out since our return."

"Nonsense, she attends church, runs errands, and she went to the Jackson girl's demise."

The Secretary of War delighted in bringing a smile to his sister's face, for it hinted of the attractive woman she once was.

"Oh Simon, you're insufferable." Returning again to her crusade, "I am serious about Clarissa. Of course, she leaves the house, but I mean for parties or to go carriage riding with young men. And," his sister emphasized, "she did not attend that 'demise' as you put it. She returned far too early from the ball that the Thomas family hosted, and she excused herself from the ceremony after she had agreed to attend the bride." Her voice began to betray the guilt she bore. "I tell you Simon, it is all my fault." She began to cry softly into a laced handkerchief.

Cameron comforted his only surviving relative. Perhaps their separation for much of their childhood endeared her all the more to him, "I will agree that she has not been as social as she was before the War, but you are hardly to blame. It has been my contention that she suffered far greater indignities as a result of the kidnapping than she expressed to us. One need only imagine what evils befell an attractive young woman..."

He stopped, realizing the effect his suggestions were having on his fragile sister. Changing his direction in mid sentence, Cameron eased himself into a more agreeable scenario for Phoebe's sake. "No, not that, my dear. I am referring to the catty tongues of busybodies who place the blame on our precious Clarissa for her role in the Lincoln capitulation and the Union defeat."

"Have people expressed this to you?" Phoebe sank back against the cushion in distress.

"Not directly, of course, they haven't the audacity, but you do see how embarrassing this has all become? Having people recognize and question her must prove dreadfully upsetting."

Had the two known that in retrospect Clarissa had actually enjoyed the entire ordeal, finding her celebrity entertaining to a point. After the voyage, she chanced to overhear two old biddies commenting on her now dubious reputation, as well as the Jackson girl's "forced marriage" to her Rebel captor. In quick order, she confronted the women, inviting them to take their evil minds and gossipy tongues to the very threshold of the devil.

"Simon, your limitless generosity shames me, but I must beg you for one more thing." There was a note of desperation in her voice that mellowed his callous heart.

"I've done nothing more than you deserve, save shooting that worthless husband of yours."

"Please don't start. Clarissa is all important."

"What would you have me to do?"

"I want you to give her a job in your office."

Cameron could not have been more surprised. "A European tour or a boarding school, but a job is totally out of the question."

Normally the anger in his declaration would have deterred her, but a mother's fear for her child precluded the wrath of her brother's infamous temper. "You've told me yourself that young women are employed in government offices."

"Yes, but they are hardly of Clarissa's background. Those women are in need of the income. Think of her reputation, for God's sake; she'll be the brunt of every gossip in the city."

"She already is. Please, I have heard your remark so many times that few men could match her intelligence and her grasp of world affairs. Besides, she doesn't have to accept a salary; she could be a volunteer." Phoebe smiled, pleased with her own suggestion. "Yes, that's perfect. Clarissa will volunteer her services to the government. Why, she'll start a new fashion among young ladies of quality. Please Simon, we must get her out of this house."

Defeated, Secretary of War Cameron nodded his head and left his sister's bedroom. On his way to the dining room the concept of Clarissa's assistance began to take root. All Phoebe had said of the daughter's abilities was not the prating of a boastful mother. Clarissa was exceedingly smart and downright insightful, for a female. Yes, it might work. Why whom could he trust more with his private affairs?

He was well into his breakfast of eggs and bacon when Clarissa entered. For the first time in weeks, he took the time to appraise her appearance. How could he have overlooked such a dramatic change? Her once dancing eyes seemed lifeless and were underscored by dark circles. Her princes styled day dress hung unfashionably loose, revealing her recent loss of weight. Cameron was convinced of his sister's diagnosis.

"Good morning, Clarissa. I am delighted you are up so early. It will save you a trip to my office."

"Whatever do you mean, Uncle Simon?"

She was puzzled by her uncle. Breakfast, or any meal of late, was an ordeal to rouse him from his constant journey into preoccupation.

Cameron placed his silverware across the Sevres china his wife recently relegated to daily use. "I find myself in a most unusual predicament, and I must insist upon your cooperation in remedying what has proven to be a most impossible situation."

Had he asked her to recreate Lady Godiva's ride, she would not have refused him, so indebted were she and her mother.

"Anything, I will be only too happy to do whatever I can."

"Excellent, I'll need you to come to my office on a regular basis, to assist me with the growing number of women with whom I must come in contact. You see, it is becoming," he cleared his throat, "awkward to deal personally with my female employees as well as female petitioners."

Witnessing her loquacious uncle stumbling over his words proved quite amusing. Looking fondly at the blush that was uncharacteristically crossing his face, she acknowledged the fact that he was the only man that had ever truly loved her. Certainly none of the young men who had professed undying affection had loved her enough to accept her on her own terms, as an equal rather than a decoration. Only Jed Thomas had appreciated her intellect and respected her opinions, or was that just another of the strategies employed by married men to seduce foolish girls. Only Uncle Simon was willing to offer her the chance to be at his side and share in his world.

"What time shall I start?" she questioned enthusiastically. "I can't wait to begin."

"Then I'll see you," he looked at his pocket watch, "In about an hour?" Cameron placed his linen napkin atop the dining table, kissing Clarissa on the forehead as he left for his office.

Alone, Clarissa Morgan's thoughts raced. Here was an opportunity she'd never dreamed possible. She would succeed on her own merits without depending upon a husband to give her an identity. She hurried through her meal and excitedly shared the news with her mother, who oddly enough, offered no objections. The passion for life that had died in England was alive once more.

Chapter Twenty-Seven

Ten miles outside New Orleans, Louisiana, March 1862

An ever thickening fog inched its way from the Mississippi River, slowly covering the shoreline and its surrounding areas. From his perch atop a nearby hill, John Wesley Porter was finding it increasingly difficult to see the Louisiana-Arkansas tracks down below. Abandoning his field glasses, he let them hang loosely around his neck angry with himself for his nervousness. When the fire was lit, he'd be able to see well enough to report the success or failure to Secretary Cameron.

Either way, Porter was exceedingly proud of his accomplishments within such a close time frame. Even the perfectionistic Secretary of War would have to recognize the obstacles he'd overcome. Hadn't he instinctively known to inquire if there was a telegraph message for him upon his arrival? And he'd sagaciously contacted the man whose name and that of a notorious saloon and casino with the French

Quarter composed the totality of the wire. His thoughts traveled back to his first encounter with the men Quentin Randolph had gathered.

*****

The double, swinging doors of the Silver Slipper flew open from the force of the drunken body flung against it. An agile sidestep on his part prevented Porter from joining the drunk on the dusty New Orleans street. Passers-by ignored the heap, a wagon barely missed his extended arm. John Wesley Porter entered the Silver Slipper, unprepared for the New Orleans nightlife. Strains from an ill-tuned piano were practically inaudible above the din of raucous laughter and voices. Gaming tables with roulette wheels emitted loud cries at the arbitrary fall of its bead.

Porter's observation was interrupted by the attentions of a heavily rouged woman in revealing dance hall attire who had draped her arms around his neck. Her breath, strongly laced with whiskey, was hot upon his neck as she shouted an offer into his ear. Pushing her roughly away, he searched the mass of swarming bodies for Quentin Randolph's distinctive presence.

Randolph stood head and shoulders above Porter, and his face bore a jagged scar across his left cheek. The mercenary was never without a leather sheathed Bowie knife, its blade razor sharp. Porter often wondered if the fiery red scar had resulted from his own weapon in enemy hands.

Finally spying Randolph, who was involved in a card game with six others, Porter eased nearer the table until his contact nodded toward a door on his left. Unnoticed by the disinterested crowd of revelers, he maneuvered the throng and stepped into a dimly lit room.

He'd give the devil his due; the cramped room was filled with some forty of the most nefarious of the criminal element the Louisiana coast had to offer. Battling his own insecurities, Porter faced the ragtag group of cutthroats, thieves, and hired guns. Only the arrival of Quentin Randolph abated his fears somewhat.

"This here's the man," growled Randolph. To their newest cohort he said, "Give 'em yer offer."

"Gentlemen," a smirk from one of the group gave Porter reason to rethink the propriety of such an appellation. "My plan is simple. A train will leave the New Orleans area. On which will ride a fortune in gold. The destination is the Confederate Treasury in Richmond. You men will see that it does not arrive."

A scraggily bearded man spoke, revealing an almost toothless mouth, "I ain't takin' on no young army types."

"That's the beauty of this operation. In order to divert attention, guards will be minimal."

"What's to keep someone frum beatin' us to it?" a young cowboy asked.

"The date of shipment is a matter of top security with the added measure of concealment of the gold in mail sacks and flour barrels."

"Don't strike me as no secret if you knows so much," spat a slender man in a worn uniform coat.

"I think the size of your cut will convince to trust that my information comes from a most reliable source."

"An what iz our cut?" a Mexican bandito questioned.

"As much as you can get away with," declared Porter, a smile breaking across his face.

A murmur went up as one turned to another, questioning every aspect of Porter's enticing yet suspicious proposal.

"Where do we meet back up?"

"We don't. Once you've gotten your fill, you take off in whatever direction you choose. None of us need ever meet again."

"You in this Randolph?" came a voice whose face was obscured in the cramped space.

"Yep, the way I see it, we got easy pickins."

"Then I'm een," the bandito acknowledged.

All but three joined ranks, leaving Porter uneasy about those who had left the room.

"Ain't no matter," an older man called Sal advised. "If word leaks out, they know we'll kill 'um. They'll keep quiet. We's gentlemen here." The group broke into uproarious laughter.

In the days of planning, none of the motley gang of rogues ever volunteered more than a first name, and more disturbing to Porter, none sought a purpose for the robbery save his own personal greed.

*****

His horse alerted him of the approaching danger, prompting the drawing of his pistol.

"Ain't no need to shoot; it's me," called Randolph through the dense mist.

"Is the blockading of the tracks complete?"

"And doused, she'll stop all right." Randolph spat a stream of tobacco juice, the remnants of which he let trickle down his chin and onto the sleeve of his coat. "You sure you won't join in the fun?"

"No, I'll watch from here." He patted the dangling field glasses. All I need to know is that the gold is removed and safely on its way with you and your men."

It was then that the sound of the train became apparent. Without further comment, Randolph was on his horse. A fire began to rise from below, reflecting upon the fog and producing an eerie light by which Porter could see the tracks once again.

His ears detected the braking and slowing of the locomotive, as shots echoed from the hillsides. Porter had the sensation that the events were transpiring in retarded motions of wounded men amid the screams of the female passengers. The Mexican known as Pancho pried loose the baggage car door, exposing the outnumbered soldiers who fought valiantly but were easily overcome. As planned several of the outlaws stood guard as others threw out the sacks and barrels which burst as they hit the ground. From a haze of white powder, floured gold bars lay exposed until the greedy grasps of raiders laid claim.

Porter emitted a sigh of relief. His faith in Dupree had never been well grounded, inspiring a lingering doubt that the bullion would be on the train at all. Only when the last of the robbers fled the train did John Wesley Porter allow his glasses to drop. He mounted his horse and rode a few feet before Quentin Randolph emerged once again from the fog.

"Excellent job, Randolph. Did all the men survive the raid?"

"Lost a few; never thought we wouldn't. They knowed the risks."

Porter heard the faint sound as Randolph unsheathed the Bowie knife, but he did not fully comprehend the source of the burning sensation that traveled to every portion of his body. As he fell from his horse, he was aware of Randolph's voice and the tobacco gush that splattered his face.

"Ain't no future in trustin' a man don't want his cut."

Porter felt the mist envelope him completely.

Chapter Twenty-Eight

Washington, D.C., March 1862

T hough the hour was late, the presence of a young man in rural riding attire would have attracted no regard by those who passed down the otherwise deserted Washington avenue. Had the early morning observer but ventured down the alley and to the rear of the stores and shops, his impression would have been hastily revised by the discovery of two similarly clad men and three saddled horses concealed in the darkness. Since Washington employed only fifty or so policemen whose primary concern was the protection of public buildings, the robbers feared only the passage of a stray citizen or a freedman searching the streets for discarded articles.

Assured that he was alone, Andrew Mallory inserted a long, metal object into the lock of the storefront. After several persistent attempts, the cylinders released.

The Major drew a pistol from underneath his coat, pointing it into the blackness confronting him. Drawing no fire, he quickly closed the door and slipped down the wooden walkway and into the alley to signal his companions, Sergeant Nathan Bradford and Private John Mason.

Both had offered to accompany the Major on his quest, despite the inherent dangers. Mallory was confident in their abilities. Bradford, as he often told anyone who would listen, had wrestled a grizzly in a traveling show that stopped at his Kentucky farming community. Though known to exhibit a short, often violent temper, the titanic Bradford was one man that Mallory wanted on his side during a fight. By no means cowardly or small, John Mason appeared so when compared to Bradford. The Major selected Mason from a list of candidates for his knowledge of Washington and its surrounding areas as well as his skills as a marksman. Mason's introverted personality drew the criticisms of some who mistook his silence as brooding or perchance as evidence of a slow wit.

One by one the trio stole into the shop, each producing a candle and a match. Mallory assigned portions of the shop, and they embarked upon a muted search of the premises.

After a seemingly endless probing of drawers, cabinets, files, and stacks of printed matter, Mason suppressed the urge to shout out his discovery of the evidence they sought. Softly but with a fervid exuberance he called, "Here they are, Sir."

Mallory and Bradford abandoned their efforts joining Mason, who was on his knees in front of a modern printing press.

"They were between the wall and the press. It's God's hand for certain that I saw them, especially in the candlelight. Why, anyone would be hard pressed to see them even in the daylight. Shine your candles here," he instructed.

The illumination of the combined candles produced enough light to discern a small space between the press and the wall through which Mason had spied the newspapers which had caught his eye. Recreating his find, Mason again inserted his arm. "Behind and to the left of the press, there's a bit more space," he explained.

The rustling of the newsprint could be heard as the Private brought forth another metal plate still house within the newspaper. Further inspection produced stacks of Confederate twenty dollar bills, matching the etchings on the two previously revealed plates.

"My compliments, Private," Andrew Mallory expressed in a hushed tone. "I'd say we have our counterfeiters. You two catch a little sleep. I'll wake you up at sunup."

Neither argued, for they had enjoyed little rest since leaving Richmond. Andrew Mallory sat in the candlelight outlining and discarding plans to capture the men responsible for the counterfeiting scheme.

The first signs of spring were unusually welcomed sights for Bill Harrison. Years of isolation in the federal prison somehow heightened his sensitivity to the tiniest flowers or the songs of birds. Observing children in a Washington park, he'd paused to catch them at play, losing track of the time. The tolling of a bell tower clock sent him hurriedly to the storefront of his unobtrusive print shop.

Passing a general merchantile, he smelled its distinctive odors of tea and spices. Noticing the twenty-eight cent price for a pound of ham, he resolved to stop by on his way home. His insatiable appetite, also a result of his prison term, produced the extra pounds he now carried in a paunch at his midsection.

A newly painted marquee bore the name *Union Printing Service*. As he fumbled for his key amid his hurry to open up before his first customer, he failed to notice the conspicuous scratches encompassing the keyhole. Entering the darkened store, which was still shaded by the window dressing he lowered each evening to conceal his presses, he reached for the cord to raise the shades. Had his old eyes adjusted more quickly to the contrasting light from the opened door and the blackened shop area, he might have staged an escape attempt of sorts. As it was, the arm groping for the cord was clasped by an iron grip from which the old man could not free himself. As he heard the door slam shut and lock, he was able to detect the forms of three men.

"Just who the devil do you think..." A hand clamped over his mouth, and he felt himself being dragged into the rear of the small shop. Kicking and struggling against a much stronger opponent, the elder of the two soon succumbed to exhaustion, allowing the intruder to carry him at will. His hands were roughly forced behind his back as he was bound to a straight backed chair. A second man secured a blindfold before he could discern a clear view of his attackers.

"We have no desire to harm you, Sir," spoke a decidedly Southern voice from the darkness. "Remove the gag."

Harrison finally regained enough energy to speak. "I don't keep money here, and I don't have anything of value."

"Oh I beg to differ," spoke the faceless voice. "It seems you have a great deal of money here, in Confederate currency."

Bill Harrison winced at the mention of the counterfeit bills. Until that point, he believed himself the victim of another robbery in an increasingly dangerous Capital. Scenarios began darting through his mind, none of which ended pleasurably. "You boys are mistaken; I run a small printing business."

Another forceful voice moved from behind to face the sightless Harrison. As he hurled his accusations in rapid succession, his talon hands grasped the man's shoulders, pinning him against the unyielding back of the chair. "You listen to me, old man. We have traced shipments of fraudulent Confederate money to your shop, and we've discovered more bills here as well as the plates concealed behind the press. Now you may have seen this as a money making little scheme, but you have robbed innocent people of their hard earned money and devaluated what they have left. And whether you know it or not, you've broken the terms of the Treaty of Manassas which prohibits Northern interference in Southern affairs." He took a quick breath. "Your cooperation here is going to determine whether we hang you or let you rot away in a Southern prison."

Bill Harrison far preferred the lynching to more endless days in prison. The days of freedom convinced him that he could never again endure the loneliness and isolation of prison life. The federal garrison had been detestable enough. What would his fate be at the hands of Rebel jailers who knew all too well what he had set out to do?

An intuition seasoned by a lifetime of criminal association told him that he held the upper hand, else why had they not killed him and merely destroyed the plates? "You've got the plates. What more do you need of me?"

A third voice, heretofore unheard dictated to Harrison. "The names of your cohorts. Not a one of us here believes that you are solely responsible for an operation this complex. No, you are in the employ of others."

"Let me assure you that I have no desire to die in a Southern prison, but if I reveal my accomplices, then I am also a dead man. You must take me South to stand trial, for I will not expose myself to the vengeance of Daniel Adamson or his cronies."

If Bill Harrison learned anything during his lifetime, it was how to manipulate those who desperately desired what he had to offer. Such a cunning "blunder" produced just the effect he sought. By carefully baiting the Southerners, he enticed them into a hasty and foolish decision.

"You boys had better check your time. I have a customer who is to collect his legitimate order at ten o'clock, and I heard the clock strike the half hour a while ago."

"Where is Adamson?" the most vindictive of the trio demanded.

"I'll not reveal another word."

"Then we'll force it…" his hands were already around the wrinkled neck of the printer.

"And take the risk of someone off the street overhearing?" The hands fell.

"You boys will have to march me to Richmond. I hear the country is lovely this time of year."

Furious with themselves and the optionless circumstances in which they now stood, Andrew Mallory accorded Harrison the first assurance that he would escape with his life.

"Untie him; we'll smuggle him South somehow."

"But Sir, how?"

"Do as I say. We have no choice but to attempt it."

Harrison felt the ropes loosen and his blindfold fall, offering his initial inspection of his captors. As he suspected, there were only three men, all young, by his prejudicial estimation. Fortunately, the largest and most dangerous was not the one issuing the orders. To further convince them of age induced infirmities, the roguish counterfeiter simulated a fall.

"We'll have to walk him out to the alley and then to the rear where the horses are." Andrew Mallory wished he'd possessed the forethought to provide a fourth mount.

With guards to his right, left, and rear, the foursome exited the shop. Oddly enough the previously quiet street and wooden walkways were now bustling with activity, primarily aimed in one direction. The pedestrians who monopolized the street were a mixture of women with small children and a smattering of men.

As the prisoner and his accusers neared the corner which led to the alleyway, Harrison began to curse and wildly attack the stunned Rebels. The desired reaction occurred, attracting the attentions of horrified women, some covering the delicate ears of their children from the onslaught of obscenities, and the protective efforts of passing men witnessing a helpless, old man at the mercies of three hooligans.

Mallory and his men abandoned Harrison, who was now prone, still kicking and reciting every example of prison vocabulary at his disposal. Running to their waiting horses, they galloped to safety as the bells of the large cathedral signaled the hour and the convening of mass.

The beleaguered printer accepted the assistance of those compassionate souls outraged by the apparent mistreatment of an elderly shopkeeper within the very shadows of the cathedral. On his way to inform Cameron of the morning's encounter. Harrison chuckled to himself. Who'd have thought that I'd ever be glad for a bunch of busybody do-gooders on their way to mass, he mused.

*****

D ressed in a red Garibaldi shirt braided in black, the pert young woman, black skirt swishing as she threaded the labyrinth of people seeking an audience with the government, commanded respect from the men and something akin to awe from the few women employed in the Federal office building. In the short time she had served the government, Uncle Simon insisted that she not use the term "employed," Clarissa Morgan had reshaped the thinking of her male colleagues due to her keen insight into the complex negotiations in both foreign and domestic politics.

Clarissa loved every aspect of the "volunteer job," finding the inner workings of public service a treasure trove of interesting activities.

Often, she would eat her lunch in the President's Park which was encircled by the State Department, War Department, Navy Department, and the White House. Finally, she felt alive and fulfilled again, grasping a place for herself where men had held exclusive control.

Silently she chastised herself about her skirts. In order to maneuver the crowded corridors more quickly and easily, she abandoned her hoops after a few days at work; however, she wore stiffened petticoats which created an illusion of fullness without the inconvenience and confinement of the hoops. Soon, she vowed, these impractical petticoats will go as well.

"Good morning, Miss Morgan."

She found herself face to face with Bryan Dowd, an up and coming bureaucrat whose constant attentions irritated Clarissa to distraction. Never breaking stride, she continued to her uncle's offices, hoping that Bryan would take note of her unwillingness to exchange pointless pleasantries; nonetheless, the ardent admirer would not be deterred.

In an effort to detain her, Bryan grabbed her sleeve with his extended arm, causing the girl to jerk to a halt in mid step. Clarissa's black satin slippers began to slide upon the freshly polished flooring, dropping her to the slick surface as she knocked Bryan's feet from under him.

Mortified by the laughter from the amused governmental employees and petitioners, she lashed out at her would-be suitor. "You are by far the clumsiest idiot I have had the misfortune to encounter. Get your hand off my arm for heaven's sake." Prying herself free, she pushed his arm coarsely away.

Bryan, unperturbed by the scene he had caused, scrambled to his feet and nobly offered Clarissa his assistance. Ignoring his overture, she stood independently and began wiping the dust from her black skirt.

"Clarissa, I need to ask you something." Dowd was shouting to be heard over the hallway clamor.

"Then make it quick," she snapped, still swatting at her soiled skirt.

"I...err... I'd like to go somewhere more..." he looked about the corridor..."more private."

Furiously she scream, "I haven't the time, Bryan!"

"Very well then," as Bryan posed his question, the noise unexplainably subsided. "Would you do me the honor of accompanying me to the theater tomorrow evening?" His words resounded through the high ceilinged passage, assuring Clarissa that only those citizens of Washington who were hard of hearing were unaware of her humiliation.

Seething, she retorted much too loudly, "No! Now leave me alone!" Catcalls trailed as she reached the office door.

"Don't be so hard on the boy."

On the verge of retaliation, the opening of the door constrained her.

"You are late," rebuked Simon Cameron.

Facing her uncle, she offered no excuses, entering the room composure unscathed. The men she acknowledged were not unfamiliar. Secretaries Stanton and Chase rose as she entered the room. When all were seated, Cameron continued. "As I was saying, the President is dispatching me to Richmond in an effort to ease the tensions created by Adamson's cotton monopoly and counterfeiting scheme. It seems that the Rebels wish to hold him accountable for these deeds as direct violations of the Manassas agreement."

"Have they demanded extradition?" questioned the Secretary of State.

"Not as yet, but their Congress is expected to request it as they meet even as we speak. My sources feel certain than official notification is forthcoming."

"Don't these buffoons realize that the culprit must be apprehended prior to extradition?" chuckled the Treasury Secretary.

"It will be my job to convince them that the infamous Mr. Adamson is as elusive as he is cunning." He turned to his niece. "Now, you must return home to pack. I will require an assistant to record the discussions with Davis, and I trust you will find the trip into the South as a further enlightenment into the workings of the Southern political system."

Thrilled at the prospect of a journey, she hugged her uncle in gratitude. "Will I have an opportunity to visit Cathey?"

"I think not. It was my understanding that she lived in Charleston, which is further south."

"Of course, how silly of me. I'll rush home."

"Meet me at four o'clock at the depot."

"I'll be there," she called, leaving the men to themselves.

"I've often felt it a great pity that she was born a female, for she would be an excellent politician," Cameron remarked sadly.

"Still, she is a credit to you, Simon. By the way, is she privy to all your activities?" Chase heavily emphasized the last phrases.

"Unfortunately my niece possesses the singular flaw which is the downfall of so many potentially great individuals." He shook his head. "I fear the girl is woefully honest."

"And what are your plans to avert the capture of our nonexistent criminal?"

"Perhaps you could perform some of your theatrics, Edwin," teased Simon, arching his eyebrows at Chase.

Cameron's reference was to an episode when Stanton, to prove his client innocent of the charge of murder by poisoning, had swallowed some of the toxin.

Stanton glared at his fellow conspirators unamused as he recalled that only a purging of his stomach had saved his life.

"I will, of course, emphasize the Union's abhorrence of the man's business practices and criminal activity, and I will promise that our most qualified men are diligently laboring to apprehend Adamson. Alas, he will elude them at every turn. We need only relay fictional reports from our agents in the field at regular intervals. Gentlemen, I have never encountered great difficulties deceiving a fool."

"Simon, I will be joining you the next time you meet with Armitage or Solomon," stated Stanton matter of factly.

His colleague's reply was a firm but gentle reminder. "Edwin, we agreed early on that the fewer of us who risked contact with outsiders, the better. Should our plans run amuck, the two of you would remain in office, and I can't tell you what a comfort that is to me."

"You are correct, of course," said Stanton, miffed at his own impatience brought out by his unusual position as a second in command.

As for Cameron, the Secretary of War considered Edwin Stanton an irrational but necessary ally. The man's frequent bouts with depression coupled with strange actions like the poisoning episode and the disinterment of a child's body for cremation and placement in his home, produced Cameron's doubts as to Stanton's sanity. Regardless, his political power, and his extreme hatred of Lincoln paled these idiosyncrasies.

Stanton continued to push for more information. "By the way, the remaining operations, how have they progressed?"

"I am somewhat distressed by the lack of communication from Porter. His telegraph message clearly stated his intention to relocate to the New Orleans area, but he has not been heard from in some time."

"Have there been reports of a strike against the Treasury?"

"Oddly enough, my agents report no such rumors. John's decision to travel does puzzle me; nevertheless, I have complete confidence in the man's abilities and judgment." As if anticipating Stanton's next inquiry, Cameron volunteered, "You'll find, as do I, that the word from Armitage is infinitely more encouraging."

Chase silently thanked heaven. Were it not for the stranglehold in which Stanton and Cameron had placed him, he would have abandoned this suicidal folly. To hear good news eased his fears only somewhat.

"According to our pious reverend, by the end of the week the South's economy will be dealt its final blow."

Chapter Twenty-Nine

Richmond, Virginia, March 1862

Jed and Stewart greedily devoured the single, tattered copy of the *Richmond Enquirer* that in part precipitated their swiftly arranged departures to the Southern Capital. According to the *Enquirer's* banner headline and ensuing article, the Confederacy had again been victimized by one Daniel Adamson. The outcries of Southerners, seething in moral indignation at the blatant violation of the accords of the Treaty of Manassas, demanded aggressive action. Previously, most had attributed the cotton fiasco to the machinations of a shrewd businessman, but the exposure of his role in a counterfeiting scheme branded him a national enemy, deserving an expedient prosecution.

The Confederate Congress, seldom in formal session, convened the day after the story broke. Warring camps, such was the ineffective practice of the Confederate Legislators, met privately in the back rooms of various home, hotels, or offices to debate strategies. Such factionalism resulted in a splintered governmental body, stubbornly refusing to compromise positions for the common good.

Two distinct camps emerged during the heated sessions, if one discounted those who demanded another attack on Washington or the installation of pickets across the Mason-Dixon Line. Senator Clement Clay staunchly advocated that a formal petition be delivered to Lincoln, requiring the extradition of Adamson on the charges of theft by counterfeiting and anarchy. His supporters, mostly pro-Davis Legislators who had taken the liberty to draft a petition the evening before, encouraged Clay's emotional recitation of the document to the assembly.

Before Clay concluded, Henry Foote interrupted, demanding immediate impeachment of Jeff Davis citing incompetent leadership and placing the blame for the Adamson affair entirely upon his shoulders. Benjamin Hill, an outspoken foe of the Confederate President, assailed Foote's position, outlined the failure of Davis and his entire cabinet.

The public's opinions were largely formed by the press. Newspapers of the Confederacy informed their readers of the personal views of its editors and or owners.

Spouting malevolent accusations toward Davis, Edward Pollard and John M. Daniel of the *Richmond Examiner* demanded action by the delegates. In concurrence with the *Examiner,* Robert Barnwell Rhett utilized his son's *Charleston Mercury* to espouse his displeasure with the nation's leadership. To counteract such diatribes, Richard M. Smith and Richard Yeadon of the *Richmond Sentinel* and the *Charleston Courier* published glowing editorials of the strengths and virtues of Jefferson Davis. All agreed on one point, that Adamson must be made to pay for his crimes.

On the floor of the Congress the all too typical name calling and shouting matches led the Charleston men to exchange looks of frustration, both believing that the lawmakers would eventually come to blows yet again.

The Speaker reclaimed control with a promise to put the matter to a vote. Such voting required the presence of each lawmaker at his assigned desk, causing Stewart to wonder aloud if the Speaker had instituted a vote only as a means to prevent bloodshed.

The polling of each elected official spent the better part of an hour, due to the windy preambles delivered by the voters. It was Jed's conclusion that the United States' counterparts of these prattling Legislators should consider themselves better off for the South's secession. When the tallying was completed, the resolution to demand extradition won a unanimous victory.

The final matter for consideration, the Texas/Mexico situation, incited similarly diverse recommendations, with the Texas delegation understandably the most ardent. Wigfall, Hemphill, and Reagan advocated deployment of Confederate troops to the Texas-Mexican border, basing the request on the proven success of the previous War. As Davis' crony, Wigfall proclaimed Presidential endorsement for the proposal.

Charles Cotesworth Pickney of Virginia opposed the mobilization on the basis of cost, not only in dollars but also in Confederate loss of life. It was his conviction that Juarez was playing the South like a gambler with a poor hand and a large ante. Such sentiments were echoed by Henry Marshall of Louisiana and the Florida delegation.

At the secret urging of Foote, Clement Clay requested an accounting of the South's financial solvency. "If we are to vote intelligently," he stated, "then each of us must grasp the economic constraints which can hinder any proposal."

An overwhelming majority agreed with Clay, resulting in the summoning of Memminger for a complete reporting.

During a recess called to locate the Treasury Secretary, Thomas and Kane left the observation gallery for the Capitol grounds where opposing sects positioned themselves, extolling the merits of their partisan viewpoints. As Jed and Stewart approached one cluster of Georgians and South Carolinians, Howell Cobb withdrew himself to acknowledge their presence.

"Whenever the Confederacy sounds the call for its sons, she can count on the two of you." He repeatedly slapped the boys on the backs in an exuberant gesture of welcome.

"Stewart and I were only too glad to honor your request that we attend the session," Jed lied. In fact, the trip to the Capital posed undue hardships on his business and personal life. With the consistent decline of the Confederate dollar, Thomas Shipping required an increased amount of attention. Even those foreign associates, with whom Ezra had dealt since the days when he had captained his only vessel, required extra incentives to prevent them from patronizing Union competitors. The worldwide distrust of the Confederacy's economic stability produced a whirlpool effect, spiraling the smallest and least stable enterprises into foreclosures.

At least with the business he could see progress from his dedicated efforts, but with Mandy he felt frustrated and helpless. There was little he could do to please her besides holding her hand as they chatted or as he read to her from the *Literary Messenger* or *Southern Review*. Not long after their return to Bellmead following Stewart and Catherine's wedding, she'd begun to exhibit symptoms, leading to Skylar's decision to confine her to bed for the remainder of the pregnancy. Despite everyone's efforts, she had sunk into bouts of depression.

From their conversations, Jed learned from Stewart that Catherine's unhappiness had cast him into a similar quandary. The adjustment to life in Charleston, bereft of family and friends, had been painful. Even the clout of an Isabella Thomas was insufficient to overcome the social stigma of her Northern origin. Naturally, the most proper levees, teas, and circles, of which Isabella held grand dame status, received Catherine. With Isabella as her sponsor, they could hardly refuse, but the old guard and its younger daughters led by Juliana Mallory refused to call at the Kane home. When Catherine attended a function with Isabella, the other women were not rude, yet an aura of hostility and coldness edged their conversations and actions toward the new Mrs. Kane. Jed liked to think that Mandy would become an ally after the baby's birth. He was pleased for sakes of both women that Catherine had agreed to stay at Bellmead while he and Stewart were in Richmond.

Howell Cobb, still grinning enormously said, "Oh I believe you boys will be of even greater service in peace than in war." Before a further explanation could be gained, Cobb was recalled to the informal lawn caucus.

In actuality the short recess lengthened into an hour's restless wait. When Secretary Memminger finally spoke before the assemblage, his audience's antagonism evidenced itself in the gestures, expressions, and remarks of the Legislators was well as those of the gallery. Memminger, totally unprepared for the onslaught of questions, stumbled and stammered under the inquisition of Howell Cobb and his allies.

"Mr. Secretary, the deadline of Juarez's ultimatum is quickly approaching. You, Sir, have been summoned to advise us as to the Confederacy's solvency so that we might arrive at a decision with full knowledge of the nation's financial perimeters."

Memminger squirmed.

"If we were to succumb to Juarez's outrageous demand, could we raise the five million Yankee dollars?"

"No Sir, we could not," was the Secretary's emphatic response. "To amass such an amount requires time. It would also necessitate a source willing to convert our currency on a grand scale to that of the Union's. In my estimation, such a process could take months and would cost the nation double the five million at the present rate of exchange."

"Then in your opinion, we should fight Mexico rather than pay?" questioned Yancey.

"Well, no...I...I'm in no position to dictate policy to you, the elected representatives of our citizenry. I merely answered as best I could, Mr. Cobb's inquiry. I don't believe anyone desires a long and costly war with Mexico."

Wigfall rose and faced the assembly. "It has been our experience that the Mexican government has been one that is based on the precarious whims of dictatorships. These despots possess a single common thread, which is their immense greed." He then turned to the Secretary whose white knuckles gripped the podium in a desperate attempt to steady himself. "If the Confederacy chose to strike a compromise for a lesser amount, what sum can be readily obtained?"

Memminger searched for a rescuer, finding none, he embarked upon a fatal course. "As I explained earlier, Mr. Wigfall, a major obstacle is the conversion to Union currency. Such transfers are costly."

"What is that rate?" interrupted Robert Johnson, a Kentucky Senator.

"As of yesterday, the Confederate dollar retains approximately seventy-five percent of its worth against the United States' dollar; however, the larger amount we seek on the open market makes us vulnerable to lesser rates due to our desperation.   That is, of course, if we can locate any financiers willing to place their holdings in our currency. Perhaps if we had more time, smaller amounts with varied sources could improve our rate of exchange."

The Mississippi Senator, James Phelan, exclaimed in outrage, "Do you mean to insinuate that the bankers and financially blessed of this nation are less than loyal to our Cause and would not strengthen our coffers in this our hour of need?"

"I mean, Sir, that they are loathe to gamble their futures on a currency system whose government cannot depend on all its states to submit tax revenue, since some withhold these resources for partisan reasons."

Memminger struck a raw nerve, for Mississippi had refused to collect tax revenues until the price of cotton rose to a more profitable rate. Phelan, in the process of delivering a vindictive rebuttal, lost the floor to Cobb.

"What need is there for an exchange, when the Confederacy is in possession of nearly $700,000 in bullion captured at the New Orleans Mint? Surely even Juarez's greed can be satisfied by this amount in gold?"

There was a note of mirth in the audience's rumblings for the next few moments. Cobb awaited the Secretary's answer, already privy to the knowledge of the otherwise secreted bullion robbery. Not willing to release his prey from the trap he'd set, Cobb rephrased his question in a more direct tone.

"Is there, or is there not, a cache of Federal gold bullion at the New Orleans Mint?"

Seeing no other option, Memminger answered, "No Sir, there is not."

Howell Cobb stepped back to relish in the havoc he'd reeked. The Speaker repeatedly pounded his gavel. Thomas

Bocock's Virginia dialect persuasively quieted the assemblage with his demand.

"Secretary Memminger, this governing body never sanctioned the expenditure of that bullion. You are hereby ordered to account for its disbursement," his voice quivering with rage.

"The bullion was neither spent nor coined."

Memminger's heart rose into his throat. His loyalty to the President did not include political suicide, thus influencing his decision to free himself from blame. Such was his intent, although there would be others to claim that he deliberately sacrificed Davis to the rabble.

"President Davis, without my approval, ordered the bullion transferred to the National Treasury to back foreign loans for military needs, should a conflict with Mexico prove inevitable. In the interest of preserving our already shaky fiscal position, the knowledge of its theft was to remain a secret until such time as the economy stabilized."

"Mr. Speaker?"

"The floor recognizes Jabez Curry."

"Thank you, Sir. Memminger," his anger barely in check, "in lieu of the theft of the captured bullion, the loss of tax revenue, and the counterfeiting operation, how much Confederate currency is backed by gold or silver?"

"I'm... well, I am not entirely..."

"Dammit, man, I am on the verge of demanding your arrest for the theft. Answer my question!"

The veins on the side of his fair skinned face bulged with the intensity of his voice.

Softly, the Secretary delivered the fatal statement. "Bearing in mind that we have no precise figures on the fraudulent monies currently in circulation, there is sufficient bullion to redeem fifty percent of the Confederate specie now in circulation."

The zealous outcries forced Memminger away from the podium and to a seat near the Speaker's abandoned chair.

From their perches in the visitor's gallery Stewart and Jed regarded the confusion wrought by the disclosure. Stewart shouted in Jed's ear to be heard above the din. "I'm going to telegraph Ezra. It's imperative that he not invest any of the funds from the Northern accounts in Confederate bonds. I'll urge him to redeem as much of our Confederate bills as possible, regardless of the losses we must assume." Jed signaled his approval, and Stewart began his trek through the mob.

The Speaker, having relinquished the dais, permitted Howell Cobb to set in motion the final segment of the strategy. Gavel in hand he exacted order from the pandemonium. "Gentlemen," he roared, "I move that an order of impeachment be brought against President Jefferson Davis and his entire administration!"

It was impossible to record the names of all those who seconded Cobb's motion.

A voice vote ensued with a thunderous chorus of "aye's" and a barely audible response of "nay's" from Davis' few remaining supporters.

"Gentlemen," Cobb continued, "we must not set the Confederacy adrift without a captain. It was after heated debate that this body agreed upon a compromise candidate under whose ineffective leadership we now flounder. I propose the appointment of an interim President to serve until such time as an election can be held. To avoid the repetitious nominations of favorite sons and other compromise designates, which experience has shown us will not be approved, let us consider nominations whose names have not appeared before us."

Scattered "amen's" lent Cobb the confidence to proceed.

"I would like to place in nomination a man who is not only a proven, qualified leader of men and a brilliant strategist, but he is a seasoned businessman as well. He was instrumental in our defeat of the North. Without his direction and cunning, we very well could be fighting the Yankees today at the cost of thousands of Rebel lives. There is but one man to lead us…Jedediah Thomas." Cobb gestured to the gallery, with all eyes following suit.

Jed sat in stunned silence, his mouth opened in an audible gasp. A myriad of thoughts rushed to mind. *This is a farce. I'm no politician. No one will take Cobb seriously.* The applause and whistles mixed with an occasional Rebel yell were deafening. Jed felt as if his head might burst. Somehow, he was moving from his position in the gallery toward the floor of the Capitol, a participant in an absurd dream.

With the assembly focused on the entry of Jed Thomas, Cobb dropped unobserved into the crowd. Near the foot of the platform, Henry Foote shook his hand. "Beautiful job, Howell. It went just as you said it would."

"I was never in doubt."

"But will Jed Thomas be as easily manipulated as this crowd?"

"Easier, Howell, much, much easier."

Chapter Thirty

Bellmead, March 1862

At an hour when the inhabitants of the two thousand acres of the Bellmead Plantation normally slept, its slaves crept stealthily from the safety of their cabins toward the larger structure which served as their place of worship. Mothers pushed their children, dazed by rude awakenings, warning them not to discard their bundles of clothing or household goods wrapped in bed clothings. Once inside the church, the children crawled atop their burdens to sleep as the adults readied for their journey to the North.

Mose stood at the door, checking off the names of those brave enough to risk their lives and those of the children for a slim chance at freedom. All knew the risks involved. If they could successfully leave the plantation without detection, there remained a mile and a half to the railroad tracks.

Though few dared express them, there were those who doubted Mr. Jasper's repeated promise that a train would be waiting to take them away from their lifetime of bondage. Still, it was the possibility of an existence free of Monroe' whip or the degradation of serving the White man that drew them.

There were those in whose memories the tortuous displays staged to punish recaptured runaways and to discourage those contemplating escapes, were vividly clear. Mose admired Posey's love for her aged mother whose frailties would impede the escape. Posey would remain at Bellmead, but her prayers were with them, she told Mose, tears streaming down her face. As Sally had pointed to her mulatto offsprings, she reminded Mose of a certainty.

"Ain't nobody ta care fer dez light uns up dare."

A few were guided by their experiences, believing that all Whites were unworthy of trust, be they Yankee or Southerners. Old Tuck pronounced the escape as foolish.

"Ain't ner' seed no white man what wanted ta helps no blacks."

The most difficult to convince, Maizy, sat isolated on one of the roughhewn benches, clutching her mistress' cast-off carpetbags. Knowing her better than anyone else, Mose perceived the indecision with which she wrestled, fully aware that leaving Bellmead wrenched her heart. Mandy was her only baby. She had cared for her every need since birth. The death of Mandy's mother cemented the girl's dependency upon the childless Black woman who loved her unconditionally, despite her spoiled tirades and thoughtlessly selfish existence. With Mandy's time so close at hand and her health so fragile, Maizy worried and fussed over her all the more, and now she was abandoning her when she needed her the most.

Jasper Erwin stepped up to the raised section of flooring that served as the pulpit. "Mose and I have grouped you by families into five groups. Each group will leave at a separate time, ten minutes apart. As you know, Abner, Monroe, and

Charles have been practicing with Mose and me at night. All of us are equally good at finding the right path to the railroad in the darkness. Last night we marked the trail in case anyone should get lost or confused. They'll explain that to you as we go. When you get to the train, there'll be folks there to get you into boxcars."

As Erwin spoke, his heart went out to those dark faces who entrusted their futures to his charge, and now that it was a reality, he began to doubt that such a massive undertaking could truly be accomplished.

"I can't tell you how important it is to stay quiet until the train leaves. You'll hear some commotion, but that will be those from Vermillion, Oak Grove, and Jasmine. There should be some others there when you get there. Just stay calm and follow your leader's instructions." He prepared to leave the platform. "One more thing, you can make as much noise as you like while the train is moving, but once it starts slowing down, you've got to stay quiet again. We don't want anyone to have call to open those cars."

Mose read off the names of the five groups which formed in the tiny sanctuary. At one, the first band of slaves stole cautiously behind the rows of quarters and into an open field. Each man carried a pistol and spare ammunition, not that any had ever fired the weapon, but all had drilled silently, knowing that his safety and that of his family might well depend upon his aim.

The night was windy, with clouds floating across a bobbing moon. Jasper thanked God for the cover in the prayer he'd offered up before the first group's departure. His voice bore a noticeable tremor as he beseeched the Lord's blessings upon these slaves, likening them to their Israelite brothers fleeing the Pharaoh's chariots.

Once across the field, the party faced the most arduous phase of the route. A thickly wooded area lay between them and the tracks. As they neared a particularly large pine, Charles spoke quietly to the band.

"Seez dis here tree? Din looks at dat ston'. Dares white stonz by pines on da way. Daares arras drawn on de groun what shoz da way we take." As he lifted the stone, they saw an arrow pointing straight ahead. The stone replaced, they continued into the thicket.

Jasper and the remaining groups nervously awaited the departure time of the fourth portion of slaves, consisting of one family with six children of varying ages, Maizy, and Mose.

Mose took his signal from Erwin. "It's time," he said to his followers.

At the opposite end of the quarters inside the overseer's house, the high winds blew a shutter from its latch, producing a startling noise. Henry Monroe sat up, mixing the squeak of bedspring with the clamoring shutter and the whine of the wind. Cursing under his breath, he stumbled to the window, his nightshirt whipping in the breeze. As he reached to close the shutter, the clouds parted, enabling him to witness the movements of the runaway slaves. Reacting quickly to the sight of the slaves carrying their possessions, he fumbled for his pants.

"Get up and sound the alarm!" he yelled to his sleeping wife as he headed for the door.

"We've got runaways!"

His wife threw a hooded cape over her nightgown and ran toward the mounted bell that served as a communications link for even the most remote sections of the plantation. Pulling violently at the rope, the peals pierced the night. In the big house candles were lighted, and in the church, the remaining slaves hurried back to their cabins to conceal their intentions lest they too be killed or punished. In separate stages along the escape route, slaves began running, knowing full well that the bloodhounds needed no light to flush their prey.

Henry Monroe rounded the corner of the last slave cabin just as the fourth group started across the open field. He fired into the cluster of slaves, dropping a child in the furrow. The mother gasped, stopping to claim her child, as the second discharge struck her in the back while she knelt to pick up the lifeless body of her daughter.

Panic-stricken, Maizy scooped up the youngest of the children sheltering them both behind one of the wagons left abandoned in the field. Clouds recovered the moon preventing a clear view of the fates of her companions. Holding the child close to her bosom, she muffled its whimperings.

"Well, if it ain't Miz Maizy."

Woman and child screamed in response to Henry Monroe's sudden, threatening presence.

"Won't the Missus be surprised that her darling mammy is one of the runaways? Guess you won't be so high and mighty now."

Maizy was unsure if her body trembled in response to her fear or the quivering of the child she embraced.

"Plenty's the time I seen you a looking down on my women folk, and now you're gonna pay for yer uppity ways."

In an instinctive effort to shield the little girl, Maizy turned slightly at the unmistakable click of the cocked trigger of his Colt six shooter. An eternity passed between the explosion that rang in her ears and the realization that she was unhurt. The thud of Monroe's body meeting the soil he'd ordered tilled by the sweat of slaves' brows caused her to open the eyes had had so tightly closed.

Steadying herself against the wagon's wheel, she stood facing Mose whose outstretched arms held one of the pistols smuggled to Erwin by his Northern friends.

Monroe managed to twist himself to a position from which he could view his assailant. Seeing Mose, he grabbed for his own gun, which the towering Black man kicked from his grasp.

"It takes a real man to beat the defenseless and shoot women and children," his statement ladened with sarcasm. "Die you son of a bitch."

Again the deafening discharge pierced the nights. Throwing the child over his shoulder, he began to drag the stunned Maizy across the field.

"Run woman!"

At the plantation house, Dorian and Sidney Mallory met Jasper in the front garden. "It's an escape!" cried Jasper. "The best I can tell, they've gone out toward the warehouses."

"Saddle some horses," bellowed the younger Mallory. "Find where the devil Monroe is and have him get the hounds."

Jasper wished he knew how he would explain sending the search party away from the runaways.

"Get moving!"

Erwin burst toward the barn.

Mandy and Catherine stood upon the columned veranda straining to hear or see the cause of the alarm. "Is it a fire?" Catherine asked.

"There's no flames or the smell of smoke. It must be a runaway," answered Mandy.

Catherine remained silent, praying for the lives of those involved and for their successes in evading recapture. She'd read horrifying accounts of the punishments that Southern masters inflicted upon errant slaves, though it was increasingly difficult for her to couple the gentile Mallory family with the heinous masters in the abolitionary press. Tonight might well stand as proof.

Mandy started down the porch steps.

"Where are you going? You're not even to be out of bed," Catherine said.

"I must find Maizy. She wasn't in her bed, and if she comes back to the house, she'll be mistaken as a runaway."

"I'll go for you."

"You haven't a clue as to where to look."

Catherine joined the woman at the foot of the steps. "At least I can go with you."

The two women walked as fast as they could, hindered by the awkwardness of Mandy's advanced pregnancy. As they started down the row of cabins, mounted sharecroppers arrived in response to the alarm. Seeing only a white clad figure turning between the cabins, the rider shouted, "There goes one of 'um!"

Intent on the reward he would receive for each slave the man helped to recapture, he reigned his horse in the direction of the fleeing figure. Overtaking it, he pushed with all his might, sending the runaway crashing into the logs of the cabin's corner. Dismounting, the rider turned the stilled form.

A piercing scream awakened him to the reality of his deed.

"What have you done too her?"

The man stared at the body of the pregnant White woman whose blood dripped between his finger from a gaping wound on her forehead.

At the train each peel of the alarm heightened the desperation of those inside the cars. To some already hidden among cargo crates, the ringing convinced them of the folly of escape. As the third group arrived and hastily loaded, those onboard clammered for news.

Mose and Maizy tore through the woods, lungs bursting, legs fighting the mind's drive to continue. When they sighted the train, the gut-wrenching sound of the engine summoned their last ounces of strength. Mose lifted Maizy into the car, pushing the child into the arms of a woman who had heard their cries for help. As the train began to excellerate, Mose was forced to run beside it. Just as he neared exhaustion, Charles' and Abner's muscular arms, strengthened by years of field labor, dragged him inside the moving railway car.

Maizy rushed to his side, and the two embraced, neither holding back their tears.

Chapter Thirty-One

Richmond, Virginia, March 1862

T aking her uncle's arm, Clarissa stepped off the train that had transported them to the Confederacy's Capital. From the barouche that delivered them, she appraised the city, comparing it to her own. To her surprise, the two cities were not as dissimilar as she had been led to believe.

Richmond's equally impressive public buildings reminded her of those of Washington, though their scales, perhaps, were smaller. There were steepled churches, elegant homes, and parks just bursting into full bloom. If anything, Richmond appeared more crowded, which she aptly attributed to a city planned for a state's seat of government that had been unprepared for its metamorphosis into national significance. The hired coach stopped in front of a quaint hotel.

Cameron explained before their departure that the accommodations he'd engaged were hardly lavish. True, the hotel's neighborhood lacked the pristine aura it once possessed, but the shop-lined avenue spoke well of itself through its friendly, inviting atmosphere.

Her uncle addressed the driver, "I'll only be a moment." To his niece he added, "We will go directly to the Capitol following confirmation of our rooms and instructions for the distribution of our baggage."

Clarissa nodded, grateful for the privacy to absorb the Confederacy about which she had heard and read so much. Craning to see ahead, she encountered a sight that became indelibly engraved upon her memory. A slovenly dressed White man led four Blacks who were shackled together at their hands and feet into an opened doorway.

Clarissa stood upright in the carriage, poking the driver's back with her parasol.

"Driver, what is that man doing?"

The driver shook his head, never able to comprehend the Yankee mentality. "Them's slaves, Miss, and that's the auction."

Before he could lodge a protest, his passenger left the carriage, dodging wagons and riders as she crossed the street in the direction of the auction site. Vainly he called after her, bemoaning the loss of what he'd assessed to be a handsome tip in Union money.

Clarissa entered the smoky room, oblivious of the stares of men who were there to deal in human flesh. Were she not so riveted to the raised platform, Clarissa would have realized that she was the only White woman present.

A thin, black woman in a soiled cotton dress, stood before the audience, tears streaming down her cheeks. Beside the woman, a White man indicated vulgar attributes whose very mention appalled Clarissa. Led away, the woman pitifully called back to one of the men, undoubtedly her husband, sending Clarissa on a desperate search for fresh air. Once outside, she steadied herself, fighting the urge to retch on the public street. Seemingly out of nowhere, a man took her arm.

"Let's go back, Miss."

She allowed the driver to guide her to the carriage, as yet unoccupied by her uncle.

"I tried to warn you," he drawled, "but ya'll Yankees don't never listen. That ain't no place for White women to be seen. No ma'am, it ain't."

Only the emergence of her uncle stemmed the flood of questions that darted through her mind. Simon Cameron clutched several newspapers, thrusting a copy excitedly into Clarissa's lace-gloved hands.

"Glorious news, Clarissa." A stark headline born the news of the hijacking of a train transferring the Union bullion to Richmond.

"Two of the robbers were jailed, but the rest evaded capture, resulting in the loss of several hundred thousand dollars in gold."

Clarissa let the newspaper lie in her lap to steady it as the carriage swayed down the rutted street. In doing so, she considered her uncle who was reading of the South's latest misfortune with a curious delight of one recanting a personal triumph.

"It appears that we will be unable to meet with Mr. Davis."

"But Uncle Simon, I understood that the appointment with you was not only agreed upon but requested?"

"Our meeting is with the President of the Confederacy, an office Mr. Davis no longer holds."

Clarissa's face voiced her confusion.

"It seems the South has impeached its President as well as his entire administration." Simon Cameron recounted the events of Davis' debacle.

"If his entire cabinet was censured, who is in charge of the government?"

"Someone with whom you are quite familiar. We'll be meeting with Acting President Jedediah Thomas."

Numbed by Cameron's revelation, Clarissa feigned interest in the *Richmond Enquirer*, allowing herself the opportunity to compose her muddled thoughts. Could she sit opposite her former lover without betraying her hostilities, and if she could not, what falsehood would compensate for her actions? The United States Secretary of War accompanied by his assistant entered the Virginia Capitol amid the confusion of an impending session.

"Secretary Cameron?" an approaching man inquired. Responding to Cameron's nod, he continued. "I am Daniel Petersen, an aide to the Acting President. I do regret that a special legislative session has been called due to the devastating events of last evening; therefore, I must request that your appointment be delayed until the session adjourns."

"And what precludes an appointment, which your government solicited, with a representative of the President of the United States?"

"My pardon Sir. I assumed you were aware of a massive slave rebellion led by the damn, excuse me Miss, abolitionists. If you will allow me, I will escort you to a gallery seat from which you may view the entire proceedings."

"Of course, Petersen, I had no idea."

Clarissa took her uncle's arm, climbing the tobacco stained steps to the balcony overlooking the assembly hall. As they seated themselves, Jed began his speech.

"Gentlemen, it is with deep regret that I must confirm the reports of an expansive slave rebellion. At this point telegraphed corroboration of escapes has been received from as far west as Jackson, Mississippi, down to Atlanta, and numerous points in between. Few plantations did not suffer losses of some of their slaves."

The characteristic waves of Legislators' voices rose and fell between each crucial declaration.

"In each instance the slaves were armed and meticulously organized, resulting in effective rendezvous with the Underground Railroad or other abolitionist factions. At Elm Fork outside Augusta, White men died at the hands of the insurgents. Still other communiqués detail the looting of homes, theft of horses, and the deliberate setting of fires. Obviously the orchestration of such a massive number of insurrections at corresponding times reeks of collusion. Would that I could pinpoint its originators."

"Captain Thomas," questioned Mr. Clay. "Not every slave vanished into thin air. Near Meredian, the slaves of Alexander Covington were discovered boarding rail cars belonging to the Southside Railroad. The crew is currently in route to Richmond. You have my assurance that all means necessary will be used to extract information from these men."

Cameron basked in the irony of the moment. As the Rebels furiously sought those responsible for the loss of their slaves, there he sat, observing the ineptness of his pursuers.

Jed started to leave the platform.

Reconsidering, he returned to the podium. "Today is to be a momentous date in the history of our nation and that of the United States, marking the beginning of amiable diplomacy. We have as our most honored guest the United States Secretary of War, the distinguished Simon Cameron." Jed initiated the applause in which the Confederate Representatives half-heartedly engaged. Cameron stood, bowing in acknowledgement.

As Jed exited, his aide directed Clarissa and her uncle down the stairs and across the assembly room floor where they proceeded to the Treasury Building and Jed's office. Seating themselves in the Presidential office, Clarissa's appraisal of the room revealed that it reflected little of the personality of the man who occupied it. On his desk, a single photograph of his wife served as a stark reminder of the barrier which separated her from the man she had grown to love aboard the *Victoria*.

As her eyes traveled to a glass encased bookshelf, she felt the hatred she had nurtured slowly begin to melt, recognizing the shelf's sole occupant to be the Brady photograph of the wedding party. To others, the picture paid tribute to a foster brother and his new bride, but to Clarissa, its position directly in Jed's line of view symbolized his love for her. She wanted to burst, to tell everyone that Jed had not forgotten, but she would never be free to do more than content herself with memories and this single affirmation of his love.

Jed dreaded the meeting with Cameron, for the man's reputation as a shrewd negotiator preceded him. He paused before the door, checked his cravat, and entered. Jed barely saw the Secretary, never remembered shaking his hand. His eyes basked in the beauty of Clarissa Morgan. When she smiled, gone were the marks of loathing and contempt that had severed his soul.

Somehow he willed himself to regard the uncle.

"How does one address an Acting President?" Cameron lightheartedly asked.

"As you have no doubt heard since your arrival, there are those who address me as *Captain*, *Mister*, or any number of unflattering and profane appellations. I prefer *Jed*, if you would grant me the honor of your friendship."

Simon Cameron seldom favored anyone whose position exceeded his own, especially when the person lacked his age or experience; however, the unpretentious gentleman whose hand he shook penetrated the armor that callously shielded the vulnerable emotions of the Secretary. *Under other circumstances, we might have been friends*, Cameron admitted to himself.

"I believe you are already acquainted with my niece, who is now my personal aide."

"Of course. Miss Morgan, I am delighted to see you again." He leaned forward, kissing her hand, longing to take her in his arms.

"Jed, I had no idea that you were Mr. Davis' successor."

Jed laughed as he offered them seats on a comfortable settee he'd added to the office, and he lowered himself into a matching chair. "I am equally surprised."

He addressed Cameron, "It seems that Daniel Adamson's vendetta against the Confederacy resulted in a loss of confidence in President Davis' administration and its ability to effectively thwart further damage to the nation's economy." He leaned forward to emphasize the import of the next statements. "Adamson's direct responsibility for the sabotage of our cotton market and currency is unquestionable. I have no means of substantiation, but my own belief is that the theft of the Treasury bullion and this slave rebellion bare his marks and total disregard for the Treaty of Manassas. I want him stopped, Secretary Cameron, and I expect no interference by the United States government in his capture and prosecution in a Southern court."

"I can assure you that President Lincoln shares your sentiments and abhors the flagrant defiance of the Treaty accords. The President has enlisted the aid of Mr. Pinkerton and his co-workers, undeniably the most skilled investigator available, to apprehend Mr. Adamson and bring him before the bar of justice."

"Please express my gratitude to the President; however, I must insist that we be allowed to dispatch a team of men to merge with Pinkerton's staff, thereby providing direct accounting to this office."

The entrance of Stewart Kane prohibited the Secretary of War's response to Jed's demands.

"Stewart, how wonderful to see you. Is Cathey in Richmond, also?"

Kissing her hand he replied, "I'm afraid not, Clarissa. She remained at Bellmead to be…" he faltered, "to be with Mandy when the baby…"

He looked beseechingly toward the friend he considered his brother. "Jed, I must speak with you in the outer office; it is most urgent."

"See here, Kane, I have been rudely treated from the moment of my arrival, and I will not be dismissed again without regard to my office," said Cameron.

Stewart's response shocked everyone for individual reasons.

"It is imperative," he snapped at the incensed Cameron, "that I speak with Jed, and we will take our leave!"

The two men left Clarissa calming her uncle.

Once inside the smaller room which Petersen normally occupied, Jed inquired, "What word did we receive regarding the escapes?"

"The message was from Bellmead."

"How many took flight?"

"All but ten or twelve are missing; a woman and a child were killed along with Henry Monroe. Even Mose and Maizy left."

"Mose and Maizy," he repeated incredulously, "there's some mistake. They would never leave Bellmead, and Maizy, well, Maizy has never been separated from Mandy, not even on what honeymoon we had. Especially with the baby due, she's not going to desert Mandy."

"She's gone, Jed," Stewart quietly stated.

"Mandy just won't be able to run the house and tend to a baby…"

"Mandy's gone!" He interrupted in a more emphatic tone. He placed his hands on his friend's shoulder, bracing Jed as he looked him squarely in the eyes. "I don't have all the details, but she left the house after the alarm sounded to search for Maizy. Somehow she was mistaken for a runaway."

He stopped, allowing his words to become reality. He felt the weight of Jed's shoulder press against his thumbs, as he shook his head in denial.

"She wasn't to leave the bed. How could she have been outside the house?" He sank into a chair, burying his face in his hands. Though no sounds were audible, Stewart watched his body heave. In a surge of expectancy he blurted, "The baby, she must have had the baby…before…"

Stewart's expression bespoke the words he could not express. "I think I'd like to sit here alone, Stewart."

After embracing Jed, he left the room.

Cameron ceased to pace as Stewart rejoined them.

Upon seeing the tears welled up in his eyes, Clarissa went to his side. "Whatever has happened?"

"I can't apologize enough for my behavior." He wiped an errant tear with his monogrammed handkerchief. "Mandy, Jed's wife was killed as the slaves escaped her father's plantation." His expression beseeched their forgiveness. "He had to know," Stewart moaned.

"But of course," muttered the Secretary.

Impulsively, Clarissa sought to comfort Jed. Without knocking she went quietly to his side, taking his arm in both her hands, she leaned her head against his shoulder. For several minutes neither spoke.

Finally, he raised his head. "The baby, too," were the only words he could muster.

"Oh Jed, I am so truly sorry. Cathey has written me so often of how sweet and sensitive Mandy was and how she had grown to love her."

Summoning all his strength, he rose and crossed to a window, opened to allow the fresh, spring breezes to freshen the musty office.

"No matter what transpired between us, Clarissa, I really did love Mandy. If someone had told me it was possible for a man to love two women, I really would not have believed him. But it is possible to love for very different reasons."

Several silent minutes passed. "She hadn't your spirit and independence," he continued. "From the day she was born, Mandy was pampered and cajoled. Skylar, her brother and physician, confessed to me that her chances of enduring the baby's birth were slim. 'Jed,' he said, 'my baby sister just hasn't the strength that a hard labor will require. You must be prepared to lose them both if nature doesn't help her along.'"

Leaning his head against the wall, he sobbed audibly.

Clarissa Morgan had never felt so utterly helpless. She longed to hold him and bear his pain if only for a moment.

Tapping softly on the door, Stewart entered the room, and his eyes pleaded with Clarissa to produce some relief for Jed's misery.

Jed slammed his fist against the wall. "By all that's holy, Stewart, how could I be so selfish? Is Catherine safe?"

"Yes, Catherine is fine. I've arranged for a private car to take us to Bellmead. We leave in an hour."

"So soon?" Jed questioned.

"There are some advantages to your position."

"But Secretary Cameron, I must…"

"Don't worry, Clarissa will soothe his feathers. He did, by the way, ask me to convey his sympathies."

"I'll let you prepare for your journey. You will inform me if I can be of any assistance…at all," Clarissa's voice trailed.

"Of course," Stewart replied as he ushered her out of the room and out of Jed's life yet another time.

Chapter Thirty-Two

Charleston, South Carolina, April 1862

Despite the thunderstorms whose winds and rain pelted the bystanders, the citizens of Charleston and the curious from North and South lined the streets which surrounded the Courthouse. Amid the backdrop of the shrouding clouds, hometowners were dressed in somber hues, symbolic of their sympathies for the young President. Even an opportunistic vendor carting umbrellas ceased barking his ware, and, along with the residents of the city, bowed his head in respect for the family's loss as those less familiar with President Jedediah Thomas craned their necks for a glimpse.

Under hastily raised umbrellas, the Thomas and Mallory families inched their way up the crowded steps and into the confines of the courtroom. Spectators lined the walls, grateful for the privilege to stand during the proceedings. By virtue of well-placed bribes, those actually seated fidgeted on the wooden benches which had long since become uncomfortable.

As the family filled into the section reserved for them, two were left unseated. Roughly removed by a deputy of the court, two gentlemen were forced to provide seating, amid lamentations of time and money spent for the opportunity to witness the last day of the trial of the Yankee scoundrel who had infiltrated their midst.

The courtroom activity heightened as the shackled prisoner inched his way to the defense table. Half dragged by the military guards procured to thwart any of the numerous threats against his life, Jasper Erwin collapsed into his chair, as much from the chains at his feet and hands as the force of the soldiers whose presence brought him very little security should trouble actually arise. Both had made no secret of their hostilities toward the abolitionist who sat accused of inciting a rebellion of Negroes and of the deaths of Mrs. Amanda Mallory Thomas and her unborn child.

Other associates of the Reverend Armitage had faced their Southern accusers with much less note by the North's press, but for the trials of the murder of one so prominent, *Harper's* and *Frank Leslie's* dispatched both artists and reporters as did New York's *Herald* and *Tribune*, and other noted publications. The pencils of the illustrators flew, capturing the emotion laden visages of the principals.

Winslow Homer, one of the illustrators, reviewed his sketchbook, as the audience awaited the arrival of the venerable Judge Milton Lowell. Staring back at him from an earlier drawing was the vindictive countenance of the state's first witness, Dorian Mallory.

Artfully guided by the questioning of the state's attorney, Nate Woodard, the deceased's brother testified with the appropriate amount of moral indignation of one who had graciously welcomed a stranger into the bosom of Bellmead

Plantation only to see the man rob his benefactor of his property and his sister.

The keen-eyed Homer observed the defendant as he admitted the truth of his accuser's accounting by his bowed head and slumped shoulders.

Nate Woodard urged his rheumatic body to its full six feet. Leaning on his cane, he prepared to present his most damnable evidence. "Mr. Mallory, when you and your brother questioned Jasper Erwin upon discovery of the slaves' escape, how did he appear to you?"

"Agitated…, confused about what to do, but he was adamant enough about which route the runaways took."

"And he advised you all…?"

"In the opposite direction; however, it was evident enough after only a short chase that we had been misled."

"How so?"

"There were no signs of recent travel on foot, such as broken limbs. So my brother and I returned to the house and released the hounds, who immediately picked up the scents of the actual trail which ultimately led to the railroad some distance away."

"And what, Sir, did you discover at those tracks?"

Mallory paused for a dramatic effect. "Jasper Erwin."

The defendant had repeatedly cursed his stupidity, that weakness of judgment, but the desire to know of the rebellion's success had ruled over reason upon the discovery of the bodies in the field. Of course, he gambled and lost that the Mallory men would ride a much longer distance. Their arrival had sealed his fate as an obvious accomplice despite his explanation that the body of his fellow overseer had drawn him to this destination, a location that the owners of Bellmead had needed a pack of bloodhounds to determine.

Judge Lowell rapped for silence from the incensed spectators.

"I am finished, Your Honor."

A query was directed by the judge to the defense attorney, the most esteemed of the abolitionist lawyers, Calvin Steed. Steed's reputation preceded his arrival in Charleston. The gifted barrister had successfully pled the cause of freedom on behalf of runaway slaves in free states and the Missouri Territory; however, this would be his first appearance in a Confederate court, against a biased jury. Nearing middle age, the counselor ran his fingers nervously through his thinning brown hair in an effort to prepare himself for the foe.

"Tell me, Mr. Mallory, have you ever been inside the Charleston Jail?"

"I believe so."

"And did your presence there indicate your status as a prisoner?"

"I object, Your Honor," roared an indignant Woodard.

"Sit back and listen a while, Nate. Answer the man, Mr. Mallory."

"Then why did Jasper Erwin's presence at the tracks that fateful evening indicate his guilt?"

Without allowing an answer, Steed pressed his point. "Hadn't you and your brother arrived at the identical spot?"

Dorian thought before replying.

"Well, my brother and I did have the benefit of a pack of hounds, but your point is well taken."

Steed, who had not anticipated such an immediate capitulation, relaxed his guard.

"Then you agree that Erwin's presence at the railway circumstantially labels him as a catalyst in the rebellion?" he stated triumphantly.

"Not any more than his defense by a high-priced friend of Jonas Armitage's implies that he is a murdering abolitionist son of a bitch."

The audience burst into laughter and cheers for a Southerner who had outwitted the silver-tongued Steed.

"The jury will disregard the witness' outburst." But even as he spoke, Lowell was aware of the futility of his charge as the jurors were as much engaged in the merriment resulting from Dorian's remark as he and the spectators.

Homer flipped past several more drawings, reaching his rendering of Mr. Curtis Le May, Master of Oak Ridge Plantation near Memphis. When he read that he had been misrepresented as a former employer of Jasper Erwin, the man had voluntarily journeyed to testify. As much in defense of his own reputation as a desire to see Erwin pay for his crimes, Le May had branded Erwin both a liar and a forger.

Bearing the agony she experienced during her hours of testimony, a torn expression distorted the visage of Mrs. Catherine Kane. Though genuinely supportive of Erwin's efforts, her replies to Nate Woodard's inquiries were equally heartfelt at most.

"Mrs. Kane, I realize the difficulty of reliving the horror of that terrible evening. You were awakened by the alarm?"

"Yes... yes, we all were."

"We?"

"The entire household at Bellmead."

"And the response?"

"I ran downstairs. Finding no one, I went out on the veranda where I was joined by Mandy, that is Mrs. Thomas, who recognized that the signal was alerting us to a slave escape. Hailing from the North, I had no real clue as to the severity of such an attempt."

"And what happened next?"

"Well, Mrs. Thomas insisted that she must locate her maid, Maizy, who was not in her bed near that of her mistress. It was Mrs. Thomas' fear that Maizy would be mistaken as a runaway and suffer harm." Stopping to dab her eyes, she began anew when the barrister interrupted.

"Rather than subject Mrs. Kane to further distress, I will conclude my questioning. I feel it is quite apparent that Mrs. Thomas ventured out into the night as a direct result of the rebellion."

Still smarting from Dorian's damaging words, Steed was not in as generous a mood. His client's case was weak, and he desperately sought a scapegoat for at least a portion of the responsibility for the Thomas woman's death.

"Mrs. Kane, were you surprised by Mrs. Thomas' decision to search for her mammy?"

"Certainly, you see, Mrs. Thomas was in a period of confinement."

"Do you reside at Bellmead?"

"Not usually. I was a houseguest. Both our husbands were away, and since the time of her baby's arrival was so near, I came to be with her."

"To look after her welfare, so to speak?"

She nodded an affirmation.

"Then why," he demanded in an accusatory tone, "did you not dissuade her from such a rash action?"

Taken aback by the viscousness of Steed's query, Catherine madly searched for words. "I.., I tried," she stammered.

"You could not exercise enough influence over the friend you came to attend to have offered to go for her, restrained her, or reminded her of her baby's health?"

Delighted by the effect his accusations produced in the witness, he drove further. "Then I maintain that you are directly responsible for her presence in the slave quarters that night and for the deaths of your friend and her unborn child."

The word "friend" was pronounced with an uncharacteristic vehemence. Catherine burst into tears and required Stewart's assistance to leave the witness chair. At his table, Steed savored his victory, oblivious to the fact that such indelicate treatment of Catherine Kane, even if she was a Yankee, was inexcusable to the twelve Southern gentlemen who composed the jury. It was one of but a series of errors that his disregard for the Southern way of life precipitated.

Flipping past the slave woman, Sally, who recounted Erwin's efforts to organize the slaves, Homer smoothed a clean sheet and prepared for a new day.

In the center of the aisle, just past the short, swinging gate that led to the focal point of the courtroom, Matthew Brady adjusted his camera, abandoning it as Judge Milton Lowell's arrival was announced.

Imported from the most liberal section of Virginia, Lowell owned no slaves. His selection to try this case, represented the Confederacy's attempt to afford Jasper Erwin a fair, impartial trial, a charge the judge undertook with solemn resolve. In the opening days of his most noteworthy case, Lowell's faith in the judicial system had slowly waned as one by one the jury box filled with staunchly reared Southerners. In the Confederacy, there were no peers for Jasper Erwin.

Formalities thus dispensed, the defense counsel rose, making know his request. "The defense calls Jasper Erwin."

The room became a cacophony of rattling chains, murmurs, and wailing benches. With much effort, Erwin sat in the witness chair to plead his own case.

"Mr. Erwin," Steed began, "in what capacity did you serve on the Bellmead Plantation?"

"As an assistant to the overseer."

"Was this your first opportunity to work on a farm or plantation?"

"No Sir."

"Then you did not 'materialize' from the blue with wild boasts about your knowledge of agriculture?"

"No Sir."

"At any time during your stay at Bellmead, did you seek to rob the Mallory family of its property or desire harm to come to any of its members?"

Erwin looked beseechingly at the family occupying the front row. Throughout his declaration, his eyes never left theirs. "The Mallory family is the kindest group of folks anyone could meet. Never once did they treat me with anything but respect nor berate me for my position as a hired man."

He paused. "I could never hurt them. What happened to Mrs. Thomas was a tragedy that none of us could have foreseen or prevented."

"How did you happen to arrive at the tracks that fateful night?"

Returning his full attention to his counsel, Erwin replied, "I was sent to find our head overseer, Mr. Henry Monroe, which I did. His body as well as those of a slave woman and her child lay in the field."

His voice took on that of an errant child hoping to convince his father to accept his reasoning. "That's when I began a pursuit in that direction." The defendant pivoted in his chair, his expression pleading with the jury for each of its members to believe him.

"Thank you, Mr. Erwin."

From his seat, Nate Woodard initiated his assault. By the time his questioning had ceased, he was learning over the witness, pointing an accusatory finger in the defendant's face.

"So you expect this jury to believe that you just 'happened' upon the spot exactly where the scents would end?"

"I knew that they must have gone that way."

"Have you any tracking experience, Mr. Erwin?"

"No Sir."

"You're part bloodhound, perhaps?"

The spectators smirked.

In a characteristic move, Woodard changed tactics quickly, confusing Erwin, which resulted in his fatal response.

"Ever been to Memphis?"

"No, Mr. Woodard."

"Then Mr. Le May never sent you into the city on some sort of errand?"

"Never."

"I don't doubt that a bit, son, but what I do doubt is whether you ever saw Mr. Le May before this trial."

His voice rose like that of a revival preacher. "You never worked a day on his plantation!" he demanded. "You've admitted that you have never been to Memphis, and Mr. Le May swears never to have met you. Now who's the liar here, boy?"

Erwin made no replies, save a fidgeting that strained the old wood chair in which he sat.

"Is it true that you counted the abolitionist preacher, Jonas Armitage, as your employer."

"Jonas Armitage was never my employer!" ralled the accused.

"Have you ever met Armitage or attended one of his rallies?"

"Yes," he weakly replied.

"And were you not one of the infiltrators sent by Armitage to coordinate a massive rebellion of Southern slaves?

The silence continued.

"You swore to God, boy. You going to lie to Him, too?"

"I was." Erwin's voice faltered. "But I never meant for anyone to die, most assuredly not Miss Mandy."

Woodard returned to his table, leaving a broken man sobbing into his own hands.

The jury wasted little time in deliberation, its foreman proclaiming the verdict as if it were a personal vendetta against the defendant.

Fearing a lynch mob, Lowell ordered the execution the following day. In anticipation, a gallows had been constructed before the trial convened.

The South Carolina sun shone brilliantly on Jasper Erwin's last day of life. He marched stoically to his fate. Before the hood was placed upon his head, he proclaimed with clarity. "God speed the day when all men shall be free."

His words and the sound of the springing trap echoed in the mind of Jed Thomas for the rest of his days.

Chapter Thirty-Three

Montgomery, Alabama, June 1863

Since his arrival in the former Confederate capital, Miles Davis became more soundly convinced of the rationale behind the nation's relocation of its foremost city. Lacking the elegance, charm, or even the sophistication of a Richmond or a Charleston, Montgomery, Alabama, in many aspects bordered on the primitive. This thought was reinforced by Miles' determination to remove the sandy poultice clinging to his once polished boots. This same mixture mired carriages and prevented pedestrian travel whenever the city was dealt one of its frequent cloudbursts.

To be fair, the first-time visitor had marveled at the view of the Roman Capitol which was built on the city's Main Street. Stretching from the bluffs that cut down to the Alabama River, the street was often crowded with the traffic of daily life, hampered by its poor conditions. The hilly terrain of Montgomery had reminded him somewhat of Richmond when he had toured the city on foot, often venturing down irregular arteries that jetted from the city's core.

As opposite in locations as in clientele were the state capital's two Main Street hotels. Frequented by those delegates who convened at the Confederacy's birth, the Exchange boasted first class accommodations. As then, the hostelry owners were Yankees, endured because of the expertise in hotel management. The Exchange was fondly appreciated and proudly extolled by patrons and townsfolk alike for its superiority to the Southern run Montgomery Hall.

A haven for saddle sore cowboys, livestock traders, and country merchants, the Montgomery House appealed to those more accustomed to bugs and bunks and most appreciative of any place to sleep off the ground. It was here that Miles spent a sleepless night anticipating this evening's encounter and swatting the invading hordes.

Climbing the stairs to his room, he noted the presence of more of the city's street than he had left out of doors. An otherwise motionless mongrel asleep on the stairs lifted one eye to glare at him as he passed, irked by the unwelcome interruption of his nap. Once on the second floor, Davis located the room, where he knocked twice.

The door was opened by a man whose obvious Hispanic features made him somewhat of an oddity so deep within the Confederacy. Juan Quintero maintained a home in northern Mexico but had proclaimed himself a citizen of the fledgling nation he now served. By the sheerest of luck, Quintero managed to volunteer his expertise to President Thomas. Under Jefferson Davis, the Confederacy had become a bureaucracy entangled in fraud and red tape. When Quintero arrived in Richmond, he called at several governmental offices, meeting with delays, blunders, and indifference to his offer to become a liaison between the Confederate states and the anti-Juaristas. After two weeks of fruitless waiting at first one governmental office and then another, the determined Quintero managed to approach the President's table at the Spotswood. Seized immediately by the startled body guards, the Mexican turned Confederate pled his case as he battled the strong arms of his captors.

Matching only his sympathies for the Confederate cause was Quintero's hatred for Benito Juarez. It was to this end that the Mexican patriot had battled, concentrating his efforts in the northern territory of his homeland. He now possessed invaluable contacts and personal friendships with those whose covert or ostensible activities united them against the dictates of Mexico's president.

Within the confines of the President's carriage, Quintero outlined his plan to the Confederate leader. A deposed Juarez would put an end to the South's woes as well as free Mexico from tyranny.

"My friend," greeted Quintero. The Mexican viewed Miles as a kindred spirit, of sorts, admiring his more humble beginnings and his fierce loyalty and dedication to his country. In anticipation of his arrival, the host had poured two glasses of whiskey, one of which he offered to his guest.

Feeling the effects of the burning liquid as it traveled down his throat, Miles remarked, "I must remember to pack a store of this for my journey."

"I fear there will be little time for pleasure."

From his companion's drawn expression, Miles' usual carefree attitude hardened in response.

"Although," Quintero continued, "Governor Vidaurri has assured me of the complete cooperation of the anti-Juaristas in Nueve Leon, the mission into Mexico will be a perilous one.

Juarez has increased patrols in the north of Mexico, striking several blows against those who are even remotely suspected of disloyalty to him." He shook his head in disbelief. "There are those who prefer gold to the freedom of their countrymen, and until those traitors are eliminated, we must be on our guard."

Quintero removed a worn carpetbag from underneath the room's single bed. Extracting a map, he rolled it across the small table, weighing the unruly edges with objects close at hand. As the men leaned over the table, the Mexican gentleman designated the specific location about which he spoke.

"In the village of San Pablo, you will find a small church."

"Are you certain that our trust in these people is well-founded?"

Though Miles' question angered him, Quintero smiled reassuringly. When would his adopted countrymen understand that theirs was not the only cause for which men would place their lives in jeopardy? Had Davis but witnessed a village after the Juaristas had abandoned it, he would have known the fervency of hatred with which his people battled this butcher and his hirelings.

"My people will not fail, for we, too, believe in honor."

Privy to the sensitive undertakings which resulted in a cargo of Southern cotton's departure from New Orleans in the bowels of a Thomas ship flying the Mexican colors and captained by an able man of Quintero's choosing, Miles suddenly realized the offensive nature of the question which had precipitated his companion's thinly-veiled remark.

Haltingly, Miles began, "Certainly... I did not mean to..."

Cut short by Quintero, he let the matter drop.

"Father Reynaldo awaits your confession. The Father is a most noble gentleman, a product of an influential Monterrey family and a man whose loyalty is without question. Through him, you will learn the location of the arms and provisions you desire."

Quintero straightened, indicating the conclusion of the briefing.

Extending his hand, Miles prepared to leave.

"When will we have the opportunity to meet again?"

"I will leave tomorrow for Richmond, where I feel assured that President Thomas will have my future well planned. Perhaps he will allow us to combine our talents in some future service to the nation."

As Quintero closed the door, his eyes fell on the map still spread across the scarred table. At that moment, the will of the curled paper overcame the empty glass which had lost the fight to control it. Snapping back into a roll, the force sent the glass crashing to the floor, where it splintered into numerous pieces. Instinctively, he crossed himself, uttering a hasty prayer. Though he placed great confidence in skill and planning, Juan Quintero was an earnest believer in omens.

Chapter Thirty-Four

San Pablo, Mexico, July 1863

Slowly rising from the altar in the front of the adobe chapel of San Pablo, Father Reynaldo's ever vigilant ears detected the closure of the door of the confessional booth. As he approached his side of the confessional, his thoughts remained on the matter he had just beseeched the Blessed Virgin to take to her Son. The concern, the fear that pervaded his every thought, was not for his personal safety. As a man of God, he knew the protection of the Saints. It was for his parishioners, a destitute flock of old men, women, and children that he prayed.

How much comfort could he continue to offer when the Juaristas raided the villages of Mexico at will forcing the able-bodied men into the army, raping the young women, and stealing what items of value they could pillage from the poor? Following just such a raid, he had journeyed to Monterrey in hopes of securing some semblance of protection for San Pablo.

Employing the influence of his family's name, the Father had gained access to Governor Vidaurri. Ushered into the library of the Governor's palatial villa, Reynaldo pulled a volume of interest from the shelf. As he caressed the costly leather binding, he saw only its worth in corn meal for the hungry in his church. That God could allow such disparity among His children plagued him and incessantly challenged his faith.

The arched door opened to admit the Governor, a portly contemporary of Reynaldo's beloved father. Santiago Vidaurri was struck at once by the boy's appearance. Comparing him to his own sons, Reynaldo was thin, his face had the calloused coarseness of a peasant's. The heartache he felt was soothed by the knowledge that with Don Sebastian's backing, Reynaldo would soon be a cardinal and perhaps attain the pontiff's throne some day, with the blessing of the Virgin and the well-placed generosity of the Cuellar family.

The Governor of Nuevo Leon embraced the young priest. "It is so very good to see you. Tell me, how long has it been, a year perhaps?"

"A little over a year, Sir, the christening of my sister's youngest, I believe."

"Of course, of course. The pride of your parents was without limit. To have your son officiate at the christening of a grandchild is a joy few can experience." Santiago seated himself, gesturing to a leather armed chair that befit the Spanish décor. "What brings you to Monterrey?" Abruptly he stopped, somewhat alarmed at a realization, "Your family enjoys good health, I hope?"

"The Lord is generous to my family; however, He sent me to you to secure your help for my humble parishioners."

Puzzled, the Governor replied, "What do you wish of me?"

Following his detailed accounting of the villagers' woes, Father Reynaldo sat back, awaiting a response.

"I am gratified that you have come to me, Reynaldo, for I have loved you as one my own sons."

He hesitated, contemplating the wisdom of his next question. "You can assure me that none of the peasants supports that criminal, Juarez?"

"Governor?"

The word was more of a plea than a question.

"Then I have a most perilous undertaking for San Pablo. If successful, the Juaristas will be dealt a severe blow."

"And if it fails?" inquired the priest.

Vidaurri shrugged. "You live in constant fear of just such a fate, do you not?" His eyes narrowed. "Then the waiting will cease." Sensing Father Reynaldo's reluctance, he plunged into his explanation. "You are acquainted with Juan Quintero?"

"Only by reputation."

"Then you are aware of his ties with the American Confederacy. You must also know that Quintero's hatred of our esteemed President began long before this war with the Southern Americans. In a very real sense, the war was the catalyst which drove Quintero to denounce his Mexican citizenship." Suddenly conscious of the impropriety as a host, the Governor interjected, "May I offer you refreshment?"

A wave of the priest's hand served to decline the offer.

"Recently Quintero met with me, in secret of course, on behalf of their President Thomas, seeking the cooperation of those Mexican citizens who oppose Juarez. As you must also be aware, the war is going poorly for the Confederacy. Badly in need of arms and other supplies its government cannot provide with its increasingly worthless currency, Thomas is most willing to negotiate a mutually advantageous arrangement which will arm both his troops as well as those patriots who oppose Juarez within Mexico itself."

Intrigued, Father Reynaldo urged him to continue.

"All that remains for the Confederacy to bargain with or sell are its cotton and tobacco stores whose commercial sale is directly controlled by the government itself. As we speak, a Confederate ship with our flag and crew is approaching California, loaded with Thomas' ante."

"But California is under United States control," said Father Reynaldo.

The older man smiled with the wisdom of age.

"As we are under Juarez's. Opportunities flourish in times of war, Father, and these men are most anxious to trade for the items we desire, especially as the Confederacy is willing to settle for half of the market value of its crops."

"And what role would a remote village like San Pablo play?"

"As I have said, the Confederate Army is in desperate need of these supplies; therefore, the return voyage around the Cape is too costly. Instead, the cargo will be shipped as far down the coast of Mexico as possible where Loyalist forces will intercept them. In short, San Pablo will store the cache until the Confederate troops arrive to collect their goods."

The young Father laughed aloud. "Surely the Confederates are not so foolhardy as to believe that such a massive store of supplies can be smuggled over miles of rugged terrain behind their enemy's own lines?"

"What alternative do they have, Reynaldo?"

Waving his hand in a gesture of dismissal he added, "What happens to these Confederates and their supplies is of no consequence to us. Our portion of the arms will remain safely concealed in San Pablo until such time as we have need."

Seated within his side of the confessional, Father Reynaldo slid open the panel which would allow a verbal exchange with the penitent sinner whose identity would remain unknown.

"Forgive me, Father, for I have sinned."

At the sound of the familiar request's delivery in an English so obviously Southern, the priest's heart caught in his throat.

"Yes, my son."

"I have failed to forgive my enemies."

"Captain Davis?"

"Yes, Father."

"Go into the chapel to pray while I determine if we are alone."

Captain Davis' reply was the opening of the well-worn confessional.

Waiting a few seconds, the Father emerged, taking what appeared to be a typical walk through his chapel. Save for a kneeling peasant whose sombrero hung down his back from a cord, the church was empty.

Cautiously, Reynaldo approached the praying figure. "Follow me."

The two men stole silently down a narrow hall and entered the Spartan quarters in which the Father lived.

Against one wall, a neatly made cot stood. Near it, a crude table and a single chair completed the furnishings. A colorful Mexican blanket closeted the priest's other raiments. Over the cot a crucifix was suspended from a sagging nail. Except for a high window, the walls of the room were completely barren.

"Your men, Captain?" inquired Reynaldo as he offered his visitor the only chair and seated himself on his crude bed.

"Quintero's maps were invaluable, allowing us to locate the trail into the mountains and the abandoned mining camp with very little difficulty."

"Excellent. If you will excuse me, I will change and we can join them." Disappearing behind the serape turned partition, Reynaldo left Miles Davis with his thoughts.

As he stood and stretched himself, Miles winced from the soreness of the trail. There was little doubt his time at Thomas Shipping had softened him. Laughing to himself, he patted his peasant attire, a far cry from his Charleston mode of day. There was a compelling urge to pace; however, the confines of the "monk's cell" prevented more than a few steps in any direction. True, the mission had proven incredibly simple. Traveling by night the troops bivouacked at Quintero's determinations. The man was a genius. With a glance toward the crucifix, he silently thanked God for the man and his service to the Confederate States of America.

Father Reynaldo's transformation from man of God to Mexican villager complete, the two mounted horses and rode toward the encampment. A continued sign of the Lord's intervention, the night was filled with starts and enough moonlight to illuminate the paths without drawing unwarranted attention to the nocturnal travelers.

The reticence of the priest discouraged Davis from conversation, thus the men rode in virtual silence deep into the bowels of the mountains. As the serpentine path narrowed, Father Reynaldo's horse reared, startled by the abrupt sighting of a trio of armed riders. In flawless Spanish, one demanded their identities.

Recognizing the three from among the Texicans removed from Hood's command for their familiarity with the enemy's tongue, Miles announced himself to his men, relieved to be reunited with his force of some one hundred men who concealed the horses, wagons, munitions, and supplies bartered for Southern cotton and tobacco.

Reaching the center of the camp, Father Reynaldo distinguished two of his parishioners as they carried hay and water for the horses contained in a hastily improvised corral. Though their labors were meant for men much younger, the stooped backs of the peasants, hardened by years of endless toil, shouldered their burdens without complaint. Tomorrow they could return to their families, having earned for San Pablo that which would protect them from Juarez's marauders.

It was the Father's first trip to the site in a week, and the alterations in appearance were startling. With the addition of the Southern troops, the area was bustling with activity even at this late hour. Lanterns swung in passing hands as soldiers readied themselves for their impending journey. Also evident was the darkened adobe dwelling which had once held slumbering miners, now enlivened by men who would extract greater riches from the nearby tunnels. As he passed its opened doorway, he saw these new inhabitants sprawled across the dirt floor and covered with coarse army blanketing. An occasional soldier stirred amid the cacophonic snoring which filtered out into the night.

Unsure of his role, the priest aimlessly followed the Southern captain as he entered a sentry guarded mine. Once inside the winding tunnel, blazing torches illuminated an unsteady path.

"Glad to see ya back, Captain," greeted a Confederate who was securing a covering over one in a seemingly infinite line of supply wagons. "We'll be ready to pull out tomorrow night, as planned."

As the soldiers conversed, Father Reynaldo reinspected the payment San Pablo would receive, reassuring himself of its existence. Lifting the shroud which protected it from the elements within the cave, he gently stroked the barrel of a gatling gun as he became lost in thought concerning its placement within the village and those he would select to man it.

"The inventory appears to have been delivered as promised, Captain. The breech-loading carbines will go a long ways to help our boys whip them Mexicans." Startled by his own offense, he quickly recounted, "them Juaristas." He needn't have concerned himself, for the padre was deep within himself and oblivious to the activity around him.

"And the medical supplies?" queried Davis.

"Are still being checked, but the doc was like a kid at Christmas. He says they're worth more to us than the rifles, but I don't see how he figures that to be."

A sudden volley of gunfire incited panic within the mine. Reacting instinctively, Miles barked orders at his subordinates, sending them to their arms and the mouth of the cave.

At the camp's center soldiers responded to the unseen foe. Several bodies lay sprawled in grotesque contortions, felled by enemy fire before they could reach their weapons or cover. Though unfamiliar with their surroundings, confused by the darkness, and overcome with the surprise of the attack, the Confederates managed some semblance of order as they returned fire. First one, then another Southerner shouted the sighting of the guerrillas, thus directing the fire of his fellow soldiers into the night.

Methodically the Juaristas eked down the mountain's side and into the encampment, easily overrunning the outnumbered defenders. Pinned inside the cavern, Miles ordered the gatling gun readied. The combined strengths of the men forced the heavy weapon to a point at the entrance. Force fed with munitions, the gun's barrel began to revolve at the urging of the hands of the man of peace.

The camp secured, the raiders initiated an assault against the mine, only to be repelled by the deadly fire of the gatling gun. The futility of repeated charges was soon evident to the Juarista commander. An instruction to his lieutenant sent a quaking private crawling toward the cavern. He was easily in range of the belching weapon, but the midnight obscured Father Reynaldo's vision as he aimed chest high. Watching intently, the soldier timed his movements with the oscillation of the turret. When the fiery blasts turned opposite his position he struck a match. Hurling the ignited explosive toward the mine, he forced himself to the ground, covering his head with his arms, prepared for what he incorrectly perceived to be the imminence of his own death.

The citizens of San Pablo rested peacefully, save for Domingo Ortiz. Sleep eluded him, causing him to rise often to gaze out his adobe hovel toward the mountains. On each trip, Domingo's eyes traveled over toward the hearth in which were now concealed five pieces of gold. When the explosion rocked the village, Ortiz crossed himself and fell to his knees. As he prayed, he wondered if even the compassionate Mother of Christ would intercede for a man who had killed a priest.

Chapter Thirty-Five

Richmond, Virginia, July 1863

Président Jedediah Thomas pushed himself away from the desk that the citizens of the Confederacy had elected him to occupy. Outside his office the constant hammering, which marked the construction of a reviewing stand, destroyed his concentration. These and similar preparations for the Confederacy's Independence Day celebration served to boost the declining morale of the Southern citizenry.

The people most assuredly were in need of something to brighten their lives. It was as though God had turned His back on the South. With the loss of the majority of their slaves, the plantations' masters, left with few options, took to their own fields. Slave traders rushed to resupply them, but even the most affluent of the owners lacked sufficient funds to replace the slaves lost to the revolt. There were rumors of slaves dying en masse, chained and abandoned in ship holds by merchants unable to market them and refusing to bear the added expense of feeding their cargos. Jed shuddered at the plights of these helpless men and women.

Those planters managing to sow their crops fell victim to insects or diseases which damaged the plants before the harvesting of any of the South's money crops.

The chances for profitable cotton sales of the healthy crops were indeed promising; however, the decreased acreage, which the absence of slave labor necessitated, would result in little more than a break even situation for most.

Yet of all the Confederacy's woes, the rampant inflation plagued the young President most. He'd witnessed the women shopping with wads of Confederate bills receiving few goods in exchange. Prices throughout the South had doubled, tripling in the urban areas. In Richmond a thirty pound sack of flour had escalated in price from one dollar and fifty cents to three dollars and seventy-five cents, coupled with coffee's rise from a four pound bag once going for fifty cents to the identical bag now bringing an unheard of twenty dollars, Southerners could not afford to feed themselves.

Congress' enactment of a law prohibiting the use of United States currency, predictably spawned a black market in which anything became available, providing the buyer possessed Union greenbacks, gold, or jewelry. But there was a limit to such resources.

To battle the stifling heat, his swallowtail coat lay abandoned on his settee, and his rolled shirtsleeves exposed his dampened arms. Reclining on the sofa, he closed his eyes as he massaged his pounding temples. Jed began to reflect upon the past two years. So much change had occurred both in his country and his personal life.

He remembered the initial firing on Fort Sumter. People danced and cheered in the Charleston streets as the cannonading reverberated from the bay. The city's most elegant ladies lined rooftops for better views of the bay and the festivities below. As he and Stewart walked by one of these homes, belles adorned with palmetto cockades threw flowers. Had it only been two years since he and Stewart led green recruits to a battlefield in search of excitement and glory? Was it within that time frame that he became both a husband and a widower?

His thoughts drifted to the conscription riots, staged to demand repeal of the law. How different from the days when he and his kind fought each other for positions in enlistment lines. North Carolina's refusal to send troops to the ever intensifying war in Texas or allow the conscription of personal arms for military use was yet another symptom of his country's widening schism. Now Mississippi and Alabama were following suit, demanding that its men be returned to plant and harvest. Jed was not unsympathetic to their needs. With most of the slaves gone, someone had to produce the nation's goods and food.

The young President considered his conflicting views. His loyalty to the Confederacy was not in doubt, but his pro-slavery resolve was dwindling, as was his belief in states' rights. Daily he saw the detrimental results of states who proclaimed allegiance to self before the national government. Could he continue to condone the punishments for runaway slaves or sanction an increase of slave importation? Should he send troops to seize much needed uniforms in the mills hoarded by North Carolina's Governor Vance? Such indecision brought Jed to his feet.

He snapped open his pocket watch, noting the hour. He should have received his daily briefings by now. Especially important was a dispatch he expected from Yancey and Judge

Post, the Confederacy's envoys to Europe, due to make shore any day. The negotiations of these men were crucial to the nation. At Jed's insistence, another effort had been launched to secure loans for the Confederacy's dying economy, heretofore denied by the countries of Europe. Influenced by the pamphleteer, Robert J. Walker, who attacked the solvency of the Confederate fiscal system, Europe balked. Not only did it refuse to exchange Confederate currency on the world market, but it feared the loss of trade with the Union as punishment for aiding the Confederacy after a collapse of the rebellious South. To combat these apprehensions, Jed had outlined a fiscal plan for the nation in which a conversion from agriculture to industry was paramount.

"Damn Daniel Adamson," he shouted aloud. "So help me, I will take the greatest pleasure in personally executing you."

Not, he mused, that the capture of the infamous man responsible for the rape of a nation and the deaths of countless individuals appeared imminent. The man was an apparition, evading the combined Pinkerton and Southern forces seemingly at will.

From the outer office, Stewart's voice became evident. Ducking his head in the door, Jed's most trusted advisor questioned him.

"Have you a minute to spare?"

"Always."

In his hand was a heavy knapsack bearing the CSA inscription. "I thought you might like to see one before they are shipped to the front."

Placing it upon the desk, Stewart began unloading its contents of writing paper, envelopes, pens, ink, pencils, blacking, tobacco, twine, cotton strips for wounds, needles, thread, button, and eating utensils. With interest, the President watched Stewart replace the articles and fold two blankets which he inserted on the outside and covered with an oilcloth. Stewart and Jed both began to laugh.

"Can you really envision a soldier carrying all this along with his rifle, cap and cartridge boxes, and a canteen in the Texas heat?" asked Stewart.

"Another example of Legislators who have never been soldiers approving supplies." Pointing to the oilcloth, Jed added, "I'm not even sure that Texas has rain."

Petersen's knock put an end to their levity. "The Major has arrived, Sir."

"Send him in."

Jed approached the opened door and embraced his brother-in-law. "Thank God you're safe, Andrew."

"Fact finding missions are hardly as dangerous as a battle, Mr. President."

After pouring them all refreshing minted tea, Jed urged Major Mallory to present his report on conditions at the front. Painfully obvious to Jed was Andrew's marked weight loss of some twenty pounds.

"It is difficult to know where to begin, Jed. As you suspected, things are worse than you had been led to believe. The men lack the supplies necessary to sustain the War."

"But we keep the Commissary Department busy day and night shipping materials," interjected Kane.

"It's reaching the actual troops, now that is the problem." Mallory began to elaborate. "The roads in Texas are often primitive at best, making wagon travel difficult and lengthy." Sighing, he continued. "The railroads are little better. Supply trains must be unloaded to wagons due to an inability to travel the tracks in some of the regions."

"Have the tracks been sabotaged?" questioned Jed.

"Hardly, the rail gauges seldom match, and when they do, there's the added problem of railroad owners demanding fees for their sections, at inflated prices I might add."

"Again the patriotism for our Glorious Cause astounds me," Jed reflected sourly. At his encouragement, laws had been enacted to prosecute profiteers and smugglers. Graft was rampant throughout the South, beginning with the common farmer withholding crops until prices soared even higher or smuggling his harvests North or into the territories. Some large plantations openly defied his orders to abandon cash crops for food stuffs. Those goods that actually reached the market fell victim to profiteers who hoarded them, all the while declaring artificial scarcities. One such operation involved the essential commodity, salt. Without it meat spoiled on its way to feed the hungry troops. Two such speculators hung for their roles in the salt fiasco.

Immune from punishment were the sutters, whose ladened wagons traveled from camp to camp peddling fresh fruits, soft drinks, candy, canned fruits, and salt fish at inflated prices. Often soldiers spent most of their pay at these wagons, and following overindulgence, spent the next day unfit for duty.

As much as he abhorred the citizens who defrauded the government and punished the soldiers, it was corrupt military personnel who angered him most. Not two weeks prior had a supply officer been court-martialed for falsely condemning barrels of food stuffs, then selling them on the black market. Even more galling was the resale of some of the barrels to the government.

"General Lee requires more troops and weapons. The conscripted soldiers just cannot replace the soldiers we lose."

Jed shook his head and pointed to his desk. "These recent casualty lists support Lee's requisition."

"It's more than just the mini-balls and artillery fire." Andrew inched forward, his expression grim. "Three out of every four deaths are from disease."

"Preposterous!" exclaimed Kane. "Andrew, I've been a soldier, and I never…"

"Fought in a conscripted army," interrupted the Major. "You fought along side gentlemen that are not volunteering as they did for Sumter and are exempt for business reasons or who pay substitutes in order to avoid service. A prime example is my brother, Dorian. Of the gentlemen there, the majority refuse to perform duties they deem beneath them, such as digging latrines. My men are mostly sharecroppers and rural, poor Whites who come to us carrying disease and unexposed to the most common disease. When you add exposure to the contrasting seasonal temperatures of Texas, the dysentery, mosquitoes, a substandard diet, why we deplete our numbers before the battle begins. And I won't even discuss the staggering rate of syphilis.

"When I talked to Skylar outside of San Antonio, he begged me to make you aware of the lack of medicines and anesthetics. Jed, if you had to witness just one of the poor devils who has to undergo amputation without anesthesia. And the disgusting reuse of dirty bandages taken off the dead. Well, it's no wonder desertion is rampant. It takes a mighty lot of loyalty to stay with an Army that barely feeds and clothes you or seldom pays you, especially when your family needs you at home to keep your farm from foreclosure."

"How are the weapons holding out?" asked Stewart after a long silence brought about by the Major's depressing accounts.

"If we could import the more modern weapons of our enemy rather than depending upon pillage during battle, it would be of great help. It's a credit to our soldiers' ingenuity the way they alter their ammunition when our supplies are depleted."

"It takes money, trade, or credit," remarked Jed, "none of which exists in any supply."

"Joe Anderson does an extraordinary job at Tredegar," added Kane. "It astounds me what he can do with melted bells and household goods. Why he's casting everything from nails and locomotive wheels to boiler plates."

Jed stood, recalling the scheduled conference with Henry Foote and Howell Cobb. The two were menaces, forever requesting, no demanding that he share their viewpoints and enact their programs for fiscal recovery which just so happened to benefit their interests.

"Thank you, Andrew. I'll expect you at dinner this evening, and you can continue. Unfortunately, I must face even more discouraging developments at the hands of Foote and Cobb."

"Let me accompany you and see that you get settled in," offered Kane.

After the men left Jed buried his face in his hands, the burdens of his office weighing heavily upon his wearied shoulders. Opening his eyes, the Brady photograph beckoned him. Removing it from its perch, he gazed at the likeness of Clarissa Morgan. Why was he unable to exorcise himself from this woman?

Even as he sat inside the picketed enclosure of the Mallory cemetery listening to the reverend extol his virtues as a faithful husband, the words spoken to comfort, racked his soul with guilt.

He never deserved Mandy, who freely gave him her heart, asking nothing in return, save his love and fidelity. The knowledge that he denied her half his heart consumed him with remorse. If there had been no War, no women lost amid a frenzied retreat, if Stewart had not granted her passage, if…if… would Mandy be alive today?

"Mr. President," Petersen called in an unusually strident voice.

"Yes?" Jed answered.

"Sir, I have beaten the door relentlessly. Please excuse me for interrupting, but I feared for you!"

Fumbling at his sleeves, Jed freed his secretary from blame. "Think nothing of it. My mind was miles away. Are they here?"

The President's growing distaste for the Legislators did not escape the sharp eyes of Petersen. "I am afraid so. With your approval, I shall announce an urgent matter requiring your attention after fifteen minutes."

Jed smiled broadly, "Petersen, you are a gift from God. Let no one tell you otherwise."

Leaving to summon Foote and Cobb, Petersen reflected upon his employer. Unquestionably, Jed Thomas was the gift. Davis could never have piloted the Confederacy through the undertows that daily threatened it.

"Jed my boy!" Cobb exclaimed as Jed braced for his characteristic back pounding greeting.

Without waiting for an invitation, both seated themselves on the sofa.

"What are your plans concerning this Mexican predicament that you've gotten us into?" asked Foote between puffs of lighting his cigar.

The decision to dispatch Confederate troops to the Texas-Mexican border had met with violent opposition led by the men he now faced. A similar meeting prior to the Legislative vote pressured Jed to appear before the Congress in support of a measure offering a compromise, relinquishing almost half the state. The President's refusal to uphold the plan he regarded as a submission to blackmail, prompted Foote's accusatory remark. Jed curbed his anger, respectful of the futility to argue with an ass whose mind was set.

"That Sir, is a matter between General Lee and myself."

"As it should be," mediated Cobb. "What Henry so ineptly expressed is our concern for the safety of our fighting boys."

"Still," Foote added, "the deployment represents a costly endeavor we can ill afford."

"And are you willing to donate to a fund to repay the Texans for their losses?"

The President's question silenced his critics.

Convinced of Jed's intentions to withhold any pertinent information, the two excused themselves for a black market bottle of Irish whiskey concealed in Foote's desk drawer.

Petersen emerged from his office. "Sir, Mrs. Kane requests a few minutes of your time."

"Show her in."

Jed again shed his coat. Catherine Kane, papers in hand, approached his desk.

"I'll only claim a moment, but I must have your approval on these purchases for the Independence Reception."

Since Jed's election, Catherine and Stewart had resided in the White House of the Confederacy to lend him moral support and to allow Catherine to better serve as Jed's official hostess, a slight his mother perpetually interjected into her letters aimed at punishing her son, only to fall far from her mark.

"Really, Cathey, whatever you desire has my sanction. I never cease to marvel at your skills and the frugality of your expenditures. I know that I don't thank you enough for all you do. The least I can manage is complete trust in your judgment."

Catherine acknowledged his compliments. Only for Jed would she endure the viscous comments, the increasing

criticism directed at a Yankee woman serving as the
Confederacy's First Lady. As for her judgment she had begun
to doubt it following the incident at the Rutherford home.

*****

Amid the clutter of rolled bandages and partially sewn
uniforms sat the flowers of Richmond womanhood. Today's
practical levee, as all such gatherings had become since the
advent of the War in Texas, was a mixture of gossip, sewing,
and bandage making. The coteries at the home of Talulah
Rutherford bore no unusual indications that would set it apart
from any other attended by Virginia socialites, save the
absence of one if its most prestigious members.

The goings on at the Capitol made it quite impossible to
include Varina Davis within this fashionable circle. To be sure,
the hostess had sent her personal invitation to the wife of their
defrocked President; however, Varina, as expected, expressed
her regrets, citing the family's impending return to their
plantation.

Talulah glanced in the direction of Stewart Kane's Yankee
wife, discovering an increasing difficulty to remain civil to the
woman. Were it not for Isabella Thomas and Catherine's
newfound position, the woman would not have been received
in this Richmond set. Now, with Jedediah Thomas'
pronouncement to have her serve as his hostess, she was
forced to endure the creature to procure the necessary
invitations to the Capital galas, for which she would have
entertained Mary Lincoln herself. At least Mary Lincoln, she
thought, was a Southerner.

"More tea, Catherine?" Talulah drawled, her manner and
smile disguising her true emotions.

"Just a bit, please. I must complement you on your table."

"Thank you, my dear. One must make such sacrifices of life's essentials, now."

As so many families near the Union boundaries, the Rutherfords suffered from the loss of their slaves. Following the success of the insurrection, vast numbers of slaves dared to stage individual and small group escapes.

"Without my Soozie, I am all but lost."

"No one would fault you, Talulah," interjected Stephanie Weston. All of us have lost at least some of our ungrateful Darkies. I suppose they are basking in the delights of freedom in the North. It just shows how little sense they have. Why, how do they ever propose to take care of themselves without anyone to tell them what to do or to provide them clothing and food when they need them?"

From across the room, a voice questioned. At seventy-five, Olivia Harold's position was hardly in jeopardy. Age, as she had often professed, allowed a woman the privilege to speak her mind regardless of whose feelings she might alienate. Thus she had exercised the prerogative for the past twenty years, much to the chagrins of those unfortunates who managed to offend the Richmond social icon. "Perhaps our new Presidential hostess will enlighten us as to the receptions our runaways are receiving in Mr. Lincoln's haven?"

The iciness unmistakable, Catherine felt a rush of color to her cheeks. In Charleston the insulating wings of Isabella Thomas shielded Catherine from overt hostilities, though she detected their existence from cautiously veiled innuendos or in snubs so slight as seating at a dinner table. Unprepared for a blatant affront, Catherine Kane responded in a manner more reminiscent of Clarissa Morgan. "How are they treated, Miss Olivia?" Catherine placed her cup daintily on its saucer, aware that all eyes were upon her and that in none lay any sympathy for her plight. "Well, first we bind their wounds that were suffered at the hands of cruel task masters. Then we give them a blessing, and like Lazarus of old, they are welcomed into Abraham's bosom."

A gasp emitted by one of the ladies caused Catherine to stop in sudden realization of her own audacity.

"And I presume that his bosom is deep within the bowels of a factory where they will labor for a pittance that will leave them hungry and threadbare and where they will most assuredly become maimed or killed in the dangerous machinery." Her speech had become adamant, and her own ample boson was heaving. "Though I suppose that their presence will free White children from a similar fate." She leaned forward, placing her gnarled hands atop a golden handled cane. "Tell us, Mrs. Kane, which makes master a better master: a Southerner who feeds, houses, clothes, and cares for his slaves or a Yankee who forces children to abandon their play and line his pockets with silver as does your own father?"

Miss Olivia's reference to the practice of child labor was indeed a bitter blow. Until the 1860 strike in Lynn, Massachusetts, the Jackson Mills had commonly employed children.

"My father is not a master of children, nor does he beat and scar his workers for minor mistakes."

Fearing irreparable results from the cat fighting Carin Wallace stood, making excuses for her hasty departure, signally the climax of the afternoon and in effect silenced the confrontation between Miss Olivia and Catherine.

As she hugged Carin in the foyer, Talulah whispered her thanks, praying that she would not be shunned by the Kane woman for allowing Miss Olivia to become so openly hostile. *Good heavens*, she thought later in the evening as she was clearing the china from the parlor, *since our victory at Manassas, the Yankees are more in control of our lives than before. Perhaps we would have fared better were we the losers?* Quickly she chastised herself for her lack of loyaly and attended to her degrading chores.

*****

But upon the matter at hand, Catherine's trust in her instincts was unshakable. "Jed, I hesitate to give you this now…"

"What is it?"

"I received a letter from Mose, and this was the envelope for you…"

"Tell Petersen to hold my appointment until I notify him."

"Certainly, supper will be waiting." She left him to his reading.

Jed examined the flawless penmanship learned at the feet of Celia Mallory. From the time he learned of his escape and that of Maizy, Jed's resentment of their desertions gradually abated, realizing that he too had risked his life and jeopardized others in the name of freedom.

Using the silver letter opener given him by his parents on the day he officially assumed the Presidency, he slit the envelope and removed its contents.

Dear Mr. President,

Maizy has asked me to write to you on her behalf. It is her one wish that you be aware of the blame she places on herself for the death of Miss Mandy. The decision to leave was a difficult one for her to make, and for that, I am directly responsible. Without my encouragement, Maizy would have remained at Bellmead.

Our flight to the North was not without great difficulties and sacrifices. The train on which we escaped was searched, but God be praised, all remained quiet, and we arrived North. Some very generous people took us to a farm where we received shelter until such time as we decided what to do with our lives.

Within a few days, Maizy and I began our walk to Washington. We were often hungry and tired during those weeks, but the Lord provided us food and shelter when our needs proved greatest.

Knowing Miss Catherine for the fine woman she is, we called upon her parents for assistance. They are good people, Mr. Jed, just like Miss Catherine. When I explained our situation to Miss Margaret and Mr. Warren, they gave Maizy a job in their home and are allowing us to live in a servant's cottage behind their home.

I am fulfilling Miss Celia's prophecy. She once told me that I would teach my people as she had taught me, and that is the purpose to which I dedicate my life. Each day I hold classes for the children of former slaves. At night their parents come to learn.

Maizy and I are married and are raising the little daughter of Pansy and Jethro. Maizy saw Henry Monroe shoot Pansy, but we had no word of Jethro. If he is still at Bellmead, please tell him that Sookie is healthy, happy, and most of all free.

Mose

Jed put the letter on his desk. At long last, he was convinced that no man possessed the right to control the freedom of another and like the feudal kingdoms of old would fall under the weight of its oppression. Such were the fates of all governments whose tyrannical rules could no longer be endured, forcing men to seek liberty regardless of the costs.

Chapter Thirty-Six

Washington, D.C., September 1863

In the twenty-five by forty, second floor office, a concerned man draped his gangly legs over a large armchair stationed in the room's center.

Through the opened windows, rays of sunlight caught the brass andirons near the marble fireplace. Spread about over the expansive cabinet table, were documents upon which the man deliberated so intently.

Abraham Lincoln abhorred the contents of the communiqué handed to him by Colonel Ward Hill Lamon. Never given to spirits, times like these could have driven lesser men to seek solace in just such a manner.

"Are you quite certain about the accuracy of these figures?" He removed his gold spectacles formerly perched upon his nose.

"Regrettably so. The South's forces are sustaining heavy losses at the hands of Juarez's army."

"But eleven thousand at Brownsville and another ten thousand at San Antonio amounts to nothing less than wholesale slaughter. Has Austin fallen?"

"At last word, the Capital remained in Southern hands; however, it too will fall by month's end."

The President shook his head in despair. "I do not understand how any army that overran the Union troops succumbs to the inferior forces of Juarez."

"Sir, the Southern supplies are woefully inadequate. As you well know, the Confederacy lacks sufficient foundaries to equip and sustain an army, especially one at its outermost borders. Considering its worth, the Confederate currency is unacceptable to foreign munition firms; therefore, the replacement of artillery and hand weapons, and other supplies are for the most part impossible."

Lincoln slowly ran his fingers through his always unmanageable hair.

"It is also my understanding that medical provisions such as morphine are in short supply. Though unreflected in the communiqué, a substantial number of casualties is the direct result of poor medical care rather than severity of wounds."

"In light of the inhumane situation, we cannot, as a Christian nation, allow such carnage to continue. I will recommend United States intervention."

"Begging your pardon, Mr. President, but I fear that little sympathy will be found for the Confederates. The memories of Bull Run are much too fresh."

The lanky President rubbed his beard in contemplation. "How long can they endure when their money is worthless, their marketable products unable to garner profits, and now an escalating conflict?" The degree of compassion Lincoln generated for all who suffered always amazed Ward Lamon.

Of anyone in the North, the President had call to rejoice at the Confederacy's troubles, yet he genuinely cared for each individual, disregarding his personal humiliation at their hands. The President's backing of aid to the slaves of the rebellion and his visits to their squatter camps touched the Colonel's heart.   Even when the Confederacy had demanded the restitution of its property as per the Treaty of Manassas, Lincoln had refused to send the slaves back to their former masters.

"Militarily, the South cannot sustain another major defeat; economically, I am not qualified to venture a guess."

Mrs. Kennedy knocked, and in response to the President's bidding, announced the arrival of his cabinet. When all were assembled, Lincoln began. "In lieu of the Confederacy's position, I requested your attendance this morning to outline procedures for readmitting the Southern states to the Union. I trust we are in agreement that a collapse of the rebellious government is imminent?" Receiving no contradictive expressions, he continued. "The proposal is simple. The individual states may comply unconditionally to these points."

He returned his glasses to their usual position far down on his nose. "Southerners must swear allegiance to the United States. Those who fail to do so will forfeit the right to vote. Secondly, those who currently or who have held offices will be unable to acquire such posts for five years. There will be a merger of the Armies with no loss of rank, and the United States will assume all outstanding debts to any nation."

Lincoln removed his glasses.

"The final provision, calling for the emancipation of all slaves, will undoubtedly meet with the most opposition."

As Lincoln anticipated, Stanton and Cameron exploded. "Mr. President, I speak for all of us when I commend your magnanimous gesture toward the Confederates; however, your proposals are entirely too lenient."

"And your terms would be, Mr. Secretary of State?"

"Most assuredly, I cannot condone the absorption of debts. The taxpayers of this country are not responsible for the financial blunders of the South. Rather the Confederacy should be monetarily liable for damages, as in any conquered nation."

Cameron added, "Nor do I trust the reinstatement of Rebel soldiers in the ranks of our military. It will lead to the rekindling of animosities, which could be disastrous should the United States find itself at war in the future." The Secretary of War looked from man to man, garnering the support they gave him in expressions, gestures, and the occasional vocal acknowledgements.

"Southern loyalty oath or not, no Rebel deserves the right to vote. Each rebellious state chose to withdraw from the Union; therefore, the citizenship of its people was invalidated."

The President calmly crossed his gangly legs and learned forward in his chair to look Stanton directly in the face. "And how, Secretary Stanton, do you propose that the Southern states pay damages when their currency is worthless? Any future revenues will be necessary to rebuild the South's economy. As far as animosities within the military," he addressed Cameron with his eyes, "I remind you that the Southern officers trained in the United States Army and at West Point, prior to secession. Regarding the validity of your last statement, our forefathers fought a Revolution to dissolve tyranny on this continent and to abolish practices such as taxation without benefit of representation." He paused to underscore his statement. "I fear, Mr. Cameron and Mr. Stanton, that you have forgotten that the South asked nothing, save peace, in the Treaty of Manassas. How can we, the losers of a conflict, demand more when we have done nothing to defeat the Confederacy?"

"I beg to differ," argued the Secretary of State. "The Union has done everything to defeat the South."

Startled by Stanton's declaration, the President's eyes flared. "If you mean to insinuate that the Union should assume vicarious credit for the abominable deeds of an opportunistic thief, then you," he pointed at Stanton, "are no better than the criminal himself. I look forward to the day he faces trial."

Cleverly concluding the debate over the South's reentry, Lincoln placed Cameron on the defensive. "Tell me Cameron, how does one individual evade capture when an entire continent searches for his whereabouts?" The President stood and positioned himself behind Cameron. "Dare I assume you have been somewhat lax in your efforts to locate Mr. Adamson?"

Lincoln's tone, unmistakably accusatory, piqued the Secretary's considerable disdain for the man he'd sworn to discredit. *How I would enjoy detailing the entirety of my debacle of the damnable Rebels he loves,* fumed Cameron. The one flaw in his scheme was his present inability to bask in the recognition due him by a grateful country.

Lincoln's assumption that the Secretary of War's silence signaled defeat, adjourned the meeting. "My proposals will be delivered to the Senators and Representatives today. Good day, Gentlemen."

Without verbal exchange, three men filed into Cameron's office. Simon Cameron addressed the Secretary of State. "Are we to sit by and allow that bleeding heart to readmit the Rebels, exempt from retribution of any sort?"

"He must still convince the Legislature of the soundness of his proposal," muttered Stanton. "After the people learn of his graciousness toward the Rebels, he'll need P.T. Barnum to hire that crazy woman opposite Mr. and Mrs. Thom Thumb. I am surprised that the master showman did not capitalize on just such a billing when the little people were guests at the White House." Then catching his own error, he recanted. "I seem to have overlooked the obvious. Barnum already boasts a trained gorilla. What are his chances with the Congress?"

"Without polling the members, it is indeed difficult to ascertain; however, we shall all call in our markers, thereby exerting pressure on them to vote against the President."

Extracting a key from his pocket, he inserted it into a locked drawer of his desk. Removing a small, tan notebook, he thumbed through its now worn pages. "I never forget those of whom a favor is owed." He stated with a note of triumph in his tone. "It is now time for some of our distinguished lawmakers to pay the piper. While you are contacting those similarly indebted to you, I will telegraph Solomon Edwards, Jonas Armitage, and others whose political influence carries a great deal of weight. Gentlemen, we have work to do."

Chapter Thirty-Seven

Richmond, Virginia, September 1863

P resident Jedediah Thomas reread the generous terms offered by Lincoln for the South's readmission to the Union. As Stewart Kane accepted the document, his friend spoke, "You find the terms more than equitable."

"Did you assume that a man like Lincoln would offer anything less?"

"No, though I did fear the more radical Republicans who control much of the government would exert enough pressure to impose strict, if not, devastating terms in order to avenge their honor at the expense of our suffering."

Stewart only nodded, sympathizing with the swelling numbers of unfortunates unable to grow or purchase the necessities of life. It was critically obvious to both men that the Congress realize the collapse of the Glorious Cause before countless innocents perished in the name of honor.

Breaking the silence, Jed interjected, "I understand Lincoln's proposal passed by the most narrow of margins."

"The numbers are unimportant; just the results matter. Nevertheless, I do fear an equally close vote this morning."

"By all that is holy, Stewart, why can't they see the futility of it all? Our economy is decimated, and the casualties in Texas are appalling. We haven't the supplies to feed and arm our troops. Why, there's nothing to prevent Juarez from amassing even more territory than Texas."

Stewart eyed his friend intently. "Perhaps the Union's intention to curtail Juarez is directly tied to its moderate readmission terms? Knowing that we cannot continue much longer, the less progress Juarez makes, the easier he is to rout. Don't you agree?"

"It certainly has merit," replied Jed. Removing his watch, he assessed the time, closing it with its distinctive click. "Well, the time has come to end a dream."

Stewart placed his arm around his friend, and the two left the office.

On the Capitol floor, the usual flurry of activity was in progress as each Legislator extolled his stance at the expense of his opposition's viewpoint. Working nonstop, printers had prepared and distributed Lincoln's plan; therefore, when the Speaker sounded his gavel, no doubt existed as to the nature of the day's business.

Though the hour was early, the intense heat drifted through the windows. Those in the gallery struggled to breathe in the oppressively heavy air, resulting in the removal of several women overcome by the temperature and their tightly laced, whalebone corsets. Those lawmakers still in possession of body servants, benefitted from their fanning, though no efforts could dispel the heat.

"Gentlemen I refer you to the copies of the Union's proposal for readmission of the Confederate states. I will open the floor to those who wish to speak in favor of the dissolution of the Confederate States of America upon the terms so offered."

A murmur arose as all eyes strained too identify any traitors in their midst who dared support the death of the Confederacy.

It was Wigfall of Texas who challenged the principles upon which the nation had been founded. "Gentlemen," he earnestly began, "as we speak men, good men, the strongest and best the South has to offer died upon the battlefields of Texas. They perish not from want of skill or courage, but from want of supplies. Their comrades in arms suffer agonies too horrible to name. Without bandages or medicines to heal their patients, the surgeons must perform needed amputations, unable to administer morphine. And still Juarez comes, freshly armed to slaughter our sons and brothers. At the fall of Austin, our boys resorted to the robbery of fallen Mexicans to obtain ammunition, weapons, and rations."

Wigfall continued, "I ask you, my fellow lawmakers, is this what we envisioned at Sumter and Manassas? Is this the noble intent of our secession, to see our lands overtaken by a dictator and our men slaughtered on the soil we strove to give them? No, the Confederate States of America was founded to enhance the rights of the sovereign states, to allow us to own our slaves and live in peace without the interference of the Yankees. Now, our slaves are, for the most part, gone. Few of you have the money to purchase more. Our way of living is dead. I never believed that I could utter these words, but I must, for the sakes of us all, for our women and our starving children. We have fought the good fight, but we are defeated."

The chamber, numbed by the intensity of the Texas Legislator's delivery and the reality of his words, grappled with its emotions. Theirs had been an effort, founded on intrinsic principles, but which was the more dishonorable, to admit defeat or to sacrifice lives in the name of honor?

Undeterred by Wigfall's passionate oration, Ethelbert Barksdale of Mississippi, requested the floor. "Sons of the Confederacy, we were all duly elected by the citizens of our states to represent the rights and wills of the people, not the interests of one state. Of course, Mr. Wigfall seeks readmission. His state is under siege. Much property has been lost to Juarez, including that of our esteemed colleague, who encourages you to dissolve the Confederacy to recoup his losses."

Wigfall rose from his seat, "How dare you slander me before this body?" he bellowed.

Amid the increasing temperature the ardent debate continued throughout the day. At times, lawmakers, sought comfort under the huge trees which lined the Capitol grounds. By early afternoon, exhaustion overcame sentiment, and the Speaker called for an individual vote.

The endless roll call, with prefacing remarks, tried the souls and patience of the Legislators. As the Speaker tallied the votes, the audience awaited the results in tense silence.

"Gentlemen, I regretfully inform you that the voting is deadlocked."

A prevalence of disgusted lamentations followed the Speaker's pronouncement.

It was a confident Cobb who approached the platform, signaling to the Speaker his desire to speak to him, rather than the entire governing body. In response, the Speaker squatted to his knees. Cupping his hands, Cobb shouted to the Speaker, who quickly rapped for the attention of the crowd.

"Gentlemen, gentlemen, I must remind you of the Constitution adopted by this governing body, in which we anticipated such impasses."

Unaware of the import of the Speaker's statements, Jed was angered at the futile efforts of these men to reach a decision while those they represented endured the ills thrust upon them. Lost in his thoughts, the Speaker's recitation of the Constitution escaped notice until the realization of its contents captured his full attention.

"… shall cast the deciding vote."

All eyes focused on the President, whose white knuckled hands clinched the arms of the chair in which he sat. As he assumed the podium, he caught sight of Steward Kane, who nodded his head in a silent affirmation for what Jed was about to do. The President faced his audience and began to speak in a slow deliberate voice.

"It was not long ago that I stood before you to accept the greatest confirmation of faith that one can receive from his fellowmen. I must confess that I am still awestruck by your confidence in my leadership and judgment. As President, in my service to the people of the Confederacy, I have striven diligently to place the needs of the people at the forefront of my decisions."

He stopped, thinking briefly about his next statements. "You are well aware of my love for the South and its way of life. I proudly volunteered to fight the Yankees and was blessed to have survived the conflict; however, my losses have been great."

His eyes began to fill with tears which he dabbed with his handkerchief. "In service to the Confederacy, I was absent when my wife and child were in need of my protection, a burden of guilt that I will forever carry. The knowledge that I am not alone in my grief compels me to what is best for this nation." Ladened with tears, the President's voice faltered. "Gentlemen, the Confederate States of America is no more."

Protected by Stewart and Petersen, he was ushered to a waiting brougham and driven to the White House of the Confederacy where he reclined upon the parlor sofa, totally drained, and drifted into a fitful sleep.

Chapter Thirty-Eight

Washington, D.C., the same morning

Clarissa Morgan called over her shoulder to a panic-stricken Bryan Dowd. "Don't fret, the Secretary left me his keys, and I'll locate his suggested agenda for the visiting British officers."

She scanned the room, on the off chance that the schedule lay amid the clutter that characterized her uncle's office. Removing his keys from her skirt pocket, she explored the contents of each drawer without locating the illusive agenda. Trying one last drawer, which necessitated several good tugs to open, she spied the agenda. *This drawer shouldn't be so difficult,* she told herself while she began to remove it in hopes of repairing the stubborn drawer. With the heavy unit in her lap, she blindly explored the recesses of the desk.

"No wonder," she remarked aloud, "here's the problem." Clarissa withdrew a small, tan notebook. "I bet Uncle Simon has been searching for this for ages." He really must do something about his housekeeping," she muttered as she began to flip through the pages.

The notebook appeared to be some sort of ledger, containing the names of several members of both houses of Congress, judges, a Supreme Court Justice, and various industrial giants. As she neared the rear of the book, her heart stopped. The entry marked *Daniel Adamson* glared at her from the page.

Intrigued, she gradually absorbed the import of each notation. Beginning in August of 1861, phenomenal sums were credited to the Manhattan Bank and Trust, First Bank of Philadelphia, and several other large financial concerns. The most recent entry bore the date of the previous week.

This must be the evidence Uncle Simon received from Pinkerton, she assumed, knowledgeable of Cameron's numerous encounters with the detective. *I had no idea such detailed information existed about the man.*

Looked upon by some as a national hero, of sorts, Clarissa deemed him an opportunist.

On the next page, inscribed with the name *Bill Harrison* and the identical date, she read of a substantial posting of funds. Repeating the name several times, she unsuccessfully probed her memory for the circumstances which evoked a vague familiarity. The notations proceeded with regularity until March of 1862.

There was no doubt as to the identity centered atop the next page. The Reverend Jonas Armitage's abolitionist efforts were well-known. A single cataloging in the amount of one hundred thousand dollars preceded *Paid in full.*

Fascinated by the possible bond between Adamson and the Reverend, she pressed further, briefly scanning the pages marked *J. W. Porter* and *Wyatt Humphries*. While the

Humphries page denoted only the October dating, the other contained the notation *for cotton purchases*. A February 1862 dating possessed no additional remarks.

Subsequent entries bore the foreign names of *Comte de Joliet* and *Lorenzo de Zavala* who received itemized monthly payments from October 1861 to the present month.

Tiring of the meaningless ledger, she closed the book, intent upon returning it to the desk, when the sudden entrance of Dowd startled her causing it to fall to the floor. As it landed, the leaves parted, exposing the entry of *Colonel Adam Dupree*. Clarissa immediately grabbed the leather-bound book, holding it face down in her lap.

"You certainly appear to be up to something, Miss Morgan." The lilt in his voice did little to calm her madly beating heart. "It is written all over your face, not that you aren't as lovely as ever."

"Really, Bryan, you ought to have the manners to knock. I was frightened out of my wits."

"Whatever are you hiding in your lap?"

"Aren't you familiar with it?"

"Should I be?"

"I discovered it as I searched for the agenda, which," she said as she offered him the paper, "is right here."

He accepted the schedule rather suspiciously. "You have been in here for quite some time." He waved the agenda. "This must have been concealed among the Secretary's disorder." His gesture encompassed the room.

"I think I'll tidy up a bit." Clarissa busied herself, arranging the desk in a more orderly fashion. "Now that you have your schedule, you may continue your duties."

A dubious Bryan returned to the outer office, grumbling over the wasted opportunity to be alone with Clarissa.

The woman's hand trembled as she rapidly thumbed the pages. Rereading the posting for Dupree, the puzzling ledger became all too simple. This was not a detective's sleuthing but the diary of Adamson himself.

Closing the book, she questioned her judgment. But why would Uncle Simon have the diary of Daniel Adamson concealed within his desk? She reasoned with herself, Uncle Simon must actually know the man. Pacing the office's length, she reconstructed the enigma. Vast sums credited to separate banks, funds dispersed to individuals, obviously from these accounts, and…

She crossed quickly to the desk, clawing her way through the pages. "March 1862, for cotton purchases," she muttered. Clarissa slapped the book shut, as if its closure would erase the staggering reality which she sought to deny. "Uncle Simon cannot be involved with Daniel Adamson," she stated emphatically.

She burst from the office, confronting Dowd and demanding an answer.

"Bryan, who is Bill Harrison?"

Her young admirer stared into space, summoning information long buried. "I'm not sure, but I believe he was the older gentleman whose printing establishment was vandalized some time back." He laughed aloud. "The old codger created quite a stir when the criminals attempted to take him hostage, and he foiled their plans. "Of course, none of this would have been newsworthy had he not been a criminal himself in years past."

"What sort of criminal?" she asked, bracing herself for the reply.

"Well, a counterfeiter, Clarissa. It was a printing business," he teased, accentuating the last words.

"I don't believe vandals would terrorize an old man, even if he had a criminal past."

"He claims he surprised them during a robbery, though I can't imagine that to be true when it was ten in the morning." Dowd returned to his work of filing. Pausing, he offhandedly offered her one last detail. "You might ask your uncle if you are really interested in the old larcenist."

"My uncle?"

"For some unfathomable reason, Harrison showed up here, raising a ruckus to see the Secretary right after his attempted abduction. He created such a disturbance that your uncle emerged and ushered him in, no doubt to quiet the old fellow so that the rest of us could work in peace." He ceased his filing, suddenly curious. "Why are you so consumed by him, Miss Morgan?"

Dowd's inquiry escaped Clarissa, whose emotions spiraled.

"Clarissa?"

Who would I inform, the President? Would he believe me or pronounce me daft?

"Clarissa!"

My own uncle, the leviathan in a vast undertaking to sabotage the Confederacy? She laughed aloud at the absurdity of the 'pursuit' of Daniel Adamson and his visit to Richmond on behalf of the Union.

She felt a tugging at her arm.

"Answer me!"

She regarded him by jerking her arm free of his grasp.

"I'm going home, now. If my uncle should ask for me, here are his keys." Removing the ledger from the confines of her pocket, she claimed the keys and deposited them in Dowd's hand.

"Clarissa, are you all right?"

"Of course, why wouldn't I be?

"Your behavior is incredibly..." he searched for the least offensive word, "unusual."

"Don't be absurd," she remarked, tossing her head in defiance.

From a nearby closet she reached for her bonnet and gloves. As she donned the stylish millinery, tying it fashionably at an angle, she informed Dowd.

"I merely have an errand to do."

The confused government clerk started after her as she veritably flew down the corridor, abandoning his chase in the realization that the Secretary never approved of his office being left unattended.

Several discrete inquiries led her to the printing shop of Bill Harrison. The mixture of the heat and her frenzied emotions left her breathless. Composing herself, she stopped under a shade tree outside a large church.

It appeared no different from any other street in Washington whose businesses catered to the middle and lower classes. Swinging from its rusted hinges, a sign cried out in advertisement of the skills of a dentist claiming painless extractions.

There was also a general merchantile and a smith's barn, facing the street where animals sunned themselves and drank from its muddy puddles. On the corner a young White boy peddled newspapers, loudly proclaiming the day's headlines.

Inside the printer's store, a clearly visible elderly gentleman in a trademark apron worked his press. Assured of his identity, she ventured across the street and into the printer's establishment.

"Good afternoon, Miss. What can I do for you?" Bill Harrison addressed the well-dressed lady who stood beyond his counter. It had been some time, he decided since such a lovely creature graced his shop.

"Do you manage all this unassisted?" she asked in feigned amazement.

Flattered, he smiled broadly, "I do for a fact, though it takes quite a bit from me; I'm not as young and energetic as I once was."

"I'm here on behalf of my uncle. It seems you have pleased him with your talents on several occasions."

"Indeed, and who might your uncle be?"

Clarissa bit her lip, then proceeded with a false confidence, betrayed by her quivering hands," Secretary of War Cameron."

If the mention of Cameron surprised him, he bore not sign. "And what would he require of me?"

"Something akin to his previous orders," she coolly replied.

"As your uncle knows, the plates were stolen in the robbery I experienced some time back. It would take a great deal of time and effort to duplicate them." He paused, allowing her to interpret his thinly veiled inquiry concerning his fee.

Clarissa was enjoying her role as a detective. *Perhaps Mr. Pinkerton will employ me as his first woman investigator*, she thought. "Your fee will reflect the difficulty of your undertaking," she assured.

"Then what are his precise specifications?"

"I'll return tomorrow with detailed instructions." Without further exchange, she left the shop.

Watching her leave, the printer regarded their encounter. Why would Cameron risk the forging of more bills when the Confederacy plainly recognized his shop as the source of the worthless bills? The conclusion he arrived upon sent chills up his spine. This woman was a Rebel spy. Throwing off his apron, he locked the shop and headed for the War Department.

Clarissa rounded the corner, pausing to collect her thoughts and calm her nerves. Of her uncle's involvement in the counterfeiting scheme, she harbored no doubt. As to his role in the Confederacy's other misfortunes, she lacked sufficient confirmation. Her mind was a clutter of indecision. She loved her uncle, who had given her everything including an unconditional acceptance in his world. Should she, could she confront this man to whom she owed so much? Would his reaction to her betrayal leave both Morgan women again at the mercy of her father?

She owed him the benefit of every doubt. Determining the extent of his involvement would require that she enlist the aid of someone she implicitly trusted. Her mind thus set, Clarissa Morgan hurried down the Washington Street.

*****

Arriving with Stanton and Chase at his office, the Secretary of War escorted them within its confines. As he neared his desk, the half opened drawer, hastily replaced by Clarissa, drew his attention. Frantically, he ripped the drawer from its cavity.

To the astonishment of the other Secretaries, he threw papers to the floor in violent agitation. "Dammit, Dowd, get in here!"

Seasoned by Cameron's previous outbursts, Dowd hesitantly entered.

"What is the meaning of this?" Cameron demanded, pointing toward the exposed drawer..

"I… I'm not at all sure, Sir. When Clarissa, I mean Miss Morgan, left I didn't think to check to see if she had tidied up after herself."

"Not the papers, you idiot! Why is this drawer unlocked?

Bryan Dowd faced an unenviable predicament. Should he shoulder the blame for the woman he most ardently pursued and suffer the Secretary's wrath, or should he profess her guilt? Assuming that the love of an uncle could forgive a minor error, he opted for the latter.

"I am waiting!" yelled the Secretary of War, leaning across his desk in the direction of the frightened Dowd.

"Miss Morgan located the British officers' agenda for me. I can only assume that she unlocked the desk. She was the only one to enter," his voice trailing into a whisper.

"Get her now!" he demanded.

Barely audible came the reply, "I am afraid that isn't possible, Sir."

Cameron emerged from behind the desk, exuding anger in his every motion. "You tell me everything!"

Without Chase's intervention, Cameron might well have resorted to violence. "See here Simon, calm down. The boy will explain himself," he soothed, as he directed Cameron back to his chair.

On the verge of tears, Dowd related the afternoon's encounter, detailing not only her strange actions but her persistent questioning concerning Bill Harrison.

As he finished, the Secretary waved his hand toward the door. "Go to my home and bring her back, and I want no excuses!"

"Yes Sir."

With Dowd safely out of earshot, Chase and Stanton restrained themselves no longer. "What the devil is wrong, Simon?" ordered Stanton.

"Clarissa has intercepted my ledger of disbursements for the conspiracy."

"Good heavens," Chase despaired. "She'll have to be silenced immediately."

"Don't be absurd!" he snapped, "She has possession of the book, but we cannot be assured that she understands its meaning."

Stanton argued, "Clarissa's a smart woman," he emphasized, "as you have repeatedly advised us."

Calming somewhat, Chase questioned the War Secretary, only partially convincing himself. "Perhaps you could explain its possession as a part of the evidence collected against the man?"

"Brilliant idea," Stanton praised, relaxing for the first time. His present lifestyle suited him, and he certainly held no desire to spend the rest of it at hard labor; he would sooner die.

Cameron contemplated Chase's suggestion, pronouncing it sound. "We'll sit back and await her return."

A pounding on the door startled the office occupants.

"Cameron, are you in there?" screamed a strident voice.

The three exchanged suspicious glances.

"It's me, Bill Harrison."

Simon Cameron opened the door.

Roughly pulling the aged printer into his office, he chastised, "My orders for you were to never appear at the War Department again!"

"I know you did, but this is a grave emergency." Suddenly realizing that they were not alone, Harrison stammered a lame excuse for his actions.

"Speak up man; you have no fear of anyone in this room."

"Well, Sir, a very lovely young woman called at my shop this morning, claiming to be your niece and asking me to remake the plates, on your order."

Chase sank into a chair.

Stanton mocked, "Oh, she might not understand the contents. She won't be able to connect any of us." His voice progressed into a thunderous explosion. "Well, she traced the counterfeiter easily enough, and the fool confirmed her suspicions!"

The Secretary of War inspected each face, hoping that one would side with him, thus sparing Clarissa's life. Even for Simon Cameron, the order to kill his own niece, for whom he genuinely cared, proved an arduous task. The loss of Clarissa would surely end the life of his dear sister, and the girl, after all, was like a daughter to him. Finally he spoke, "We will wait until Dowd returns. There is nothing the girl will not do for her mother. Realizing what harm might befall her with my arrest, Clarissa will be persuaded to do the right thing," the Secretary reassured everyone save himself.

If any trait outshined her beauty, it was her tenacity. Once that girl set her mind on a course of action… Well, he would see to it that they charted the same path.

Some twenty minutes elapsed, marked by mounting tension. When Dowd arrived with the report that the girl had not returned home, Cameron was finally moved to action.

"Dowd, write down exactly what she was wearing and distribute copies to each of us. We'll comb the city; she can't have gone far."

In his months of service to the capricious Secretary, Bryan Dowd had never questioned an order or pressed for an explanation. In light of the man's foul humor, he saw no reason to begin.

Cameron sectioned the city, allowing himself the most likely sector, the railway depot.

*****

Approaching the depot, Clarissa Morgan bypassed the peddlers who lined the streets selling their wares to travelers. Resisting the alluring aroma of the chestnut vendor and the distinctive crackle of the taffy seller breaking the candy with his hammer, she pressed on to the B&O Station.

Easily discernible by its gingerbread trim and dilapidated, arched doorways facing the rail side, the structure suffered from the neglect so prevalent of many of the Capital's public facilities.

Clarissa searched the slate board that identified the times and destinations of the evening trains. A train heading South ran within the hour. Starting into the depot, she spotted her uncle's landau approaching. Gathering her skirts, she darted between the trains and ran for the first that was pointing in a southerly direction.

Fearing discovery in a passenger car, she ran the length of the train until she saw a boxcar whose doors were opened. Glancing over her shoulders, she took hold of the rim of the gaping spaced and pushed herself upward. Her first attempt, failed, landing her in a heap of skirt folds upon the rocky rail bed.

Removing her gloves, she forced her body forward, lunging head first into the car. Had someone chanced to witness, he would have seen Clarissa in an unladylike pose, revealing the bottoms of leather boots as they protruded from a mass of crinoline, brown skirt, and a lace chemise. Wiggling and thrusting herself further, she maneuvered into the recesses of the boxcar. Thank God, she praised, that I abandoned those confining hoops.

Adjusting to the dim light, she surveyed her surroundings. Bales of hay, whose straggling bits covered the dirty floor, lined the width of the cars, several stacks deep. To her left, crates marked *Richmond* brought a sigh of relief. At least I'm on the right train, she thought. The sound of men's voices sent her scurrying behind the crates. Heart pounding, she crouched, straining to hear their conversation.

"All ready from this end."

"Then give 'um the signal."

Clarissa prayed that the door would remain unclosed, fearing the creatures that might lurk on board and the weather, which was unusually warm for September. Mercifully, the workmen passed, and the train's whistle announced the eminence of their departure.

Inside the station, Simon Cameron badgered the clerk for details concerning a beautiful girl in a brown dress and matching bonnet. Convinced of the man's inability to recall any ladies of quality purchasing passage that day, he left the depot and the clerk as he labored to explain his insulting choice of words to the husbands of two female ticket holders.

Cameron climbed the steps of a stationary passenger car, only to be barred by the uniformed conductor. Unable to produce a ticket, the Secretary was forced from the car amid protests which evoked both his kinship and concern for a lost daughter and his governmental office.

Impressed by neither, the conductor held fast. As the train began to inch forward, the Secretary ran beside the windows, leaping occasionally in a vain search for Clarissa Morgan.

Not until fields replaced the Washington landscape, did she venture from her hiding place. Dragging a stray hay bale in front of the door, she positioned herself to attain full advantage of the breeze and the passing countryside. Pulling her skirts above her knees and taking stock of her situation, she pried into her drawstring purse, reclaiming five dollars, an embroidered handkerchief, and the apples she carried for an afternoon refreshment.

She patted her skirt pocket, reassuring herself of the ledger's survival of the ordeal. Shining the apples against her sleeve, she considered her appearance. As she began plucking straw form her dress, the streaks of dirt and a dark, sticky substance caused her to sigh. How could she ever carry out her plan in such a state of disarray? Removing her hat and setting it to the side, some of its loosened feathers fluttered in the breeze. Five dollars would not be sufficient for a ticket, clothes, and food. I've been in more difficult straights, she reasoned. Only there was always someone for me to protect and for whom to remain strong. Now, I'm completely alone.

It was then that she heard the rustling of some hay at the right of the car. Scrambling to her feet, she concealed herself yet again. Within a few seconds she regained control and chided herself for panicking over what was undoubtedly a mouse or even a result of the constant swaying of the train. Slowly Clarissa rose to her feet. A lone board from a previous cargo in her right hand, she carefully approached the area from which the noise resulted.

Peering over the hay bales, she cringed at the sight of a ragged man sleeping on a crudely arranged straw bed. Beside him, overturned and drained, lay a crockery jug, which accounted for his continuous sleep during her arrival. Perched upon the bales below her were a rucksack, and a pearl-handled knife, further evidence of his character.

Afraid to move lest she awaken her fellow stowaway, Clarissa sat motionless, her mind racked with indecision. Lifting herself upon her toes, she methodically inched her hand over the stacked bales toward the hilt of the dagger. As she grasped the handle, a fitful twisting of the drunken form sent a paralyzing wave of dread throughout her body. Comfortable on his back, he began to snore loudly, in a slow, even rhythm.

Tightening her grip, Clarissa withdrew the blade, collapsing against the hay bales. Her heart trapped within her throat, she sat emotionally spent.

The rustling of straw, accompanied by a repulsive belch, anounced his awakening. Trapped, she covered the knife with her skirt folds.

Unseen by Clarissa, he reached for his jug, holding it high overhead in an attempt to extract any elusive drops of the corn brew. Finding it empty, he cursed his luck and sailed the crock across the car, smashing it into the wall and causing Clarissa to wince upon its impact.

He stumbled toward the opened door, oblivious of the woman's presence and began to drop his trousers. Unable to remove her eyes, lest he catch her unaware, the woman forced herself to endure the repulsiveness of his actions.

As he turned, his eyes fell upon the woman crouched amid the straw.

"Well, well, what has we here?" His mouth parted in a lecherous smile, a wave of nausea claimed Clarissa's stomach. "What be yer name, girlie?"

She wanted to scream, but a huge knot formed in her throat, preventing all hope of speech. Scooting herself backward, Clarissa began to rise to her feet. The futility of escape or the hope of a rescuer kindled the fiery spirit that had so often sustained her.

Moving close, the smile transformed into a hardened frown, as he began to remove his shirt. "If ya don't feel like talkin' to ole Virgil," his voice becoming more threatening with every step, "then we won't do no talkin'." He was close enough for her to smell the foulness of his breath and the stench of his body. Clarissa could not recall with any exactness the progression of events that instinctively transpired. She saw the distortion of his features and heard the wild expression of pain as his body doubled over in agony. He looked in disbelief to the dagger whose pearl hilt and partially exposed blade protruded from the bloody wound in his abdomen. "Ya damn, bitch," he moaned as his knees buckled, and he fell forward, driving the blade still further into his body.

Clarissa sidestepped along the wall, whimpering softly, her eyes never leaving the quiescent body that lay upon the flooring of the boxcar. Each time the swaying of the train jarred the corpse, she emitted a sharp cry. Retreating as far as possible, Clarissa fell to her knees, sobbing uncontrollably. Staring at the pool of blood which formed underneath the dead man, she fought to regain control of her emotions.

He's dead, you fool, she repeatedly told herself; *you killed him.*

"I killed him," she announced. "I murdered him."

As the reality took hold, she jumped to her feet. When the train stops, they will know I killed him; I'll hang. A new rush of terror stirred her to action.

Kneeling beside the loathsome form, she turned her face in disgust, nudging the lifeless man toward the door. With the weight of his bulk hindering her progress, she stood, taking his feet in her hands and dragging the corpse to the edge of the railway car. Gasping for breath, she rested herself in preparation for the efforts that lay ahead. As she wiped the perspiration from her face with the back of her soiled sleeve, Clarissa mustered her last vestige of strength. She shoved the dead man's shoulders until he plummeted to the ground. While the train sped southward, Clarissa watched the corpse roll down the railroad incline into the wooded land beyond.

With tatters of her petticoats, she wiped the blood as best she could from the boxcar floor and tossed the bloodied rags from the train. As she slumped against the wall, she recalled the haversack. Forcing herself to his makeshift bedroom, she prepared to rid herself of the final reminder of Virgil.

The yellow bag's rattle aroused Clarissa's curiosity. Opening the bag, she exposed two five dollar gold pieces, a tattered shirt, and a pair of equally well-worn trousers. The wretched condition of her own clothing, now smeared and caked with blood, compelled her to abandon them in favor of those of the dead man.

She stripped to her chemise, fingering the shirt as though it were some abhorrent creature. Even the feel of it against her skin chilled her despite the oppressive temperature inside the car. After she finished rolling up the legs of the pants and the sleeves of the shirt, she placed her head against the rucksack and feel into a deep sleep.

As the motion of the train slowed, Clarissa bolted from her dream. Darkness had descended, contributing to the few seconds of panic that elapsed before she reassured herself of her plight. Taking the haversack, she stuffed it in her handbag along with Cameron's ledger. On her hands and knees, Clarissa scrambled to locate her bonnet. Thus found, it was tenderly deposited within the bag, a gesture lost to those unfamiliar with the complex workings of the feminine mind.

The shrill whistle of the locomotive signaled its intention to stop. In the moonlight, the outlines of houses emerged. Holding to the door, she leaned out in hopes of more accurately determining her whereabouts. Little more than a scattering of houses and a tiny depot, the adjacent watering tower served as the village's only enticement. A gnawing hunger drove her from the confines of the railway car. A hasty inspection of both directions completed, she jumped from the train, barely maintaining her footing on the loose rocks that formed the track's bed.

Clarissa Morgan awaited the train's departure in a grove of trees which lined the track. A lantern signal given, the engineer urged the locomotive forward. From the clapboard depot a light shone, casting its illumination upon the ground. Approaching the window, Clarissa sighted a boy whose age she suspected was not quite sixteen.

The boy appeared genuinely surprised to have a visitor at such a late hour. "What can I do for you, Ma'am?"

"I need to catch the next train to Richmond," Clarissa responded in her best Southern accent.

"Oh, I am sorry," he expressed in a sincerity that was truly touching, "but the train left just a few minutes back. Didn't you hear the whistle?"

"Certainly, but I had no idea where it was heading."

He smiled. "Well, yer welcome to wait here until tomorrow morning about ten. That's when the next one's due in." He gestured to a row of rude, wooden chairs that lined one wall. "Make yourself ta home. The name's Eldridge, Eldridge Mayhew."

She deposited her knapsack and offered young Eldridge one of her coveted smiles. "Mine's Cathey Jackson."

"Ya'll from around here?"

"No, I'm from a little further up north. What do you call your town?"

"It ain't no town, just a few houses and a railroad watering tower. We have to go the ten miles into Fredericksburg to get to a real town." His eyes traveled the length of her body. Realizing that she had taken notice, he blushed and looked away.

"Eldridge?"

"Ma'am?"

"I haven't eaten all day, and I wonder if there's somewhere I could get something?" Noticing his hesitation she added, "Oh, I can pay."

"No, no, I…it's just that folks have so little these days. My ma fixes me a supper of sorts. I'd be right honored if you'd share it."

He produced a molasses pail which contained several biscuits and some preserves. Offering the entirety to Clarissa he boasted, "My ma puts up the best peach preserves in the county." Watching her devour the biscuits, his remark demonstrated heartfelt concern. "Guess you ain't ate in a while, have you?"

Realizing what a pig she was making of herself, she lowered her eyes in shame. Eldridge mistakenly assumed that her hunger and her attire were direct results of the South's poor economic times.

Patting her hand, he did his best to cheer her. "Don't worry none, Miss Cathey. Now that we're rejoinin' the Union, there'll soon be food enough for everbody."

"Whatever do you mean, rejoining the Union?"

"Well, a man fresh outa Richmond this mornin' told me." He rose in search of proof. "When I told him, my pa wouldn't believe such, he left me this copy of the Richmond newspaper." Eldridge thrust it toward her. "My pa don't read none, but I'll be doin' the readin' for him."

The rest of his words were lost to Clarissa Morgan as she scanned the *Richmond Enquirer.* Incredible as it seemed the Confederate Congress had voted to seek readmission to the Union. She read with interest how President Thomas' pivotal vote determined the nation's fate. Knowing how much his country meant to him, she realized the agony he must have endured as he pronounced the Confederacy's death sentence.

The article confirmed a scheduled meeting between the two Presidents to be held in Fredericksburg the next day. Pressing the newspaper into her lap, she turned to the young clerk. We have to stop him."

"Now Miss Cathey," he said in a soothing tone, "I know it's hard to give up the Cause."

"But you don't understand," she pleaded. "I have information that will change Jed's, that is the President's mind."

The backwoods clerk shook his head in disbelief, unable to fathom what information a ragged, hungry woman could possibly possess to alter President Thomas' decision.

Sensing his distrust, Clarissa determined to gamble on the rural lad she scarcely knew. "Please Eldridge, you must help me."

She crossed the room, tearing open the rucksack and producing the diary.

Handing it to the confused boy, she pleaded her case. "This is the diary of Daniel Adamson." His eyes widened with the incredibility of her declaration. "Open it," she ordered.

As he thumbed the pages, she interpreted. "These are members of a conspiracy headed by Adamson to devastate the South. Look at Porter's entry. It shows he purchased the surplus cotton in England to corner the market."

Still skeptical, Eldridge argued. "That don't mean nothin'. Anybody can put words in a book."

Undaunted, Clarissa persisted. "That's what I thought at first, but look."

She took the book from his hands.

"Here's a vast payment to the Reverend Armitage. Do you know who he is?"

"Who don't? He's that damned abolitionist who claims to have organized…" he stopped in mid sentence, the reality of the situation taking hold.

Triumphantly Clarissa pressed on. "This man, Bill Harrison, is a counterfeiter who flooded the South with worthless paper money. I talked to him, Eldridge, and he mentioned the plates."

Repeatedly pointing to the pages, "Here is one of the South's own," she stated, her voice indicative of the loathsomeness deserving of a traitor.

Running his hand through his sandy hair, he looked at the woman, then to the book. "He sold out the Confederacy." He repeated in an effort to convince himself. Finally, he faced Clarissa. "What will we do, Ma'am?"

Jumping from her seat, she ran and threw her arms around Eldridge. The astonished boy blushed profusely.

"Now we head to Fredericksburg to stop President Thomas. With this evidence, the people of the Confederacy will understand that the country's failure is not of its own doing, and, left alone, it can survive." Clarissa was jubilant. She sat back and laughed to herself. Was it really she who was fighting to save the system she denounced so bitterly in the men's salon aboard the *Victoria?* It would be days later when she would take the time to reflect upon her motives. There was a part of her who wished to undo the damage of her uncle and his conspiracy, but it was her love for Jed and the desire to preserve what he held so dear that sent her South at the risk of her own life.

Eldridge Mayhew donned a Rebel cap and bolted toward the door.

"Where are you going?" Clarissa demanded.

Exasperated that she failed to read his mind, "To get two horses, a course. We can't wait for no train!"

"But what if someone comes in?"

"Miss Cathey, you're the only person's what come in at night in the last year."

Chapter Thirty-Nine

Fredericksburg, Virginia, that same night

At Marye's Heights, the four-columned brick home stretched over a verdant hillside. Through its arched entry, many a guest had been treated to a relaxing, hospitable stay; however, sleep eluded the President of the Confederacy. In the waning hours of his term, he stared into the moonlight from a four-postered bed. His sleeplessness could not be attributed to misgivings regarding the dissolution of his country, but it reflected his concern for the futures of those left destitute by secession, inflation, war, and freedom.

From an early age, he'd been groomed to assume his father's position at Thomas Shipping. Thanks to Ezra's investments in Northern banks, the Thomas family did not share the fates of so many of their contemporaries like the Baker and Hoffman families whose homes were auctioned to Northern speculators to clear their debts. Even Bellmead had faced sale, until Jed paid the mortgage in Union currency.

Never would he allow the soil in which his wife was buried to be owned by Yankee "carpetbaggers," as they now called such men who raped the South of its lands by paying only fractions of their true values.

He anguished over the plight of the slaves so soon to be freed. Uneducated, with no place to go, they would be easy prey, perhaps more abused as freedmen than as slaves. Already pockets of Whites were forming groups whose sole purposes were to deny Blacks the liberties they would soon be granted. It sickened Jed to see what the South had become. He struggled to convince himself that life would be better when the Stars and Stripes once again flew over a united country. At least the War with Mexico would end and with it the sacrifices of Southern lives.

Yes, he could return to Thomas Shipping, but his brief tenure in government had kindled new desires and ambitions that could not be satisfied by managing his father's empire. He wanted, he needed, to be at the forefront of rebuilding the South, yet his position as President prohibited his holding of public office for five years under the readmission terms.

Jed pulled the covers around his shoulders. Though the day had been warm, the setting of the sun had cooled the evening. He turned to the opposite side and finally fell into a restless sleep.

*****

Aboard the Presidential train enroute to Fredericksburg

The President scoffed at the measures constantly undertaken to insure his security. Though he was far from a popular President, Lincoln could not accept that anyone would harm him. At all hours of the day and night, he ventured out into the Washington streets to clear his head of whatever perplexing matters plagued him. Yet, he agreed to this early morning trip to Fredericksburg, allowing for the ill feeling of the South toward any representative of Northern power.

A smile formed across the lined face of the nation's leader as he recalled the measures undertaken to avert an assassination attempt. On his way from Illinois to Washington for his inauguration, his railway cars had been filled with family and friends. Stopping at regular intervals, the President often stepped out upon the platform of the last car to briefly speak to his cheering constituents.

One such stop afforded Allan Pinkerton the opportunity to board. Confronting Lincoln with the plot he and his men had miraculously unearthed, the detective suggested that the President place his fate in his competent hands. The President acquiesced, at the urging of Colonel Lamon, and the three left the train, boarding a special sleeper car with four berths previously reserved by Pinkerton. As the Presidential entourage steamed into Baltimore, the site designated for the assassination attempt, Lincoln was safely concealed as an invalid passenger on a separate train. With none the wise, Lincoln arrived safely at the Capital, forever in Pinkerton's debt.

Abraham Lincoln wished for a respite from the confines of the trains that sped down the newly complete tracks which linked Manassas Junction to Fredericksburg. As always the Illinois farm boy felt decidedly out of place in such opulent surroundings. Reminiscent, he stroked the red velvet upholstery upon which he sat and surveyed the crystal candle enclosures, the richly grained woods of the furnishings, and the finely woven rugs which carpeted the flooring. It was far removed from the cabin of his boyhood where he had studied by the firelight. His thoughts turned to his son, Tad, whose health was a constant worry. It troubled him to travel when the boys were ailing, despite his knowledge that they had the best of care.

Still, he was thankful for the brevity of the ceremonial dissolution of the Confederacy and the symbolic oath its former President would take. It was Lincoln's own suggestion that the two Presidents meet at a mid point to further the Union's willingness to accept its Southern brothers. Already Texas, Tennessee, and Georgia had applied for readmission, and it was his hope that the remaining states, following Thomas' example, would quickly follow suit.

Abraham Lincoln greatly admired young Thomas. It was his opinion that few men, young or old, possessed Jed's courage and foresight. *Were I in his position,* questioned Lincoln, *would I abandon honor and pride for the common good?* Realizing that he had done just that while he was held captive in the abandoned barn, the President concluded that he and Thomas were not dissimilar in many regards.

*****

Even her mother would not have recognized the pristine Miss Morgan clad in men's clothing as she rode the back road into Fredericksburg astride an old plow horse. A hastily borrowed felt hat contained the lengthy tresses whose pins had been lost long before. Few words passed between Clarissa and Eldridge that did not pertain to directions or his repeated warnings of the hazards that characterized the seldom traveled road.

Eldridge reigned his bay and pointed into a grove of trees. "Fredericksburg is bout a half mile other side of them trees yonder. You'll have to take the bridge over the Rappahannock River, and it'll take you right to the center of town."

A look of disappointment crossed her face, "Aren't you going on with me?" a note of urgency in her voice connotated her dependency upon the boy.

"No Ma'am I ain't. I done all I can by getting you here. I got chores and my job at the depot. Besides, my pa made me promise to have the horses back for the late afternoon plowin'."

She leaned forward in her saddle and kissed his cheek. "Thank you Eldridge. I'll never forget what you've done." Clarissa believed that she could still see the flush of his cheeks as he rode toward his home, leading the horse upon which she had ridden. *Thank God for you, Eldridge Mayhew*, she thought as the boy and horses disappeared from view.

Throwing the rucksack over her shoulder, she started her walk toward Fredericksburg. Jaws set in fixed determination, Clarissa cleared the trees and viewed her destination for the first time. The city, which sat on the southeastern shore of the Rappahannock, was somewhat larger than she imagined. From her vantage point, she could discern several tall structures, any of which might serve as Presidential meeting places. Locating Jed would prove more difficult than anticipated. If only I'd thought to question Eldridge concerning specific locations of hotels or meeting halls, my task would become much less daunting. Surely someone will know the whereabouts of the ceremony, she reasoned.

Just across the bridge, she leaned her burden against one of the towering oaks that lined a row of picket-fenced homes on Hanover Street. The leaves were beginning to fall, having turned from their verdant greens to the coppers and rusts of autumn. Somehow they cast a prevailing sense of despair, as if they knew their once vibrant days of glory had passed. Picking up some of the fallen leaves, she examined their hues. *Yours was a hopeless cause from first budding*, she mused, *yet leaves burst forth in a fury, defying the elements and weathering the storms until the inexorable power of nature holds dominion over them.* Clarissa stared at a particularly large tree which had survived countless autumns, only to bud again, stronger and more firmly rooted than before. *The South, too, will weather this storm*, she thought. *It may have lost its brilliance, but it will emerge all the better for its sufferings.* She patted the trunk and hurried down the cobbled street.

A portly gentleman appeared on the porch of his home, posting the Stars and Bars proudly. As if sensing her presence, he turned from his task.

"What do you need, boy?"

A few seconds elapsed before Clarissa acknowledged that his inquiry was addressed to her. Attempting a more masculine voice, she replied. "Have you heard where President Thomas and Mr. Lincoln will meet?"

"You planning on declaring yourself a damned Yankee?" his question ladened with disgust.

"No..., I ... I just wanted to see it for myself."

"Have the need to see if it's really so, eh?" He left the porch by way of a tier of wooden steps. Passing the fading garden flowers, he met Clarissa at the fence, leaning across it.

"They tell me Thomas stayed the night at Marye's Heights. I expect he's closer to the railway depot by now. That's where the curious will be gathering. Not that there'll be much to see. The Yankees are a might skittish about that lanky gorilla." He paused, "So Thomas will be joining him aboard that fancy train of his. It's a pity," he despaired. "It would do me good to think one of our own laid him in the ground." With a rising vehemence the man declared, "He's at fault, and the whole Confederacy knows it."

Without thinking, Clarissa came to Lincoln's defense, "Oh, but he isn't..."

"And who the devil else would it be?" he interrupted. "That Daniel Adamson is a puppet for Lincoln. How else do you explain why he's reeked so much havoc on the South but has never been found, despite," he growled sarcastically, "all the great man's promises?"

Wisely keeping her tongue in check, Clarissa thanked the man for his help and followed his instructions toward the train station. The Southerner's hatred of Lincoln astonished her. Dismissing it as the opinion of one bitter man, she hurried her steps.

When she arrived at the depot area, a large crowd had formed. Several held signs blaming Lincoln for the Confederacy's misfortunes. There was a boisterous speaker garnering listeners from his makeshift podium atop a baggage wagon. He denounced the President of the United States as a treaty violator and demanded that the crowd rush the train and lynch Lincoln at the town square. A chorus of angry Southerners announced agreement, echoing approval with clinched fists and Rebel yells.

A gnawing fear gripped Clarissa, as she began to doubt her ability to reach Jed. What if the mob saw fit to blame him as well?

The shrill whistle of the train, mixed with the raucousness of the crowd, spurred the mob into action. Clarissa became engulfed in the crush of people as it neared the tracks. Seemingly from nowhere, rifles appeared as armed men took positions across the tracks.

Without warning, shots rang out from the depot. Soldiers in Confederate uniforms lined the rooftops and the surrounding areas. General Stonewall Jackson's men had created a formidable line of sentries. From the back of his mount, he commanded his soldiers to shoot any citizen seeking to storm the train or impede the progress of President Thomas and his staff.

Slowly the throng parted as soldiers, acting upon Jackson's orders, confiscated the vigilantes' weapons. Somehow Clarissa made her way to an elevated platform from which she could survey the station grounds. When Lincoln's train came into view, splatterings of blue dots about the locomotive proved puzzling. She could easily spot the baboon stack of the 4-4-0 wood burning engine. As she concentrated on the train and its blue masses, Clarissa failed to notice the arrival of the Confederate President, encircled by armed escorts.

Now clearly visible were Union soldiers positioned about the train, their bayonets reflecting the morning rays of the sun. Scanning the crowd yet another time, Clarissa spotted Stewart Kane amid the Rebel forces. Clutching her knapsack to her bosom, she threaded the labyrinth of people, inching ever closer to the iron steps at the rear of the clerestory-roofed Presidential car.

An undulating wave of bodies forced back by the Confederate guards nearly sent her to the ground. Steadying herself against the railing at the rear of the car, she wedged between it and the throng. As she struggled to free herself from the entanglement of arms and legs, Jed Thomas' face appeared. Clarissa was struck by his pale, sunken features, her heart overflowing with compassion and love.

He was almost beside her, buffeted by his entourage when she screamed over the clamor, "Jed, it's I, Clarissa Morgan!"

The conflicting newspaper accounts of the next events would spawn debate for years to come. Most witnessed the Confederate President turn in toward the railing, bewildered, then becoming ecstatic about something he spied in the crowd.

When Jed failed to recognize her, Clarissa had discarded the faded hat, allowing her cascading black hair to fall loosely to her shoulders.

As Jed began his approach, Secretary of State Edwin Stanton exited the coach, positioning himself on the landing to extend greetings on behalf of President Lincoln. His attention drawn by the mention of the missing woman's name, he watched in amazement as a dirty-faced boy became Cameron's elusive niece.

Forcing his way toward Clarissa, whose arms groped blindly in his direction, Jed's ankle turned, propelling him to his right, just as the Secretary removed a derringer from his morning coat and fired it at Clarissa. The thrust of the turning ankle plunged Jed between his guards, placing him in the path of the bullet. As a shot pierced his shoulder, he fell forward, shielding the girl.

Clarissa heard the discharge of the gun and felt herself propelled to the ground. She was aware of a sharp pain in the back of her head, as the world became darkness.

Women screamed, as rifle blasts exploded from Union and Rebel marksmen, none clearly aware of specific targets. Bodies fell to escape the hail of bullets, others lay stilled unable to avoid the random shots, as the truly fortunate escaped to cover.

When the officers gained control of their men, the chaos ceased. The bodies of four Union soldiers littered the grounds. Two Rebels died in the exchange, as well as four civilians. Of the five wounded, only the President of the Confederacy and the unconscious woman that Stewart Kane carried were taken aboard the Presidential train to be administered to by Lincoln's personal physician.

As Stewart gently placed Clarissa's limp body on a sofa, he pried the worn haversack from an iron-willed grasp. He could hear Jed's protest as the physician, Doctor Roderick Hammonds, removed the blood-soaked coat and shirt to expose his wounded shoulder.

"I tell you, I am perfectly fine. You must see to Miss Morgan."

Dr. Hammonds, disregarding his patient's objections, examined the wound. The bullet penetrated the right shoulder, lodging against a bone. Jed refused the medication to ease his pain, in hopes of speeding the doctor to Clarissa. Delving into the tissue, the physician felt the muscle tense, reacting to the intense discomfort of his probe.

To Jed, the pain in his shoulder was incomparable to the anxiety he was experiencing over Clarissa's fate. As he gripped the rim of the impromptu examination table, he called to Stewart, "How is she?"

"I think she's coming around," he said as he peered into the compartment where Jed sat. "How will you be?"

The doctor replied, "I am finished. Aside from some stiffness and a little pain, you should heal nicely."

The door behind Stewart flew open as two armed Federal soldiers and Colonel Lamon escorted President Lincoln into the car. Lincoln took stock of the woman who lay on his settee while extending his hand to Stewart. In an attempt to defuse the tension of the morning, Lincoln declared, "The four of us do seem to cross paths under the most unusual of circumstances."

"Yes Sir, we do have that knack," Stewart agreed.

"Miss Morgan's condition?" queried Lincoln.

"Doctor Hoffman has yet to examine her; however, she does stir from time to time." Both gazed helplessly at the young woman.

Their conversation was interrupted by Jed's entrance. Still wearing his soiled clothing, has arm bandaged to his chest, he was unsuccessfully maneuvering his morning coat over his shoulder.

"Let me assist you," offered the President, taking the coat and draping it over both shoulders.

Jed acknowledged his gratitude.

"President Thomas, please forgive my absence. You see my men," he gestured in the direction of the uniformed sentries, "refused to let me leave the front of the train after the gunfire began."

"I am only too glad that they did, Sir. Tell me has Secretary Stanton been located?"

"Perhaps we should sit down."

He indicated to the men his preference of seating. "You are certain that Secretary Stanton was the assassin?"

"I am afraid so, Mr. President," replied Kane. "I watched him remove the gun from his coat and fire, though I cannot fathom his motive for wanting Jedediah dead."

Lincoln shook his large head. "Stanton has never been a supporter of the South, but I should think he would applaud you rather than blame you for your effort to bring the South back into the Union."

A low moan from Clarissa, who was being attended by the President's physician, set all eyes upon her.

Jed rushed to her side.

"Clarissa, it's Jed."

In a haze of pain and confusion, she struggled to sit up. As the identity of the man kneeling beside her became clear, she threw her arms around him, sobbing uncontrollably, "Oh, Jed I found you."

Suddenly the reality of her whereabouts and the persons surrounding her became evident. Pushing him away, she looked down at her clothing, deeply ashamed to be inside the Presidential car, clad in the cast-off garments of a drifter. Instinctively her hands smoothed her hair. Without meeting their eyes, she sought to justify herself. "I... you must excuse my appearance." Then casting Jed a pleading look, "You see I ruined my dress when..." her voice trailed.

Stewart Kane crossed over and playfully mussed her hair. "We've nothing to fear about her health," he teased. "When a woman is aflutter over her clothes, she's perfectly normal."

In friendly retaliation Clarissa slapped his arm away.

"Clarissa," Jed questioned, "whatever possessed you to come to Fredericksburg alone?"

"I came to... my...knapsack!"

She jumped to her feet, then fell back into Jed's arms. "The diary is in it!" she cried, steadying her head to stop the spinning carousel the room had become.

Stewart bent beside the sofa, producing the rumpled haversack from underneath.

"Thank heavens," she gasped.

As she tore into the rucksack, the men watched, dumbfounded by her actions. "This," she proclaimed dramatically, "is the record of the financial transactions between Daniel Adamson and his fellow conspirators."

As she presented the ledger to Jed, Stewart and Lincoln crowded at either side of him, prompting Clarissa's cautious movement to another seat.

The three examined the entries, occasionally commenting on a name or a date.

"Miss Morgan, how did you come into possession of this book?" inquired the resonant voice of Abraham Lincoln.

From the moment she embarked upon her course of action, this was the moment she most dreaded. To expose her uncle as a criminal would ruin his career, which was his entire life. Concern for her aunt and her mother tempted her to ignore Cameron's role in the Adamson cabal, yet the toll his actions had taken on thousands of innocents left her but little choice.

"I discovered it quite by accident in my uncle's desk." Clarissa proceeded to relate the events which led her to Fredericksburg, carefully avoiding the details surrounding the death of the drifter.

"By all that is holy!" Lincoln exclaimed.

Failing to convince anyone, least of all herself, Clarissa speculated, "Surely there is some sort of reasonable explanation for his…"

Lincoln cut short her attempt to exonerate his Secretary of War. "My dear, loyalty to one's uncle is commendable; nevertheless, there exist no excuses for his withholding of such evidence from me and the rest of my administration.

"His unwillingness," Stewart cited, "to disclose this ledger confirms his guilt." He took her hands in his. "I realize how difficult this must be for you, but you were certain of his guilt or you would have confronted him yourself."

"I know," she softly said as tears began to trail from her eyes.

Jed Thomas remained silent throughout the long exchange. His hatred for Simon Cameron increasing as the woman's account assured him of her uncles' responsibility for incalculable miseries. That the man had actually watched from the observation gallery as the Confederacy fought for its very existence further enraged the young President. He chided himself for his inability to see through Cameron's hypocritical façade. Of course, he was unable to capture Adamson, at the same time discouraging him from sending Southern investigators to aid in the search. He would see this man again, and he would know what drove him to such lengths.

Lincoln was dictating instructions to Colonel Lamon concerning Cameron's detention in Washington. "He will be placed under house arrest within the White House!" ordered the President, uncharacteristically agitated.

Lamon had never known the President to express such vehement anger.

His virulence was directed at himself as much as with Cameron. From the onset of his term, Abraham Lincoln sensed the rift that existed between his cabinet and himself, but a realization of the extent of this division by the outright betrayal of Cameron infuriated the ordinarily docile Lincoln. Somehow he should have perceived the Secretary's deceit. The signs were obvious, the inability to produce Adamson, the smug expressions, and Cameron's frequent absences.

Jed stood behind Clarissa's chair, his hand resting reassuringly upon her shoulder.

"Mr. President, my primary interest is for Miss Morgan's safety."

She pivoted in her seat and expressed her shock. "My safety? Really Jed, I am quite all right."

"I fear that Stanton's intent was to kill you, not me." He proceeded to explain himself to her perplexed companions. "You told us of seeing your uncle at the B & O Station. Evidently, he knows the ledger is in your possession and is determined that it not come to the attention of anyone else. Unless he followed you, which I consider is highly unlikely given your mode of travel, Stanton must be a cohort of your uncle's."

"He merely seized the opportunity to silence you when he recognized your face in the crowd," interjected Stewart, beginning to assume Jed's reasoning.

Clarissa protested adamantly, "I do not believe for one moment that Uncle Simon would harm me."

"Miss Morgan," Lincoln explained, "when a man as willful and ambitious as a Simon Cameron or an Edwin Stanton faces political ruin and a federal imprisonment, reason and compassion are outweighed by the will to survive. I am ordering Colonel Lamon to place you under guard and initiate a search for Secretary Stanton."

Lincoln rose. As he and his soldiers were about to leave the car, the President added, "If I might be so bold, I will send into Fredericksburg for you more suitable attire, and if you need...any further... articles..." his voice trailed in embarrassment.

"Thank you, Mr. President. I do long for somewhere to freshen myself."

"This gentleman will escort you to the sleeping quarters. I'll remain here." Lincoln poured a glass of lemonade and lowered himself onto the settee. With Clarissa out of the car, he addressed the two Southerners.

"I would feel less apprehensive for her if you gentlemen were to accompany us back to the Capital. She will be, of course, in an unfortunate situation with her aunt, and perhaps her mother as well. Secretary Cameron has long been their benefactor, and his arrest will no doubt cast a troublesome shadow upon Miss Morgan."

"I think we all agree that she has done both nations a great service by exposing the Adamson scheme." After Lincoln and Kane expressed their agreement, Jed added, "With your permission, Stewart and I should like to be present when you question Cameron. Aside from the obvious destruction of the Confederacy, Adamson is directly responsible for the deaths of my wife and child during the slave rebellion. I am also interested in the detention of the Reverend Jonas Armitage."

"I have failed to properly express my sympathies to you, and I do understand your interest in the conspirators. I welcome your input and opinions regarding any of these men." The President paused, rubbing his eyes. "I am most curious about your feelings toward Colonel Dupree."

"It would appear that the man is guilty of treason; however, the dissolution of the Confederacy brings into question where the authority for prosecution of such betrayal rests."

"Indeed," mused Lincoln.

The three discussed the legalities at length and were vaguely aware of the train's departure from Fredericksburg.

Chapter Forty

The Virginia countryside

Edwin M. Stanton urged the horse he had stolen from a Fredericksburg hitching post. Driven by the instinct of self-preservation, he headed westward. From that fateful moment that he recognized Clarissa Morgan amid the mob of angry Rebels, his destiny had been sealed for he could not allow this woman to expose the intricacies of the conspiracy. The echo of the derringer's discharge still rang within his head as did the subsequent firings of the soldiers, causing him to kick the helpless animal all the harder.

Reaching the top of a hill, he disregarded the placid, majestic setting of the Virginia village lodged within the valley. The telegraph wires alone intrigued him. Tracing them to a general merchantile, he dismounted the winded horse and approached the store. Stanton grimaced in pain, the combination of age and years of carriage riding making him less than an adept horseman.

Once inside he scrutinized the faces of the rural customers, lest any recognize him as the man responsible for the death of a woman in Fredericksburg. Aside from a country matron and a few aged duffers, the store contained only a white aproned shopkeeper whose plodding gait served to somewhat ease his panic. Secretary Stanton approached the wooden counter which was flanked by partially filled barrels that once overflowed with beans and other products offered for sale. Had Stanton been less distracted, he would have noticed the shelves lacking the abundance enjoyed by Northern concerns.

At his request to send a telegraph message, the shopkeeper gestured toward the machine house within a cage. If the stranger's obvious impatience with a lackadaisical clerk and his constant glances toward the street incited any suspicious notions within his fellow customers, none were outwardly divulged. Rather, these rural Southerners focused on their inabilities to secure the items they needed.

Stanton hurriedly scrawled the message which the shopkeeper turned telegraph operator reread much too loudly for the fugitive's taste.

"To Mr. Lawrence Mims in Washington, D.C."

The Secretary, fighting the urge to break and run, paid the fee and immediately departed. As he rode toward the setting sun, his thoughts were with his beloved wife and children. There was money enough in the bank to support them until, with Cameron's assistance, he could return to the Capital and enjoy his own political prowess. *Cameron had been correct in his thinking*, mused Stanton, when he insisted that the conspirators work as independently as possible so that at least one member could retain his political power in lieu of unforeseen difficulties. Yes, Cameron was indeed a brilliant man.

Chapter Forty-One

Washington, D.C.

As Simon Cameron rolled down Fourteenth Street and approached the Willard Hotel, his euphoria was marred only by his missing niece. The fabrication he'd delivered to his wife and sister would not conceal her absence forever. There was, after all, a limit to how long he could keep her in New York on the pretext of representing his personal interests. To break the news to them of her accidental death would be premature, since she was cleverly evading those dispatched to locate her.

The realization of the fact that all his efforts were finally at an end and that the Confederacy's President might be taking his oath of allegiance at that very moment overshadowed his concerns for Clarissa. He'd won a great victory. The South was on its knees in capitulation for its arrogance and was suffering devastation far exceeding his design. So be it, he thought, and all the better for the Republicans to seize control of Southern politics and propel me into the Presidency.

The Willard's dining salon, a favorite of the Secretary's, seemed an appropriate setting for the celebration marking this

unparalleled political maneuver. Secretary Chase and
Solomon Edwards, already seated near the dining room's large
window, noted his arrival and the approach of three gentlemen,
one of which was Pinkerton.

Unable to hear the fervent conversation, Chase and
Edwards exchanged puzzled queries. Seeing the detective
roughly grasp Cameron's arm and the Secretary's angry
reprisal, Chase started for the door. Only Edward's calm
intervention prevented Chase from sharing Cameron's fate.

"Are you mad?" he barked in a hoarse whisper. "Something
has gone amiss. No doubt his damnable niece has persuaded
someone to believe in the authenticity of the ledger. Though
it serves him right, only an arrogant fool would keep records
of his nefarious dealings."

Chase slowly reclaimed his seat, suddenly aware of the
crowd of onlookers gathering outside and in close proximity of
their table. "Then we are in danger ourselves from the diary or
Cameron's betrayal."

Dubiously Chase agreed, eyeing Cameron's departure in
his landau with Pinkerton and his men as added passengers.

"The devil with you, Pinkerton. I'll see to it that you never
draw another penny from governmental service, and I will ruin
you in the private sector as well!" roared Cameron.

Oblivious to the Secretary's rantings, Pinkerton nodded
politely to a trio of passing ladies. His silence and apparent
disinterest drove Cameron into a deeper frenzy of more violent
words and gesticulations.

Pinkerton was savoring this encounter. The telegraph
message had been delivered by one of Lincoln's most trusted
aides, delighting the detective who relished the prospect of
arresting the Secretary of War. Pinkerton had made it his
personal goal to research as many governmental officials as

possible, starting with those foremost in hierarchy. In doing so, he had uncovered facets of Simon Cameron that he deplored.

The man's past was a labyrinth of political dealings, especially favorable to the iron moguls of his native Pennsylvania. Furthermore, Cameron was, in the detective's opinion, disloyal to the President and most willing and capable of manipulations and strategies whose aims were to discredit Lincoln and expedite his own lofty political aspirations. Until the telegraph's arrival, he had been unable to amass sufficient evidence of any specific crime to dislodge such a powerful politician.

Thus, the rantings of the caged lion in whose carriage he now rode did little to frighten Pinkerton. Actually he found Cameron's predicament quite amusing. It would be a singular pleasure to supervise the man's house arrest and be on hand when the President arrived from Fredericksburg.

The nation's premier investigator found his career both exciting and personally rewarding as a direct result of moments like these.

*****

The armed sentries who lined the hallway leading to the executive offices snapped in a cycle of staccato salutes as the President and his entourage traveled its length. Behind the guards the usual office seekers and petitioners gaped in stunned silence as the President escorted an uncommonly attractive woman, who drew the admirations of even the most happily married of the pickets. Following them, a fair-haired gentleman with his arm encumbered walked quietly beside a darker version of himself.

Of course, the sentries recognized Colonel Lamon and appreciated his approving nod as he passed in an informal review.

The sentry positioned on the right side of the double doors opened them, stepping back to allow sufficient room for the President and the lady's fashionably large, hooped skirt. Each of the wearied travelers experienced renewed energies in anticipation of the audience about to take place.

Clarissa's eyes went immediately to her uncle, who deliberately avoided their contact. He seemed unusually confident for a man whose status as a prisoner was betrayed only by the denial of his morning toilet.

"Mr. President," he bellowed as soon as Lincoln entered. "I demand an explanation for this outrageous treatment." He had attempted to rise from his seat but was unceremoniously thrust back by Pinkerton's men.

Calmly Lincoln deposited Clarissa in the room's most comfortable chair and turned to face his traitorous official. "And you shall have it, Cameron; we all demand a similar accounting…from you."

Jed surveyed the man who deprived him of his child and its mother. Only the constant throbbing within his shoulder restrained him from carrying out his desire to place his hands around Cameron's neck and slowly watch his life ebb. Stewart guided Jed toward an overstuffed settee, realizing from their conversations of the previous evening that his friend would require his support to endure the presence of Simon Cameron.

Clarissa had hoped to share some time alone with Jed as they journeyed to the Capital; however, the President had monopolized him and banished her to the Presidential quarters. Before she was lulled to sleep by the motion of the rhythmic clicking of wheels against rails, her thoughts had been of him.

Watching him eye her uncle with vehemence, she feared his attitude toward her would be altered because of the actions of a man she could not control.

"Mr. Cameron," the President continued in the same deliberate tone. "I have in my possession a ledger accounting the expenditures of Daniel Adamson." Lincoln gestured toward Lamon who produced the book from a pocket inside his uniform.

The revelation produced the appropriate amount of righteous indignation expected from a pious individual falsely accused. His subsequent denials did little to dissuade his complainants, who fired volleys of questions against the as yet undaunted Cameron.

As Lincoln discussed the ledger's specific pages, the Secretary of War determined that Providence had, in fact, set in motion these events of which he was now a part, presenting him with the opportunity to claim the recognition he rightfully deserved.

With unbridled arrogance, Cameron answered the charges. "Actually, I am quite pleased with Clarissa's meddling," he smiled pleasantly at his niece, "for now I can receive credit due me for my acts of patriotism."

Clarissa gasped; the men observed the Secretary with astonishment.

Cameron rose, unimpeded by the detectives and approached his niece. "It seems that I owe you a great debt, my dear. Without your interference and flight, these men would never have known to whom they owe their gratitude for reuniting the nation and putting the South in its place." He bowed deeply in a satirical tribute.

Addressing Lincoln, he proceeded. "The Northern voters will rally behind me, the man with the backbone to stand against the damnable Rebels. Unlike you, I did not accept the

Union's defeat or the principles of a worthless treaty. I took control while you dribbled forgiveness." He searched their faces, believing that he was winning their admiration as he presented each aspect of his actions. "It always amazes me what a small amount of money will buy; the loyalty of a senator, the cooperation of a foreign official, or even a war to vex one's enemy," he boasted.

Cameron continued, "As for the Confederacy, my loyal Republicans have begun to live on its sacred soil. Soon, as per your readmission terms, Mr. President, they will occupy its state offices and work its freed darkies. The next election will be mine."

He sauntered toward the President's desk and rubbed his hands reverently across the top of Lincoln's chair. He looked at Jed and Stewart in a gloating moment of supreme triumph.

"So help me, I'll kill him with my bear hands." Stewart was across the room before the detectives could restrain him. Cameron stood his ground, breaking into absurd laughter.

"I don't think you will be so amused when you face a gallows," snarled Kane wrestling himself free of the men who prevented him from the confrontation he zealously desired.

"And from whose gallows and for what crimes shall I swing, Mr. Kane? Have I committed treason against the United States of America? Did I seek to bring about its downfall?"

He crossed the room to face the seething Rebel.

"You seem to have forgotten that the Confederate Congress has voted, thanks to our Mr. Thomas, to dissolve the Confederacy."

Cameron smiled, thoroughly satisfied with himself. "And who will find fault with the great emancipator? Without me, the Negro would have faced the whip for countless generations. History will record me well and in more favorable terms than," his tone marked with disgust, "Honest Abe or the second President of an impotent nation."

The sting of truth in Cameron's words cut to the hearts of those around him. Rising slowly, the Confederacy's last President walked methodically to face the individual who had robbed the South of its birthright.

He glared at a man who had manipulated political bargains in the name of his party and nation, wondering how such a Judas could rationalize the unconscionable actions he proudly proclaimed.

During the days of secession, War, and his Presidency, Jed had struggled with decisions of ominous magnitudes and consequences, yet they paled in comparison to the one he now faced.

Though contrary to every fiber of his being as a gentleman, a Southerner, and an advocate of justice, Jed was left optionless by the dictates of Simon Cameron.

"Knowledge of your crimes must never leave this office." Jed ignored the fervent objections from the office. "And if they should, we will all disavow your claims!" his voice threatening, his face marked with savage determination. "I want nothing more than to see you answer for the lives of countless Southerners, but to do so would furnish the Confederacy with a rallying point, encouraging it to battle for a Cause that is lost."

His voice became stronger as his eyes left Cameron and traveled about the office. "I cannot, in all good conscience, allow the War with Mexico or the Black man's slavery to continue, nor will I see our people suffer another day more than is necessary."

He addressed the President, who was sitting at his writing desk, "I do request that this man and his fellow conspirators be stripped of any governmental offices."

Lincoln leisurely unfolded his long legs encased in perpetually wrinkled, dark trousers. "And who are your fellow conspirators in my cabinet?"

Cameron spoke with convincing assurance, "You command such loyalty in your Secretaries that I feared disclosure if I confided in any of them."

The President scoffed at Cameron's statement, "I command such loyalty in everyone but you it seems. Then tell me, Simon, the funds that you secured originated from what sources if Chase were not in leagues with you?"

"Surely Sir, you do not imagine that such sums could be secreted without your knowledge? All of Washington is keenly aware of your fastidious scrutiny of expenditures by all branches of government."

Both Pinkerton and Lamon shared private notions that the President would be well advised to so examine his wife's accounts. Her debts for clothing alone were the scandal of the Capital, and the recent purchase of numerous pairs of gloves fueled the gossip concerning the state of her mental health.

"Pinkerton?"

"Yes Mr. President."

"I should like for you to investigate all the members of my administration, especially the Treasury Secretary. If any evidence exists of collusion with this man, I will expect you to notify me personally."

"Of course," Pinkerton grinned slyly at Cameron. "It will be a singular pleasure."

"Lamon, order mobilization of Federal troops and extra supplies dispatched to Texas. We have an aggressor on American soil."

Lamon beamed, "Yes Sir."

"And have Mrs. Kennedy summon the French minister, the Comte de Joliet. He will find himself hastily recalled to Paris, thus terminating his ministerial duties. I shall also issue an order for his arrest should he ever return to this country."

As the door closed behind the Colonel, the President draped one leg over the arm of his chair, adopting the pose so often seen by those closest to him. Lacing his words with pointed sarcasm, he addressed Cameron. "Mr. Secretary, it is with great pride that I announce your appointment to the Imperial Court of Russia. You will assume your duties within one week, provided a passage can be secured."

"Indeed it can," spoke Stewart. "I will personally assure that a Thomas ship will be leaving on that date."

"Such an appointment is a sentence of virtual exile. I will not accept the post, nor will I ever resign my cabinet position." He crossed his arms defiantly as he glared at the President.

Approaching the ebuillient Cameron, Allan Pinkerton questioned, "Do you recall the report I made to you concerning the vigilante organizations springing up throughout the Confederacy?" Undaunted by the lack of a response, he pressed further. "As I recall, we discussed in rather graphic detail the tortuous murders, lynchings, and beatings of your so-called Carpetbaggers and Southerners assumed to be in sympathy with the Union." Perceiving a slight tremor in the Secretary's hands, Pinkerton persisted.

"It would seem entirely within reason that a person of my means, who already posses the names of these 'patriots,' could easily filter enough information to make you a prime target for these men." He withdrew a handkerchief and offered it to Cameron. "You seem to be perspiring, Sir."

Cameron pushed the proffered article away, enraged. Several tense minutes elapsed as the Secretary contemplated his destiny. Then, his bearing divulging no aspect of the defeat he had just suffered, he announced. "Undoubtedly my wife will require a somewhat lengthier time frame in which to set our household in order."

Lincoln did not acknowledge Cameron for several seconds. When he did, the President continued to stare down at the paper on which he was writing. "Your wife may remain as long as she deems necessary. Now, I am certain that you have a great many details that will require your attention before you sail."

The new Russian Minister stormed from the office, slamming the heavy door behind him.

As he turned his attentions to Clarissa Morgan, Lincoln expressed, "Mrs. Lincoln and I would be honored if you and your mother would be our guests until such time as you can arrange for suitable lodging. It is the very least that this nation can do for such a brave woman. I only wish that I could publicly recognize your valiant efforts."

Her emotions ravaged, Clarissa could do little in the way of a reply. Until now she had not begun to formulate plausible excuses for avoiding her Uncle Simon or to explain her absence from home. It was not that she feared him any longer, but her revulsion for the man and what he had done would be all too evident should they meet in the presence of her mother or aunt.

Jed came to Clarissa's side, taking her by the arm. "Mr. President, I wonder if Miss Morgan and I might have a few moments together?"

"There's a small room for receiving visitors," Lincoln gestured, "that should meet your needs."

Holding open the door, Jed permitted Clarissa's passage into the Presidential reception room. Like so many others in the Executive Mansion, this room resembled a lady of quality who had fallen upon hard times. The bull's-eye molding bore paint chips, and the delicately patterned wallpaper was beginning to show its seams.

Clarissa seated herself in one of the five chairs, slipcovered to disguise the tattered upholstery. The marble-topped table beside two of the chairs reflected the tarnished round globes of the chandelier.

"Clarissa," Jed spoke, "I can't begin to thank you for what you did for the Confederacy. Knowing your views concerning slavery, I can't begin to imagine what drove you to expose your uncle at the risk of your own life. By all that is holy, you despise the Confederacy and all that it represents."

She turned her head at a slight angle. Arching her eyebrows, she offered Jed the alluring smile which he found so beguiling. "I did it for the man I love."

She stood, allowing him to take her in his arms. Their kisses betrayed the passions repressed over the endless months of separation.

"I want you to marry me," he whispered.

It required enormous will for her to push him gently away. "You can't marry a woman like me." She buried her face in her crossed arms, supporting herself on the mantle above the marbled fireplace.

"Of course I can."

He followed her to the hearth. "I have dealt with Mandy's death, and there is no more Confederacy to come between you and me now."

He placed his strong hands upon her trembling shoulders. "I can be the man you've searched for," he pleaded. "You are everything to me, Clarissa. No one, nothing, is or ever will be more important."

She looked upward, speaking to his reflection in the ornately carved mirror which hung above the fireplace. "Jed, I killed a man. He had every intent of harming me; I swear."

Her eyes begged him for help and forgiveness. As she related the incident aboard the train, he held her all the tighter, as if shielding her from the man whose body lay concealed within the underbrush. Her confession and exposure of her emotions, revealed for the first time the vulnerability Clarissa Morgan kept carefully masked, but whose existence was so very near the surface. All her life this façade had sheltered her against the heartless rejection of her father, the frailties of her mother, and even the advancing Rebel Army. Only with Jed Thomas had she relaxed her defenses and allowed him into her soul.

Gently he turned and embraced her. "You have me to protect you now." As Clarissa rested her head upon his chest, she was comforted by his reassuring words. "And no one will ever be able to harm you again."

With the evening shadows falling upon the Capital of a nation once more united, the lovers left to begin their lives together.

Chapter Forty-Two

Richmond, Virginia, three days later

A squad of gray-clad soldiers primed their weapons in preparation for the ordeal at hand. Roused from their tents at dawn they knew little save that they were to administer the sentence of death to a fellow soldier.

As the poor fellow was guided to the wall of the prison courtyard, the six privates noticed the heavy blindfold covering the man's face. The Captain barked his orders, releasing a volley of gunfire which propelled the body into distorted poses as it fell.

The burial detail was closely guarded by Major Andrew Mallory.

As the chaplain was about to read the Twenty-third Psalm over the pine box, he questioned the Major as to what name he should use to address the deceased.

"Traitor!" was his harsh reply.

Aghast by the brutality of the Major's words, the minister hurriedly read the verses and left the scene.

When the detail was putting away its spades and boarding the wagon, Andrew Mallory stood at the foot of the grave for which no marker would ever be erected.

He spat defiantly on the soil and muttered, "May you rot in hell, Adam Dupree."

*****

The Virginia countryside

Leaning back against the feather pillows which elevated his head, Edwin Stanton rested from his latest bout of asthmatic wheezing that had impaired his escape. Unused to his beardless chin, he instinctively groped at its former location.

For as long as he could remember, his health had been the greatest obstacle to his success. The throbbing in his head intensifying, the Secretary cursed his infirmities and dwelt upon the circumstances which left him in this Virginia hamlet rather than nearer his destination. With asthma racking his body, he had barely the strength to climb the stairs and settle himself. The innkeeper and his wife, a doting old couple named Bennett, saw to his needs and were well satisfied with the manner in which he presented himself. Sensitive to his desire to hastily recover and speed to Texas to nurse his wounded son, there was no request denied Stanton by the empathetic couple, for they had lost a boy to the War. Still, they had pleaded for him to stay yet another night to assure his full recovery before continuing his difficult journey.

A sharp rap at the door was welcomed in hopes of the arrival of a breakfast he craved. In response, the door opened to admit the bowleged form of Allan Pinkerton and two of his men.

"Good morning, Edwin," the detective called all too cheerily. Reacting to Stanton's stunned expression, Pinkerton closed the door and approached the bed. "Oh, it wasn't so difficult a task. First there was the telegram, a few stops for food and water, and now your respite here."

Doubling over from an asthmatic siege, the Secretary was unable to respond.

"There are a great many loyal Rebels like the Bennetts who have been only too happy to assist the Yankee likes of us," he gestured to his men, "in apprehending the man who attempted to assassinate their President Thomas."

"Jed Thomas?" he weakly questioned.

"Fell into the path of the bullet," explained the detective who added matter-of-factly, "Miss Morgan is alive, well, and extremely informative. Now Sir, if you will dress, we will escort you to Washington."

As Pinkerton and his men neared the door of the second-story room the detective spoke to his men. "Station yourselves outside the window."

With his back to Stanton, he added, "Oh, you might not have heard of Mr. Lincoln's latest decision." Without waiting for a reply, Pinkerton continued. "It seems that Secretary of War Cameron has accepted an ambassadorial post at the Czar's court. Rumor has it that several South American nations have similar vacancies."

Tapping his bowler, Pinkerton left.

Without hesitation, Edwin Stanton opened the armoire and removed the derringer.

Pointing it at his head, he pulled the trigger.

The discharge startled Pinkerton, who methodically walked down the stairs to summon his men.

*****

Washington, D.C.

At his office in the Treasury Building, Salmon Chase paced the length of his office yet another time. Unable to eat or sleep since Cameron's arrest, he awaited the fall of the Damoclean sword. Auditors of the President's choosing confiscated his clerks' offices where they had worked in shifts for the past two days, scrutinizing expenditures and searching for evidence to link him to Cameron.

It was Chase's repeated prayer that he had been clever enough to conceal the funds he had funneled into Cameron and Stanton's conspiracy.

"Damn you both!" he cried.

With his role in the cabal thus exposed, would come the forfeiture of his dream of the Presidency. As much as he coveted the nation's highest office, he dreaded the loss of Kate's esteem. Of his six children, four of whom had died, Kate was his joy. Her giftedness apparent at an early age, she had become his favorite and later his protégé. To bring shame upon her, he could not bear.

His secretary's discrete knock caused him to react like a frightened animal.

"Mr. Secretary, the President is here to see you."

Chase hastily dried his sweating palms against the side of his trousers and braced for the worst. Abraham Lincoln strode in and seated himself near the window.

"I was about to take a ride with my boys and decided to speed things up by paying a call," he declared.

Chase searched his face and words for some inkling of his fate. "How kind of you," he managed to express.

"I must commend you, Salmon, and ask for your forgiveness."

"Sir?"

"It shames me to admit that I doubted your honesty and your loyalty to our government by assuming that you had a hand in Cameron's plot."

The Secretary lowered himself into his chair. "Please don't think of it...really, Mr. President," he stammered.

Watching the President rise and take his leave, Chase could no longer curtail his curiosity. "Have you uncovered others?"

Lincoln rubbed his beard, "Only Stanton, and his death will prevent Pinkerton from obtaining any additional names from him."

"His death? I had no idea."

"Suicide. As for the Reverend Armitage, the outcries of his large following would jeopardize the veil of secrecy which we are forced to impose. Harrison and the others mentioned in the ledger..?" The President shrugged his shoulders. "Cameron was clever enough to handle personal contacts himself. I fear we are at an impasse if de Zavala cannot be captured at the War's end."

Thank God, Chase repeated to himself.

"Good day, Mr. Secretary, and again, my humblest apologies."

As the door sounded its closing, Salmon P. Chase buried his face in his hands and wept tears of relief.

*****

The neighborhood housed Washington's poor. Crumbling structures of several stories towered over wooden shanties. Escorting the hired barouche, a mixture of ragged children both black and white, ran alongside. Such elegance was a rarity. Eyes traveled up to the liveried man who sat high above his passengers, his back erect and his decorum flawless. The grand lady's watered silk dress rustled faintly in the wind.

It was a section of Washington that Clarissa had never frequented, the home of European immigrants and newly emancipated slaves. Its people shared a common dream of a better life for themselves and their children.

Because of its stark contrast to its surroundings, a red-bricked building trimmed in white attracted the eye from a great distance. A large crowd gathered in front of the structure and parted as the carriage driver halted his team.

A dignified Black man in a dark morning coat, accompanied by a pregnant woman in calico, approached. He offered his hand to Clarissa, who stepped from the barouche. The Black man turned to Jed Thomas, who was now at his side.

The two embraced as Mose remarked, "It's a great day."

"I am glad that I'm able to witness it firsthand. You've worked a miracle."

"The parents all worked, and Mrs. Jackson and her friends raise extra funds for the furnishings. I can't take credit; so many have sacrificed to see this school's completion."

Their eyes turned to the building where the words *Celia Mallory School* were inscribed above its entry.

"She'd be honored that the school bears her name." Jed could see the tears welling up within Mose's eyes.

They entered the school, followed by the women, the children, and their parents. After the commotion of seating the audience of some two hundred on wooden benches died away, Mose rose and began his address to the assembly.

"When I was the age of these children, I thirsted for knowledge and dreamed of learning to read the books that lined the shelves of Bellmead Plantation's library.   One morning when I was assigned the task of dusting those shelves, my mistress found me sitting on the floor turning the pages of one of the books. Instead of punishment for disobeying, she sat me down on the sofa and began the first of many lessons.

"You see, Mrs. Celia Mallory recognized the potential in a young slave boy, just as I recognize the great treasures that sit upon these benches today in the school that bears her name. We have with us Mrs. Mallory's son-in-law. Mr. Jed Thomas is a familiar name to you all. Were it not for his courageous oath a few days ago, our nation would still be divided, and our people still under the yoke of bondage."

He stopped momentarily and looked in Jed's direction. "What most of you do not realize is yet another debt we owe him, for this school was his idea."

A round of applause arose amid the murmur of disbelief.

"When an envelope arrived several months ago from the President of the Confederate States of America, I found within it both a letter of request and an authorization to withdraw funds from a Washington bank on a monthly basis. His request was that I administer these funds to continue the education of the children that I was teaching. He further proposed that I increase the number of students by building this school." Extending his arm in a form of presentation, he concluded by saying, "Our benefactor, Mr. Jed Thomas."

The former Confederate President acknowledged his audience and began his speech directed to those who despised him as a representative of slavery and the cruelty of masters and slave traders. It seemed impossible that the man who led the South could be responsible for this school to educate their children, but their faith in Mose Douglas, who had recently adopted the surname of the great Frederick Douglas, assured them that it was so. Even for the most skeptical and bitter, there was no denial of the evidence of Mr. Thomas' sincerity. About the large classroom, rows of desks, stacks of books, and a large supply of papers, pencils, and slates were neatly arranged and awaiting the children for whom they were intended. As they listened to his words, each heart was touched by his concern and encouraged by his words.

"...I see a day when children rich or poor, Black or White, will sit side by side, and schools like this will be unnecessary. Perhaps we will not witness such a time, but our children, or their children will apply the principles learned here to make this dream a reality."

As the audience applauded, Jed and Clarissa made their journey back to the National Hotel. Since living in the Cameron home was quite impossible, Jed had reserved two suites, using the newly appointed ambassador's preparations as a ruse to remove both Clarissa and her mother from his influence.

These new arrangements suited Clarissa perfectly. Not only was there a staff to see to her mother's needs, but she shared her days and evenings with the man she adored. There were dinners and parties to attend; however, she enjoyed most the evenings in the National's suite when they played cards or read.

To the great relief of Phoebe Morgan, her daughter was deliriously happy, yet at the same time she was exhibiting an inner peace Phoebe had never dreamed possible in her daughter. To be sure, Clarissa was still opinionated and stubborn. Absent was the perpetual searching that had characterized her for most of her life. As for the young man, who could find fault in a prospective son-in-law like Jed Thomas?

She only hoped that Simon would be equally content at his new post. His acceptance of the Russian ambassadorship seemed somewhat puzzling, but there was no outguessing a complex man like her brother.

As the carriage progressed at a leisurely pace through the streets of the Capital, Clarissa contemplated the next chapter in her life. By the end of the week, they would all be bound for Charleston, where Isabella and Catherine were preparing the Thomas home for their wedding. Clarissa was lost in thought until the carriage stopped in front of an exclusive Pennsylvania Avenue milliner.

"Jed, why are we stopping here?"

He smiled affectionately. "You'll see," he said mysteriously.

Presently, a clerk left the shop carrying a hatbox bearing the name *William*, the designer's name.

"Here we are, Mr. Thomas. I do hope Miss Morgan is pleased." She winked slyly at Clarissa.

"Thank you." He looked toward Clarissa, whose face was flushed with anticipation. "I assure you, she will adore it. All the women at the theater will be clamoring to know where she purchased it." He smiled at the clerk, "and she won't forget to mention William's name."

The barouche proceeded down the Avenue as Clarissa tore open the box and removed a pale blue bonnet with contrasting ribbon. "Oh, Jed!" she gasped. "I've never owned a hat done by William, and this one is particularly exquisite. It will..."

He finished her sentence, "Just match my new gown. Of course it will. Would you mistake me for some backwoods

Southern boy?" They both laughed remembering the battlefield and her initial appraisal of all that was Southern.

"I do love you, Jedediah."

He squeezed her hand. "And what," she asked, giving him a playful glance, "did you mean about the theater?"

Jed looked toward the western side of Pennsylvania Avenue as they were nearing the State Department. "Oh, I must have neglected to mention to you that we have been invited to Ford's Theater this evening."

She tugged at his sleeve. "You know full well that you haven't informed me. Now, tell me this instant, by whom have we been invited?"

"By the fine couple who live there." He pointed toward the White House.

"The Presidential box!" she cried falling back against the burgundy cushions. "My goodness, Jed, I never dreamed of sitting in a Presidential box with the eyes of Washington on me."

"Some might take a look my way," he teased.

A gloom came to her classic face. "Though I don't fancy an evening with the mad woman of Washington. But," she flashed her captivating smile, "I'll suffer through it."

"I'm sure it won't matter, but I understand the play is quite entertaining. It is the final night of the engagement, and tickets for this comedy are much in demand."

"*Our American Cousin,* she interrupted. "Everyone says that Laura Keene is magnificent."

Arriving at the National, Jed paid the driver as he watched his fiancé, who was in a rush to change, enter the hotel. *How very dim things were just a few days ago*, he thought. The weight of the Confederacy with its bloody war and ravaged people, his guilt over his betrayal and the death of Mandy, and his inability to remedy any of them robbed him of any joy. Clarissa Morgan had changed everything.

This morning as he waited for Clarissa to dress for the ceremony at the Celia Mallory School, he had read of Lincoln's dispatch of train loads of staple goods destined for the main rail arteries of the South. At the President's urging, planters would soon be able to borrow money at low rates of interest to rebuild their livelihoods. Most amazing was the man's proposal that the poor who overflowed the tenements of the Northern cities be awarded incentives to travel South and work on plantations and the new industries that had he promised to build below the Mason-Dixon Line.

With the cessation of Cameron's payments and the intervention of the United States Army, Juarez was negotiating peace and agreeing to Lincoln's demands of a full withdrawal of Mexican forces and the return of all lands. As the remaining states applied for readmission, the freeing of slaves was required, though the President had previously issued an Emancipation Proclamation. *Thank you, Lord, for Abraham Lincoln. The nation truly owes its survival to him* thought Jed.

Despite the many Southerners who misunderstood his motivation, preferring to maintain the illusion that the Confederacy could survive on honor and arrogance, Jed was content that he had done what was best for the people of the South, both free and slave.

He paused for a moment, looking at the marble and gold staircase she had taken. Smiling, he shook his head, as he recalled her ragged attire aboard the Presidential train. She had abandoned her family and risked her life in an attempt to save the collapse of the nation he had placed between them. He shuddered as he remembered the incident in the boxcar that she had recounted to no one else. And why had she done all this? She loved him. Did any man truly deserve such a mixture of beauty, compassion, and fortitude that was Clarissa Morgan? *I'll devote my life to trying*, he vowed.

So lost in his thought of the woman he loved, Jed was oblivious to those he passed in the National's lobby, including a dark-haired man with a black moustache that he nearly forced to the ground.

"I am genuinely sorry," apologized Jed to the well-dressed man he found vaguely familiar.

The man grumbled, "Get out of my way!"

Jed could detect by his accent that he was a fellow Southerner, but this was nothing unusual, for the National always catered to the gentility of the South. Yet, there was something about the man that troubled Jed. Watching him leave the hotel, Jed failed to pinpoint anything about the man that would constitute such uneasiness on his part. He did notice that the man's attempt to conceal his bowed legs in baggy trousers and a longer than stylish coat was in vain.

Dismissing the irritable man from his mind, Jed began his ascent to make his preparations for the theater. There was little that could mar his mood. A lifetime of happiness with Clarissa was assured as were the prospects for a remarkable evening.

John Wilkes Booth headed toward a rendezvous with his fellow conspirators who would play key roles in the most memorable performance of his life.